His Sweet...

LUCY MONROE
MAYA BLAKE
KATHERINE GARBERA

First Published in Great Britain 2017
By Mills & Boon, an imprint of HarperCollins*Publishers*
1 London Bridge Street, London, SE1 9GF

ISBN: 978-0-263-92982-9

05-1017

WEDDING VOW OF REVENGE

BY
LUCY MONROE

Lucy Monroe started reading at age four. After going through the children's books at home, she was caught by her mother reading adult novels pilfered from the higher shelves on the bookcase. . .alas, it was nine years before she got her hands on a Mills & Boon romance her older sister had brought home. She loves to create the strong alpha males and independent women that people Mills & Boon books. When she's not immersed in a romance novel (whether reading or writing it) she enjoys travel with her family, having tea with the neighbours, gardening, and visits from her numerous nieces and nephews. Lucy loves to hear from readers—e-mail her at LucyMonroe@ LucyMonroe.com or visit her website: www.LucyMonroe. com.

For my Grandmother Lucille and my Great Aunts. . .
you are women who have inspired me my whole life
with your wit, your work ethic, your intelligence, your
generosity and your zest for living. I want to thank you
for that from the very depths of my heart. I love you all.
Blessings, Lucy

CHAPTER ONE

ANGELO GORDON'S blue eyes narrowed with interest.

"You're sure of this information, *amico mio*?" he demanded, his American accent spiced with Sicilian overtones that denoted his reaction to the news more strongly than words could have.

Hawk nodded. "Positive. Baron Randall has been keeping tabs on Tara Peters since their affair ended two years ago."

"How did you find out?"

"The owner of the security agency Randall has on retainer talks more than he should after a couple of whiskey sours." Hawk didn't make those kinds of mistakes, but didn't mind taking advantage when someone else did.

"That's convenient."

"I thought so."

"Okay. Give me the scoop and don't leave anything out."

Hawk tossed the file on Angelo's desk and waited for the tall Sicilian-American to open it.

He pointed to the news story on top that showed his client's enemy with his arm around a woman more than a decade his junior. "Randall and Miss Peters met four years ago at a fashion show in New York. He was there with another model, but left with Miss Peters. By all accounts, he swept the young Miss Peters off her feet and into his bed. She gave up modeling and started taking college courses. They were together for eighteen months and broke up when he became engaged to his current wife. Rumor suggests he asked Miss Peters to remain his mistress."

"She refused."

"Yes."

"She was stronger than my mother." Grudging respect laced Angelo's voice. "Why is he having her watched?"

"According to my informant, Randall still wants her. He's given instructions to scotch any possible romantic entanglements. So far, my colleague hasn't had to make the effort."

Angelo surged to his feet and turned to look out the window behind his desk. His brooding six-foot-two-inch frame blocked the light and Hawk's view of upper Manhattan. "What the hell does he expect to accomplish? That's what I want to know."

"Obviously reentrance into her life."

Angelo turned back, his patrician features creased with a frown of disbelief. "That doesn't make any sense. She said no and apparently meant it."

"Right. It makes one wonder how long Baron Randall expected his marriage to last in the first place.

When he married, his wife's father had been recently diagnosed with an inoperable heart condition."

"But good living and exercise have given him a clean bill of health, or at least a new lease on life."

Hawk smiled cynically. "Much to Randall's dismay no doubt. The marriage has never been a happy one."

For which Angelo could take some credit.

Tara wasn't the only woman Randall had propositioned for the role of his mistress. Others had accepted and thanks to some judicious behind the scenes handling on both Hawk and Angelo's part, the young Mrs. Randall knew it.

"According to my sources, she will be filing for divorce within the month."

Angelo inclined his head in acknowledgment of information that would not have come as a surprise. "You think he wants to take up where he left off when he's free?"

"I can see no other explanation for his behavior. Miss Peters is the only long-term relationship Baron Randall has had in more than a decade that did not profit him business wise. He cheated on her only when he was away from her. For an amoral womanizer like him, that is bloody significant."

Hawk had never before seen Angelo Gordon wearing that particular expression. *"You think he loves her?"*

"Love?" Hawk flicked his hand in a dismissive gesture. "Not bloody likely, but I do think he's obsessed by her. From what information I can gather, she is unique, if only in her ability to walk away from him. My instincts tell me it's more than that, though. She was very

career minded as a model. He was her first serious boy-friend."

"You think she was a virgin when they met? *How old is she?*"

"Twenty-four and yes, I think Randall's the only lov-er she's ever had."

"That does make her unique, especially in Randall's jaded world."

"There's more."

"What?"

"You aren't going to believe this." Hawk had had a hard time believing it himself. "It is simply too damn perfect."

"And *it* is?"

"She graduated with her degree in business six months ago and has been in Primo Tech's management training program for the past four of those months."

Angelo had bought the hi-tech company in Portland, Oregon, three years ago. Just like all the other compa-nies he bought and resuscitated, it was becoming a lead player in its industry. However, the success of his com-pany was no doubt not nearly as interesting to him in that moment as the fact Tara Peters was employed there.

"It's fate."

Hawk's laugh was every bit as skeptical as Angelo's. "That is one way of looking at it."

Angelo sat at his desk after Hawk left, perusing the file on Tara Peters. Hawk had included still shots from sev-eral of her fashion shows. They showed a woman of ethereal beauty, shrouded by innocence, but wearing clothing that would tempt a saint to sin. On her tall, model slim body, that nevertheless had curves in all the right places, they were more than a temptation…they were downright provocation.

Her dark brown eyes in the perfectly proportioned oval face, surrounded by a cascade of silky chestnut hair intrigued him…even knowing she had once been Baron Randall's.

He flipped through the photos until he came to those included with the tabloid articles that had sensational-ized her breakup with Randall. The difference between the two sets of pictures wrenched at something inside Angelo he thought long dead. Those same chocolate-dark eyes now reflected the pain of betrayal and lost in-nocence.

Just like his mother's had.

He needed to assimilate this piece of information and decide how best to act on it. He didn't have much time, either. If for no other reason than that Baron Randall would go looking for Tara Peters the minute his wife filed the divorce petition.

That gave Angelo a month, maybe less to act on his newfound knowledge of Randall's unexpected weakness.

The man who had stolen his company and destroyed his mother deserved to be ruined on every level and An-gelo was going to make damn sure that happened.

Tara Peters laughed at the other junior execs around her, at least the female ones. They were primping for the ar-rival of Angelo Gordon like he was a rock star or some-thing.

"Aren't you even going to put on lipstick?" Danette Michaels demanded with her usual forthrightness after glossing her own lips and putting her compact mirror away in her desk drawer. "He's supposed to do a tour of this floor sometime today."

"No lipstick." Tara had spent years wearing just the right makeup, dressing with flair, and flaunting the assets that had made her a top model at the age of twenty.

They had also brought her to the notice of Baron Randall and for that alone, she would spend the rest of her life devoid of makeup and dressing in conservative business attire.

Never again.

She straightened the papers on her desk. "My only interest in impressing Mr. Gordon is with my work and I don't need lipstick to do it."

Danette rolled her eyes. "You are such an all work and no play kind of girl. Did you ever hear that makes you boring and can give you ulcers before you're thirty?"

Coming from a woman who had her first serious boyfriend at the age of twenty-one, that was pretty funny.

"My twenty-four-year-old stomach is just fine, thank you and better boring than stomped on I always say."

"Not every man in the world is like that jerk, Baron Randall."

Like most people, Danette had read the tabloid accounts of Tara getting dumped by Baron so he could marry his oil heiress. However, unlike most people, the younger woman had not let the stories color her view of Tara. She thought Baron was a world class pig and that her friend was better off without him.

Tara agreed. Now.

But two years ago, she'd felt like she would die from the pain and humiliation of the all too public breakup.

"Of course they aren't," she said, trying to stave off another lecture about getting back on the horse so she wouldn't forget how to ride. Between Danette and her mother, she'd heard it about a thousand times too many. "But right now I'm not interested in finding out. I don't have time for a man in my life and honestly, I don't see how you can, either."

Danette shrugged, her amber cat eyes twinkling.

"Some of us are better at multitasking than others," she said with a grin. "Anyway, even if your career is all you care about, you should want to make a good impression on Angelo Gordon. He owns this company and several like it."

"I do want to impress him…with my business acumen."

"He's already impressed, Tara."

Tara spun in her chair to face her manager, surprised Mr. Curtiss was here instead of in the schmoozing session with the upper managers and the company owner.

"Mr. Gordon wants to speak to you privately."

Tension stiffened her spine as the words reminded her of a similar conversation she'd had with her modeling agent. The woman had told her that Baron Randall wanted to meet her. Tara, naïve idiot that she had been four years ago, had been both flattered and impressed.

"Why alone?"

If her manager thought that an odd question, he

didn't let it show. "He's impressed with your report on workplace effectiveness. He wants to discuss it with you."

Relaxing, she smiled. Business. It was just about business, nothing like that other time when the introduction had been a prelude to seduction.

"That's great, Tara," Danette said, "I heard the guy is a genius. If he appreciates your brains already, I guess it's true."

"Does he want to see me right now?" she asked, feeling a little light-headed.

Sure, she'd daydreamed about the owner of the company being so impressed with her recommendations he wanted to talk to her. What junior executive didn't? But that kind of stuff didn't happen in the real world.

Her manager looked at his watch and frowned. "Five minutes ago, actually. I got waylaid by a phone call on my way to tell you."

Tara Peters walked into Angelo's temporary office with her back straight and a credible expression of confidence. The only giveaway to her nervousness at being summoned by the owner of the company was the tight clenching of her fingers into small fists at her sides.

Her bone structure was delicate for a woman of her height, which no doubt explained her success as a catwalk model.

Yet, she looked very different from the still shots of her fashion shows that Hawk had included in the *Tara Peters* file. Nor did she resemble the pictures that had accompanied the tabloid articles after her breakup with Randall.

All the photos had shown a stunning woman who made the most of her beauty, but no one would accuse this Tara Peters of trading on her beauty to succeed in her job.

She had confined the glorious length of her signature chestnut hair in a tight French braid that fell down her back. She wore no makeup and the small ovals of her nails were unpolished, but buffed. The navy-blue slacks and blazer she wore disguised her figure very well.

He hadn't been sure what to expect, but her current no-nonsense, almost androgynous attire fit Hawk's report on her behavior since Baron Randall married another woman.

Tara didn't date and appeared uninterested in attracting men. Was she still hung up on the monster? The thought did not sit well with Angelo and his usually impassive face creased in a frown before he realized it.

"Mr. Gordon?" The voice was questioning, but not hesitant and he liked that.

He admired strength because weakness…of any kind…cost far too much.

He looked up and met her faintly quizzical brown eyes. "Miss Peters. Please take a seat."

She moved across the room and slid gracefully into a chair opposite his desk. His opinion changed on the suit. The jacket dipped in at her waist. Her movement had revealed curves that were neither pronounced nor were they so slight her blouse could disguise them completely. The way the clothes tried to hide, but could not help hinting at her femininity made him want to strip them off and see the beautiful body beneath.

It did not help that pictures from her file of her clad in bikinis and other almost-there outfits flashed in his mind's eye.

Desire vibrated through him with shocking swiftness and urgency, making him glad for the concealment of his desk. He hadn't responded with this level of physical intensity to the mere sight of a woman since puberty.

He forced his mind through the mental exercises he had learned in the Aikido training he had started as a young boy. He continued to train, using it as a way to keep his body fit and mind focused. Normally it worked without him even having to think about.

This time, he had to wait for the stunning response of his body to subside breath by breath before he could begin to concentrate on his agenda. "I've been reading your report on workplace effectiveness. You've drawn several interesting conclusions and made an equal number of suggestions that are worthy of note."

Her eyes lit with pleasure and she smiled, her feminine fragrance teasing his nostrils as she leaned forward. "There's a wealth of data to be analyzed and interpreted from recent studies on the subject, much of which has been ignored by current management theory."

He nodded. Whatever else Miss Peters was, she had shown herself to be a natural in her chosen field. "I particularly found your suggestions regarding vacation time of interest."

"Several studies have shown that employees who put in less overtime, take their vacation yearly and don't consistently work through their lunch hours are actually more productive than their counterparts who work the longer hours and never take any time off." She smiled. "Healthier, too. They have fewer heart attacks and are less likely to develop ulcers."

"You've definitely done your homework."

She blushed at the compliment and he filed the reaction away for future reference. From the way she presented herself, he had to assume her beauty was of much less significance to her than doing well at her job.

Interesting.

And unusual.

"Many of your suggestions fly in the face of corporate policies the world over."

She leaned further forward in her chair, her oval face animated and flushed in a way he'd like to see somewhere besides the boardroom. "Those management styles are as outdated as the all-male executive staff. They don't work in today's dynamic workforce, particularly the organic environment found in the hi-tech industry."

"Why did you go for a job in hi-tech? Your résumé shows a strong liberal arts background for your business degree."

She looked disconcerted by his question and settled back in her chair, biting her lip uncertainly. "The job description did not include a requirement in technological education."

"I'm aware of that, but you did not answer my question."

She smiled slightly. "Sorry. You're right." Her smile grew and her demeanor relaxed. "I like the stimulating atmosphere. Things are always changing, not just the products, but the face of the workforce as well. The job is challenging. But most importantly, I wanted to work someplace I could make a difference."

"And you thought Primo Tech would be it?"

"Yes."

He lifted the report that would have caught his attention even if it hadn't been the ideal conduit for their first meeting. "I would say you are well on your way to doing so."

"I'm glad you think so." She beamed and he found himself smiling in return, something he rarely did.

His phone buzzed at exactly the moment he had instructed his secretary to ring through.

He lifted the receiver. "Gordon here."

"Mr. Gordon, I'm ringing as instructed."

"Thank you. And my other arrangements?"

"The reservations are made. Dinner at seven-thirty in the restaurant of your hotel."

"Hold on just a moment." He pressed the hold button and schooled his face into an apologetic expression, another one he used infrequently. "I'm sorry, I have to take this call."

Tara stood hurriedly. "Of course."

She was halfway to the door when he said, "Miss Peters."

She turned. "Yes?"

"I would like to discuss the report further. Can you meet me this evening for a business dinner at my hotel?"

Despite the fact he had specifically referred to it as business, her eyes filled with wariness. "Dinner?"

"Yes. Is that a problem?" he asked, inflecting his voice with just the right amount of superiority and disapproval to remind her who he was.

She took a deep breath and squared her shoulders, her lips flattened in a determined line. "No. I'll be there. What hotel and what time?"

He told her and then watched her walk out of his office, his attention on the way her slacks outlined her heart-shaped behind. This aspect of his plan for revenge was shaping up to be more pleasure than work.

Seducing Tara Peters would be no hardship at all.

Tara got ready for dinner, her nerves more on edge than they had been in two long years. Why? Because the minute another magnetic, sexy tycoon came on the scene, her body had started reacting. She couldn't believe it and was thoroughly disgusted with herself.

Worse, she'd seen immediately the unexpected feelings of attraction were mutual. She might have very little practical experience with men, but she'd been on the receiving end often enough to identify when a man was attracted to her. She'd learned early in her modeling career to recognize and avoid it.

Her one failure being both spectacular and devastating.

She hadn't spent the last two years avoiding men and entanglements just to fall for another Baron Randall. No way. She was smarter than that.

Even brief contemplation of a relationship with a man like Angelo Gordon would be stupidity itself.

Right. Remember that.

Only instincts that had nothing to do with intelligence and everything to do with emotion were sending all sorts of messages to her brain. They urged her to put on a little makeup, change into a more feminine dress and brush out her long hair for goodness sake! She'd done her best to sublimate such impulses for two years.

Her mind said now was not the time for a resurrection, but her heart and body said otherwise.

Stupid, stupid, stupid, she muttered under her breath as she put the final pin in the sleek French roll on the back of her head and surveyed her appearance. She'd changed her slacks for a black skirt and her blouse and blazer for a matching jacket meant to be worn buttoned up as a top.

With her understated black heels and sheer stockings, she had a distinctly Jackie-O appearance without the feminine softening of lipstick and accent jewelry.

Perfect.

No way could her boss misinterpret her outfit as any sort of attempt to entice him on a personal level.

She didn't care if Angelo Gordon affected her in ways she'd thought deadened by Baron's betrayal. Wanting him scared her far more than it enticed her and she wasn't giving into it.

Desire was an emotion that encouraged smart women to make dumb decisions.

Hadn't she seen that enough growing up with her mom bouncing from one destructive relationship to the next? Her mom had never understood why none of the men stayed. She hadn't comprehended that the type of powerful, charismatic male she was attracted to traded on those very traits to get what he wanted—sex with a beautiful woman.

However, they'd all been incapable of giving her mom what *she* needed…love.

Tara's mom had only broken the cycle by default when miracle of miracles, a strong, sexy man also turned out to have a heart.

It was Darren Colby's influence in Tara's life that had led her to believe that kind of man wasn't always bad news. She was no longer so naïve. Darren was an anomaly in the male species, an alpha male with a heart…but she didn't figure anomalies like that came along more than maybe once a millennium.

She would stay focused on her job and not the way Angelo Gordon's dark good looks affected her libido.

Tara walked into the posh downtown hotel, projecting an unshakable confidence that was only skin deep. Inside, she was as nervous as she'd been her first day on the job. More even, because then all she'd been fighting was a fear of the unknown. Tonight, she fought her fear of being weak.

Angelo waited for her at a table in a small private alcove of the hotel restaurant. A historic landmark, the hotel's rich décor of carved wood paneling leading to cavernously high ceilings was original to its nineteenth century construction. Despite the distance to the ceilings, the rich detail of the da Vinci-like scenes painted there caught her attention.

But even the artwork's beauty could not keep her focus when she could feel Angelo's regard across the restaurant. He watched her with unreadable blue eyes as she made her way toward him between linen topped tables graced by well dressed diners. Even from this far away, he exerted an aura of masculine power that sent her heart tripping.

Just like Baron.

Only unlike Baron, she would not allow herself to be fooled into believing Angelo was more than what he appeared on the surface, a ruthless corporate shark.

He stood when she reached the table, his height startling at close quarters. At five foot nine, she was no shrimp, but the top of her head barely reached his shoulder.

She had to tilt her head back to look him in the eye. It was a very odd feeling. "Good evening, Mr. Gordon."

He waited for the maître d' to seat her before sitting down again. "Angelo, please. I prefer a more relaxed environment in my companies."

"Your approach appears to be quite effective. You've never lost a company yet."

Something swirled in his indigo gaze as he poured her a glass of wine from the bottle already sitting on the table. "Actually, I have lost one, but that was a long time ago."

Sensing he had no desire to discuss it further, she took a sip of the fruity wine and then asked, "Angelo is an Italian name?"

Other than the blue eyes, which were not entirely uncommon in Italian men—with his dark hair and tanned good looks, he had a very Mediterranean appearance.

"My mother was Sicilian."

That explained a lot, but remembering a fashion shoot she'd done outside of Palermo one summer, she said, "Most Sicilian men are a lot shorter than you."

"My father was American."

"And tall," she guessed.

He smiled, making her breath catch. This man was beautiful.

"Yes. According to my mother, that was one of the first things she noticed about him. There was more than a foot disparity in their sizes, but I can never remember them seeming like they did not fit."

"I've heard love can be a great equalizer," she said with a tinge of mockery she wished she didn't feel.

But after her childhood and one disastrous personal affair, she had little belief in the emotion so many touted as the panacea for all ills.

"So they say." His tone was no less cynical than her own.

The waiter came to take their order and she made a point of selecting her own meal. This was not a date and even if it was, she didn't go in for the old world custom of the male ordering for the female. She'd spent too many years taking care of herself.

"You wanted to discuss my report?" she asked after the waiter left.

"First, I think I should like to know a little more about you, Tara."

"I'm sure all the pertinent information is in my employee record."

"Perhaps I prefer to hear it firsthand."

"I was under the impression this was supposed to be

a business dinner." She kept her tone light, not wanting to offend her boss, but not so light he wouldn't take the comment to heart.

His midnight gaze caressed her with tactile force and it was all she could do not to shiver. "My closest friends started as business associates."

"You don't strike me as a man with a lot of close friends." She'd meant the words to come out worldly and sophisticated, but instead her voice was two octaves lower than normal and sounded flirtatious, darn it.

"You're very perceptive." He cocked his head slightly, his expression challenging her. "That does not mean you could not become one of them."

"You're very bold."

"I didn't get where I am hesitating to go after what I want."

"If you want my business expertise, you can have it. If you're looking for a personal relationship with an employee, I decline." She couldn't be more direct than that, but then this man apparently needed blunt.

He nodded, his expression showing no offence. "I can respect that." Then he smiled. "That does not mean I won't try to change your mind."

"I would prefer if you didn't."

"I would prefer you did not treat me like a pariah simply because I own the company you work for."

"Wanting to stick to business is hardly treating you like an outcast."

"And denying me the possibility of friendship?"

"You don't need my friendship."

"You are wrong." And the intensity in his expression said he was telling her the truth, but how could that be?

Unless his definition of friendship and hers were not quite the same thing. Maybe he was between *girlfriends* at the moment.

"I have no interest in becoming a business tycoon's pillow friend."

CHAPTER TWO

"Do you judge every man you meet by Baron Randall's standards?"

She should not be surprised he knew about her past. Half the modern world had read the tabloid stories. Or at least it seemed that way sometimes. It was a good thing she'd learned early on in her modeling career that someone asking an awkward or painful question did not equate to an obligation on her part to answer it.

"That's really none of your business, Mr. Gordon."

"Angelo."

She barely refrained from rolling her eyes. "Angelo. I work for you and to my knowledge a personal relationship with my employer is not a requirement on my job description."

His amused but piercing gaze did things to her insides she desperately wished it didn't. "You are not only forthright, but you're damn certain of yourself."

"Yes." He wasn't the only person who knew what he wanted and went for it. Rather she knew what she didn't want—a repeat of her disastrous affair with a ruthless business tycoon.

Despite the fact that Angelo made a pointed effort to restrain his conversation to her business report over dinner, Tara found herself unwillingly enthralled by the man himself. He was intense, dynamic and smart. Smarter than any person she'd ever met and yet, he didn't dismiss her opinions if they differed from his. She appreciated that more than he could know, truly enjoying the evidence that he respected her even if she wasn't quite in his league.

That was something she'd always felt was in doubt in her relationship with Baron.

She hadn't been sure how Angelo would take her not-so-gentle refusal to get personal, but he'd responded with a professionalism and maturity she couldn't help admiring. She'd known men a lot older than him that reverted to spoiled little boys when thwarted in their pursuit of a woman.

For that reason, she found herself relaxing as the evening progressed, less concerned when their conversation took temporary by-ways not related wholly to human resource management.

They'd spent an hour over dinner before she even realized it.

The waiter asked if they wanted dessert and Angelo looked at her. "Do you have a sweet tooth? I've had their raspberry crème brûlée and it is some of the best I've tasted anywhere."

"Crème brûlée is my favorite," she admitted, her mouth watering at the prospect of indulging in the treat.

With one of his rare, but devastating smiles, he ordered one for each of them.

The desserts arrived and she had to stifle an animal groan of anticipation when she saw the perfect caramelization of the glaze on top.

"You look like you've just been offered a dish of ambrosia."

"Haven't I?"

He laughed, the sound doing things to her even more insidious than the sight of the decadent treat.

She felt compelled to explain her over the top reaction. "I spent years eschewing refined sugar and processed food of any kind for the benefit of my figure and complexion."

Appreciative eyes burned over her and she felt like she was wearing a spandex mini that revealed every curve rather than the black Jackie-O suit.

"You must still refrain quite a bit." His voice caressed her with obvious masculine approval.

For the first time in years, she found herself blushing about a comment made regarding her physical appearance. She'd gotten very used to seeing her body as her tool in trade, but this man made her very aware of herself as a feminine being.

She shrugged, projecting the air of insouciance she *should* be feeling about his comment. "I didn't stop modeling all that long ago."

His eyes narrowed. "I was under the impression you came to Primo Tech straight out of college."

"I did, but the last couple of years I supported myself with my modeling."

"After your breakup with Randall."

She grimaced. "Yes."

"He paid for your schooling before that?"

She didn't know why, but she found herself wanting to answer his question, when normally she would have cut such personal conversation off at the knees.

"He wanted to maximize our time together, so I agreed not to work."

"I'm surprised he didn't want you to give up school."

"Oh, he did." But as much as she'd thought she loved the swine, she'd been unwilling to give up her independence completely, or her dreams for her future.

"You refused."

"Adamantly."

"Did you retire from modeling because he wanted you to?"

Again, the question didn't offend her so much as give her an opportunity to talk about something she'd kept locked away inside for two long years. "I'd always planned on retiring young enough to go to school and move onto a second career. So, when he said he wanted to be the only man in my life, not one in a cast of thousands, I agreed and quit a few years and a few goals before I'd planned to. I was actually flattered he felt so strongly."

She knew her voice echoed her disgust with herself over her naiveté. Even so, her insistence on taking college courses had been a bone of contention between them until their break-up.

"Do you regret that decision?"

"I find regret a wasted emotion. When I had to go

back to work to support myself again, it was harder to get the lucrative jobs, but I survived and I learned a lot in the process."

Angelo studied her, what looked like real respect warming his gaze. "Yet even after going back to work, you excelled in your studies. I have heard modeling requires a great deal of dedication."

No doubt he'd dated a few models in his time. Most rich men did, seeing beautiful women as adornments as surely as designers saw models as mannequins to display their wares.

Still, she couldn't help liking the knowledge he was impressed with her efforts at school rather than offended by them as Baron had been.

"I don't think I could have modeled full-time and gone to school as well, but I earned enough working through the summers to support myself during the school year."

"You're a very determined woman."

"I'd say that was something you probably understand well."

"You'd be right." He pointed his spoon toward her brûlée. "Taste."

Did he have any idea what the sexy timbre of his voice did to her insides? Of course not, and no way was she letting on either. Better to get over the strange, melting reaction than expose it in any way, but every word was like foreplay to her sexually deprived body.

Bad. This was very bad.

She grabbed her spoon, conversation ceasing while she obeyed his order to taste. She gave a helpless moan of pleasure as the first bite of the perfectly prepared sweet filled her senses. Her eyes closed and she savored the taste she indulged in so rarely.

She'd once had another model describe a chocolate torte as orgasmic, but until this moment she'd never had an erotic reaction to food before. The sensual slide of the vanilla custard across her tongue was just that though and goose bumps formed on her inner thighs as her womb clenched in an astonishing reaction to the delicacy.

Belatedly coming to terms with how her not-so-innocent enjoyment could be misinterpreted, she quickly opened her eyes. Straightening in her chair, she tried to wipe the pleasure from her expression and willed her unruly body to calm down.

Her spoon clattered to the table in her haste to let it go. "Um, it's very good. You were right." She forced her gaze to meet his, afraid of what she would see, but unwilling to play the coward. "I guess I got a little carried away there."

Blue eyes looked back at her with hunger, but he shook his head. "Relax. You look like you think I'm going to pounce."

"Aren't you?" She wasn't an idiot and she wasn't a tease. She knew what her reaction had to have looked like to him.

A total come-on, despite all she'd said about not wanting to get involved.

"You've made your view of a relationship between the two of us very clear, Tara." He spoke as if instructing a small child and perversely she wanted to tell him she was anything but. "I'm not going to read an invitation in a former model's obvious love of feeding her starved sweet tooth."

"Thank you." And she should feel grateful. Extremely grateful.

Not disappointed.

"No problem. Now, enjoy your dessert."

He'd let her off the hook with his assurance, so why did she feel even further enmeshed in his web than before?

"So, how was dinner?" Danette asked in a low undertone as she and Tara worked on slides for a presentation their manager was supposed to give to Angelo and the top management string the following morning.

Tara looked around, thankful no one was nearby enough to overhear her friend's question. The dinner last night had been strictly business, but that wasn't necessarily how others would interpret it.

After her affair with Baron, she'd been the butt of enough gossip to last her a lifetime. "Shh. I don't want to talk about it right now."

Danette's hazel eyes widened, darkening to green with a knowing gleam. "So it wasn't just business."

"No," Tara snapped, then realized her answer had come out wrong. "I mean yes…I mean it *was* business and *only* business." If she didn't count the orgasmic dessert. "Okay?"

"I don't know. Angelo Gordon is a real hottie and you seem pretty frazzled for a woman who had a *strictly business* date last night."

"It wasn't *a date* at all."

"Are you saying he didn't make a move on you?"

How did she answer that? Had their conversation at the beginning of dinner been a move? She thought maybe it had, but then he'd backed off pretty easily.

She took too long to answer and Danette's expression turned gleefully calculating. "So, he is attracted to you."

That was something she couldn't deny without lying. "Could we drop this discussion? We've got work to do."

"Sure, but, hon, just answer one question…if last night was all business and no play, why are you blushing to the roots of your gorgeous hair?"

Tara still hadn't come up with an adequate reply to her friend's teasing comment by the time the other woman left work to get ready for her very real date with a budding journalist.

It had bugged her all day. For something like the hundredth time since waking that morning, she shoved thoughts of Angelo to the back of her mind. She forced herself to concentrate on the papers in front of her.

With no distractions around her and fierce effort, it worked. She was so engrossed that security came to tell her all external entrances but the main one had been secured for the evening before she realized what time it was. She looked at her watch and was shocked to see it was well after seven.

She should have left over two hours ago.

Muscles cramped from long hours of sitting in the same position protested and she stood to stretch. Her tummy growled, but her eyes were drawn back to the almost completed report on her desk. Just another hour or so and she would be done.

"Why are you still here?"

She jumped at the sound of Angelo's voice, her entire body flushing with warmth and she hadn't even turned to look at him.

When she did, she felt like she'd been hit by a truck. Why did the man have to be so darn sexy? Most of his management team was at least a decade older, balding and showing the effects of middle age in their belt size, but not Angelo. He was tall and lean with muscles to die for and if he was much over thirty, she'd eat the report she'd been editing.

"I was working on a project and got lost to the time."

"What about this workplace effectiveness model you've been trying to sell to management? Doesn't that include going home on time?"

She shrugged guiltily. "Theory doesn't always work in reality."

He smiled, white teeth flashing in his gorgeous face. "No, it doesn't, but if you're going to convince my management team of your theories, you're going to have to live and work by them."

"You're right, of course." She sighed, wishing life was as easy as putting ideas down on paper. "I guess you got caught up in something, too?"

His expression cooled for no reason she could discern. "I was putting together the plans for a new acquisition."

"You're buying another company?"

Satisfaction flashed in his eyes, but they remained strangely chilled. "Yes."

"Um…congratulations."

"Thank you." He ran his fingers through the short, dark curls on his head, leaving them mussed and looking way too enticing for her own good. "Have you had dinner?"

"No. I'll stop and get something on the way home." She turned and grabbed her suit jacket off the hook on the cubicle wall behind her desk.

As she did so, she realized the sheer white camisole that looked perfectly acceptable under the jacket was much too thin for a business environment without it. It had gotten warm and she hadn't even been aware of taking the jacket off, but now she wished she hadn't gotten quite so engrossed in her work.

Looking down, she could see the shadow of nipples that had hardened upon her boss's arrival and was darn sure he could, too.

"Have dinner with me." His voice betrayed nothing, but he made no pretense of ignoring the display. Dark indigo eyes flicked from her breasts to her face. "Well?"

Sensation zinged through her, making her tight peaks sting and she shoved her arms into the sleeves of her suit jacket.

Panicked at how tempting the invitation was and the desperate reaction of her body, she blurted the first excuse that came to her mind. "I'm really not all that hungry."

Her stomach gave immediate lie to her words with an audible growl and she had to bite back a groan of embarrassment.

"Are you sure about that?"

"Uh…"

"Look, Tara, I'm simply interested in sharing some company for dinner. I eat enough meals alone to get tired of it. Stop worrying. I'm not going to pounce."

That was the second time he'd assured her on that score, but she was beginning to think it wasn't him pouncing she had to be concerned about.

"I'm sure you're not short on companions you could call on." She couldn't keep the cynical conjecture from her voice.

"You'd be surprised. I've never found the company of women with dollar signs in their eyes all that alluring."

She gave him a frank once-over. "Like women are only interested in you for your money."

"Is that a compliment?"

"Yes." She'd never been good at prevaricating. She hated lies, no more so than since she'd been lied to so spectacularly by Baron Randall.

"If you find me attractive, why not have dinner with me?"

"Because you are who you are and I am who I am."

"You mean the whole multimillionaire and junior-management trainee thing?" he asked with droll humor.

She found herself smiling. "Yes, that thing."

"Why don't we pretend to be nothing more than an unattached man looking for the company of a woman he admires a great deal for dinner?"

He admired her *a great deal*? That was a different line than Baron's had been anyway. He'd been so focused on her beauty and then her sexual innocence, he'd barely given credence to her brain.

"All right, but let's keep it simple. It's late."

"Do you have any suggestions?"

She did and couldn't help being surprised when he willingly let her direct him to a chain restaurant known for its quick and friendly service. The food was good, but not exactly five-star. Apparently, Angelo didn't care about eating only in the best restaurants.

She liked that and told him so.

He shrugged. "When you have the freedom and finances to eat where you want, why limit yourself? Besides, this was one of my dad's favorite restaurants when I was growing up."

"You grew up in the Pacific Northwest?"

"Seattle."

"Wow…I guess I thought all big business tycoons came from New York."

He laughed. "I have an apartment there. Does that shore up your image of me?"

"That depends…do you call it home?"

"I don't call anywhere home. I travel too much. I have a house in Palermo that would probably be the closest thing."

"Do you speak Italian?"

"Fluently."

"Oh…I took French in high school, but I was always more interested in numbers than languages."

"I'm fluent in several. It comes with the territory, but my mother spoke Italian to me always and we spent part of every year in Sicily with her family."

"You said she *was* Sicilian earlier…is she no longer alive?"

"She and my father died within two years of each other."

"I've heard about that kind of devotion…one can't go on living without the other." She'd always questioned it though…wondering if two people could ever really be that necessary to each other.

His face contorted as if in pain, but then went so blank she had to wonder if she'd imagined the first expression. "They loved each other very much."

He said it so coldly, as if he was unmoved by his parents' emotion.

Still…"Their deaths must have been very hard on you."

"I survived."

She nodded. He was too strong not to have done, but she wondered for just a second what the cost had been for him to be so detached about it now.

"My dad walked when I was two." Tara said after a silent pause. "He didn't know the meaning of the word devotion." Or commitment. Or love for that matter.

"Did your mother remarry?"

"Eventually. I had a few *uncles* who were every bit as allergic to the c-word as my dad before Darren Colby, my step-father, came into our lives."

"That doesn't sound like an ideal childhood."

"That's one way of putting it." She laughed, shocked at herself for sharing so much with a man she was determined not to get involved with.

The same thing had happened the night before. It bothered her, but a barrier that existed between her and the rest of the world seemed to be missing with him. Odd, but apparently it wasn't something she could do much about.

It was like her normal privacy filter was switched off around him.

Thank goodness he was only in Portland for a visit to his company and would be gone soon.

"Your mother must have had lousy taste in her partners," he said.

"That depends on how you look at it. She's drawn to dynamic, powerful men. Men a lot like you."

"For you to have had several male figures in your childhood, they must have been drawn to her, too."

"For a while anyway. She's beautiful."

"You say that like it's a curse."

"None of the men who dumped on my mom would have given her the time of day if she'd been plain."

"And perhaps Baron Randall would not have been attracted to you if you were not equally as beautiful?"

"I prefer not to talk about him."

"But he is the reason you are so reticent about becoming my friend."

"I never said that."

"Do you deny it?"

"No."

"And the man your mom married, Colby. I bet he was also attracted to her beauty."

"Darren would love Mom if she was fifty pounds overweight and had a mole on her chin."

"He sounds like a great guy, but wasn't he first attracted by her beauty?"

"I suppose."

"So, it isn't always a curse."

"No, but then there aren't that many men in the world like Darren."

"Maybe there are more than you think."

Did Angelo want her to believe he was one of them?

The prospect that he might was even scarier than her own urge to find out.

Over the next few days, Tara couldn't help feeling he was trying to convince her of that very thing.

Against her will, she found herself more and more attracted to the business tycoon who admired her brain and never criticized the fact she played down her beauty. He was charming to everyone, making Danette practically faint with excitement when he accepted an invitation to an informal barbecue at her place on Thursday night.

Under her brazen front, Danette was actually pretty shy and this would be the first major event she'd hosted at the condo her parents had insisted on helping her buy. Members of the city's elite, they had no problem providing their daughter with a home most people couldn't afford after working twenty years.

Even so, Danette had been worried about the success of her party and told Tara so. Having Angelo's attendance was a major coup, especially since so many other partygoers would be from Primo Tech.

"And don't you even think about trying to get out of coming now that you know he's going to be there," Danette said seconds after Angelo exited their work area.

"I told you I don't want to end up with another Baron Randall."

"Good gosh, Tara! Are you blind, or something? Not only is Angelo a good ten years younger than that swine, but the two men are so different they could be opposite species."

"Oh really? How are they so different?"

"First of all, it's no secret Baron Randall built his empire using other people."

A piece of information Tara wished she'd been privy to *before* meeting him.

"Angelo buys and salvages struggling companies. He's gotten where he is through the sweat of his own brow."

"Please."

"You know what I mean. He worked to build those companies up, just like he worked on this one. He's earned his tycoon status, not stolen it. And he's also not a womanizer."

"Oh, really?"

"Really. Ray did some checking for me at his newspaper. Angelo hasn't had a steady girlfriend in more than two years and he doesn't sleep with other men's wives."

"Like Ray could know that for certain."

"Angelo's newsworthy enough that if he had been caught with the same woman more than once it would have made at least one headline."

"The operative word being caught and one of the great benefits of being filthy rich is the ability to buy a newspaper's silence."

"Baron Randall is rich too, but there are still stories

about his womanizing ways in more than a few scandal sheets."

"Maybe he didn't care enough to have them squelched."

"What makes you think Angelo would?"

"Okay, so you've got a point. He's probably not a womanizer. Happy?"

"If you'll cut the guy some slack, yes."

She wasn't going there. "Is Ray going to be at the barbecue?"

"Sure. He's bringing his camera and taking pictures for my scrapbook." Danette smiled dreamily. "It isn't every day you get such a hunk of a multimillionaire in your backyard eating grilled steak."

Tara couldn't help laughing. "You are incorrigible."

Her friend grinned, her eyes filled with infectious laughter. "That's why you like me so much."

"So, are things serious between you and Ray?"

It had been her experience that when her friends started making cooing noises about settling down, they went into matchmaker mode with a vengeance and this barbecue invitation couldn't be seen as anything but.

Danette chewed on her bottom lip. "I think so. At least for me. He hasn't said anything about love, but he spends all his free time with me."

"That's a very good sign."

"I hope so."

And if it were true…what did that say about her and Angelo? They weren't dating, but he certainly managed to fill up most of her free time.

* * *

Thursday dawned bright and clear, the Oregon sunshine for once unclouded by threats of rain. Tara walked to work from the light rail terminal with a smile on her face. It was a good day to be alive.

A strong masculine hand gripped her shoulder before she walked into the building. "You look happy."

She smiled up at Angelo, for once allowing herself to enjoy her body's reaction to the devastating man's presence. It wasn't as if anything could happen in front of the building in plain view of the parking lot and the rest of Primo Tech's employees. "I love the sunshine."

"It's a great day for your friend's barbecue."

"Yes, it is. Danette will be pleased."

"Speaking of, would you like me to pick you up on my way?"

"I don't…"

"I'd feel more comfortable arriving with someone."

"I don't see you as the shrinking violet type."

"I'm not." His expression said he couldn't imagine such a thing, either. "But I would still like to bring you with me."

They were both going and a car ride there and back could hardly do any damage. After all, she'd been in the car with him twice now and come away unscathed. "Sure, why not?"

His hand slid up her shoulder and cupped her nape, sending her thoughts skittering to the four winds. "I'll look forward to it."

She watched him walk away thinking maybe unscathed was too strong a term to describe her living on the edge of going for another tycoon.

CHAPTER THREE

THE phone was ringing when Tara walked through the door of her apartment at twenty-five minutes after five. She sprinted across the small foyer and picked it up from the hall stand. "Hello?"

"Hey, hon…just wanted to make sure you're not going to dress like a bag lady now that the big boss is coming."

Danette.

"Sheesh…you called me to bug me about what I'm going to wear to your *casual* barbecue? Don't you have better things to do?"

"Right…it's casual and that means shorts and a T-shirt. Don't you dare show up in one of your casual-but-really-they-are-for-work-outfits."

Tara rolled her eyes. "What difference does it make?"

"Well, now that's an interesting question. It shouldn't make any difference…to you. I mean, if you're really not interested in the boss, then you shouldn't be bothered exposing a little flesh around him."

The idea of being around Angelo and wearing a pair of hip-hugging shorts and T-shirt that showed a glimpse of her stomach when she raised her arms made Tara's body flush with heat…and not from embarrassment.

"Come on," Danette added, "it's over eighty degrees outside. Be practical."

"I won't show up in a skirt and hose!"

"You'd better not and don't forget your swimsuit." Danette had sole use of the pool area at her condo complex to host her barbecue.

Tara loved the water, but if wearing shorts around Angelo made her jumpy, how would she deal with a swimsuit? "I'm not going to be swimming."

"Oh, please…did I mention it's eighty-some degrees out there? Of course if you get too hot and want to cool off, I could lend you one of mine."

Remembering her friend's penchant for string bikinis that showed more flesh than some bandages, Tara made a note to grab her own suit.

Just in case.

Angelo rang Tara's doorbell with more anticipation than he'd felt for a date in years.

Tara Peters was every bit as beautiful as her photos had shown, but she was also a very intriguing woman. He had no difficulty understanding Randall's fascination with her.

Angelo wanted her, too, which made this aspect of his revenge against the other man sweet indeed.

The door to her modest brownstone swung open and his breath suspended in his chest, all thought ceasing in a wave of shrieking male hunger that had him wanting to push her back into the apartment and claim her body as his own.

Denim shorts clung to her curves, stopping high enough on her thigh to make her well-toned, honey tanned legs look miles long. Her lemon-yellow T-shirt did some clinging of its own, revealing the fact her bra was so flimsy he could see her nipples peaking through the soft cotton.

Tara's arms came up and crossed over her breasts in a protective gesture that brought home to him the fact he'd been staring at her like a crass teenager watching a striptease.

Angelo's gaze traveled up to her face. She'd pulled her hair up into a ponytail. Still wearing no makeup. "You look about eighteen."

A damn sexy eighteen and he was glad he knew she was twenty-four or he would feel like a lecher with the thoughts going through his mind.

"And you *don't* look like a corporate magnate," she said smartly.

He leaned against the doorjamb, interested in the way she backed up a step as if his closeness bothered her. "Are you saying my business suits are all that stand between me and mediocrity?"

She laughed abruptly and shook her head. "You could never be an average guy. And I hate to tell you this, but most of the men at the barbecue are not going to be wearing Armani T-shirts and Ralph Lauren shorts."

His brows rose.

She grinned at him. "I used to be a fashion model. Identifying designers is my stock in trade. I can tell a knockoff designer bag a mile off."

"I'm not similarly gifted."

Her look said she doubted his words and he almost smiled. Men in his world often knew a great deal about women's fashion for the expedient reason that it made it easier to buy gifts a certain type of female would truly appreciate.

That sort of woman had never appealed to him.

"Are you ready to go?" he asked.

She nodded, grabbing her tote bag from the floor beside the door.

She waited for him to back up, but he merely shifted his body slightly so she could get by him. Tara gingerly stepped around him, as if afraid to touch him, but equally determined not to show it. He inhaled her scent, letting it tease his senses, before stepping back so she could shut the door.

Angelo's position forced her to stand mere inches from his body as she locked up. Then he led her outside to his car, where he took pains to invade her personal space buckling her in and adjusting her seatbelt. She was breathing in shallow pants, her eyes vague with suppressed desire by the time he straightened and shut her door. Good.

She wanted him and it wouldn't be long before he would have her—despite her aversion to wealthy tycoons.

The thought brought him harsh satisfaction. His revenge against the man who used and discarded people like trash was close at hand. However, unlike Baron Randall, once Angelo had Tara, he wasn't sure he'd let her go.

And that might be the best revenge of all.

"How many pictures do you need for your scrapbook?" Tara demanded of Danette as the woman's annoying boyfriend snapped yet another shot.

Angelo didn't like Ray's preoccupation with Tara, either, and was on the verge of making his displeasure known in a very basic way.

Danette shrugged her slim shoulders. "You can never have too many. And you've got to admit, even without makeup, you're awfully photogenic."

About that, Angelo had to agree.

But Tara grimaced. "I think I'm going to rue the day you took up your new scrapbook hobby."

"Hey, we aren't all so focused on work that we don't have outside interests."

"I have outside interests."

"Name one."

"I volunteer at the Boys and Girls club once a week."

That hadn't been in her file, Angelo took a mental note.

Danette snorted delicately. "Right, but you're doing almost the same thing at the club as you do at Primo Tech."

"Hardly."

"You manage staff resources. How is that different?"

"The staff is made up of volunteers."

Even Angelo could tell Tara was stretching the truth

and it made him smile. For a woman dedicated to work-life effectiveness, she was lousy at practicing what she preached. "So, you volunteer at the Boys and Girls club, but you don't connect with the kids?" he asked.

She turned to face him, her expression mirroring her surprise and some embarrassment. "I didn't realize you were there."

He handed her a cranberry spritzer over ice. "Your drink, as promised."

He'd been taking care of her in small ways like this one since they arrived at the barbecue and she didn't seem to know how to take it. Apparently other men in her life had not pampered her. However, he was intelligent enough to know that pampering and seduction went hand in hand.

She smiled, her rich chocolate eyes warm. "Thank you."

The snick of another picture came from her left and she jerked her head around. "Do you mind?"

Ray had the sense to look abashed. "Sorry. Photography is a fairly new hobby for me."

Tara sighed expressively. "You and Danette and your hobbies. Give it a rest, would you?"

"Sure."

Angelo gave the man a steely look that had sent more than one boardroom discussion going in the direction he wanted it to. "I wouldn't mind getting copies of some of the photos. Would that be possible?"

"You want pictures of the barbecue?" Tara asked, her voice pitched high in surprise.

"Not really, but there are one or two guests I wouldn't

mind having a photo of." He gave Tara a significant look.

"If you want a picture of me, I've got an entire portfolio full I'm not using anymore." She said it like a joke, but he didn't smile.

"I'd love to see them. Maybe you can get the portfolio out when we get back to your place."

Her mouth opened, but nothing came out.

"If you can get her to show it to you, you'll be getting further than most of us. For a former top model, she sure is shy," Ray said, sounding put out.

Danette smacked him in the arm, her eyes filled with teasing laughter. "Hey, you are supposed be interested in seeing my baby photos, not my best friend's modeling shots."

Ray grinned and shrugged.

Angelo frowned at him and the grin swiftly disappeared.

"Are you going to swim?" Danette asked Angelo, going for a swift change of subject, apparently realizing he wasn't as amused by her boyfriend's interest in Tara as she was.

The prospect of seeing Tara in a swimsuit sent his libido into overdrive. He met her wary brown gaze as he answered Danette. "I'd like to."

"Good." She grinned at Tara. "How about you?"

"I don't think I will this time."

"Oh, come on." Danette waved her hand in front of her face like a fan. "It's hot and I know you brought your suit."

"If you don't want to swim, we won't," he said making it clear he considered them a couple at this party and had no intention of participating in activities that didn't include them both.

If anything, her expression turned more wary. "You don't have to refrain from swimming because I am."

"It's not a problem."

She gave the sparkling water a look of longing and he moved closer, until he could touch her shoulder.

Her head snapped up and their eyes locked.

"Are you sure you don't want to swim?"

"I…"

"What are you afraid of, Tara?"

She licked her lips and let out a short sigh before averting her gaze. "You."

He hadn't expected her honesty. "I promise not to dunk you."

"That's not what worries me and I think you know it." Tara spoke in a low voice so Danette and Ray, who were now arguing over when to start grilling the steaks, could not hear.

"A life worth living requires taking a few risks." Somehow, he was even closer than a moment ago.

"I've taken my share."

"Not with me."

"And you want me to believe you're different?"

"I am."

Tara's heart contracted at those two simple words. In a way, he'd already proven that. Other men would have tried to dismiss her reluctance to go swimming as trivial. Angelo saw the decision for what it was, an opportunity to either keep shutting him out or to let him one step closer to the private Tara Peters.

It represented a willingness to socialize with him, not only as a couple, but also in a situation that left her vulnerable. Few women looked their best with their hair hanging down their back in a wet rattail. And no woman put on a swimsuit in front of a man she was hugely attracted to without taking a risk.

Maybe after two years, taking this one small risk wouldn't be so bad. She might be inviting Angelo closer, but she wasn't going to bed with him. She wasn't offering to have his babies or buy his staff presents at Christmas.

"I'll swim."

He nodded, his expression every bit as serious as hers. "Okay."

Tara hadn't bothered with a wrap because her suit was pretty conservative, but as she walked toward Angelo, who watched her with blatant male appreciation, she wished she had. The navy-blue shorts and halter style suit covered almost as much as her clothes had, but it clung to her curves like a second skin and it was pretty obvious her sexy boss liked the view.

When she came within reach, he casually reached out and placed his hand on the bare flesh between her shoulder blades. "Nice suit."

Her breath caught and it took effort to force out a response. "Thanks. It's one of my favorites."

He guided her toward the poolside. "The body beneath it is fantastic."

She stiffened under his hand, the comment catching her off guard.

He gently increased the pressure and kept walking. "Don't tell me you aren't aware of how incredible your figure is. You've been a model for years."

"Was a model."

"Semantics shouldn't change your awareness of your own beauty."

"Beauty doesn't mean much in the scheme of life." And in her opinion, it often got in the way.

"Coupled with brains and a passionate nature, it's a pretty potent package."

Was he implying he saw her that way? "Few men care about what's under the surface."

"I'm unique."

"I get that you'd like me to believe that."

He didn't stop beside the pool, but kept walking, until he led her through a glass door into the building that housed half of the huge swimming pool. The condo complex was not only exclusive, its luxury amenities were without equal in the area. Residents could swim in whatever weather the Oregon skies chose to offer.

Danette had told Tara that was one of her favorite things about her new home.

Since the day was hot and sunny, no one else was availing themselves of the covered portion of the pool however. The illusion of total privacy heightened Tara's awareness of Angelo in a way she wished it didn't.

He paused on the edge of the empty water and looked down at her. The intensity of his gaze burned away her awareness of the sounds coming from the party outside. "You're not very trusting are you?"

"If I was after the way I grew up and what I went through with Baron, I'd be an idiot."

"You're far from stupid, but you're also blind."

She opened her mouth to argue, but he pressed his finger against her lips and she had to fight the urge to suck it into her mouth and taste his skin. "You can't see beyond your past. I am not from your past. I am right here, right now and I want you to see *me*."

She reached up and grabbed his wrist, the simple connection feeling too good, too *right* for comfort. She tugged his hand away, but kept her hold on his wrist and his fingers somehow went from pressing against her lips to cupping her cheek.

Her eyes locked with his. "I can't see anything else."

"Good." He leant down until his lips hovered just above hers. "That's the way it should be."

"You're awfully arrogant at times."

"I would bore you to death if I were any other way."

Was he right? Did she crave the same kind of man her mother had always been attracted to? Somewhere deep down inside she'd always known she did, which was why she'd shied away from men in general. She hadn't trusted her own judgment.

Could she now?

"I'm going to kiss you."

He waited, watching her with searing patience. He was giving her plenty of time to pull away, but right now that was beyond her. She wanted him, wanted his kiss. She needed to know if the feelings inside her were a figment of her imagination, or if connecting to this man would truly be as soul-altering as her senses were telling her it would be.

Then he kissed her.

Carefully.

Slowly.

Thoroughly.

He didn't demand, didn't push for more. However, he still managed to take gentle possession of her mouth, imprinting his taste and the very essence of himself on her consciousness.

The almost soothing press of his lips against hers was not in the least aggressive and yet she felt completely, utterly claimed.

The expression in his eyes when he lifted his head said that as far as he was concerned, she had been.

"Are you ready to go swimming?"

The kiss had been so profound that the mundane question did not at first register. When it did, it also reminded her that they were not really alone.

For a woman who hated having her personal life in the spotlight, she'd certainly given the other partygoers an eyeful.

However, on closer inspection, she realized that at the place they were standing inside the building, hardly anyone could see them even though the door that led outside was made of clear glass. Ray with his annoying camera, seemed to be the only one even looking, the expression in his eyes smug.

Obviously he'd gotten a shot of the kiss. She wondered if that picture was going to make it into Danette's scrapbook. Considering her friend's sense of humor, it probably would.

The pool looked more inviting than ever. "Yes. I'm definitely ready to get cooled off."

She realized the implication of her words as soon as Angelo's low chuckle reached her ears. Annoying heat surged into her cheeks. She'd blushed more around this man than she had since taking her first modeling contract more than ten years ago as a gangly adolescent.

"Then shall we go?" Angelo asked, tugging her toward the deep part near where it flowed to the outside, obviously intending to jump in.

She pulled back. "I'd rather enter at the shallow end."

He turned to look at her, his expression indecipherable. "Why?"

She shrugged. "I guess I'm the cautious sort, but I like to get used to the water a bit at a time."

"That's torturous."

He was right, but she'd never been able to force herself just to jump into cold water.

Something shifted in his penetrating blue gaze.

That was all the warning she got before Angelo swept her up in his arms and tossed her in the pool.

Cold water shocked her system. She sank toward the bottom, legs and arms flailing. Tucking her legs in, she executed a neat roll and shot toward the surface. It wasn't far, the pool was only six feet deep to begin with. She came to the surface gasping for air and ready to take an inch off his hide.

Impatiently brushing the water from her eyes, she

looked around, treading water and ready to yell at him, but he wasn't poolside anymore.

A sudden shower of cold droplets from behind her had her spinning around in the water. He was there, so darn tall, he could touch bottom and still keep most of his face above the water. He moved to her right, ending up not a foot from her in more shallow water. His expression was so relaxed and mischievous she couldn't begin to hold on to her anger.

She didn't think Angelo Gordon looked mischievous very often. Something spasmed in her heart that she was the one to bring out this side of him.

She sent a cascade of water directed at his head with the sweep of her hand. "You fiend." But her heart wasn't in it and the words came out sounding a lot more teasing than accusatory.

He grinned, not bothering to wipe the water from his face. "Feels good doesn't it?"

"It would have felt better if I'd been able to get used to it before being dunked."

He shook his head. "You would have wasted time playing in the shallows, torturing yourself with every small foray deeper into the pool."

"The shallows aren't always a waste of time."

"They are when diving into the deep end is so rewarding."

Neither of them was talking about swimming and from the seriousness of his expression now, they both knew it.

"I dove in once before and learned to rue my impetuousness."

"Which doesn't mean you should never go diving again."

"I almost drowned the last time."

He shook his head. "Not you. You got the breath knocked out of you, but you're fighting fit again."

He was right. Baron had hurt her, but her nature didn't allow for wallowing in misery. She'd picked up and moved on, in every way but her willingness to risk her heart again.

Angelo tapped her nose. "You're enjoying the water now, admit it."

"Yes, I am." What had felt frigidly cold against skin heated by the sun now felt refreshing.

"Diving into deep waters can be terrifying or rewarding depending on who you do your diving with and what kind of water he leads you into."

Oh, gosh. She didn't know if she could handle this. He'd been challenging her to see him as a unique individual since the moment they met, but this was more. This was a direct attack on the way she'd been handling relationships for two years.

Or rather avoiding them.

"What kind would I find myself in with you?" she couldn't help asking.

Strong fingers curled around her waist under the water and she found herself being pulled against him. "The kind that will leave you sated with pleasure."

"I've been sated before, but that didn't make up for the hurt that came later."

"No one can guarantee the future, *bella mia,* but the present is here for us to enjoy."

There was something extremely intimate about being called an endearment in his mother's native language. It made her feel special to him. Only that was probably wishful thinking. No doubt, he slipped into Italian with every woman he wanted to bed. It was sexy.

The cynical thoughts made her angry. Was she going to spend the rest of her life thinking the worst of every man who came into it? That made her a victim of her past, not victorious over it and Angelo had been right. She was a strong woman, too strong to let her past control her.

"Yes, the present is here for us to enjoy."

When his lips covered hers this time, there was no hesitation, no gentle persuasion. It was all raw passion and masculine claim-staking, a sensual demand that she acknowledge his ability and right to give her pleasure.

And she gave it to him through a mouth that willingly molded to his.

Lips cool from the water soon heated against hers and his tongue pressed against her mouth, this time demanding entrance. With a groan of needs long denied, she opened to him. Unlike Baron's carefully orchestrated seductions, Angelo took her mouth like a conquering marauder. Imprinting himself on every millimeter of the interior, he devastated her lips with a carnality that left her weak.

He lifted her more firmly against him, his reaction to their kiss pressing blatantly against her thighs.

Her breasts ached and swelled in the confines of her halter top, while her most secret flesh grew hot and wetter than the water surrounding them. She laid her hands against the sculpted muscles of his chest, her fingers delighting in the sensation of wet, slick skin covered by curling black hair. The kiss deepened into territory she'd never explored and she dug her nails into his pecs. He groaned against her lips.

A shower of water broke them apart, the sound of laughter around them grating on nerves sensitized by his lovemaking. And it had been lovemaking even if he hadn't done any more than kiss her. Some of the other partygoers had swum through the low arched partition to the outside and were engaging in a game of tag.

Incapable of the coordination it took to tread water, Tara took advantage of her proximity to the edge to grab it with both hands. She hung there while her body struggled for breath and she tried to regain control over her emotions.

"Do you want me to apologize?" He spoke very close to her ear.

She shook her head, not looking at him. "I was with you all the way."

"I didn't mean to lose control, *stellina*. Public displays of affection are not my thing. The thought of embarrassing a lover leaves me cold."

But then neither of them had expected the other guests in the pool to follow them inside.

"*Stellina?*" she asked, not ready to dwell on the implication of her own loss of control or his insinuation she was his lover.

His lips quirked. "Little star."

Thinking of her five-foot-nine stature, she shook her head. "Hardly that."

"It fits you."

"Maybe to a giant like you, but the rest of the world sees me as rather tall."

"How the rest of the world sees you is unimportant to me."

"Your arrogance is showing again."

"And we both know how you feel about that."

She turned away from the heat in his gaze. "I think your Sicilian blood is showing."

"Maybe a little, but don't chalk that kiss up to my Latin temperament."

"You want me to believe I'm wholly responsible for your passion? Isn't that giving me an awful lot of potential power?"

"Why should I attempt to hide what must be obvious?"

This was getting stranger by the second. Baron had always been careful to minimize the effect she had on him, or at least her impression of it. He had played control games, wanting her to believe the greater need was on her side. He'd spouted platitudes about love while withholding the security of knowing she impacted him with the same potency he did her.

Either Angelo was way more sensitive than Baron Randall or he was more confident. The latter was far more likely.

She turned her head and gave him a sideways look. "You're a unique man, Angelo Gordon."

"I'm glad you can see that." He waited a beat. "Finally."

No, no lack of confidence there.

A feminine hand landed on Angelo's shoulder. "You're it." The buxom brunette swam away at speed, her string bikini leaving nothing to the imagination.

To Tara's shock, Angelo joined in the game of water tag with enthusiasm and showed that he played shark in the water every bit as well as he did the boardroom.

CHAPTER FOUR

WHEN they climbed out of the pool forty minutes later to eat, Tara was panting from the exertion. She grabbed her towel and started drying off. He did the same.

She leaned over to wring her long hair out. "I wouldn't have pegged you for that kind of water play."

"What, you thought I only knew how to swim laps in a pool?"

"I would have thought water polo would be more your style—highly competitive and a definitive winner at the end of the day."

"Actually I was on a team through high school."

She straightened, surprised by the admission. "Were you really?"

"Yes, but the traveling schedule interfered with my studies and I dropped it my freshman year in college."

"I was right then."

He acknowledged it with a slight inclination of his head and then draped his towel around the back of his neck. "But I can also play a mean game of tag."

"Definitely." He'd tagged her several times, and unlike some of the men, made no attempt to cop a feel when doing so.

He really was different…from anyone she'd ever known. Even her stepfather…because as wonderful as Angelo was proving himself to be, she could sense he had a ruthless streak that would leave even a man of Darren's strength in the dust.

That ruthlessness was in evidence when they arrived back at her apartment later that evening. "Invite me inside."

"I don't think I should." She wasn't sure she was ready to take the next step in their relationship, or if she ever would be.

"Because of the kiss in the pool."

"Because of how much I want to repeat the experience."

He got out of the car and came around to her door. He opened it and leaned over her to unbuckle her seat belt. He stopped with his face inches from her own. "I won't continue to pay the price for another man's stupidity."

"You're so sure I don't want this because of what I went through with Baron."

"You do want this." His mouth claimed hers for another kiss that left any spoken denial useless. "You're afraid of me because of him."

"I told you about my mom."

"She had bad taste in men."

"Apparently so do I."

The chill in his eyes made her shiver. "I resent that remark. You want me."

"I didn't mean to imply you're a bad risk."

"But that's what you believe."

Frustrated anger welled up inside. "Are you saying you're interested in commitment? Marriage? That you'll stick around if a business opportunity comes up that makes our relationship impossible?"

"Most men marry someday and I don't do business in the bedroom so our relationship will never be compromised by my commercial interests."

"What do you want from me?"

"Invite me inside and we'll explore the possibilities."

"I don't believe in casual sex."

"There is nothing casual about where you fit into my life." The gravity of his expression and tone convinced her he was telling the truth.

As impossible as it might seem, this man was serious about her. He wasn't making any promises, but he wasn't denying the possibility of a future either. A very skilled seduction campaign or was he showing the marks of integrity she could rely on?

"If I invite you up, it isn't to share my bed."

"I'll settle for some coffee to start with."

"All right."

Angelo pulled back, shocking her by not cementing his victory with another kiss.

They had coffee and to her further surprise, he left around eleven without making a pass. Oh, he kissed her again and her lips were still tingling the next morning from it, but he hadn't tried to get her into bed.

Which had left her confused and unable to sleep for dwelling on the implications of everything that had happened at and after the barbecue.

* * *

She was yawning the next day when she sat down at her desk and looked over to see Danette doing the same thing.

They both laughed.

"Tired?" Tara asked.

"Yes, you look like you are, too, but I bet it's for different reasons."

"You're so bad."

"Well, admit it…you probably went home and worked on a project until bedtime, while I worked on Ray."

Tara laughed again, this time shaking her head. "You are incorrigible."

"And you aren't answering. Dare I hope you and the boss hit it off last night?"

"I'm sure Ray told you we kissed…I'd say it was pretty obvious we're attracted to each other."

"That doesn't mean a whole lot when it's you we're talking about. You've got more fortitude than anyone I've ever known."

"Are you saying I'm stubborn?"

"If the conservative shoe fits…"

Tara just shrugged, not wanting to get into a long discussion about her date with Angelo and knowing that was where this conversation was headed if she didn't watch it.

She and Danette worked for a while before her friend piped up with, "Ray thinks you two are a great couple."

"Ray needs to spend more time focusing on you than what's going on around him. I was ready to throw his camera in the pool last night."

Danette gave a gasp of mock horror and clutched at

her heart. "He paid a thousand bucks for that baby. He would have cried like a lost orphan if you'd drowned it."

"I guess it's a good thing your hobbies feed each other."

The phone rang before Danette could reply to Tara's teasing.

She picked it up. "Tara Peters here."

"Good morning, *stellina.*"

"Angelo." She turned so her back was to Danette's now avidly curious gaze.

"Did you sleep well?"

"If I answer that honestly, you'll get a swelled head." Where the flirtatious words came from, she didn't know.

She'd never been particularly flirtatious and in the last two years, she'd been positively subdued in her behavior toward men, but he brought out a side to her she'd considered gone forever.

"I did not sleep." The words were given in such a seductive voice, she about melted in her chair.

"Um…I'm sorry?"

A wicked chuckle made her insides shiver. "I'm not sure I believe you."

"You doubt my sincerity?"

"Perhaps I wouldn't if you answered my original question…did *you* sleep well?"

"No."

"Ah. I like that. It was because of me."

"Conceited man."

"Am I?"

"Maybe not." She had spent her night thinking about him.

"I need to be back in New York on Monday."

"Oh." Gosh, how original, but what was she supposed to say to that? *Don't go?*

"My flight was scheduled to leave this afternoon."

"It was?" As in he'd changed it?

"Yes."

She waited in silence, not sure how he wanted her to respond. Hoping she'd interpreted his use of the past tense correctly.

"I had it postponed."

Relief surged through her and she knew she was in deep trouble with this man. "You did?"

"I wanted to spend more time with you."

"I like *that*," she admitted.

"So, you'll let me take you out tonight?"

"Yes." She was making an irrevocable decision, but maybe it was time she started taking some risks.

If she didn't, she might spend the rest of her life regretting yet another bad choice.

"I'll pick you up at seven."

"All right."

"You have a date with the boss?" Danette demanded the minute Tara hung up the phone.

"Yes."

Danette's whistle echoed the shock reverberating through her own brain.

She was still reeling from her decision to actually go on a date with Angelo when she dressed for the evening.

Unlike their business dinner, she had no desire to dress in a way that downplayed her femininity tonight. Pulling a garment she hadn't worn in a very long time from the back of her closet, she smiled. The quintessential little black dress, its spaghetti straps and skirt that hit her midthigh were elegant and sexy despite the simplicity of the dress's design.

She brushed her hair into curling waves that reached the middle of her back, slipped on a pair of black stiletto sandals and stood to look in the mirror. Oh gosh, she'd forgotten the way it looked. The way she could look.

Had it always been this sensual? Half of her body was on display and the neckline showed a lot more cleavage than she remembered.

Even without makeup, the woman staring back at her appeared ready for a very hot date and she wasn't sure that was the image she wanted to provide. Angelo didn't need a whole lot of encouragement in this area. She was reaching for the zipper on the back of the dress when the doorbell rang.

He was early.

She looked longingly at the less revealing dresses hanging in her closet and started to jerk the zipper down when the doorbell rang again. She pulled the zipper back up and after giving her reflection one last despairing glance, she headed for the door.

When she opened it, she almost fell backward from the intense appreciation in his gaze. He looked like he wanted to eat her alive. Zings of forbidden pleasure arced through her at the thought.

Taking a deep breath, she tried to ignore the incredible reaction of her body to his presence. "Hi."

"Hello." He looked her up and down, his fiery gaze touching her with tactile force and leaving goosebumps in unimaginable places in its wake. "I like the way you look."

"Thank you."

He'd changed from a business suit to a v-necked, lightweight, black sweater that molded his muscular chest and charcoal gray slacks that emphasized the sheer masculine perfection of his form. "You don't look so bad yourself."

His smile was more like a wicked invitation to sin. He put his hand out. "Ready to go?"

"I don't have any makeup on yet." Not that she normally wore it, but this was a date.

Not counting yesterday, which had not been official…it was her first one in two years.

"You don't need it."

She cocked her head to the side and studied him like he was an alien species. Sometimes, like now, it felt like he was. He certainly didn't fit the mold of the other males she'd known. "Most men want their dates to be as gorgeous as possible."

"You aren't an ornament on my arm. You look beautiful to me and that is all that should matter."

"Thank you."

"Besides, makeup cannot improve on perfection." It was a corny line, but he said it was such offhand seriousness; she couldn't dismiss it as mere flattery.

"Wow…you know just the right thing to say."

"The truth often comes out that way."

"But not always. Sometimes the truth hurts." She didn't know why she said it, maybe as a reminder to herself.

His mouth set in a grim line. "You're right, but I still prefer it over dishonesty."

"Me, too." A sudden urge made her blurt out. "Promise you'll always tell me the truth."

He stared at her as if testing her motive for the request, but then he nodded. "I won't ever lie to you."

"I'll never lie to you either." She said it quietly, fervently and he received it without comment.

Taking her arm, he tugged her out the door. "Now that we've established that, let's go eat dinner."

She laughed, a feeling of buoyant happiness bubbling through her. Unless he was the best actor on the planet, he'd meant his vow of honesty and she knew she had. No matter how odd the pact might seem to others, it gave her a sense of peace and a spark of hope for their future.

They were in Washington Park before she thought to ask where he was taking her for dinner.

"We're almost there."

To her knowledge, there was no restaurant near where they were, unless you counted the concession stands in the Rose Garden. Which seemed to be where they were headed, but she couldn't imagine he was taking her there.

She saw that she was right about their destination however as he pulled the purring Mercedes into a parking spot near the gardens. He came around to open her door and the scent of roses washed over her senses. Midsummer, the air was laden with their sweet fragrance.

She closed her eyes and inhaled. "It's what I think Heaven will smell like. So sweet and good."

"I'm glad you like it."

He helped her out of the car and then led her through an archway and down into the gardens. He kept going until they reached one of the private gardens enclosed by a tall green hedge. He stopped and she saw a linen covered table set with china and lit with candlelight in the center of the small garden bedecked with a thousand more flickering candles. Two antique dining chairs were on opposite sides of the smallish table and he seated her in one before taking the other.

A black clad waiter immediately poured them each a glass of champagne and then set starters of chilled crabmeat over a bed of lettuce.

She looked at Angelo, too stunned to pretend to be the least bit casual about his efforts. *"This is amazing."*

"I wanted tonight to be special."

"Any particular reason?"

"Because what is going on between us is special."

His words seduced her utterly.

Dinner was an incredible experience. They talked about everything including Angelo's plans for Primo Tech. He listened to her ideas on the subject and then brought up two more companies he was currently resuscitating.

That discussion took them all the way to dessert when Angelo said, "Tell me about Baron Randall."

Her muscles tensed. "I already did."

"Only some of it."

"Do you spend your other dates quizzing women on past liaisons?"

"Only when those liaisons are still impacting the present."

"He doesn't. I'm here aren't I?"

"He does. You're here against your better judgment. Because of your experience with him, you wanted to write me off."

"I've been writing *all* men off for two years. It's not personal."

"It became personal the moment I got lumped in with the rest." And in his arrogant view of the world, that was unacceptable.

She almost smiled.

"Your refusal to date makes it sound like you're not over him." He didn't sound pleased at that idea.

"I am, trust me."

She couldn't read his expression, but she wasn't sure he believed her.

"I told you I wouldn't lie to you."

"But if you are lying to yourself, how will you help it?"

"I'm not that much of a fool."

"I hope that is true."

She wasn't offended by his words. In fact, their urgency touched her. "Trust me. It is."

"How did you meet?"

"At a show." Perhaps talking about it would set Angelo's mind at rest. Goodness knew she felt more comfortable sharing her secrets with him than anyone else, though she still wasn't sure why. "He asked for an introduction from my agent and then swept my then naïve self right off my feet."

"He's quite a bit older than you."

"Sixteen years and that was a big part of his success where other men had failed. Not only did he know just what buttons to push to get a response from me because of his experience, but I made the mistake of assuming age meant maturity. That he knew what he wanted."

"Didn't he?"

"Yes, I guess he did…but in the end, it wasn't me."

"So you broke up."

"Yes."

"He married an heiress within a month of the break-up."

"Don't ask me how he accomplished that. She had to have heard the stories. We were splashed across every newspaper. Why would she want a man who had to have been having an affair when they met?"

"He was living with someone else when he met you."

"How did you know that?" She hadn't even learned that juicy tidbit until she read one of the nasty articles done on their breakup.

He shrugged. "I read."

"Well, I didn't know about her until later."

"I see."

"I doubt it."

"You sound bitter."

"The tabloids slayed me…portrayed me as the skirt

on the side while Baron had been courting his one true love. They dubbed me *Tempting Tara* when I was the one who'd been tempted and then tossed aside."

"Anyone who knows Baron Randall would know that he's absolutely incapable of having one true love."

"You know him?"

"We've met." The cold dismissal in his voice left no doubt what Angelo thought of the other man.

"So, you don't think I'm some sort of floozy, ripe for the picking by another charismatic tycoon?"

"Floozy?"

"You know what I mean."

"Yes, I do and no, I don't."

"But—"

"I want you. That's not a crime."

"No."

"So you think I'm charismatic?"

"On occasion, yes."

"That's good to know."

"I'm sure you think so."

"If it means I get the girl, I do."

"The jury is still out on that one."

"Then let's see if I can't rig it."

"What?"

He was standing up and his hand was outstretched. "Come for a walk with me and let me turn some of this charisma on you."

He was teasing, but it wasn't a joke. The man was way too attractive for Tara's own good. And as docile as any lamb, she still put her hand in his and let him lead her toward the main part of the rose garden—that had been closed off for their enjoyment alone. Its lush beauty in the fading light awed her.

"It's incredible here," she said after several minutes of silence.

"I think so, too. It's one of my favorite places."

"Did you visit when you lived in Seattle or discover it when you bought Primo Tech?"

"When I was a kid, we came every summer. It was like a pilgrimage."

And he was sharing this special place and his precious memories with her. That meant something. It had to.

"My mother loved the Rose Festival and we drove down for it," he continued, "I liked the rides."

"I can't imagine you on a carnival ride."

"I was a little boy. Even tycoons had to be children at some point."

"It's hard to picture. I see you trading companies from your crib."

"Actually I didn't get interested in the business side of things until I was twenty. Before that, I thought I would be an engineer like my father had been."

"What changed your mind?"

"Life." He put his arm around her waist and pulled her into his hard, warm body. "My father was technically brilliant. He developed several new designs and started his own company."

"I'm surprised he was a success. A lot of engineer types aren't good when it comes to the day to day operations." She'd seen it over and over again at Primo Tech.

"He wasn't the greatest businessman, but he made do."

"Whereas you are brilliant business wise."

"And a mediocre engineer."

"There are always trade-offs in life."

"Yes, there are."

"What's the name of your father's company?"

"It doesn't exist anymore. It was absorbed into a bigger company."

That surprised her. "I would have thought you would keep it intact. A pride thing."

"I didn't own it at the time."

"I'm sorry." She sensed that caused him a lot of pain.

He turned to face her. "Let's not talk about business right now."

"What do you want to talk about?"

His head lowered. "This," he said as his lips pressed against hers.

It was unlike any of the other kisses had been. This was both tender *and* passion driven. Desire vibrated off of him and against her mouth, but he didn't push for a deeper kiss. When he was done, he lifted his head. "You are so sexy, *stellina*."

"You make me want to be."

Triumph rippled through Angelo. For two years this woman had wanted to be anything but sexy. She had avoided men and intimacy completely, but in his arms, she wanted to be a woman.

She was so close to being his—he could sense it.

"Come on, there is something I want you to see."

She let him guide her toward the lower part of the rose garden. He kept his hand on her shoulder, his thumb brushing her nape. Triumph flared through him when she shivered despite the warmth of the air and shifted toward him infinitesimally.

Experience had taught him that often it was the small touches which seduced a woman, not a blatant show of passion. She already knew how much he wanted her. He'd shown her that in the pool. Now he had to show her it was okay to want him too…because he knew what to do with her wanting.

He leaned down so his breath caressed her ear when he spoke. "I know how to satisfy your craving to be a sensual woman, Tara. It will be very, very good between us."

"I…" Her voice trailed off as if she didn't know how to respond to his comments.

He wasn't so reticent. "I will give you more pleasure than you have ever known. Believe it."

This time it was a full blown shudder that rippled down her spine. *"Angelo."*

He was not even kissing her, but already her arousal was making her voice husky and her heartbeat quicken. He smiled. She didn't know it, but they had just passed first base on their way to a home run.

CHAPTER FIVE

By the time they returned to the car, Tara was a mass of throbbing sensation.

Angelo and she had lingered in the garden for quite a while. He had shared a surprising knowledge of the different species of roses, having her smell them and feel the softness of their petals as he explained their differences.

All the while, he had been touching her and saying things in that husky, deep voice of his that promised the sun, the moon and the stars all wrapped up in one ultra masculine package.

As battle strategies went, it had been extremely effective. He'd vanquished her resistance and moved her toward surrender with the speed and efficiency of a well-armed, seasoned campaigner. It was the recognition of her comparative lack of experience that made her hesitate to give total surrender.

Could she really be sure of what she wanted and what was best for her when she was under the influence of his charismatic presence? When her hands were literally shaking with the need to touch him?

She turned toward him as his car slid into a parking spot in front of her brownstone and was struck anew by his sheer masculine perfection. So sexy. So strong. So much a man. She wanted him more than she'd ever wanted anyone, including Baron.

Which made it all the more imperative that she not dive into an emotional commitment without knowing where he was at in that regard.

She could remember all too clearly the times she had said she loved Baron and gotten no response or an, "I know." She could see now that he'd only said the words to her when it suited his strategy for manipulation.

She no longer had such naïve illusions about love, but sex wasn't a simple slaking of physical needs for her, either. It never could be. She needed to know that more than Angelo's hormones were engaged. She wasn't giving her body to another man without being sure he saw her as more than an occasional bed partner.

Angelo switched off the ignition.

"I'm not going to ask you up."

He tensed and turned to face her, his jaw set, surprise making his eyes darken. "Why not?"

Time for total honesty. She sensed any attempt at prevarication would only give him the final leverage he needed to bring about her surrender. "Because if I do, we'll make love and I'm not ready to do that yet."

He reached out and cupped the back of her head, his thumb tracing the shell of her ear and making her tremble even more. "You want me."

No way could she deny it. "Desire isn't enough."

"What *is* enough?"

She stared at him, nonplussed by the question. She hadn't expected him to want to discuss the intricacies of a relationship. Most men shied away from that sort of thing.

But, goodness knew, Angelo Gordon was unlike any other man of her acquaintance. "I don't want to be treated like a one night stand."

Which was as far as she'd gotten in her thought process…or as far as she had allowed herself to go.

"I want more than one night."

"How much more?"

"How much more *do you want?*"

"I'm not sure."

"That's not good enough."

"I can't quantify it."

"Sure you can. What do you want? Protestations of love?"

She, who no longer believed in love, felt her heart rate double at the mention of the word. Was he saying he was falling in love with her? How could he be?

"What do you want, Tara? A promise of fidelity, or do you want more?" he went on relentlessly. "Perhaps an offer of marriage. Is that what you need to feel good about giving yourself to me? Commitment with a capital C?"

Was he saying he would give those things to her, or was he testing her, pushing to figure out the parameters of the deal?

"I just realized I wanted to pursue a relationship," she said, frustration at being put so firmly on the spot lacing her voice. "How am I supposed to know what form

I need it to take before I'm ready to be intimate with you?"

"You're too smart not to know your own mind."

Only right now, her mind was muddled by desire and the need to conquer fear. She doubted he ever got muddled in his thinking. Probably, he thought he was being extremely reasonable asking her to define what she needed, but he wasn't the one with doubts. Somehow, she couldn't see this man ever being the one with the doubts.

Her only defense against his relentless logic was more honesty. "Look, you were right, Angelo. I have been letting my past control my present. I don't want to do that anymore, but that doesn't mean I'm ready to jump into bed with you. I need time."

His smile was all sensual, predatory, and it confused her, because it wasn't the expression of a man who had just been turned down. "Oh, you're ready all right, but you're hesitating because you don't know where it will lead."

She throbbed low in her womb and she knew he was right. "Fine. You're right. There aren't a lot of options for where sex between us could go."

"This is always true. Those options do not change over time."

"Some of them become less palatable."

"You do not want a one night stand, but I gather you also don't want a few long weekends with us both moving on to other partners?"

The mere idea made her shiver with revulsion. She'd never taken sex casually and the idea of going into a relationship that intimate with the expectation of ending it repelled her. "No."

"That leaves two other outcomes…we move in together—"

"No," she practically shouted.

His brow raised in question.

She took a deep breath and let it out. "I stupidly went that route once before…even after watching my mom make the same mistake over and over again. I won't be controlled by my past, but I won't refuse to learn from it, either."

"Then there is only one alternative left: marriage."

"I—"

"You see, it was not so hard to define. In order to give yourself to me, you want a lifetime commitment."

"I'm not angling for marriage." But her words came out a mere whisper of sound, the direction the conversation had taken shocking her to the core.

"Aren't you?"

"No." She wasn't, darn it. Frustration welled up in her. "If you weren't trying to go so fast, this wouldn't even be an issue, so don't try putting all the blame back on me. I only said I'm not keen on having casual sex with a man who will disappear from my life very soon."

"I wasn't aware I was trying to blame you for anything and I agree, casual sex is not what I had in mind."

A maelstrom of emotion churned through her. *"We can't get married just because you want to have sex with me."*

"People do it all the time actually, but I think we've got a lot more than sexual desire going for us."

"Let me get this straight," she said, feeling more bewildered than she ever had in her life. "Are you saying *you want to marry me?*"

"Yes."

Suddenly she felt claustrophobic in the interior of the car. She couldn't get enough air and the world was going black around the edges. "You didn't say that," she breathed.

"I don't just want you, I like you, Tara. It's been a long time since I felt that way about a woman. I'm thirty years old and I've never been in love. I don't think I'm wired that way. There are a lot worse things I could do than marry a woman I want as much as I want you."

She couldn't think of a single thing to say in response. Baron had put off making any major commitments with a constant stream of excuses. So had her mother's boyfriends. She'd never known a man like Angelo that wanted to jump feet first into long-term commitment…except Darren.

Her stepdad had asked her mom to marry him on their second date. But that was because he loved her and Angelo had just said he wasn't wired that way. It didn't make any sense.

He sighed at her silence. "I respect your integrity and your intelligence. I enjoy your company and I think you feel the same way about me. You probably thought you loved Baron Randall, but look at where that got you. Marriage to me would be a lot better for your emotional well-being than waiting around for another man like him to show up."

"If you feel that way about it, we can keep dating… take our time deciding if a future makes sense."

Something came over his expression, the ruthlessness she'd always been sure lurked under his civilized exterior.

He shook his head decisively. "Some of the best decisions I've made in my life have been spur of the moment based on my gut instincts. Those instincts are telling me that a marriage between us would work."

This was beyond anything she could've imagined.

"So, what? You want to fly to Las Vegas and get married tomorrow?" she asked sarcastically, trying to point out the ridiculousness of his attitude.

"That would work," he said musingly. "I think I could wait one more night to have you."

"You're insane."

"Not even close. I'm merely sure of what I want."

She shoved her car door open, feeling as if she didn't get out of that car immediately, she was going to lose it. "I need to think."

"You sure you won't ask me up? I could work on convincing you."

"No!" She clambered from the car. "I don't think that's a good idea."

He didn't appear worried by her rejection. In fact, he gave her another look filled with sensual confidence. "I'll be by to take you to breakfast. We'll spend the day together."

She nodded and reeled like a drunk up the walk and into her building. Luckily someone had left the front door unlatched because keys would have been beyond her right after she got out of the car.

She wasn't much better when she reached her door on the top floor. The phone was ringing when she got it unlatched.

She rushed inside and picked it up, still feeling dazed. "Hello."

"*Stellina.* I wanted to make sure you made it inside all right."

"Yes, I'm here." Which was definitely an exercise in the obvious, but scintillating, even intelligent conversation was beyond her.

"I do not like the fact your building has only one locked exterior door and I noticed it was left open. It is old…even locked, it could easily be broken into."

"This isn't New York, Angelo."

"Bad things happen here, too."

"I'm fine."

"Yes, but I'll be glad when we're married and I can know you are always safe."

She tried her best not to dwell on his use of the word *when* instead of *if.* "You mean if I married you, I could look forward to your hiring me a bodyguard?"

"That's an idea worth considering. I have plenty to go around."

She was still gasping with indignation and leftover shock when he said goodbye and hung up the phone.

Surprisingly she slept well and woke up feeling refreshed before the alarm went off.

The phone rang as she was getting out of the shower. It was Angelo telling her he wanted to take her to the beach and to dress appropriately. He also suggested she bring spare clothes in case they got wet or sandy. She couldn't help wondering if he didn't have plans to try to stay overnight, but she found herself packing the clothes and other necessities anyway.

Was she engineering her own downfall? His proposal had fried her brain cells.

Angelo parked his car in a spot near the entrance to the beach. Despite the warmth of the day and it being a Saturday, the spot was deserted. It was the reason he favored this beach over others and why he'd built a vacation home not far away. He liked the solitude.

He'd take Tara to his house later, when her initial reticence to being alone with him had diminished.

They got out of the car and stopped in unison to take stock of the view before them.

"It's gorgeous," Tara breathed, her voice filled with awe.

Blue water stretched out as far as the eye could see and waves crashed against huge, mountain like rocks jutting out of the water a couple hundred feet from the shore.

"Yes." He looked down at her. "But the view isn't the only beautiful thing around here."

She averted her face, but he could see his compliment had pleased her. Once again, she'd gone for a very feminine look, wearing a cropped tank top and low rider shorts that showed lots of leg and the smooth skin of her stomach. Her sandals were strappy bits of nothing that accented the delicate lines of her feet.

She'd pulled her thick chestnut hair up into a youthful ponytail again, leaving the slender column of her neck exposed.

He leaned forward and placed a warm, lingering kiss against the sensitive spot behind one ear. He inhaled her fresh, sweet fragrance and nuzzled her. "You smell good."

"Thanks." She pulled away with a jerky, nervous movement. "We'd better get down to the beach."

"We're not on a timeline." But he let her lead him away.

He could afford to wait to solidify his advantage. He had no doubts about how this day would ultimately end. And he was enjoying the wait.

They walked down a path from the parking lot to the beach. As soon as they hit the sand, Tara stopped and pulled her sandals off. She let them drop behind a log near the path entrance.

"Are you sure they'll be safe there?"

"Do you see anyone around to steal them?"

There was only one other car in the small parking area and the only other occupants of the beach were nothing but small dots in the distance. "Point taken."

"You should take off your shoes, too."

He hadn't walked barefoot on the beach since he was a kid, but there was something about an untamed beach and sunshine that brought out even a tycoon's need to connect more closely to the elements. He slid his sports shoes and socks off and left them next to Tara's sandals.

Then he put his hand out and she took it. They walked hand in hand to the shoreline, their silence sur-

prisingly companionable considering the heavy subjects they had been discussing when they parted the
night before.

The sand was warm against his feet, but the heat
generated from their palms pressed together was
greater. He got a primitive charge out of touching Tara
in any way. Even the slightest connection sent electric
impulses along his nerve endings and knowing that
making her his took her away from his enemy gave
him an equal charge.

He hadn't been nearly as surprised by his proposal
as she had been, but then he knew what lengths he was
willing to go to get his revenge against the man who had
destroyed the grief-stricken and vulnerable woman who
had given Angelo his life.

Marriage would be a much more effective tool in removing the possibility of reconciliation between Randall and Tara than mere seduction.

"How seriously do you take the commitment of marriage?" Her words told him her thoughts had been going
along the same course as his own.

"It's the ultimate commitment between a man and a
woman."

"Do you consider divorce an easy out if things get
difficult?"

"No."

She stopped and looked up at him, her brown eyes
questioning. "What do you really think about marriage?"

"I want a companion."

"There's more to life than bed." Their thoughts had
been traveling along *very* similar paths.

"I said a companion, not a bed warmer. I like talk-ing business with you. It's stimulating."

She grinned, a naughty gleam in her dark eyes. "I've never had my opinions described that way before."

"They're that, too," he said, easily sliding into the game. "You're the first woman to turn me on while talking about the merits of on-site employee day care."

She laughed, the sound warm and inviting. "What else?"

"Children. I want a family. I've built an empire I have no desire to leave it to some hospital who will build a wing with my name on it." As he said the words, he realized how true they were.

Why not Tara as the mother to his children?

He certainly had no illusion about falling madly in love and living happily ever after with some dream woman. And he'd be destroying his enemy in the pro-cess.

She nodded, looking thoughtful. "So you see mar-riage as pretty much permanent."

"Don't you?"

"Yes. The worst part about growing up was the up-heaval every time one of Mom's boyfriends left. I won't put my children through it. I want a marriage that is going to last."

"Ditto."

She smiled at that, but didn't say anything else and they walked along the shoreline for several minutes, the call of seagulls and the surf the only sounds around them.

Then she stopped abruptly and leaned down to pick up a red bucket some child must have left behind. She looked at it as if the bright plastic somehow held the answers of the universe.

She turned and tugged his hand. "Come on."

"Where?"

"I want to build a sand castle." She led him to the spot where the sand was still wet but no longer brushed by waves from the outgoing tide.

Stunned, he just stared at her when she plopped down to her knees and started scooping damp sand into the bucket.

She peeked up at him, her eyes wide behind her sunglasses. "Are you going to help?"

"Why?"

"Why help or why build?"

"Why build?"

She shrugged. "I've always wanted to build one and I never have."

"Never?"

"I grew up in the Midwest. I didn't even see the ocean until I started taking modeling jobs that required travel. I moved to Portland for Primo Tech, but I've spent most of my life living in land-bound states."

If someone had told him that seducing a former model included building a sand castle, he would have dismissed the idea as nonsense.

"Come on," she cajoled, "don't be a spoil sport. If you can build companies, you can build one small sand castle."

It didn't turn out that small. She wanted turrets and a moat, as well as a courtyard and a castle that any royal family would be proud to live in.

It took them two hours to complete. When they were done, she sat back on her haunches and surveyed their handiwork with satisfaction. "Very nice."

"It looks formidable."

"Like a princess could live protected behind its walls all the days of her life." A strange expression shot through her brown eyes. "But it's only sand. Just like most fantasies in life, it looks great, but it won't survive the incoming tide."

"Not all dreams disappear when tested by reality."

"Most of mine have."

"What kind of dreams?"

"Oh, I don't know. I was going to grow up and be a supermodel."

"You were very successful."

"But no Cindy Crawford."

"Why would you want to be anyone else?"

She laughed at that. "It's a girl thing."

"What other dreams got washed away on an outbound tide?"

She sighed and then sat back on her already sand covered bottom, her gaze fixed on the castle. "When I was a little girl, I dreamed of having a family. By the time Darren came along, I no longer trusted the dream." She fiddled with one of the sticks they'd discarded as too crooked to stand atop the turrets as a flagpole. "I'd moved out before I accepted he wasn't going to."

"But he didn't."

"No. He stayed with Mom, but then I made the mistake of dreaming of my own future with a man I loved. It took almost two years, but eventually I realized that whole Prince Charming fantasy was just that. It was no more real than this." She pointed to the molded turrets and empty moat.

"What exactly are you saying?" Did she want to avoid marriage altogether?

Now that he'd decided it would be the best form of revenge and that marrying her wouldn't exactly be a hardship, he would not accept a refusal.

She looked at him then, her dark gaze intense. "I'm not looking for love and a perfect happily ever after anymore."

"And yet you are hesitant to marry me. Why?"

"I need to know that what we have is more than a sand castle on the beach."

"How many years was Darren your stepfather before you moved out?"

"Six."

"You spent six years wondering if he was real...you could spend just as long wondering about me, but I am real and so is my proposal."

Then he did what he was best at and kissed her slightly parted lips.

Angelo's mouth took possession of hers as he dragged Tara into his lap.

And that fast, she was lost. It all felt so incredibly right. The heat of his body against hers, his uniquely masculine scent surrounding her and the spicy warmth of his mouth both comforted and enticed her. The feel of his rock hard muscles holding her gave her a primitive sense of security no modern woman would admit to.

As much as her mind told her attraction to this man spelled danger in capital letters, her body responded to his as if she'd found the other half of her whole. The half she hadn't known was missing until this very moment.

She wanted to dismiss such thoughts as juvenile and fanciful, but they permeated her being with rock solid staying power. Her *soul* knew this man.

Hard, mobile lips molded hers perfectly and with just the right amount of pressure that she moaned under the onslaught to her senses.

He growled in response to the sound, his hand gripping her waist tightly. She felt like she was being kissed by a wild predator claiming his mate, not a refined businessman. She responded on a level she had never allowed herself to explore before, digging her fingertips into his shoulders and reveling in the leashed power she sensed there.

He lifted her by the waist, repositioning her so she straddled his hips and their torsos were pressed close together. She could feel the threat of his hardness against her most sensitive flesh and the layers of clothes between them did nothing to negate the heat that connection generated.

Jolts of sensual awareness rippled through her body, making her arch toward him and shudder while his lips continued to entice her passion to greater heights.

Suddenly his thumb brushed upward from where his big hand rested against the indentation of her waist. It caressed her in an up and down motion, teasing at her rib cage just below her breasts before dipping down over the curve of her hip.

Her breath suspended in her chest as she waited for him to explore further, to actually touch swollen flesh chafing at the restrictions of her bra. But he didn't and she found herself breaking her lips from his to suck in much needed oxygen.

"Angelo," she panted.

She didn't know what else she wanted to say, couldn't form a cohesive thought to save her life.

His hands curved around her in a hold so possessive, she gasped. "This thing between us is good. Don't dismiss it, *stellina*."

She had no answer, so she remained silent.

He kissed her temple and then the corner of her mouth as if he couldn't help himself before guiding them both to their feet. She dusted the sand from her clothes and her legs, while he pulled something small from his pocket.

It was a mini digital camera. He aimed and took a shot of their sand castle, then took a picture of her looking at him.

She wasn't smiling. She had no idea how she looked. Her thoughts were deep and her body was still vibrating with sensual awareness.

"You wanted a picture of our sand castle?" she asked, surprised by the gesture.

"There is more than one way to preserve a dream."

The message in his eyes was one she was terrified of interpreting so she turned away.

He laughed, the sound husky, as she started back up the beach. "I won't let you run from me, Tara."

She didn't answer because if she was honest with herself, she'd have to admit she didn't want to.

CHAPTER SIX

TARA wasn't exactly shocked when Angelo pulled his luxury car into a spot in front of a Frank Lloyd Wright style house positioned on a cliff overlooking a private beach not far from where they'd built their sand castle.

She'd half expected him to offer to rent a hotel room so they could shower the sand off before dinner, but the privacy and subtle magnificence of the home was beyond anything she would have envisioned.

"Is this yours?" she asked as he turned off the car.

"Yes."

"I'm surprised you keep it considering how little time you must have for vacations."

"I've found it useful in hosting negotiations with West Coast companies."

Ah. That made sense. Seclusion and the home court advantage…both great assets to have on his side when working on a business deal.

The inside reflected the stark simplicity of Wright architecture, but the quality of both the house's furnishings and minimalist décor pointed to Angelo's wealth.

He led her to a bedroom with a huge plate glass window that overlooked the ocean. "You can shower and change in here."

"Thank you."

She watched him walk away, her feelings no more settled than they had been on the beach.

After her shower, she brushed her hair out in front of the mirror in the large en suite bathroom. She left it down, shimmering in silky waves over her shoulders, contrasting against her white dress. She'd thought this dress was more conservative than the one she'd worn the night before even though it also had spaghetti straps.

It fell to her ankles in a form fitting line that was nevertheless not clingy. However, the row of tiny buttons that began at the sweetheart neckline stopped eight inches above the hem, leaving a slit that parted when she walked. And it struck her that a man of Angelo's temperament would see the buttons as some kind of challenge.

She bit her lip, wishing she'd brought something less in your face feminine.

Just then, he walked into the room. The lack of a warning knock said more about his sense of possessiveness than it did his lack of manners. She had a feeling the oversight had been very deliberate.

"Ready?" he asked, dressed in a pair of dark chinos and white Polo shirt that set off his dark skin while accentuating the sculpted muscles of his chest.

Talk about sexy.

She put her hands out in a stock modeling pose. "What do you think; am I ready?"

His eyes flared with blue heat as he gazed at her. "You look beautiful."

"Thank you." She slipped her feet into a pair of heels. "Now, I'm ready to go."

He put his arm out and she took it, saying nothing when he casually suggested she leave her things in the room for later.

She was curious to see what his plans for the night were. After his comments before they left the beach and the way she had responded to him, she wondered if he was considering using sexual intimacy to convince her of their compatibility.

She'd made the mistake once of believing great sex meant a great relationship. She wasn't that naïve anymore, but she couldn't deny the surge of sexual awareness she had every time he was near, either. Even Baron had not impacted her so startlingly with his mere presence.

Dinner was fabulous and she couldn't help thinking about how Angelo had told her that he enjoyed her company. She liked being with him, too.

As much as she wanted him, it wasn't all about sex.

Though that was what was primarily on her mind in the confines of the car as he drove them back to the beach house.

"It's late. Do you want to spend the night?" he asked as he pulled into the parking spot he'd used earlier.

"Wasn't that your plan all along?" Her tone wavered somewhere between censorious and teasing.

He shrugged. "It occurred to me, but if you aren't comfortable, we'll drive back to Portland tonight."

At least he was being honest.

"There are multiple bedrooms," she said, knowing even as she made the remark that the likelihood of more than one being used was very small.

"Yes."

"We'll probably end up in the same one, though."

"That is entirely up to you."

And her libido, which was as out of control as it had ever been in her life. Even so, she didn't want to spend what remained of the night in the car driving home and then seeing him off at her front door.

She wasn't sure what she did want, but saying good-bye to him was not it.

"It makes the most sense to stay."

"Excellent." He opened his door and swung his legs out of the car. "I wasn't looking forward to driving back across the mountains this late."

But he would have done it if she asked him to. That was worth something. Her trust was gently building without her really realizing it.

He built a fire in the great room's fireplace and opened the sliding glass door that led to outside. The sound of crashing surf filled the room and cold air rushed in to make the heat from the fire welcome, even though it was summer. Not atypically on the Oregon coast, it had started getting chilly the moment the sun went down.

She slipped her heels off and stretched her toes in the plush carpet before moving to stand near the floor to ceiling window beside the open door. She loved summer because of the long days and gorgeous sunsets.

This one was almost over, but it had been spectacular. The deep red and orange reflected off the water as the light faded. She didn't know how long she stood there, how long Angelo let her simply watch out the window, but the sky faded to a deep purple and then there was nothing but black night out the window. Soon, the moon would be out, but for now, the darkness made it seem as if they were alone in the universe.

It gave her a strange feeling, one she needed to counteract, and fast.

She remembered spying a familiar game case on one of the built-in shelves. "Do you fancy a round of Backgammon?" she asked without looking to see where he was.

There was nothing but silence behind her.

She turned to see why he hadn't answered and ran smack into his chest.

He cupped her shoulders and looked down at her, his expression doing impossible things to her insides. "I want *you,* Tara."

"So, you do plan to try to convince me with seduction." She couldn't quite decipher the change in his expression and that made her nervous, bringing out the cynicism she'd used so many times in the past to hide behind. "Or is it the other way around? Are you hoping your proposal will smooth the way for getting me into bed? And then maybe tomorrow, or the next day, or whenever you get ready to move on, you start making noises about how maybe we aren't really all that compatible."

Her tone was nothing short of an accusation, her

words deliberately offensive, but he didn't get angry. In fact, he didn't tense at all. He simply looked at her like he knew something she didn't, something really important. Something she wanted to know but was afraid of finding out.

His mouth came down and hovered just above hers.

"You—" a barely there kiss against her lips "—are—" his tongue flicked out to taste the corner of her mouth "—going to—" another kiss, this one more firm "—to have—" again his tongue…this time exploring the seam of her lips "—to trust—" his hands landed on her hips and pulled her into intimate contact "—me."

He tilted his pelvis toward her, leaving little doubt of the level of his arousal. Then, another kiss, this one demanding entry to her mouth while his hands rotated her hips against him. How could being pressed into such intimate contact with such blatant male sexuality feel so natural, so right?

Just like on the beach, her body reacted to his nearness as if it had found its sole home in the universe. She had no defense against something so profound.

She parted her lips on a sigh of surrender she prayed she would not regret.

His tongue took possession of the heated interior of her mouth and increased the temperature several degrees. He tasted so good, better than the slice of banana split cheesecake he'd cajoled her into having for dessert. Her arms snaked around his neck and she went up on tiptoe to duel with his tongue in an ancient dance of erotic desire.

The world tilted and she realized she was being carried. She didn't know where and didn't much care. She was too busy trying to devour a pair of sexy, masculine lips that she thought she just might be content to lock with for the rest of eternity.

He stopped moving, bent slightly and then no light filtered through her eyelids. Even that reality couldn't hold her attention for very long, but when he laid her down on the plush carpet, pulling his mouth from hers, her eyes flew open and she moaned in protest.

They were in front of the fire, its orange glow the only light remaining in the room. It flickered over his features like a magical ebb and flow of illumination and shadow. She lay on her back staring up at him, her heart beating wildly while her lips pulsed with the need for more of his kisses.

He came down beside her, propping himself up on his elbow. So close their bodies touched, his leg slightly covered hers, and his chest pressed against her arm.

She felt surrounded by him, completely closed in, and her breaths came in shallow pants.

"Afraid?" he asked, not sounding particularly concerned.

"You said I should trust you."

His dark brow rose, the firelight lending a primal cast to his face. "Do you?"

"I'm working on it."

He smiled one of his rare smiles. "Good."

She said nothing and he brushed her face with his fingertips, leaving a trail of tingling sensation in their wake. "You are so beautiful."

Those words had been said so many times to her over

the years, they'd almost ceased to have meaning.
However, he was not seeing her as a body prepared to
show some designer's creation off to advantage. He
was looking at her as a lover and no man had been allowed to do that in two long years.

Even before, Baron's appreciation of her beauty had
been wrapped up in his own pride of ownership. Something she had never been comfortable with, no matter
how much she had thought she loved him.

Angelo looked at her as a man looked at a woman
he could not look away from, not a woman he desired
to show off to others.

The words unfurled inside her with a burst of pleasure and she savored them in silence for several seconds
before replying. "Thank you." She brought her hand up
to trace the chiseled features of his face and down his
neck to his collarbone. "You are a beautiful man."

The corner of his lips quirked in amusement. "I've
never thought of myself in those terms."

"Most men don't." She grinned, feeling ridiculously
happy for no reason she could discern. "However, you
can trust me on this. Aesthetically you are extremely
pleasing. Feature for feature you have the most masculine beauty I have ever seen. And I saw a lot of beautiful men in my former profession."

"So, you think I'm the sexiest guy you've ever met?"

"Yes."

"It's those Sicilian genes." The smug arrogance in his
voice was more amusing than annoying.

She laughed. "Both of your parents must have been
devastatingly attractive people."

"I suppose."

"Don't you know?"

A dark shadow crossed his features and his mouth flattened into a grim line. "Yes, but it isn't something I've thought about in a long time."

"You don't like talking about them, do you?"

"No."

"Maybe it would help whatever bothers you so much if you did." She was no amateur psychologist, but she couldn't help feeling he kept too much of himself hidden.

Said the pot to the kettle.

She almost sighed, but bit it back. She wasn't any better than him, but she had told him more about Baron than she'd even told her mother. And she felt better for it.

He traced the neckline of her dress, allowing his finger to dip into her cleavage for a breathless second. It felt amazing, just that small touch, but she sensed they were on the verge of something more important and she willed herself not to get sidetracked by how good it felt to be next to him.

"Angelo?"

"It's too private."

"Even to share with the woman you want to marry?"

An arrested expression came over his features and his gaze shifted from her breasts to her eyes. "You want me to talk about them to you?"

"Yes."

"It's important to you?"

"I think it is."

He sat up, looping his arms around one raised knee and ran his fingers through his hair. "I don't know where to begin."

"Wherever you want." She scooted into a sitting position beside him, glad for the warmth of the fire now that he wasn't touching her.

Her nipples peaked from the cold air blowing in through the open doorway. She didn't want it closed however. The sound of the surf was soothing.

"My dad met my mom when he was in Sicily negotiating a contract." Angelo's voice was void of emotion…no remembered pleasure, no residual pain, nothing. "He fell for her like a ton of bricks within minutes of their meeting. At least that's how he used to tell it. He went after her as only a brash young man sure of what he wants can do."

"You wouldn't know anything about that," she teased.

He shrugged, not even cracking a smile at the small joke. "It's not the same. This was love—the kind you hear about in fairy tales I guess."

Something clenched inside her at his words.

He'd fallen silent, maybe sensing her inner turmoil.

"Go on," she urged.

"Dad talked Mama into marrying him and returning to the states with him."

"That sounds pretty romantic," she had to admit. She might not believe in love and happily ever after for herself, but it sounded like his parents had certainly known what that was all about. "Were they happy?"

Pain spasmed across his face and laced his voice

when he spoke. "Yes. They were deeply in love for all the years of their marriage, but Dad died of a heart attack when I was twenty. Mama was lost without him."

"I'm sorry."

"I was, too. She didn't know how to run a company and I was still in school. I wasn't ready to take over the reins."

"That would have been hard for you."

"Even harder when I realized what that had cost us."

"What did she do?"

"She hired someone, a man who came highly recommended. He was brilliant and seemed to really know his business. *I liked him.* I worked alongside him at the company during my summer break that year. I thought he was teaching me the ropes so I could take over as soon as I graduated." Self-disgust dripped from Angelo's words.

"Is he the one responsible for you losing your family company?" she asked with an awful premonition.

"Yes."

"Because he wasn't as good as you thought?"

"Because he was a lying, using bastard who did whatever it took to get what he wanted."

"That doesn't sound good."

"He seduced my mother into selling him the company at half its worth and then dumped her."

The words hung in the air with poison still capable of causing pain. Tara could feel it. *She* hurt.

This guy had been worse than Baron. She shuddered at the thought. She hadn't thought they got any slimier.

"He was ten years her junior, but it didn't matter,"

Angelo went on, his voice flat now. "She was so grief stricken, she was easy prey for him and all the while I thought he was being a good friend to her while I was away at school."

"You blame yourself."

"Not as much as I blame him."

"So, he just walked away from her after he got his hands on your company?"

"Not before destroying my mother. He mocked her for believing a man a decade younger would want to marry her. He ruined her sense of honor and womanhood." His fist hit the floor. "I thought he was my friend, but when I found out he'd been screwing my mother, I wanted to kill him."

"You didn't."

"I might have. I was angry enough and there are a lot of primitive urges passed down by my Sicilian ancestors, but I was too busy dealing with her suicide."

Horror clawed through her heart and she felt nausea well up inside. "She killed herself. Over him?"

"She still loved my dad when this monster came into her life. He used her loneliness against her and when it was over, she felt she'd betrayed Dad's memory. She came from a very traditional Sicilian home and she couldn't face what she'd done."

"Did she tell you this?"

"She left a note...wanted to explain to me so I wouldn't hate her. God knows I never hated her, but she couldn't live with herself...with the memories, the humiliation and hell, probably the loneliness."

"So she gave up?" At least her mom had kept fight-

ing. No matter how many mistakes in judgment she made about men, she'd never given up and abandoned Tara.

"He killed her." The words came out like bullets and she knew Angelo believed them implicitly.

Tara didn't say anything. In a sense he was right, but in her opinion, his mother had let him down, too. Women got hurt all the time by men they trusted. Just look at her own mom…and her own past. His mom's choice had been cruelly selfish toward her son, but Tara couldn't condemn her…had no interest in doing so.

She saw immediately that Angelo's belief he wasn't wired for the more tender emotions came from a bone deep determination never to be at risk to them like his mother had been. His steely determination was palpable.

"Thank you for telling me."

He looked at her coldly. "No more questions? You don't want to know how she died or what happened to the bastard who used her so mercilessly?"

"Only if you want to tell me."

"She took pills. They'd been prescribed by her doctor to help with the grief after Dad's death. She went to sleep curled around his pillow and never woke up again."

"I'm so sorry." It was inadequate, but she didn't know what else to say.

Some things were just too big for mere words.

"It's been ten years."

"And it still eats at you."

"But not for much longer."

"You plan on getting revenge against the guy who did it?"

His gaze became shuttered. "You know me well. Yes."

Somehow, she wasn't surprised he'd waited so many years to get the guy back. Angelo was a heck of a businessman and that meant he left nothing undone. Any revenge plot he devised would have every angle covered.

"You're Sicilian. It's in your nature," she tried to say lightly, but it came off flat and she sighed. "I hope it gives you the satisfaction and closure you need."

Angelo's jaw could have been hewn from granite. "It will."

She bit back an argument. Vengeance wasn't going to bring his mother back or restore his family company to him, but maybe it would allow Angelo to move on. She was surprisingly unconcerned by the fact the man who wanted to marry her was caught up in a revenge plot.

A dedicated businessman, she was sure he'd choose that avenue for retribution. His empire was built on saving failing companies and she didn't see him destroying an empire and all of its employees to crush a single man. More likely, he'd take it over. And considering what kind of man Angelo would be taking it from, she had no trouble thinking the unscrupulous toad deserved it.

Then Angelo turned toward her and the sensual predator was back gleaming at her from those indigo eyes.

She sucked in a breath at the swift change. "Angelo?"

"Old grief has no place in our present, *stellina*."

She would have replied but he was pressing her back to the carpet, his lips applying pressure to hers, while sexual intensity rolled off of him in palpable waves. It was so overwhelming, she was shocked by the gentle way his mouth explored hers.

She could not imagine what kind of training he had gone through to learn this kind of self-control, but it awed her.

So did his sexual expertise. She thought she'd known all there was to know from a man experienced in the art of seduction, but Baron didn't have a patch on Angelo.

He built her desire with caresses that touched everywhere and lingered nowhere. The fire crackled in the hearth beside them, the wind blew in the scent of the ocean to wash over their heated bodies and every nerve ending she possessed came to life with stunning power. Surge after surge of electric desire rushed through her until she panted and shook with need.

He palmed her breast, his big hand engulfing the swollen flesh. Her nipple, already beaded, now ached with the need for more stimulation. Only, the careful pressure of his hand muted by the layers of her top and bra was not enough. She arched up into his hand anyway, striving to increase the friction.

He rotated his palm. Sensation shot from her nipple straight to the core of her and she pressed upward, moaning.

"I want to touch your skin," he whispered in an erotic growl.

"*Yes.*"

He unbuttoned her bodice, one small button at a time. He paused between each one to place a baby kiss on the skin revealed.

"Oh, Angelo…" Her fingers scrabbled in the carpet beneath, vainly trying to find purchase—something to anchor herself to with the storm of emotions raging through.

"This is a very sexy dress, sweetheart." He spoke against her chest, the hot air from his mouth making her shiver in a response as far removed from being cold as possible.

"Thank you."

"You may wear it again."

She laughed at the sheer arrogance of his statement, the sound strangled.

Finally, he peeled the front of her bodice away from her body to reveal her white lace bra that conveniently hooked in the front. Had she worn this particular bra and panty set on purpose? Had she subconsciously hoped he would do exactly what he was doing, which was un-latching the bra with one-handed dexterity she couldn't hope to emulate?

He took his time peeling back the bra cups, using each movement of the fabric to increase her arousal, while teasing her with what was to come.

Oh, gosh…this man knew exactly how to touch her.

He looked down at her naked torso framed by the white fabric of her dress with blatant male appreciation burning his gaze. *"Bellisima, cara."*

"You sound so sexy when you speak Italian," she said on a sigh. "What are you saying?"

"Most beautiful. And you are that, Tara."

He hadn't translated the *cara,* but even she knew what that meant. Darling. Was she darling to him?

She hoped so because the more time she spent with Angelo Gordon, the more she felt for him.

His fingertip traced circles on her breasts, first one and then the other...back and forth...first left...then right...but never touching the hard nubs that ached for his attention.

"Please, Angelo."

"What do you want, *cara?* Tell me." His voice was thick with passion, the subtle Italian accent coming out.

"I need you to touch me."

"I am touching you."

"More. I need more."

"What more?"

"You know."

"Perhaps I do, but just to be sure, I want to hear you say it."

"No." Suddenly she felt all too vulnerable. He was wringing a response from her that was greater than anything she'd ever known. "Don't make me say the words."

He lifted his hand away from her and met her gaze square on. "Why not?"

She had to suck in air before she could speak. "It gives you all the power."

"No, it does not. Whatever you ask for, I will give. That puts the power directly in your corner."

"You won't make me beg?"

A feral grin slashed across his gorgeous face. "Only if you want me to."

And he was just the man that could make her want such a thing.

"How could you possibly know I want you to?" Even Angelo was no mind reader.

"You won't ask directly for something. You'll say words like *more* and *please* and make me guess what more it is you want." His voice was every bit as devastating as his touch—so rich and smooth and full of erotic promise.

"So, anything I ask for you will give me?"

"Anything."

Baron had never given her that kind of power in bed. She couldn't think of any other man who would. It took a tremendous amount of confidence and consideration to make the offer.

"Even if I ask you to stop?" she pressed.

"Especially if you ask me to stop."

He really was putting the control in her hands. No man had ever done such a thing. He might seduce her body, but he wanted her to give permission with her mind before he did it. It was such a tantalizing concept, she shuddered in renewed need.

"I want you to touch my nipples." Heat that had nothing to do with sexual arousal flooded her cheeks, but excitement at saying the words out loud also coursed through her body.

"Your wish is my command." He rotated his fingertip on the very tip of her hardened peak.

Excitement crashed over her in wave after wave of incredible pleasure, but it still wasn't enough.

"Harder, please." Then remembering what he'd said, she husked, "Pinch it."

He did, gently and then more firmly and she couldn't

help the soft animalistic sounds rasping out between her parted lips. He tortured her with soft then firm touches until the sensitive flesh throbbed with aching intensity and her breath was coming out in hitched little gasps. Then he moved to her other breast and did the same thing while her head thrashed back and forth on the plush carpet.

"You look like a sensual fantasy in the firelight."

The words shocked her, so lost was she to her feelings. "I feel like a woman on the verge of ecstasy," she breathed out.

His hand moved to the remaining buttons on her dress and started undoing them with the same enticing kisses between each button until her lace panties were revealed. He stopped then and brushed across the front of the lace and she jumped from the sensation.

He smiled. "Nice. They match your bra."

"Yes." Was that her voice—so husky it was practically a whisper?

He finished unbuttoning the dress, baring her completely to him but for the scrap of lace covering the heart of her.

Her legs parted of their own volition from the heat of his gaze.

He took the silent invitation with a speed that made her cry out as his fingers slid between the lace and her skin to dip into the warmth of her feminine center. His mouth moved down her body until it closed over one distended nipple and this time her cry was so harsh it made her throat ache.

He sucked and she whimpered.

His fingers did magical things to her sensitive flesh. She started gyrating against them, her hands gripping the back of his head and keeping him pressed to her breast in frenzied strength. A tension she hadn't known in two years built and built until it broke over her like a tsunami wave.

There was no way she could contain it and she bucked against Angelo, crying out his name and demanding more with an abandon she had never felt before.

He kept up the nerve-racking touches until her body jerked with each light caress and shook from an overdose of pleasure.

She grabbed his wrist. "Stop!" she begged.

He did, cupping her with possessive tenderness that made her eyes sting.

CHAPTER SEVEN

SHE didn't know how long they lay together like that before it occurred to her what she had just experienced had been very one-sided. And he hadn't said a thing…had not demanded entry to her body or anything!

What kind of amazing man was he? Certainly, he was unlike any other she had known or heard about.

She reached down with the hand closest to him and brushed the back of her fingers along the rigid length of his erection.

A low sound of pleasure rumbled in his chest. "Mmm…that feels good, *cara*."

"Do you want to make love, Angelo?"

"We are already making love, but if you are asking if I want to have intercourse…" He paused and she waited with bated breath for him to go on.

"Without a doubt, I want you, but I promised you. No seduction. After what just happened between us, it could be nothing but."

He was right, but… "Maybe I've changed my mind… maybe I want to be seduced."

"I don't break my word, Tara." Despite the obvious arousal of his body, his tone was absolutely firm.

She respected that. A lot. Only that didn't mean he had to lay here like a statue in sexual agony.

She brushed her hand back and forth, loving the way his big body jerked from the small caresses. "I c…could please you in other ways."

Angelo's only response was a very primitive growl deep in his throat. Taking it as acquiescence, she turned on her side, pleased with the way he kept his protective and highly erotic hold on the apex of her thighs. It felt like they were connected intimately.

She undid his trousers and slipped her hand inside. He was big and hard against the silk of his boxers, tenting the fabric significantly. She gulped at the thought of making love completely, but sensed he would never hurt her, not this man who had been so careful to keep his word even when she tempted him not to.

She caressed him and he went even more rigid.

She reluctantly pulled his hand away from her and sat up to kneel beside him. She grabbed the waistband of his trousers.

He rolled onto his knees and then stood so she could slide his trousers down and then the boxers, taking care not to catch his hard length on the waistband.

Her breath expelled from her lungs in a long whoosh at the sight of his hard flesh so close to her face. "You're um…very prepared."

He chuckled. "I've never heard it put that way before."

She leaned forward, but he reared back. "Please

don't. If you put your mouth on me, my good intentions are going to take a vacation and not come back until I'm buried deeply inside you."

She nodded her understanding and stood. She let her dress slide from her body completely.

His eyes glowed his appreciation.

She smiled. "I want you to take off your shirt, too."

"Hot?"

"You don't know how much."

She choked on a laugh before joining him on the carpet, this time with him on his back and her snuggled up beside him.

"That feels good."

"I haven't done anything."

"You don't have to. Just having your body beside mine is a turn-on."

No beautiful Italian speech there, but she appreciated the sentiment and curled her fingers around him in reward. "Amazing. You're so soft."

"Soft?" he choked out.

"I mean your skin…like silky velvet. Can there be such a thing?"

"If you say it is, I believe you. Right now, I would believe anything you want me to."

She laughed. "I doubt it, but you just keep saying stuff like that."

He didn't laugh. He moaned as she started stroking him. She listened to the hitches in his breathing pattern to determine how he liked to be touched. It was the most incredible experience she'd ever had, having this powerful man put himself at her mercy.

"Tara…"

"Yes, *cara,* yes! *Don't stop.*"

She didn't and he erupted with a masculine shout that rang in her ears. Her body went stiff against him as if sharing an echo of his ecstasy. She'd never felt anything like it and collapsed against his side as if she'd found her own completion.

Eventually, they snuggled in front of the fire for a long time before he got up and carried her into the bedroom. As she had suspected, they ended up sharing a bed.

Tara saw Angelo off at the airport with the promise to have an answer to his proposal by the following weekend.

She couldn't believe she was making him wait, even harder to believe he was letting her.

He'd made it clear he wanted her decision now, but he hadn't pushed for it. It had to be obvious she wanted him enough to risk pretty much anything…even marriage. But he had agreed to wait for her decision and that made her feel really good.

Baron had always insisted on having his own way, so had most of the men her mother had lived with.

Angelo wasn't like that. He wanted her compliance sure, but not at the cost of her self-respect and that meant the world.

Not wanting to make the same mistake with Angelo, she had with Baron, she spent a good portion of her off-hours that week researching him. Everything she found, which wasn't much…the man was very private, pointed to him being the opposite of Baron.

He was absolutely ruthless when taking over a company and making it profitable, but he was also known for his ability to turn all a company's assets to a profit, including its current workforce. He gave regularly to charities, was honest as far as she could tell, and as Ray had told Danette, Angelo was not a playboy.

In fact, there was almost nothing that she could find about him in the social columns. He didn't have much of a personal reputation at all.

Everything she could find on him was related to his almost supernatural ability to make money and turn a dying company into something great.

She'd searched for information on his father's company, but without knowing its name, she'd had no luck. And its loss was never referred to in the articles written about him now. Except for what he'd told her, his past was shrouded in mystery.

His present was filled with business, but his life was not littered with people he'd used and discarded once he'd gotten what he wanted from them.

The turnover rate in his corporate headquarters was very low. Another good sign, if she needed one. He was a trustworthy man.

Thursday evening, she stood in the grocery checkout line, tiredly waiting for her turn. It had been a long day, an even longer week. She'd missed Angelo more than she'd thought possible. How could someone become so necessary in such a short time? She'd lain awake every night wrestling with her inexplicable desire to acquiesce to his marriage proposal. It made no sense and yet, her heart told her she needed the man.

She didn't trust that organ, but found its promptings impossible to ignore...thus her sleep deprived exhaustion.

She yawned behind her hand while the checkout clerk argued with the man in front of her over the sale price on a can of chili. Someone had to be sent to verify the price listed on the shelf.

Knowing that nothing was going to happen until the matter had been resolved, she let her gaze roam over the magazines and weeklies displayed at the check stand. Her eyes skimmed the headlines, noticing two Elvis sightings and one alien baby claim before she was arrested by a picture that looked like...no it couldn't be.

But it was.

A full color image of Angelo kissing her in an obviously heated embrace in Danette's pool filled the front of one of the weekly tabloids. The headline read, *Tempting Tara Takes Another Rich Lover...*

Would she never be rid of that awful nickname? Darn it, she wasn't the one who had done the tempting in her relationship with Baron, or the one with Angelo for that matter.

The tag line under the photo was worse. *Will going to bed with the boss put this former model on the fast track to success in corporate America?*

She grabbed the tabloid with a jerk that almost tore its front cover and yanked it open. She flipped the pages with angry flicks until she found the article. It was a two page spread with more pictures. Lots of them. Every one insinuated sexual intimacy between her and Angelo.

One showed them coming out of their hotel room at the coast. Angelo's arm was around her, his body language and expression possessive. The implication was unmistakable, but the editorial copy spelled it out anyway.

Like two years before, she was painted as a money-grubbing whore, only this time with her eye to the main chance at Primo Tech. An unnamed source in the management training department was quoted as saying it looked like Tara was hoping to gain her promotions via an avenue even older than hard work and perseverance.

It was all there…her affair with Baron, further speculation on her being the other woman when he courted his oil heiress. There was even some nonsense about how he'd been keeping her under surveillance since the breakup and innuendo that she might be at fault for the rumored possibility of imminent divorce.

Tara's stomach somersaulted and it took a full minute of shallow breathing before she was sure she wouldn't lose what little she'd eaten that day. She'd skipped lunch, trying to get ahead at work so she could take a half day off on Friday and keep her weekend free. Angelo was due in early the following afternoon.

Had he seen the article? She had no way of knowing. Surprisingly he had not called her all week. She had expected him to at least attempt to sway her decision with frequent phone calls, but he hadn't. She only knew when he was due back because he'd told her before leaving when to expect him.

Her gaze re-focused on the article. *How many people had seen it?*

The weekly didn't have the highest circulation in the country, but it was a national publication.

She couldn't believe this was happening all over again and it made her furious. She hadn't done anything wrong, but she was being painted as a scheming tramp who used her body to get ahead instead of relying on her brains. That made Tara angriest of all. She'd graduated at the top of her class and was darn good at her job. She didn't need the company owner's *patronage* to get a promotion.

She was perfectly capable of securing one on her own merits, thank you very much.

The whole situation would be ludicrous if it didn't hurt like a knife to the gut. Twisting that knife was the knowledge that whoever had sold the picture and information to the tabloid had been at Danette's party. And one of her co-workers had been willing to be quoted, if anonymously, saying something extremely nasty. Betrayal burned through her.

She didn't know who she worked with that felt that way, but only one person had gone around taking picture after picture at the party. Ray…the budding journalist.

He'd told her he was a *serious* journalist and that photography was only his hobby. The weekly was hardly an impressive example of journalistic solemnity and those photos had been paid for, which made the little hobby *a job*.

An ugly, despicable job…but one that could not be denied. Her stomach cramped again as an even less palatable thought assailed her. Had Danette known about it?

Two years ago, a couple of models that Tara had thought were friends had betrayed her to the press. One going so far as to tell out and out lies about her, exacerbating the piranha like media frenzy feeding off of her misfortune. That had hurt almost as much as Baron's rejection.

So, maybe Tara was being hopelessly naïve now, but she simply could not accept that Danette had been in on Ray's scheme. Danette was too forthright and she had too many stars in her eyes when she talked about Ray.

Which meant she was probably hurting as much as Tara was right now...if she'd seen the article.

It wasn't fair. The rat. The absolute rat! She'd like to see him right now and she'd cut off his tail.

"Miss, it's your turn!"

She looked up, realizing from the expression on the faces around her that was not the first time the checker had told her to move forward. Apparently the big chili controversy had been settled.

She tossed the weekly down in front of the checker. "I'll take this, too."

He nodded, his expression bored and then finished ringing her up. She paid and left, anger and hurt sizzling through her in alternating waves.

Those waves took on monumental proportions when she got to work the next day to discover she was being fired. She was told the order came from Angelo's office in New York, but she refused to believe it. First of all, the man was too smart to fire a woman he'd slept with over getting caught out by the media.

Such an action put both him and his company too much at risk for retaliation and a sexual harassment lawsuit, if the woman in question was in the least bit dishonest.

The human resources manager assigned to the task of letting her go had finally admitted that Angelo was currently in Puerto Rico dealing with a natural disaster emergency that had affected one of his supply plants. Apparently even phone communication was iffy.

Which explained why he hadn't called all week.

When he didn't arrive that afternoon, or call, she tried his office. His secretary confirmed that he was calling in only sporadically for messages. Tara left one, bothered by his absence and her inability to get ahold of him. And she had to admit that an emergency like the one he faced in Puerto Rico wasn't something he could dismiss or delegate.

She'd made a decision not to be hampered by her past in every judgment she made. That meant continuing to believe in the tycoon she missed more than she wanted to.

At least until he proved himself unworthy of her trust.

Wanting to get one issue of trustworthiness resolved, she tried to call Danette, but got her friend's home voice mail instead and was forced to leave a message.

The phone rang the next morning and woke her out of a fitful sleep. She'd spent too many dark hours thinking about her best friend and the man who wanted to marry her.

Hoping it was Danette, she grabbed it. "Hello?"

"Tara?"

The voice was familiar, but she couldn't quite place it.

"Yes?" Her voice came out scratchy and she cleared her throat.

"I need to see you, darling."

"Who is this?" she demanded, her sleep fuddled mind sure of one thing.

The voice at the other end of the line was not one of the two men in her life with a right to call her by endearments: Angelo and her stepfather, Darren.

"Don't tell me you've forgotten the sound of my voice. I haven't forgotten anything about you, Tara. I never could. Not the sweet way you smell, or the taste of your lips—"

"I am not in any mood for obscene phone calls," she inserted with speed, recognition finally enlightening her rapidly wakening mind.

Baron's laugh was seductive and low, like he thought she was flirting with him. "How about a visit? Would you prefer I say these things in person?"

"No! Are you in Portland?" she asked, worried that might be the case and wondering how he'd gotten her number.

"Not yet, but I can be. We need to talk."

"We finished talking two years ago."

"Tara, I'm divorcing my wife."

"How fortunate for her," she quipped, unable to help herself. Did he really think she cared?

"I understand your bitterness, darling. I made a terrible mistake two years ago. I want to make it right."

"You don't know the meaning of making things right. You did me one favor two years ago, Baron. You walked away. I'm not about to let you undo possibly the only good deed of your life. You're a user. You suck other people dry and smile while you're doing it."

She had no idea how she'd ever loved this man, but after one week in Angelo's company, the difference between the two types of tycoons was crystal clear to her.

"I don't want you in my life. I don't want you calling me and I swear that if you show up in Portland stalking me, I'll go to the authorities for a restraining order."

"Tara, you're angry, but you don't understand—"

"You're wrong," she interrupted again, not wanting to hear a single line of his con story. He'd deceived her before with that tone and his too believable excuses, but never again.

"I'm not angry. I'm disgusted you could think for one second I would want to hear from you again after the way you used me and then threw me to the wolves in the press with a steak tied around my ankle."

"I can explain that."

"No. You cannot." She exhaled a frustrated breath. "Leave me alone, Baron, or this time I'll be the one giving sympathy producing interviews to the press."

He made a harsh sound. "Tara, you can't trust Angelo Gordon."

So, he'd read the tabloid stories? That was one more thing Ray-the-rat had to answer for. "My private life is none of your business."

"I used to be your private life."

What colossal nerve. "That was a long time ago and it is certainly not true any longer. Goodbye, Baron."

She hung up.

The phone rang five minutes later and when the number only came up as *out of area* on her caller ID, she ignored it.

CHAPTER EIGHT

CHECKING her voice mail after her shower, Tara ground her teeth in vexation when she realized the second call had been from Angelo. But his message gave her her first smile in over thirty-six hours.

He was headed back to Portland and would arrive later that evening. He said nothing about the gossip stories, but he did apologize for not calling when he'd been unable to fly out the day before.

She listened to the message three times just to hear his voice and then erased it with a jab of a button, irritated with her lame, sappy behavior.

The phone rang again, this time a local newspaper name showed up on the caller ID and she let it go to voice mail again. The rest of the day, the phone rang off the hook and the two times she made the mistake of answering it, a reporter was on the other end of the line.

She was in the middle of preparing a tray of snacks for Angelo's arrival and muttering to herself about Ray-the-rat and Baron when something struck her.

What made her angriest about Baron's phone call

earlier had nothing to do with the past. No pain from his betrayal lingered to catch at her heart. No longing for what might have been tugged at her thoughts, but she was furious he had implied Angelo was untrustworthy.

And she was feeling downright feral that her attempt to avoid another phone call from Baron had made her miss one from Angelo.

Baron couldn't begin to understand, because he didn't have a protective bone in his body, but she was sure Angelo wouldn't hurt her. Nor would he allow her to be hurt by others. He was going to be enraged when he found out she'd been fired and she had no doubt Ray-the-rat was going to heartily regret making her and Angelo the crux of his career advancement…such as it was.

Another sudden, not so welcome thought scorched through her consciousness.

She trusted him.

She really trusted a tycoon.

That's why she'd given him the benefit of the doubt about her employment termination. That was why she was waiting for him to show up with a heart full of hope instead of a loaded shotgun. Against all odds, something deep inside of her had bonded with him and told her she could believe in him.

That was scarier than having Baron trying to come back into her life. Her ex-lover posed no threat to her emotional health, but Angelo was something else altogether. She wasn't at all sure how much damage to her current happiness letting him go would do, but she had a feeling it wouldn't be negligible.

She did not want to fall in love again. She did not ever want to be that vulnerable.

Before she started hyperventilating, she reminded herself that trust was not love. They weren't mutually exclusive emotions of course, but neither were they absolutely mutually inclusive.

Were they?

How could she have let herself come to this pass? She'd only spent a few days with him. She knew powerful men like him weren't innately trustworthy. She hadn't needed Baron to tell her that, but when he'd said it, she'd been offended. Was still offended.

Her heart insisted that Angelo was different. Unlike with Baron, she didn't have to convince herself…she had to fight belief. Maybe it was the things Angelo had told her about his past. He hadn't condemned his mom, but he was determined to make the man responsible for her pain pay.

That made him protective, even if it was of a memory.

She should never have researched him. All that stuff about what a ruthless but really fair guy he was had turned her head, or her heart. He'd told her he didn't give up, that he made things work and she had no option but to believe him.

And seriously, a man who spent ten years preparing for revenge didn't change his mind on a whim. If he wanted to marry her, he planned to make it stick.

Was she trying to convince herself to accept his proposal? Or facing the inevitable?

She trusted him, she wanted him and in a way she did not understand, but could not deny, she needed him.

The decision she'd been wrestling with all week was really no decision at all. In a way, Baron's call had put it into perspective. Angelo was nothing like the older man and Tara was sure that if she refused his offer, she would regret his leaving much more than she'd ever regretted her failed relationship with Baron.

The buzzer sounded, scattering her thoughts and letting her know she had a visitor. She rushed into the entry hall to press the black button which would unlock the front door. Sure it was Angelo, she opened her door and waited just inside so she could see down the hall.

Within seconds his tall, muscular body came into view. His eyes looked tired and his skin was pale, but he strode toward her, his body vibrating with purpose.

She didn't smile, didn't speak. She just waited.

He reached her and without a word, yanked her into his arms and kissed her with claim staking intensity. She locked her fingers behind his neck and kissed him back.

When they finally came up for air, she was in his arms and he was leaning on the inside of the closed door to her apartment. She wasn't going to waste time wondering how they'd gotten there. He made things happen.

This was just one of those things.

Nuzzling her neck, he squeezed her. "I missed you, *stellina*."

"I missed you, too, Angelo."

He lifted his head, his gimlet stare enough to make her heart contract in her chest. "Don't ever buzz your apartment open without using the intercom to see who it is again."

She laughed, relieved that was all it was. "All right."

He kissed her again. Hard and fast. "I mean it."

"I know."

He carried her into the living room and sat down on the sofa with her in his lap. His thighs weren't the only hard things under her bottom. Heat flashed through her, sensitizing nerve endings already on edge.

"You really did miss me," she teased.

He didn't smile in response. "I have severely reprimanded my second in command."

"He's the one who ordered I be fired?"

"Yes."

"Then you know about the articles as well."

"I saw something at the newsstand in the airport."

She cringed at the reminder how widespread was her humiliation. "Did you flip?"

"That's one word for it, but my reaction to the initial article was nothing compared to my fury when I was told you'd been fired as a crisis containment measure. If you were a different woman, that kind of crisis containment could have blown up in our collective faces."

She knew he'd been too smart to take such a step.

"My managers will not act so impetuously on my behalf again."

She shivered at the chill in his voice.

"Why did they?"

His brows rose. "What do you mean?"

"It just seems to me that they had to have some reason for believing you would approve their decision."

"Ignorance."

"Well, yes, but…"

"They were ignorant because they've never been in this situation before."

She waited in silence for him to continue explaining and was surprised when he did after only a brief pause.

"They know only that I hate personal publicity of any kind. I've never dated a woman employed by one of my companies and I don't usually make it on the front pages of the weekly tabloids. My last magazine cover was *Newsweek*."

"I read it. That article had a lot more truth to it."

"No doubt. I'm going to kill Ray." From the way Angelo growled the words, she could almost feel badly for the rat.

"So you think it's him, too?"

"Who else could it be?"

"I can't think of anyone, but I'm sure Danette didn't know about it." Fairly sure anyway.

Once again she was operating on the principle of giving her friend the benefit of the doubt. It had worked with Angelo.

Looking unconvinced by her assurance, he asked, "Have you spoken to her?"

"No. She wasn't at her desk when security walked me out and she hasn't returned my call."

"My second in command will be attending the remedial management training course on human resource development."

She felt a twinge of sympathy for the general manager. "That will be quite the come-down."

"Particularly if you teach it."

She laughed. "I no longer work for Primo Tech."

"This is true." He buried his hand in her hair and brushed his fingers through it to the ends. "That's so damn silky. I'm hoping you'll take a position closer to me."

"What?" First he was talking about her hair and then a job offer? "Are you offering me a position in your main office?"

"In my life."

"You mean you *don't* want me working for you?"

"Of course I want you working for me. Do you think I want a brain like yours going to a competitor?"

She warmed at the compliment, but still wasn't sure what he was driving at. "Um…I'm getting confused here."

"I'm hoping you'll take your next job…working for me…as Tara Gordon rather than Tara Peters."

She swallowed and then plunged. "Yes."

He looked like he'd been turned to stone. "You will marry me?"

"As soon as you like."

"You are serious."

"Very."

"No big production?" he asked, sounding very satisfied.

"No, but I'd like my mom and Darren there, and Danette."

"Done." He kissed her again and this time they were both disheveled and missing some clothes when they came up for air.

She still had her bra on, but her shirt was gone and his was completely unbuttoned. His tie hung over the back of the couch and his suit jacket was in a crumpled pile on the floor.

He was looking at her like a starving man facing a five-course meal. "I want you."

She rested against the hard warmth of his chest. "I want you, too."

"But we're waiting."

"Until we're married?" she asked, an unnamed emotion making her heart squeeze.

"Yes."

It felt right and she smiled, glad that she'd agreed to marry quickly. She liked the idea he wanted to wait, but she didn't think either of their self-control could stand up to a long engagement. "We're going to have one heck of a wedding night."

"Count on it."

The buzzer for the front door sounded again.

"Are you expecting anyone else?"

"No." But she got up.

"This time use the intercom."

She pressed the gray button, thinking she should have done it before. Never mind it being some deranged criminal, what if Angelo had been a reporter? "Who is it?"

"Tara?"

"Yes."

"It's Danette. Can I come up?"

"Of course, hon." She buzzed the entry lock and then dove for her shirt.

"Button up, Angelo. Danette's on her way up."

"Worried if she sees my manly chest she'll swoon?"

"Maybe." She winked. "But mostly I don't want to advertise what we've been doing for the last half hour."

"You're a conservative little soul, all things considered."

She shrugged, but bit her lip. "Does that bother you?"

"No. I was raised by a traditional Sicilian woman, you've got to remember. Before my father died, she defined the term conservative."

"I wish I could have met her."

His eyes clouded over. "Me, too."

There was a knock on the door and Angelo answered it because he was closer.

Danette stared at him as if she was seeing a ghost. "Mr. Gordon?"

"Angelo. I've eaten meat from your barbecue. That puts us on a first name basis."

At that, Danette's eyes filled with tears and her fist flew to her mouth, but the sound of a sob escaped.

Tara rushed across the room and threw her arms around her friend. "It's okay, hon. Truly. We know you didn't have anything to do with it."

She wasn't totally sure about what Angelo believed, but he wasn't acting all cold and accusatory, for which she was grateful.

"But Ray did." And then the sobs escalated.

Tara held Danette until she calmed down and stepped away, wiping her eyes with a handkerchief Angelo handed her.

She took a deep breath and then let it out, her eyes wounded pools in her tear ravaged face. "He doesn't understand why I'm so angry."

"The idiot. I'm sorry."

"Me, too. I broke up with him." Her lip quivered, but she maintained control. "I can't believe I let myself love that slimeball."

"Aw, hon…"

Her gaze darted to Angelo. "I quit my job, too. Told Primo Tech what they could do with their management training program after I found out you'd been fired."

"I'll get you reinstated," Angelo said without hesitation.

Danette shook her head. "Thank you, but I need to get away. I've lived here all my life and been protected for most of it." She bit her lip and swallowed. "I want adventure. I thought Ray was it, but I was wrong."

Tara's heart broke for her friend.

"Maybe I could help find you something." Angelo said.

A glimmer of hope sparked in Danette's eyes. "Seriously? You mean it?"

"Yes."

"Aren't you mad at me?"

"You are not responsible for the malicious behavior of your former boyfriend."

"I'll never make another scrapbook page again."

Tara gave her a hug around her shoulders. "Let's not get hasty. One scheming photographer does not the death of a hobby make."

Danette gave her a weak smile.

They talked her into staying for dinner. When Angelo discovered she spoke both Spanish and Italian, he said it would be a piece of cake to get her a job abroad if she'd like.

Danette left with a smile on her face, despite the sadness in her eyes.

Tara frowned at the closed door Danette had just walked through. "I'd like to punch Ray right in the nose."

"I've done better than that. I've instigated proceedings against him for getting the photo under false pretenses."

"I doubt the charges will stick."

"Maybe not, but I'm doing my best to make sure they do and the experience of going to court and having to hire a lawyer to defend his actions definitely will."

"True."

"So, about this wedding."

"Fly to Reno, get married and check into a swank suite for our wedding night?" she asked, more convinced than ever that waiting would be taxing her control on her feminine impulses.

He grinned, his expression more carefree than she'd ever seen it. "We are going to have a very good marriage, *stellina*. You fit me like a glove."

Angelo looked around the exclusive wedding chapel with satisfaction. A big wedding was out of the question. Not only would it take too long to prepare, but he didn't want the publicity that would accompany it to alert Baron Randall of Angelo's plans to marry Tara.

When he'd seen the innuendo laden articles with pictures of him and Tara kissing, his first thought had been the money he'd paid to bribe Randall's private detective not to mention his involvement with Tara had been wasted.

The whole flight back to Portland, he'd been worried he would only land to discover Randall had gotten to her first.

Randall hadn't gotten to her and Angelo was determined he wouldn't get the chance.

Hence the hasty wedding, but it didn't have to be a shabby, hole-in-the-wall affair. And it wasn't.

He'd offered his second in command a way to get back into his good graces...arrange a wedding fit for a princess in less than twenty-four hours. The wedding chapel was actually outside Reno, in the mountains toward the more affluent and less touristy Lake Tahoe.

The cathedral style chapel was decorated inside with dozen and dozens of white and yellow roses and purple irises. Lit with candlelight and recessed sconces that made the stained glass behind the altar glow, it was the perfect setting for his soon to be wife to walk down the aisle.

Tara's mother and Danette were seated in front on one of the polished wooden pews. Angelo's private investigator and long-time friend, Hawk, sat across the aisle from them.

The music of a pipe organ swelled, filling the space with the strains of the wedding march.

Angelo's gaze snapped to the back of the church where the open double doors framed Tara, her head held high, her dark brown eyes pools of feminine mystery and her hand curled around her stepdad's arm.

They started forward and a wave of something indefinable washed over Angelo.

Possessive desire was certainly part of it. Soon, this woman would be his to have, to hold and to make love to...over and over again.

Tara wasn't wearing a traditional wedding gown, but the designer original filmy white concoction she had on clung to every single one of her curves. It dipped in the front to reveal the top swells of her creamy, smooth breasts. Sexy and feminine, the dress was the stuff masculine fantasies were made of.

Those fantasies vied for his attention with the minister as he went through the wedding service. Angelo managed to give all the right answers, however, and smiled in victory when Tara did the same thing.

Afterward, he took everyone out for a celebratory dinner at the five-star restaurant his assistant had made reservations at. All he really wanted to do was take Tara up to their suite and make her his completely.

The glow on her face made it worth it however. Her mom and Darren were important to her, which was something he needed to remember. It had been a long time since he'd had close family.

After his parents' deaths, he'd pushed away his Sicilian family, only going home to visit infrequently.

"You know, when I gave you that information on Randall, I never would have guessed this is where it would lead you to," Hawk said from beside Angelo.

Tara's mother and her husband were dancing while Danette and Tara had gone to the ladies' room.

Angelo turned, lifting a sardonic brow. "What better way to ensure he doesn't get his hands on her again?"

His friend's eyes narrowed. "I know you can be a cold and ruthless bastard, Angelo, but tell me that's not the only reason you married her."

"Do you think she would be better off having that egomaniac people user back in her life?"

"Tara doesn't strike me as a woman stupid enough to make the same mistakes twice."

"He can be damn convincing."

"Not enough to get her to agree to be his mistress."

"No, Tara would never agree to that kind of arrangement." But once Randall was divorced, the rules would change.

He'd just taken steps to make sure the other man could never again enter the game.

"Do you feel anything for her besides the need to get the better of your enemy?" Hawk asked, sounding like a man with a stronger conscience than Angelo had ever suspected.

"I want her."

"Is that all?"

"None of your damn business."

"I'm your friend, Angelo."

"But you aren't my confessor."

Hawk just stared at him, the look disconcerting, even for Angelo.

"I want her. I respect her. I like her. It's enough."

"I wonder."

"I'm not going to hurt her."

"Have you taken any time to consider how she's going to react once she learns about Randall?"

"With any luck, she'll never have to know about Randall. I'm sure as hell not going to tell her."

"I've never been much of a believer in luck."

Angelo wasn't, either.

CHAPTER NINE

TARA was as nervous as a virgin when Angelo carried her into their honeymoon suite, his midnight gaze burning hotter than any blue flame. The sexual energy emanating off him had been growing all night until she fairly sizzled from the impact.

Despite the elegance of their surroundings, she felt like she was about to be devoured by a mountain lion. A very hungry, powerful lion with sharp teeth and claws that could tear through the barriers she had erected around her emotions.

That shouldn't frighten her.

She'd married him, after all.

But it did.

He stopped on the other side of the threshold, kicked the door shut and then looked down at her, predatory intent and primitive satisfaction exuding from his every pore. "You are mine now, Mrs. Gordon."

"Am I?"

"Yes." Then he kissed her.

It was hot; it was carnal; it was a statement of intent to possess.

His hot mouth molded hers, letting her taste the essence of this man she'd married. Could determination have a flavor? Strength? Desire? Intelligence? Masculine dominance? She could taste all of that and the spiciness of his need in his kiss. They'd never shared a kiss like this and yet her soul responded to it on a level of recognition she could not begin to dismiss.

Swirling sensation spiraled to the core of her and then outward in radiating waves of delight until it was all she could do not to cry out.

He carried her to the bed and stood her on her feet at the end of it and then gave her a once-over that left her trembling. "You arc incredibly beautiful, my wife."

"Thank you. You clean up nice in a tux yourself."

His smile slashed through her with heat, leaving her stomach quivering in a way she'd only ever experienced with him.

He reached around her, enveloping her in his warmth and teasing her with his nearness. He started tugging her zipper down. His fingertips played along her spine as each new inch of flesh was revealed.

"Angelo?" Was that hesitant, high-pitched voice hers?

"Yes?"

"Other than the other night, it's been two years and then we didn't...you know."

"Make love?"

"Right."

"You are telling me it has been a long time for you."

"Yes."

"I'm glad."

"Um…that's nice, but I wanted…"

How did she tell her new husband—a man who had married her for the sole purpose of bedding her, or close to it anyway—that she needed him to go slowly? It was so obvious that was not what he wanted to hear at that very moment.

"What did you want, *cara*, this?" He leaned down and kissed her shoulder, nibbling at the sensitive area above her collarbone, before lifting his head. "Or this?" His mouth closed over hers again while his hands slipped down inside her dress and cupped her backside with sensual mastery.

He caressed and squeezed her, his fingers dipping dangerously close to the warm, humid spot between her thighs. Memories surged through her from their time at the beach. Jolts of pleasure zinged through her sweetest spot and her entire woman's flesh. He teased her with his touch, making her want more, making her arch her spine, pushing her bottom back, trying to increase the depth of his penetration between her thighs.

But his hand moved with her, stopping her from achieving the intimate caressing she craved. She moaned against his lips and tried a new tactic, widening her stance so she was open completely to him. He rewarded her with a risqué massage on the highly sensitive flesh of her inner thighs and outer perimeter of her delta.

She groaned at the throbbing pleasure that grew with every tiny caress.

Maybe slow wasn't what she wanted after all. She broke her mouth away, letting her head fall back in abandon. "Angelo, please…touch me."

"I am touching you." His voice was laced with masculine amusement and dark gratification.

He liked driving her crazy. He started kissing her again, but this time, he touched everywhere, but her mouth with his talented lips.

How could she have wanted slow? She was ready to expire and she still had her panties on.

It took him forever to get her dress off, every bit of new flesh revealed had to be kissed, tasted and nibbled until the silky white fabric lay in a puddle around her feet and she stood shivering violently from her need. She wanted to be more active in their lovemaking, but she couldn't make her body cooperate. She was too shaken by the feelings roiling through her with the surging power of an electric blast.

"Angelo, I want you."

"Remember what I told you the other night?"

It was all she could do to remember her own name. She frantically tried to think of what he'd said the night they'd made each other climax.

"You want me to ask?"

"Yes."

With another man, asking would have made her feel like she was begging, but she remembered what else he'd said. "You'll give me whatever I ask for?"

"Yes." The sexual promise in his voice was almost her undoing.

This game made her feel like he was ceding his control to her and when making love with a man like him, that was heady stuff.

"I want you to take your clothes off."

He towered over her, his expression dangerously elemental. "You want to see me naked?"

"Oh, yes."

"Then undress me."

She swayed on her feet. "Is that a dare?"

"A request."

One she couldn't and didn't want to deny.

She started with his tie, undoing the bow and pulling it gently from his neck. She flipped it on the bed, an idea for later forming in her mind.

Then she went to the studs on his shirt, carefully slipping each one from their hole before leaning over to set it on the dresser not far away. The entire time, she pressed into his lower body, swaying side to side every so often to caress the hard ridge against her. By the time she had the whole shirt undone, he was making animal sounds and a white ring of stress had formed around his lips.

"You have formidable self-control.'

"And you are a born seductress."

She laughed, the sound throaty and sensual. "Perhaps…just for you."

She peeled his shirt off, revealing bronzed skin over sculpted muscle that took her breath away.

"Do you work out?"

"Aikido."

"Martial arts?"

"Yes."

"I wouldn't have guessed that of you." He was such

the quintessential businessman, but then it fit with the aura of dangerous male animal that always seemed to be hovering under the surface.

She never wanted to be this man's enemy, but she had no fear of totally infuriating him as his lover—more proof of her innate trust of him on a very basic level.

"We have a lifetime to learn one another's secrets."

"True." Her hand dropped to his trousers. "But even though this is one I've seen once before, I would very much like to explore it again."

"Go for it."

She laughed at the tension vibrating in each of the three short words. "I plan to and this time I want to feel it inside of me."

"Good, because that's exactly what is going to happen." The potent promise in his voice sent warm moisture flooding through the core of her.

He'd ceded control, but not power. How much control would he let her have tonight?

He started to help her with his trousers, but she pushed his hands away. "I want to do it all." She peeked up at him, her breathing coming in ragged gasps that matched his. "Okay?"

"Whatever you like."

"Really?"

"Yes."

She leaned over and took the tie off the bed. "Will you let me tie your hands?"

It was a fantasy she'd had for a long time.

Angelo had gone completely still. "You want to tie me?"

"Um…yes."

"Why?"

"I want to know you trust me."

"And your trust?"

"If I didn't trust you, I would not have agreed to marry you."

"I could say the converse is true."

"You could, but we both know it's not."

"We do?"

"Yes."

He eyed her for so long, she thought he was going to refuse and she was getting ready to drop the black tie. She wouldn't push it. She wanted him and he wanted her and really, she couldn't blame him for being a little leery about her request. It wasn't exactly your average wedding-night foreplay. He didn't understand what motivated her—she needed to know he trusted her. Baron had never trusted her, because he knew how untrustworthy he was. He always had to be in control.

"Do you want my hands in front or in back?"

Her head snapped up at the question, her mouth dropping open in wonder. "You don't mind?"

"I trust you, *stellina*. Do what you like."

He was so darn strong…even acceding to her wishes, she sensed that he was still in control here.

"B—" She had to clear her throat. "Behind you please."

He turned around, his trousers undone and hanging low on his gorgeous hips. Admiration and warmth flowed through her at his acquiescence.

"There aren't a lot of men who would be confident

or trustworthy, therefore trusting enough to let their lover do this," she whispered.

"Not just a lover. You are my wife."

She smiled. "Yes. Your wife."

She pulled his wrists together and tied them, securing it with a bow. It would be very easy for him to undo it, but the illusion of his helplessness was more exciting than anything she'd ever done. Because it was accompanied by a very real faith in her.

She gently turned him back around and finished taking off his clothes. When she was done, she looked her fill at the incredible male perfection before her.

"The other night…"

"Yes?"

"You said if I kissed you there…" She nodded toward his erection. "You would lose control and come inside me."

"Yes."

"Can I kiss you tonight?"

"Yes." This time the word came out more a growl and the hard male flesh in front of her bobbed its agreement.

She dropped to her knees and began her exploration with her fingertips. Velvet encased steel. There was no other description that she could think of for how it felt in her hands. She curled her fingers around him, caressed the full length and he groaned.

"Does that feel good?"

"You know it does."

"For me, too."

"I'm glad."

She nodded and then leaned forward to press a chaste kiss to the very tip. He smelled so good, she nuzzled him, inhaling a fragrance unique to him that affected her every bit as powerfully as his earlier caressing had.

Then she tasted him and he made a noise like a bitten back shout. She wanted to hear him really shout and set about making that happen, using her hands and lips and tongue. His body shuddered and he tilted his pelvis toward her, making his need more than clear.

"You have to stop," he said in a hoarse voice that told her more about how much he'd been holding back than anything else.

She tilted her head back and looked up his beautiful body to his face. Sweat had broken out on his brow and the flush of arousal had darkened his skin.

"Do I?"

"Yes."

"And if I don't want to?"

His arms moved and then the sound of a silk bow tie whispering to the carpet could be heard. "I will have to make you."

She would have grinned, but she was too excited and her mouth was too busy trying to suck in much needed oxygen. He understood her game exactly.

He had trusted her enough to give her control and put him in a pseudo-submissive position, but he was also strong enough to take charge when she needed him to.

"Come up here."

"I can't."

"Why?"

"My legs won't hold me," she admitted, knowing the only reason she was upright was because she was kneeling.

She felt dizzy even in this position.

He reached down and lifted her under her arms, his big hands clasped around her ribs. He lifted her all the way until their mouths were parallel and then he kissed her.

She curled her arms around his head and tried not to faint from a wave of love so profound, she almost drowned under it.

This man was perfect for her in every way. Of course she loved him and it would be okay. He was worthy of her love.

He laid her on the bed and removed the pretty white underthings she'd worn just for him.

When she told him so in a husky voice unrecognizable to her, he smiled.

"You're welcome to wear them again, but tonight, I don't want anything between us, even provocative bits of lace."

She agreed. She wanted nothing between them, either, not even the barrier of unspoken love, but that was one thing she could not remove.

She'd gone that route before, admitting her love and leaving herself vulnerable. She was married to this man. She had all the time she needed to show him it was safe to love her, too, that she wouldn't leave him voluntarily like his mother had done or involuntarily like his father had done.

He made love to her then, starting off gently, but rapidly moving to a passion and urgency that left her sated and exhausted in the middle of the huge king-size bed.

Afterward, he wrapped himself around her and they slept in each other's arms, only to awaken twice more in the night to make love again.

Angelo woke to the smell of coffee and the yeasty aroma of cinnamon rolls. He stretched, feeling more depleted than he ever had from the toughest Aikido session. Remembered pleasure made him groan as he opened his eyes, looking for his new wife.

Tara smiled at him from where she was lifting silver lids from the dishes on a room service cart. "I ordered breakfast."

"It smells delicious."

"I thought after last night that we both could do with sustenance."

"Wore you out, did I?"

"You made me hungry anyway." She winked saucily and he was reminded of her surprising friskiness the night before.

There had been something important to her about tying his hands and he'd worried when he untied them, he would be failing her, but she'd liked that part, too.

A charming, enigmatic, surprising creature was his wife. No wonder Baron had not wanted to let her go. The thought sent a shaft of annoyance through him and he dismissed it.

She'd never be Baron's again. Tara was his now. That was all that mattered.

Angelo clasped his hands and stretched his arms,

then tilted his head from side to side, working the kinks out. "I am hungry, too, *stellina*."

"Then come have some breakfast," she said breathlessly.

He looked at her and found her beautiful brown gaze riveted to his body. "Ahh…but that isn't what I'm hungry for."

She blushed delightfully and laughed. "That's all that's on offer at the moment. We need fuel. Or maybe you don't," she amended, looking at where the sheet tented from his body, "but I do. Have pity, Angelo, and come eat with me."

He shook his head, laughing in a way he could never remember doing with a former lover, as he got out of the bed.

She was scandalized when he came to the table naked, but almost fell off her chair with laughter when he conceded to her modesty by tossing a napkin down over his lap.

They bantered and made love for the rest of the morning, never leaving their suite until they had to depart for their scheduled take-off time at the airport.

Tara was both obviously thrilled and sweetly nervous when he informed her they were flying to Sicily so she could meet his family.

"Finally."

Tara looked up from her laptop. "Finally what?"

They'd been in Sicily for three weeks, but it hadn't all been honeymoon and sexual intimacy. When she had expressed concern over her career, Angelo had been quick to offer her a dream job and set her up with her own mini office on the opposite side of the study from him in his villa.

She'd never lived or worked in such an opulent setting. What other junior manager worked at a desk that was an original Chippendale and slid her pumps off under said desk to curl her toes against genuine Italian marble? Not to mention having a staff of servants available to care for her every whim?

Was it any wonder she adored Angelo? He spoiled her rotten and every day, her love grew. She was starting to wonder if she really needed to hold back the words until he said them first.

Their relationship was unlike anything she had ever known before and he made it obvious he saw her as an equal, not a woman to be manipulated into being what he wanted.

Her husband's voice had been so filled with satisfaction when he spoke that she wasn't surprised by the look of triumph on his chiseled features.

She smiled at him. "You look like you just bought another company."

"How well you know me." That seemed to give him as much satisfaction as whatever news he'd just gotten. "I haven't, but I'm about to."

Something about the way he said it made her pause.

"What company is it?"

"One I've wanted for a very long time."

"You're taking down the guy who seduced your mom into selling him the family company, aren't you?" She didn't know how she knew, just that she did.

A strange light glittered in his eyes. "Yes."

"How?"

"He's gotten cocky. He never thinks his schemes can fail, but he's wrong."

"In what way?"

"His father-in-law leads a group of investors that make up the bulk of his financial house of cards. Once they withdraw their support, his highly leveraged company will be worse off than a lame duck on the first day of hunting season."

She shivered at the analogy. "Why would his father-in-law remove his support?"

"His daughter has finally wised up to what a bastard the guy is and is filing for divorce."

Just like Baron's little oil heiress…only Baron said he was divorcing her, but she was willing to bet it was the other way around. Unless he'd found a richer prospect. Considering the fact he'd called, trying to see her, she doubted it.

Anyway, Baron wasn't who she needed to be focused on right now.

The strange intensity emanating off of her husband was far more interesting to her. "That makes you happy?"

"Hell, yes. I helped to make sure it happened."

A chill skittered down her spine. "What do you mean?"

"The guy had affairs."

"That kind of man would."

"I took advantage of the fact."

"How?" Then she latched on to his meaning. "You made sure his wife knew about the other women?"

She felt slightly nauseous at the prospect. Angelo's

capacity for ruthlessness was way beyond what she had ever guessed at.

"Yes."

"That was cruel."

"Do you really think so?" His eyes darkened with strong emotions, one of them unmistakably anger. "Wouldn't you have preferred to know what kind of bastard Baron Randall was before getting so involved with him?"

"Sure, but that's different...a wife is already involved. She loved him."

"And he would keep hurting her if she didn't face the truth. They could have had children before she woke up to what kind of man he is."

"You can't justify such cold behavior with that kind of reasoning. You didn't tell her about him for her sake, you did it for yours."

"I didn't tell her anything." He got up and came to lean against her desk. "I made sure she found out through friends, that there was always someone there to comfort her as each new layer of his sleazy behavior was revealed. If my mom had found out the same way, she would have been saved a lot of humiliation and might be alive now."

She wished that were true, but chances were, there had been clues that his mother's lover was an evil man, whoever he was. Just as there had been clues to what kind of man Baron was. Things she'd ignored for the sake of her love.

"I had friends around me when Baron did his public rejection campaign and trust me, it didn't make it any easier to bear."

"You don't know that. You didn't have to face the other."

"No, I didn't, but I did learn that friends can be worse than strangers, or even enemies."

"Do you really think a wife is better off not knowing of her husband's infidelity?"

"No, that's not what I meant at all." But she could see how it sounded like it. "It just bothers me that was part of your revenge against him. I pictured you taking over his company, not laying waste to his personal life."

"No man deserves to be ruined as much as this guy. I'll never forget my mom's sobbing, hysterical confession, or her deep shame and guilt because of what she'd done. His cruelty killed her. You can't get more personal than that."

And it had left Angelo in a world where business and vengeance ruled and love had no place. No wonder he was so ruthless, but he couldn't go on being that way. If he learned to love her, would he soften...at least a little?

"He didn't give her the pills," she pointed out.

"No, just the reason for taking them."

"That could have been as much about her grief over your father than over what this guy did to her. She made the choice, Angelo." She hated saying it, but he couldn't spend the rest of his adult life hating this other man.

A heart full of hate had no room for love and she needed his love.

"Why are you defending him?" he asked sounding both confused and strangely wounded by her words.

"I'm not." She laid her hand on his thigh in comfort. "I'm trying to make you see reason."

"In what way?"

"Revenge can consume you and I don't want you consumed." She pleaded with him with her eyes, hoping he would read the message there and heed it.

He gave her one of the slashing smiles she'd come to adore. "Don't worry, it's almost over and the only thing that consumes me lately is when I get to make love to my beautiful wife next."

"I want that to be true."

"It is. Believe me when I say I spend a lot more time thinking about you than *anything* else."

That was a huge admission and she gave it the response it deserved, standing up to kiss him with all the passionate love beating in her heart.

CHAPTER TEN

"TARA?" They were naked, snuggled against each other on the oversized reading chair in the far corner of the study with their legs entwined and stretched out on its matching ottoman.

Angelo had responded to her kiss with flattering enthusiasm, locking the door and then proceeding to demonstrate just how much he thought about her during the day.

She nuzzled his hair roughened chest. "Mmm-hmm?"

"Why was your breakup with Randall so public?"

The languorous aftermath of their lovemaking dissipated like the steam on a latte. This wasn't something she'd talked about to anyone, even her mom. It had hurt too much.

He rubbed her back soothingly. "I'd really like to know."

"At first, it wasn't. Baron told me he was getting married, but that he wanted to keep our relationship going."

"You said no."

"Right. Up to this point, everything had been pretty low-key between us media wise. The apartment we shared was in the suburbs, we didn't do high profile dating. I thought I was safe from the paparazzi and their blood sniffing."

"Something had to happen to change that."

"It did. I had a couple of friends, or at least they were women I thought were my friends, from the modeling community. They sold the story of my affair with Baron, along with some embellishments, to the press after his marriage was announced. When it became obvious he'd been sleeping with me while courting her, he had to do damage control."

It was Angelo's turn to go stiff, his palpable fury enveloping her. "Painting you as his sexpot mistress who wouldn't listen to the word no, was it?"

"Yes." She sighed, the pain of her friend's betrayal and Baron's willingness to destroy her good name to protect himself only a dull ache, but still there as a reminder to what a naïve fool she'd been. "It hurt so much."

"Because you loved him?"

"Because both he and my so-called friend betrayed me, devastating my life and for what?"

"Money?"

"Right, but it didn't do any of them all that much good. The two models are working fifth string trunk shows and hardly living the high life. Baron's divorcing his wife. Their betrayal didn't take them as far as they expected it to, I bet."

"What?" His hold on her tightened and he went on

before she could answer his question. "How do you know about Randall's divorce?"

"He called me."

"He called you?" Angelo's fury was incandescent now. He sat up, pulling her up so he could see into her face. "Why the hell didn't you say something?"

She frowned at his over the top reaction. "I didn't think it mattered."

"Of course it mattered."

"No. It didn't. Listen, Angelo, Baron might have some idiotic notion about renewing ties, but I wasn't interested."

"You told him no."

"Do you think I would be married to you if I hadn't?"

"What else did he say?"

"He warned me off you as a matter of fact."

Angelo looked a little gray around the edges and she thought that was sweet.

"Don't worry about it. His opinion is the last one I would take on relationships."

"What did you say to him?"

"To leave me alone and then I hung up."

"If he calls again, I want to know about it."

She narrowed her eyes at him. "Don't go all macho controlling on me, Angelo. I'm a grown woman and no one, not even you, is going to boss me around."

"That's not what you said last night."

They'd played a variation on their favorite game the night before with him doing the *directing*. She hadn't minded one bit, particularly when she'd gone to sleep so sated and exhausted she'd had a hard time waking up when their alarm went off that morning.

"It's not the same thing and you know it."

"No, it is not. For that was a game and this is very serious. I don't want you to have anything to do with Baron Randall."

"Do you really think I'm such a masochist I'd want to?"

"So, you believe he could still hurt you?"

This conversation was taking some very bizarre turns.

"No. I don't care about him, therefore he cannot hurt me."

"You said—"

"It was a figure of speech and don't think you're going to sidetrack me from the original topic getting all fixated on it. I'm not your pet dog to order around."

Suddenly she was under him and his lips were hovering just above hers. "Trust me, I see you as anything but a pet dog."

She was relaxing beside their private pool the next day when it occurred to her that Angelo had never once mentioned the name of the man he wanted to take down. She didn't dwell on that for very long because something else came to mind that had the power to blast all other thoughts from her brain.

"Angelo…we need to talk."

The urgency in Tara's voice sent dread skating down Angelo's spine. What could be wrong?

He cut his call short and turned to face her. She was wearing a yellow bikini that set off the sexy lines of her body as well as the tan she'd acquired since arriving in

Sicily. However, her expressive eyes showed none of the latent desire that usually shimmered there.

"What is it, *stellina?*"

"We never talked about kids."

"And this is so urgent because?" Was she pregnant?

The thought sent warmth skirling through him. It had been a very long time since he had been part of an intimate family. He liked the idea of her being pregnant with his child very much.

"We haven't been using any form of birth control."

She was just now noticing this? "I know."

"You know?"

"Well, we were both there." He smiled lazily. "It wasn't something I could miss."

"I didn't notice!" she shrieked, not sharing his humor at all.

"Why are you so upset?"

"What if I'm pregnant?"

"Don't you want to be pregnant?" That prospect had never occurred to him.

There was more of the traditional Sicilian male in him than he thought sometimes.

"That's not the point."

"Then, what is?"

"We didn't even talk about it and for all we know, it's a fait accompli."

"Would that be so bad?"

His question seemed to shock her. "Did you do it on purpose?" she asked accusingly.

He was trying to hold on to his temper, but it was getting harder by the second. *"Did you?"*

"You know I didn't!"

"Look, honey, the last thing I was thinking about on our wedding night was preventing conception. I wanted you so much, you had me tied in knots. Or don't you remember? We were in Sicily before I even thought of it."

"How could you be so irresponsible?"

"Me?"

"*You.* The only other lover I've ever had was Baron and that ended two years ago. Birth control wasn't exactly a blinking blip on my radar."

"And you believe it should have been on mine?"

"Wasn't it?"

"You're my wife."

"So?"

"So, if you get pregnant, it will be a celebration."

"It's not the idea of me getting pregnant that has me worried!"

"That's what you came in here going on about."

"It's the fact you didn't even think about it, which makes me wonder how many other times you haven't thought about it."

"The answer is never."

"But…"

"Contrary to what you apparently think, I'm no more interested in casual sex than you are and since a relationship is pretty difficult to develop when you're working sixty-plus-hour workweeks, I've spent a good part of the last decade celibate."

"But you're not the celibate type."

"A man, even a man like me, only has so much energy. I've poured mine into work." Which no doubt explained his explosive reaction to her.

"You don't make love like a novice."

"Who the hell said I was a novice?" Where did she get her ideas?

"Don't start yelling at me again."

"I wasn't yelling at you." But he had to lower his voice a few notches or he was going to bring one of the servants running.

"If you've been celibate for ten years…"

"I said largely celibate, not…" Suddenly he realized how ridiculous this discussion was becoming. "Never mind. I have never had unprotected sex. All right? You are safe from disease if not pregnancy. By the time I thought of birth control with you, we'd already made love many times. If you do not wish to get pregnant and are not already, we can discuss forms of birth control."

She deflated like a pricked balloon. "I suppose waiting to discuss it until we know if I'm pregnant makes the most sense."

"You're right. Maybe I should get a pregnancy test kit and then we can start making decisions."

"Wouldn't you rather see the doctor and be sure?"

"It takes forever to make an appointment and the test kits are something like ninety-nine percent accurate."

"I'm sure the family doctor will be able to see you tomorrow."

"The big reception thingy is tomorrow night. I'd rather wait until the next day."

"I'll have it taken care of."

"Thank you." She turned to go, but then stopped and spun back to face him. "Angelo?"

"Yes?"

"Do you want children?"

"Very much."

She smiled. "Me, too. I would never consider a pregnancy accidental."

"Nor would I. If you are pregnant, it is a blessing."

She seemed to relax. "Yes. And if I'm not, we'll decide if we want our blessings sooner than later."

"I'm pregnant? You're sure?" she asked the doctor, butterflies taking off in her stomach like Kamikaze pilots on a rampage.

"*Sì, signora.* It is good we can tell these things so early now, yes?"

"Yes."

She stumbled out of the doctor's office, her mind in a whirl. She was pregnant. With Angelo's baby. Her hand dropped to her tummy. She didn't feel any different, but she carried life inside of her, the product of her marriage to a very special man.

Angelo was going to be thrilled.

In fact, he was ecstatic. *"You are pregnant with my baby? Already?"*

She grinned at his jubilant response. "Yes."

"I guess I am very potent for you." His Sicilian accent suddenly evident.

She pressed herself against him, feeling evidence of

that potency intimately. "Yes, dearest Angelo, I think you are."

He growled and started kissing her.

They flew to New York two weeks later. Angelo insisted she take settling into her new home slowly, sleep late and arrive at the office no earlier than 10:00 a.m. because of her pregnancy. When she argued she was pregnant, not an invalid, he told her he wanted to pamper her.

How could she refuse him?

She was eating her breakfast on their balcony that overlooked Manhattan when the doorbell rang. She got up to answer it, but Maria, the housekeeper got to it before she did.

She halted in the living room when she heard a familiar voice that made her muscles tense. What in the world was Baron doing here?

He walked into the room, his eyes fixed on her in some kind of ludicrous appeal. "Tara."

"You have no business in my home, Baron. You know I don't want to see you."

"I came to save you from a monster much worse than the one you believed me to be." He stood there, looking as handsome as he ever had, but she wasn't moved in the slightest.

She just wanted him gone.

She rolled her eyes at his dramatics. "Godzilla?"

His jaw tautened. "Angelo Gordon."

"My husband is not a monster. Get out of our home. Right now." She called Maria's name. "This man is about to leave. Please see him out."

"Tara, you've got to listen to me. It's for your own good."

She totally ignored him and went back to her breakfast, shutting the terrace door on his voice.

She didn't tell Angelo about the other man's visit when she got to work because she figured later that night, when they were home, would be soon enough.

Looking scrumptious in a dark suit and pristine-white shirt, Angelo came into her office and asked if she wanted to join him for lunch.

She smiled up at him, wondering how much of what she felt for him glowed in her eyes. "I'd love to."

"Great."

They went to one of her favorite seafood restaurants and she was feeding a seemingly insatiable craving for rock shrimp in cocktail sauce when a shadow fell over their table.

"Tara."

She looked up and barely stifled a groan of irritation. "What are you doing here?"

"You need to know the truth about your husband."

"Go away, Baron."

Angelo stood, towering over the older man menacingly. "Leave my wife alone, Randall."

Baron backed up a step, but he didn't leave. "Or you'll do what? Ruin me?" He laughed, the sound hollow. "I'm already ruined and don't think for a second I don't know who is responsible."

"You are responsible. Everything happening to you right now, you brought on yourself."

What was he talking about? Baron was ruined? And

he held Angelo responsible? "What's going on?" she demanded.

"Does she know why you sought her out?" Baron asked, nodding toward Tara.

"Our relationship is none of your business," Angelo bit out, sounding so feral, she shivered.

"Neat evasion tactic." Baron sneered. "But since we both know you detest deceit of any kind, it isn't going to work. Tell her the truth."

"What truth?" But a sick suspicion was growing like a mushroom cloud after a nuclear explosion inside her. "Baron's the man who seduced your mother, isn't he?"

Angelo looked down at her. "Yes. I have more reason to hate the bastard than you do."

Remembering all that he had told her, she could do nothing but agree. "Yes."

But that told her nothing about how she fit into all of it and she was horrifyingly sure she fit somewhere.

Her agreement seemed to take Baron back for a moment, but then his expression turned ugly. "Maybe. But that means she's going to despise you just as much for using her the same way."

Angelo had used her? How?

"You're way off base. Tara didn't have a company I wanted so much I was willing to drive a woman to her death to get it."

The words should have given her comfort, but there was too much tension in them for her to take them at face value.

"I didn't kill your mother," Baron snarled. "She was

weak. She sold you out for a body to warm her lonely bed."

Angelo punched him and Baron went down. "Don't you ever speak of her like that. She was worth a hundred of you and her only weakness was her inability to see you for the selfish blood sucker you are."

Baron got up, grabbing the table for support and then wiped at his now bloody lip. "You think you're so damn good, but what you've done to Tara is no different. You used her to get what you wanted, didn't you?"

Angelo ignored the other man's accusation and put his hand out toward her. "Let's go, Tara."

She shook her head. She'd refused to listen to Baron twice now, but she wasn't walking away from the accusations this time. Her husband had withheld the name of his enemy and now she knew why, but she wanted to know more. Like why Baron was so convinced Angelo was using her.

"What did I have that Angelo wanted?"

"The chance to get revenge on me."

"I already had that," Angelo said deridingly. Then he turned to her again. "It's time to leave. Now."

"But you wanted it all," Baron said before she could react to the chilly command in her husband's voice. "You wanted to take away everything I valued."

"You didn't value me. You dumped me."

"Tara." It was Angelo again. Demanding.

But she was done doing things his way. "Leave if you want, Angelo, but I'm not going until I have some answers. And right at this minute I don't trust you to give them to me."

Baron's look of triumph almost changed her mind. "My marriage was temporary. I planned to come back to you and Angelo knew it."

The man was unhinged and incredibly calculating. He'd married his wife planning to divorce her? Tara shivered in revulsion. "You're not serious."

But she had the awful feeling he was.

Deadly so.

"Oh, yes, very serious. Your precious husband went looking for you the minute his private investigator found out that I was still keeping tabs on you."

The room suddenly felt too warm and dizziness washed over her as the full implication of what was being said hit her.

"*You were keeping tabs on me?* Like some creepy stalker?" She turned to Angelo. "*And you knew about it?*"

Angelo's mouth set in a grim line. "He's had you under surveillance since you broke up. His private investigator had instructions with the incentive of a bonus to squelch any romantic entanglements you might try to get into."

She glared at Baron, ready to finish what Angelo had started. "Who do you think you are, the Godfather?"

"More like a man who doesn't care who he hurts to have what he wants." Angelo's voice dripped acid.

"How did you know about it?"

"Hawk."

"Your friend from the wedding?"

"His private investigator," Baron replied before Angelo could answer. "Tell her how you bribed *my* private investigator to keep quiet about your relationship with Tara."

"I can't believe you've been watching me all this time. That's illegal, you miscreant."

He looked at her like he couldn't comprehend why she was hung up on that detail. She could have told him if he asked. The truth that was being revealed about her husband's pursuit of her hurt so much, she simply could not deal with it. She felt like a million little knives were shredding every happy emotion inside her.

"Tara, Angelo only went after you to get back at me."

Angelo cursed, a word she'd never heard him use, forcing her to acknowledge his presence and the pain slashing at her insides.

She turned from Baron, dismissing him from her mind as if he no longer existed and faced her husband. "The first time we met…you used my report as an excuse to see me, didn't you? You already knew who I was and what I had been to Baron."

Angelo's jaw set with rock like tension. "Yes."

"I told you."

The sound of Baron's voice was like nails scoring a chalkboard on her nerves. She rose from her chair, her body vibrating with unbearable tension and fury, and faced her ex-lover and her husband.

"Listen to me closely, Baron, because this is the one and only time I'm going to say this."

The look of smug satisfaction he'd been wearing disappeared at the tone of her voice.

"According to both you and my husband, he was aware of your bizarre efforts to keep track of me. That means that either he or Hawk has sufficient evidence to support charges being brought against you for stalking. Is that true, Angelo?" She asked the question without taking her baleful stare from Baron.

"Yes, *stellina*. True."

She flinched at the endearment, but kept her gaze firmly fixed on Baron.

He had blanched, apparently finally coming to terms with the fact he had boxed himself into a dangerous corner where she was concerned.

"I want you to leave. I don't ever want to hear from or see you again. If you ever attempt to contact me in any way or resume your pathetic little game, I will not only file both civil and criminal charges against you, but I will make darn sure your wife's divorce attorney has all the evidence she needs to paint you in a light so deranged and amoral, you'll be lucky to walk away from that marriage wearing socks under your shoes. Do I make myself clear?"

"Tara—"

"Do, I, Baron?"

"You've changed."

"And you haven't, but that's not the issue, is it?"

"No, it is not," Angelo answered, his voice colder than an Arctic wind. "The issue is that if Randall comes near you again, the picture you have painted for him will seem like the Elysian Fields compared to what I will do to him."

"I'm leaving," Baron gritted out, "but ask yourself if you should stay with a man capable of using you the way Angelo Gordon has."

The parting words sent wounding shards into her already bleeding heart. She refused to give Baron the satisfaction of seeing her hurt, but what made it hard for her to even breathe was that no matter what sick motivation had prompted his revelations, he had been speaking the truth.

Angelo had used her to exact revenge against his enemy.

She didn't mean anything to him. Not really. And that truth tore through her with all the emotionally destroying force of a level ten earthquake. She gripped the table rim in an effort to stay upright.

"Angelo?" she croaked.

He was by her side in a second, his big hands gripping her waist and shoulder. "Yes, *stellina?*"

"I want to go home now."

She felt like she was being ripped apart. She knew Angelo didn't love her, but to be nothing more than an instrument of revenge for the man who owned her heart was more than she could bear.

CHAPTER ELEVEN

WHEN THEY REACHED the apartment, she went to the bedroom and started packing. She didn't pay attention to what she grabbed, she just pulled clothes from drawers and dumped them in the big suitcase she'd tossed on the bed.

"You are not leaving me."

She didn't acknowledge him with so much as a glance.

Long tanned fingers wrested the top she had just grabbed from her fingers. "No. We are going to talk."

"We have nothing to talk about." Remembering saying those same words to Baron made her flinch. "I'm not staying."

"So, you let him win."

She spun to face him at that, fury so intense she was shaking with it, filling her to the brim. "No one wins in the sick scenario. Not you. Not him. And certainly not me. You used me, Angelo. You lied to me and you promised me you never would."

"I did not lie to you."

"A lie by omission is still a lie."

"No. It is not. Not unless you ask for the answer and I deny it. You did not ask. Nothing I have said to you has been untrue. Nothing."

"Justify it however you like. It won't change what you did to me. Baron is right. You are no better than he is."

"Like hell. I did nothing to hurt you. I am not rejecting you. I married you!"

"To keep me away from him."

His silence condemned him.

"Trying not to lie to me again?" she asked sneeringly.

"It does not matter."

"You're wrong and you're wrong about me leaving. I'm going and you cannot stop me."

"Damn it, Tara, you are pregnant with my child. You cannot just walk away from me."

"I wouldn't condemn my worst enemy to a father with your moral poverty."

It was his turn to flinch. "You would…" He didn't finish his sentence, but she didn't care.

She just wanted out of there. She realized she didn't need her clothes. She didn't need anything but to be somewhere away from him.

She spun on her heel and marched from the room.

He grabbed her shoulder. "Where are you going?"

"Let go of me."

"No."

She yanked her shoulder from his grasp and fell against the wall from the momentum.

His face leached of all color. "*Stellina*, are you all right?"

"What do you care?"

"I care." He leaned back against the wall as if his legs wouldn't quite hold him up. "You don't have to go. I'll leave…stay at a hotel. You're safer here. Please, Tara, let me do at least this much for you."

"No." She couldn't stay where the memories of her doomed happiness with him would haunt her.

He didn't say another word as she walked out of the apartment. She took a taxi to a hotel, checked in and went up to her room to cry her heart out.

She stayed in the hotel for three days, eating room service for the baby's sake, ignoring Angelo's calls on her cell phone and crying until her throat was so raw, she could barely speak to order food over the phone.

On the third day, there was a knock at her door. Her stupid heart leaped, thinking it might be Angelo, but then she told herself it wouldn't matter if it was. She would just send him away. Her heart returned to being a cold lump in her chest.

She looked through the peephole and recognized Hawk, her husband's friend from the wedding. His private investigator.

"Go away," she yelled through the door…more like croaked.

"I can't do that, Mrs. Gordon."

She didn't have the voice to argue. That's the only reason she opened the door, she told herself.

"What do you want?"

"Are you okay? You sound like you're sick."

She shrugged. She was. Sick at heart.

He was carrying a suitcase. It looked like the one

she'd been packing when she left Angelo. Because she had no clothes to change into, she'd taken to wearing the terry robe provided by the hotel with her suite. She was wearing it now, her hair hanging down around her face in stringy tangles.

He put the suitcase down. "Angelo looks worse than you."

Her eyes widened at that. Her husband never looked less than perfectly groomed.

"He's worried about you."

She glared, not buying it.

Hawk shook his head, his expression vexed. "You're both a couple of idiots."

"I am not…" Her voice refused to function any more.

Hawk shook his head. "Why don't you let me do the talking?"

Did she have a choice? She shrugged again.

"I know why Angelo came after you initially. Hell, I helped him do it, but he cares about you now. He needs you."

She shook her head vehemently.

The big man facing her frowned fiercely. "You walked out and I have been with him in that mausoleum of an apartment for three days."

"Not…mausoleum…"

"It is now, with him mourning your loss like a grief-stricken widower. I haven't seen him like this since his mother died. It's always a woman," the tall man said with disgust and shook his head. "Do you know he has not gone to work since you left him?"

When she didn't reply, Hawk sighed with frustration.

"Whether he's too stubborn to admit it, or you are too angry to accept it, he needs you. The real question is whether or not you care enough about him to give him the chance to prove it to you?"

"I'm not too stubborn." The voice came from the doorway and she turned to look, gasping at what she saw.

Hawk hadn't been lying. Angelo looked like he hadn't eaten in a week, not a mere three days. His cheeks were hollow and lined with strain. His jaw line was shadowed with three days of stubble…it was almost a beard and his jeans and sweater looked slept in. But it was his eyes that were the worst.

They reflected the tortures of the damned in their indigo depths. "I do need you, Tara. More than I can ever say with simple words."

"I thought you weren't coming," Hawk said, as if Angelo hadn't just made an impossible declaration.

"I couldn't stay away. I had to see her." Angelo's gaze was glued to her face.

"Well, it looks like she's not faring any better than you."

"My fault." Angelo turned away, his proud shoulders slumped. "I should go."

Hawk said something ugly under his breath. "Don't be an idiot, Angelo. Does she look like she'll be better off if you go?"

Angelo turned back. "I had Hawk bring your clothes. If you need anything else…" His voice trailed off, his throat working like he was trying to hold in some intolerable emotion.

"You," she croaked, unable to let him walk away.

He'd used her and that hurt. So much. But she'd spent three days grieving that pain and there was more here than a man who had callously used a woman to exact revenge. This man was hurting and vulnerable in a way a man like Baron never could be.

"Me?" Angelo asked.

"Stay."

"Very good." That was all Hawk said before walking toward the door. When he got there, he looked back at Angelo. "Don't screw this up. I'm not baby-sitting you through another day of mourning. Men in love give me a stomachache."

Men in love?

Angelo heard the door click shut, but his attention was fully on his wife. She looked like hell and it was all his fault. He'd hurt the woman he loved and hadn't even known he loved her until he did it.

How could it have taken Baron's revelations and their painful impact on Tara for him to realize he loved her?

If he lost her over his own stupidity, his heart would turn to stone. For the last three days, he'd thought it had. He'd hoped she would call, but when she didn't…when she ignored his calls to her cell phone, he'd known what he'd done had been too heinous for her to forgive.

He didn't know why he'd come, except that like he'd told Hawk, he couldn't stay away.

He needed her.

And she did not know it.

She thought he had married her as an act of revenge

and he would give anything to be able to deny that claim, but since he had hidden his own feelings from himself with the excuse, it now stood between them like an uncrossable chasm.

Only he had to cross it. Somehow.

He had to reach her and convince her of his love because the alternative was unthinkable.

He'd lived three days in hell and he knew he couldn't stand one more.

Tara stumbled to a chair and sank into it as she considered the possibility Hawk had been right. That her husband was actually in love with her.

He *looked* like a man who had loved and lost.

He came forward as if drawn by an invisible string and knelt beside her, but did not touch her. "I'm sorry."

"You used me, just like he did." It hurt to talk, her throat was so dry.

She'd left a glass of juice on the small table beside the chair earlier. She lifted it now and drank it down, desperate for the ability to talk this out with her husband.

"Not like him."

She glared at Angelo, not willing to accept anything less than total honesty. "Yes, like him."

"He doesn't feel. I do."

She shook her head. "You can't. You married me to keep me away from him."

"I thought so, yes." His voice was low, full of anguish. "I wanted him to lose everything he valued."

"It worked."

"But I lost more. You never would have gone back to him. I know that now. You are too strong…too smart. Because my motives were wrong, you left me and I don't know how to get you back."

"You want me back?"

"Yes." She'd never heard a single word spoken with so much fervency, filled with such desperation and yearning.

"Because of the baby?"

"Because I love you." Even now, she could tell the words were hard for him to say.

"You don't love me," she whispered in denial, unable to accept that after all the pain and betrayal, he could actually feel what she so desperately wanted him to feel.

"I do. I love you more than my own life, Tara, and I would take back everything I have done that has caused you pain if I could."

"You expect me to believe that?"

"I have never lied to you."

"You would undo our marriage if you could?"

"If it would take the expression of pain from your beautiful brown eyes, yes."

He really meant it…he would give her up if he could undo the past and save her pain.

"The baby, would you undo that?" she pressed.

If he had looked like the damned being tortured before, he looked worse now. "I thought you might…"

"What?"

"Then I realized you never could. Not you and I was glad and I'm ashamed that I was so relieved not just for the sake of our baby, but for my own sake. As your baby's father, I would always have a role in your life. And yet, if I could save you this pain, yes...I would make it so we never met, so you never married me and let me into your body."

If he meant those words then he had to really love her. "How can I believe you?"

His face twisted in sorrow and he averted his gaze, strain coming off of him in tangible waves. They remained like that, her on the couch, him kneeling before her, for several silent minutes and then he turned to face her.

"I loved you when I married you even though I did not admit it to you or to myself."

"I wish that were true." It would make the pain so much more bearable.

"Do you remember our prenuptial contract?"

"We don't have one."

"Wouldn't we, if I only married you to spite Randall? I'm a very rich man. If I didn't love you, if I had the least intention of ever letting you go, wouldn't I have done something to protect my empire? I'm not a stupid man...in the normal course of things anyway."

"You said you wanted the marriage to last. You weren't planning on divorce."

"No, but only love would make me trust you enough to leave something so vital to a man in my position undone."

She bit her lip remembering the prenuptial contract her mom and Darren had signed. The man had been top over tails in love, but businessman first last and always, he'd had one drawn up. It had protected her mom, too, in a way, but still the implication had been the marriage had a chance of ending.

Considering the number of relationships her mom had had between her dad and Darren, his subtle concern had been justified, but Angelo had shown no such concern. And he had a lot more to protect than Darren had.

"You married me to keep me away from Baron."

"I married you to keep you near myself." The urgency in his voice rang true.

"But—"

"Tara, I met you and I wanted you. I got to know you and I knew having your body would not be enough. I've spent ten years spurning emotion, staying apart from my family, never letting anyone as close to me as I allowed you within a week of meeting."

It had been the same for her. "But the revenge…"

"What revenge? Did I do a single thing to Baron Randall that he did not bring on himself?"

Tara considered her husband's words and his need for revenge and realized that he was right. He might have brought the pieces together, but Baron had put them all on the game board. "No."

"If I had met you under any other circumstance, I would have wanted you for mine for all time."

"How can I be sure?"

But even as she asked the question memories bombarded her. Angelo was capable of utter ruthlessness, but he had not seduced her when it was obvious he could. In fact, the whole time he had known her, he had done nothing to hurt her.

He had given and given and given and that kind of behavior from an alpha guy like him denoted she had a very special place in his life.

A place that could not begin to be defined by his need for revenge.

"It is a matter of trust, *stellina*. If you love me, then you can trust me…your heart will beat with mine and know the truth despite what logic might say." The vulnerable expression in his indigo eyes said more eloquently than any words how unsure he was of her feelings, how much she could hurt him right now if she rejected him.

His mom had done that. She hadn't loved him enough to stay and face her own demons, but Tara was stronger than that. If they had a chance at happiness, she couldn't bear to let him go.

"I do love you, Angelo. So much."

His throat convulsed. "Enough to stay with me even though I am not the perfect man you deserve?"

"None of us is perfect, my darling, but I couldn't leave you without ripping my own heart out."

The kiss was a mutual melding of their mouths and their lovemaking afterward was beautiful and tender enough to make even a stone heart cry. Her heart was not made of stone, so tears seeped from her eyelids and Angelo rubbed a wet cheek against her own.

"I have been alone so long."

She held him to her as he loved her with tender, pleasure filled strokes. "You aren't anymore."

"No, I am not." The joy and satisfaction in his voice was unmistakable.

As the pleasure spiraled out of control she cried out, "Angelo, I love you."

His hands cupped her face and he met her eyes, his burning with emotion she'd never thought to see there. "And I love you, Tara. My wife. *My life.*"

Their son was born on a spring morning. As the doctor laid the superbly healthy infant onto her chest, Angelo placed one hand on her head and the other on their baby's back.

"Thank you." He mouthed the words, his voice so low it could not be heard.

She smiled at him, this man who loved her so completely. "We are a family."

"Not alone."

"Never alone."

"I love you, Tara."

"I love you, Angelo."

And their baby made a snuffling sound as if agreeing to the preciousness of the circle of their family.

They belonged together, the three of them and God willing, one day there would be more children. Her tycoon would never again have to live in a world void of love and tenderness.

Men like Baron Randall would never understand that gift, but Angelo did.

Because her ruthless tycoon had something the other man did not. A heart.

HIS ULTIMATE PRIZE

BY
MAYA BLAKE

Maya Blake fell in love with the world of the alpha male and the strong, aspirational heroine when she borrowed her sister's Mills & Boon at age thirteen. Shortly thereafter the dream to plot a happy ending for her own characters was born. Writing for Mills & Boon is a dream come true. Maya lives in South East England with her husband and two kids. Reading is an absolute passion, but when she isn't lost in a book she likes to swim, cycle, travel and Tweet!

You can get in touch with her via e-mail, at mayablake@ymail.com, or on Twitter: twitter.com/mayablake

To Lucy Gilmour, for making my dream come true,
and also because I know she loves bad boys!

CHAPTER ONE

'PUT YOUR ARMS around me and hold on tight.'

The rich, deep chuckle that greeted her request sent a hot shiver down Raven Blass's spine. The same deep chuckle she continually prayed she would grow immune to. So far, her prayers had gone stubbornly unanswered.

'Trust me, *bonita*, I don't need guidance on how to hold a woman in my arms. I give instructions; I don't take them.' Rafael de Cervantes's drawled response was accompanied by a lazy drift of his finger down her bare arm and a latent heat in ice-blue eyes that constantly unnerved her with their sharp, unwavering focus.

With gritted teeth, she forced herself not to react to his touch. It was a test, another in a long line of tests he'd tried to unsettle her with in the five weeks since he'd finally called her and offered her this job.

Maintaining a neutral expression, she stood her ground. 'Well, you can do what I say, or you can stay in the car and miss your nephew's christening altogether. After agreeing to be his godfather, I'm sure you not turning up in church will go down well with your brother and Sasha.'

As she'd known it would, the mention of Sasha de Cervantes's name caused the atmosphere to shift from toying-with-danger sexual banter to watch-it iciness. Rafael's hand dropped from her arm to grip the titanium-tipped walking stick tucked between his legs, his square jaw tightening as his gaze cooled.

Deep inside, in the other place where she refused to let anyone in, something clenched hard. Ignoring it, she patted herself on the back for the hollow victory. Rafael not touching her in any way but professionally was a *good* thing.

Recite. Repeat. Recite. Repeat—

'I didn't agree…exactly.'

Her snort slipped out before she could stop it. 'Yeah, right. The likelihood of you agreeing to something you're not one hundred per cent content with is virtually nil. Unless…'

His eyes narrowed. 'Unless what?'

Unless Sasha had done the asking. 'Nothing. Shall we try again? Put your arms—'

'Unless you want me to kiss that mouth shut, I suggest you can the instructions and move closer. For a start, you're too far away for this to work. If I move the wrong way and land on top of you, I'll crush you, you being *such* a tiny thing and all.'

'I'm not *tiny*.' She moved a step closer to the open doorway of the sleek black SUV, stubbornly refusing to breathe in too much of his disconcertingly heady masculine scent. 'I'm five foot nine of solid muscle and bone and I can drop kick you in two moves. Think about that before you try anything remotely iffy on me.'

The lethal grin returned. '*Dios*, I love it when you talk dirty to me. Although my moves have never been described as *iffy* before. What does that even mean?'

'It means concentrate or this will never work.'

Rafael, damn him, gave a low laugh, unsnapped his seat belt and slid one arm around her shoulders. 'Fine. Do with me what you will, Raven. I'm putty in your hands.'

With every atom in her body she wished she could halt the stupid blush creeping up her face, but that was one reaction she'd never been able to control. In the distant past she tried every day to forget, it had been another source of callous mirth to her father and his vile friends. To one friend in particular, it had provoked an even stronger, terrifying reaction. Pushing away the unwelcome memory, she concentrated on the task at hand, *her job*.

Adjusting her position, she lowered her centre of gravity, slid an arm around Rafael's back and braced herself to hold his weight. Despite the injuries he'd sustained, he was six foot three of packed, lean muscle, his body honed to perfection from years of carefully regimented exercise. She needed every single ounce of her physiotherapist training to ensure he didn't accidentally flatten her as promised.

She felt him wince as he straightened but, when she glanced at him, his face showed no hint of the pain she knew he must feel.

The head trauma and resulting weeks-long coma he'd lain in after he'd crashed his Premier X1 racing car and ended his world championship reign eight months ago had only formed part of his injuries. He'd also sustained several pelvic fractures and a broken leg that had gone mostly untreated while he'd been unconscious, which meant his recovery had been a slow, frustrating process.

A process made worse by both his stubborn refusal to heed simple instructions and his need to test physical boundaries. Especially hers.

'Are you okay?' she asked. Because it was her job to make sure he was okay. Nothing else.

He drew himself up to his full height and tugged his bespoke hand-stitched suit into place. He slid slim fingers through longer-than-conventional hair until the sleek jet-black tresses were raked back from his high forehead. With the same insufferable indolence with which he approached everything in life, he scrutinised her face, lingered for an obscenely long moment on her mouth before stabbing her gaze with his.

'Are you asking as my physiotherapist or as the woman who continues to scorn my attentions?'

Her mouth tightened. 'As your physio, of course. I have no interest in the…in being—'

'Becoming my lover would make so many of our problems go away, Raven, don't you think? Certainly, this sexual tension you're almost choking on would be so much easier to bear if you would just let me f—'

'Are you okay *to walk*, Rafael?' she interjected forcefully, hating the way her blood heated and her heart raced at his words.

'Of course, *querida*. Thanks to your stalwart efforts this past month, I'm no longer wheelchair-bound and I have the very essence of life running through my veins. But feel free to let your fingers keep caressing my backside the way they're doing now. It's been such a long time since I felt this surge of *essence* to a particular part of my anatomy, I was beginning to fear it'd died.'

With a muted curse and even redder cheeks, she dropped her hand. The professional in her made her stay put until Rafael was fully upright and able to support himself. The female part that hated herself for this insane fever of attraction wanted to run a mile. She compromised by moving a couple of feet away, her face turned from his.

For the second time in as many minutes, his laugh mocked her. 'Spoilsport.'

She fought the need to clench her hands into agitated fists and faced him when she had herself under sufficient control. 'How long are you going to keep this up? Surely you can find something else to amuse yourself with besides this need to push my buttons?'

Just like that, his dazzling smile dropped, his eyes gleaming with a hard, cynical edge that made her shiver. 'Maybe that's what keeps me going, *guapa*. Maybe I intend to push your buttons for as long as it amuses me to do so.'

She swallowed hard and considered staring him down. But she knew how good he was at that game. Heck, Rafael was a maestro at most games. He would only welcome the challenge.

Reaching behind him to slam the car door, she started to move with him towards the entrance of the church where baby Jack's ceremony was being held. 'If you're trying to get me to resign by being intolerable, I won't,' she stated in as firm a tone as possible, hoping he'd get the hint. Aside from the need to make amends, she needed this job. Her severance package from Team Espíritu when Marco de Cervantes had sold the racing team had been more than generous, but it was fast running out in light of her mother's huge treatment bills. It would take a lot more than Rafael's sexual taunts to make her walk away.

He shrugged and fell into step beside her. 'Good. As long as you're here tormenting yourself with your guilt, I feel better.'

Acute discomfort lodged in her chest. 'I thought we weren't going to speak about that?'

'You should know by now, rules mean nothing to me. Unspoken rules mean even less. How's the guilt today, by the way?'

'Receding by the second, thanks to your insufferable tongue.'

'I must be slacking.' He took a step forward, gave a visible wince, and Raven's heart stopped, along with her feet. He raised a brow at her, the hard smile back on his face. 'Ah, there it is. Good to know I haven't lost my touch after all.'

Ice danced down her spine at his chilled tone. Before she could answer, the large bell pealed nearby. Pigeons flew out of the turrets of the tiny whitewashed church that had been on the de Cervantes's Northern Spanish estate for several hundred years.

Raven glanced around them, past the church poised at the summit of the small hill that overlooked miles of prime de Cervantes vineyards, to the graveyard beyond where Rafael's ancestors lay interred.

'Are we going to stand here all day admiring the landscape or do we actually need to go *inside* the church for this gig?' A quick glance at him showed his face studiously averted from the prominent headstones, his jaw set in steel.

She drew in a deep breath and moved towards the arched entrance to the church. 'It's not a *gig;* it's your nephew's christening. In a church. With other guests. So act accordingly.'

Another dark chuckle. 'Or what, you'll put me over your knee? Or will you just pray that I be struck down by lightning if I blaspheme?'

'I'm not rising to your baits, Rafael.' Mostly because she had an inkling of how hard this morning would be for him. According to Rafael's housekeeper, it was the first time he'd interacted with his family since his return to León from his private hospital in Barcelona. 'You can try to rile me all you want. I'm not going anywhere.'

'A martyr to the last?'

'A physiotherapist who knows how grumpy patients can be when they don't get their way.'

'What makes you think I'm not getting exactly what I want?' he rasped lazily.

'I overheard your phone call to Marco this morning… twice…to try and get out of your godfather duties. Since you're here now, I'm guessing he refused to let you?'

A tic in his jaw and a raised brow was her only answer.

'Like I said, I know a grumpy patient when I see one.' She hurried forward and opened the large heavy door.

To her relief, he didn't answer back. She hoped it was because they were within the hallowed walls of his family's chapel because she was close enough to feel his tension increase the closer they got to the altar.

De Cervantes family members and the few close friends who'd managed to gain an invitation to the christening of Sasha and Marco de Cervantes's firstborn turned to watch their slow progress up the aisle.

'Shame you're not wearing a white gown,' Rafael quipped from the side of his mouth, taking her elbow even as he smiled and winked at a well-known Spanish supermodel. But, this close, Raven could see the stress lines that faintly bracketed his mouth and the pulse throbbing at his temple. Rafael *really* did not want to be here.

'White gown?'

'Think how frenzied their imagination would be running right about now. It would almost warrant a two-page spread in *X1 Magazine*.'

'Even if I were dressed in bridal white with a crown on my

head and stars in my eyes, no one would believe you would actually go through with anything as anathema to you as a wedding, Rafael. These poor people would probably drop dead at the very thought of linking you with the word *commitment*.'

His grip tightened for a minuscule moment before that lazy smile returned. 'For once, you're right. Weddings bore me rigid and the word *marriage* should have a picture of a noose next to it in the dictionary.'

They were a few steps away from the front pew, where his brother and sister-in-law sat gazing down adoringly at their infant son. The sight of their utter devotion and contentment made her insides tighten another notch.

'I don't think that's how your brother and his wife see it.'

Rafael's jaw tightened before he shrugged. 'I'm prepared to accede that for some the Halley's Comet effect does happen. But we'll wait and see if it's a mirage or the real thing, shall we?'

Her breath caught at the wealth of cynicism in his tone. She couldn't respond because an usher was signalling the priest that it was time to start.

The ceremony was conducted in Spanish with English translations printed out on embossed gold-edged paper.

As the minutes ticked by, she noted Rafael's profile growing even tenser. Glancing down at the sheet, she realised the moment was approaching for him to take his godson for the anointing. Despite her caution to remain unmoved, her heart softened at his obvious discomfort.

'Relax. Babies are more resilient than we give them credit for. Trust me, it takes a complete idiot to drop a baby.'

She was unprepared for the icy blue eyes that sliced into her. 'Your flattery is touching but the last thing I'm thinking of is dropping my nephew.'

'You don't need to hide it, Rafael. Your tension is so thick it's suffocating.'

His eyes grew colder. 'Remember when I said weddings bore me?'

She nodded warily.

'Christenings bore me even more. Besides, I've never been good in churches. All that *piety*.' He gave a mock shudder. 'My *abuela* used to smack my hand because I could never sit still.'

'Well, I'm not your grandmother so you're spared the smacking. Besides, you're a grown man now so act like one and suck it up.'

Too late, she remembered certain words were like a naked invitation to Rafael. She was completely stunned when he didn't make the obvious remark. Or maybe it was a testament to just how deeply the whole ceremony was affecting him.

'I just want this to be over and done with so I can resume more interesting subjects.' Without due warning, his gaze dropped to the cleavage of her simple, sleeveless orange knee-length chiffon dress. The bold, heated caress resonated through her body, leaving a trail of fire that singed in delicate places. 'Like how delicious you look in that dress. Or how you'll look *out* of it.'

Heat suffused her face. It was no use pointing out how inappropriate this conversation was. Rafael knew very well what he was doing. And the unrepentant gleam in his eyes told her so.

'Rafa...' Marco de Cervantes's deep voice interrupted them.

Raven glanced up and her eyes collided with steel-grey ones which softened a touch when they lit on his brother.

Like most people who'd worked the X1 Premier circuit, she knew all about the de Cervantes brothers. Gorgeous beyond words and successful in their individual rights, they'd made scores of female hearts flutter, both on and off of the racing circuit.

Marco had been the dynamic ex-racer team boss and race car designer. And Rafael, also insanely gifted behind the wheel, had at the age of twenty-eight founded and established himself as CEO of X1 Premier Management, the multi-billion euro conglomerate that nurtured, trained and looked after racing drivers. Between them they'd won more medals and championships than any other team in the history of the sport.

The last year had changed everything for them, though. Marco had sold the team and married Sasha Fleming, the racing driver who'd won him his last Constructors' Championship and stolen his heart in the process; and Rafael had spectacularly crashed his car, nearly lost his life and stalled his racing career.

The icy jet of guilt that shot through Raven every time she thought of his accident, and her part in it, threatened to overwhelm her. Her breath caught as she desperately tried to put the incident out of her head. This was neither the time nor the place.

But then, when had timing been her strong suit?

Over and over, she'd proven that when it came to being in the wrong place at the wrong time, she took first prize every single time. At sixteen, it was what had earned her the unwanted attention that had scarred what remained of her already battered childhood.

As a grown woman of twenty-three, foolishly believing she'd put the past behind her, she'd been proved brutally wrong again when she'd met Rafael de Cervantes.

Rafael's mouth very close to her ear ripped her from her painful thoughts. 'Right, I'm up, I believe. Which means, so are you.'

Her heart leapt into her throat. 'Excuse me?'

'I can barely stand up straight, *pequeña*. It's time to do your duty and *support* me just in case it all gets too much and I keel over.'

'But you're perfectly capable—'

'Rafa...' Marco's voice held a touch of impatience.

Rafael's brow cocked and he held out his arm. With no choice but to comply or risk causing a scene, Raven stood and helped him up. As before, his arm came around her in an all-encompassing hold. And again, she felt the bounds of professionalism slip as she struggled not to feel the effortless, decidedly *erotic* sensations Rafael commanded so very easily in her. Sensations she'd tried her damnedest to stem and, failing that, ignore since the first moment she'd clapped eyes on the legendary racing driver last year.

What had she said to him—*suck it up*? She took a breath and fought to take her own advice.

They made their way to the font and Raven managed to summon a smile in answer to Sasha's open and friendly one. But all through the remainder of the ceremony, Raven was drenched with the feeling that maybe, just maybe, in her haste to assuage her guilt and make amends, she'd made a mistake. Had she, by pushing Rafael to take her on as his personal physiotherapist, jumped from the frying fan into the proverbial fire?

Rafael repeated the words that bound the small person sleeping peacefully in the elegant but frilly Moses basket to him. He firmed lips that wanted to curl in self-derision.

Who was he to become *godfather* to another human being?

Everything he touched turned to dust eventually. Sooner or later he ruined everything good in his life. He'd tried to tell his brother over and over since he'd dropped the bombshell on him a month ago. Hell, as late as this morning he'd tried to get Marco to see sense and change his mind about making him godfather.

But Marco, snug in his newfound love-cocoon, had blithely ignored his request to appoint someone else his son's godfather. Apparently, reality hath no blind spots like a man in love.

Was that a saying? If not, it needed to be.

He was no one's hero. He was the last person any father should entrust with his child.

He gazed down into his nephew's sweet, innocent face. How long before Jack de Cervantes recognised him for what he was? An empty shell. A heartless bastard who'd only succeeded at two things—driving fast cars and seducing fast women.

He shifted on his feet. Pain ricocheted through his hip and pelvis. Ignoring it, he gave a mental shrug, limped forward and took the ladle the priest passed him. Scooping water out of the large bowl, he poised it over his nephew's head.

At the priest's nod, he tipped the ladle.

The scream of protest sent a tiny wave of satisfaction through him. Hopefully his innocent nephew would take a look at him and run screaming every time he saw him. Because Rafael knew that if he had anything at all to do with his brother's child, the poor boy's life too would be ruined.

As well-wishers gathered around to soothe the wailing child, he dropped the ladle back into the bowl, stepped back and forced his gaze away from his nephew's adorable curls and plump cheeks.

Beside him, he heard Raven's long indrawn breath and, grabbing the very welcome distraction, he let his gaze drift to her.

Magnet-like, her hazel eyes sought and found his. Her throat moved in a visible swallow that made his fingers itch to slide over that smooth column of flesh. Follow it down to that delectable, infinitely tempting valley between her plump breasts.

Not here, not now, he thought regrettably. What was between the two of them would not be played out here in this place where dark memories—both living and dead—lingered everywhere he looked, ready to pounce on him should he even begin to let them...

He tensed at the whirr of an electronic wheelchair, kept his gaze fixed on Raven even as his spine stiffened almost painfully. Thankfully the wheelchair stopped several feet behind him and he heard the familiar voice exchange greetings with other family members. With every pulse of icy blood through his veins, Rafael wished himself elsewhere...anywhere but here, where the thick candles and fragrant flowers above the nave reminded him of other candles and flowers placed in a shrine not very far away from where he stood—a constant reminder of what he'd done. A reminder that because of him, because of callous destruction, this was his mother's final resting place.

His beloved Mamá…

His breath caught as Sasha, his sister-in-law, came towards him, her now quietened son in her arm.

Sasha…something else he'd ruined.

Dios…

'He's got a set of lungs on him, hasn't he?' she laughed, her face radiant in the light slanting through the church windows. 'He almost raised the roof with all that wailing.'

He took in the perfect picture mother and child made and something caught in his chest. He'd denied his mother this—the chance to meet her grandchild.

'Rafael?'

He focused and summoned a half-smile. '*Sí*, my poor eardrums are still bleeding.'

She laughed again as her eyes rolled. 'Oh, come on, my little champ's not that bad. Besides, Marco tells me he takes after you, and I don't find that hard to believe at all.' She sobered, her gaze running over him before piercing blue eyes captured his in frank, no nonsense assessment. 'So…how are you? And don't give me a glib answer.'

'Thoroughly bored of everyone asking me how I am.' He raised his walking stick and gestured to his frame. 'See for yourself, *piqueña*. My clever physiotherapist tells me I'm between phases two and three on the recovery scale. *Dios* knows what that means. All I know is that I'm still a broken, broken man.' In more ways than he cared to count.

She gently rubbed her son's back. 'You're far from broken. And we ask because we care about you.'

'*Sí*, I get that. But I prefer all this caring to be from afar. The up-close-and-personal kind gives me the…what do you English call it…the *willies*?'

Her eyes dimmed but her smile remained in place. 'Too bad. We're not going to stop because you bristle every time we come near.' Her determined gaze shifted to Raven, who was chatting to another guest. 'And I hope you're not giving her a hard time. From what I hear, she's the best physio there is.'

Despite telling himself it wasn't the time or place, he couldn't stop his gaze from tracing the perfect lines of Raven Blass's body. And it *was* a perfect body, honed by hours and hours of gruelling physical exercise. She hadn't been lying when she said she was solid muscle and bone. But Rafael knew, from being up close and personal, that there was soft femininity where there needed to be. Which, all in all, presented a more-than-pleasing package that had snagged his attention with shocking intensity the first time he'd laid eyes on her in his racing paddock almost eighteen months ago.

Of course, he'd been left in no uncertain terms that, despite all indications of a *very* mutual attraction, Raven had no intention of letting herself explore that attraction. Her reaction to it had been viscerally blunt.

She'd gone out of her way to hammer her rejection home… right at the time when he'd been in no state to be rejected…

His jaw tightened. 'How I choose to treat my physiotherapist is really none of your business, Sasha.'

A hint of sadness flitted through her eyes before she looked down at her son. 'Despite what you might think, I'm still your friend, so stop trying to push me away because, in case you need reminding, I push back.' She glanced back at him with a look of steely determination.

He sighed. 'I'd forgotten how stubborn you are.'

'It's okay. I'm happy to remind you when you need reminding. Your equally demanding godson demands your presence at the villa, so we'll see you both there in half an hour. No excuses.'

'If we must,' Rafael responded in a bored drawl.

Sasha's lips firmed. 'You must. Or I'll have to leave my guests and come and fetch you personally. And Marco wouldn't like that at all.'

'I stopped being terrified of my big brother long before I lost my baby teeth, *piqueña*.'

'Yes, but I know you wouldn't want to disappoint him. Also, don't forget about Raven.'

He glanced over his shoulder at the woman in question, who now stood with her head bent as she spoke to one of the altar boys. Her namesake hair fell forward as she nodded in response to something the boy said. From the close contact necessitated by her profession, Rafael knew exactly how silky and luxuriant her hair felt against his skin. He'd long stopped resenting the kick in his groin when he looked at her. In fact he welcomed it. He'd lost a lot after his accident, not just a percentage of his physical mobility. With each groin kick, he ferociously celebrated the return of his libido.

'What about Raven?' he asked.

'I've seen her in action during her training sessions. She's been known to reduce grown men to tears. I bet I can convince her to hog-tie you to the SUV and deliver you to the villa if you carry on being difficult.'

Rafael loosened his grip on his walking stick and gave a grim smile. '*Dios*, did someone hack into my temporary Internet files and discover I have a thing for dominatrixes? Because you two seem bent on pushing that hot, sweet button.'

Sasha's smile widened. 'I see you haven't lost your dirty sense of humour. That's something to celebrate, at least. See you at the villa.'

Without waiting for an answer, she marched off towards Marco, who was shaking hands with the priest. His brother's arm enfolded her immediately. Rafael gritted his teeth against the disconcerting pang and accompanying guilt that niggled him.

He'd robbed his family of so much…

'So, which is it to be—compliance without question or physical restraints?' Raven strolled towards him, her gaze cool and collected.

The mental picture that flashed into his mind made his

heart beat just that little bit faster. Nerves which his doctors had advised him might never heal again stirred, as they'd been stirring for several days now. The very male satisfaction the sensation brought sent a shaft of fire through his veins. 'You heard?'

'It was difficult not to. You don't revere your surroundings enough to keep your voice down when you air your... peccadilloes.'

The laughter that ripped from his throat felt surprisingly great. He'd had nothing to laugh about for far longer than he cared to remember. Several heads turned to watch him but he didn't care. He was more intrigued by the blush that spread over Raven's face. He leaned in close. 'Do you think the angels are about to strike me down? Will you save me if they do?' he asked sotto voce.

'No, Rafael. I think, based on your debauched past and irreverent present, all the saints will agree by now you're beyond redemption. No one can save you.'

Despite his bitter self-condemnation moments ago, hearing the words repeated so starkly caused Rafael's chest to tighten. All traces of mirth were stripped from his soul as he recalled similar words, uttered by the same voice, this same woman eight months ago. And then, as now, he felt the black chasm of despair yawn before him, growing ever-wider, sucking at his empty soul until only darkness remained. Because knowingly or unknowingly, she'd struck a very large, very raw nerve.

'Then tell me, Raven, if I'm beyond redemption, what the hell are you doing here?'

CHAPTER TWO

I'M NOT HERE to save you, if that's what you think.

The words hovered like heat striations in Raven's brain an hour later as she stood on the large sun-baked terrace of Marco and Sasha's home. This time the rich surroundings of the architecturally stunning Casa León failed to awe her as they usually did.

I'm not here to save you...

She snorted. What a load of bull. That was *exactly* why she'd begged Marco to let her visit Rafael in hospital once he'd woken from his coma all those months ago. It was why she'd flown to León from London five weeks ago, after months of trying to contact Rafael and being stonily ignored by him; and why she'd begged him to let her treat him when she found out what an appalling job his carers were doing—not because they were incompetent, but because Rafael didn't seem inclined in any way to want to get better, and they'd been too intimidated to go against his wishes. It was most definitely why she continued to suffer his inappropriate, irreverent taunts.

She wanted to make things right...wanted to take back every single word she'd said to him eight months ago, right before he'd climbed into the cockpit of his car and crashed it into a solid concrete wall minutes later.

Because it wasn't Rafael's fault that she hadn't been able to curb her stupid, crazy delusional feelings until it was almost too late. It wasn't his fault that, despite all signs that he was nothing but a carbon copy of her heartless playboy father, she hadn't been able to stop herself from lusting after him—

No, scratch that. Not a carbon copy. Rafael was no one's copy. He was a breed in his own right. With a smile that could slice a woman's heart wide open, make a woman swoon with bliss even as she knew her heart was being slowly crushed. He possessed more charm in his little finger than most wannabe playboys, including her father, held in their entire bodies.

But she'd seen first-hand the devastation that charm could cause. Swarthy Spanish Lothario or a middle-aged English playboy, she knew the effect would be the same.

Her mother was broken, continued to suffer because of the very lethal thrall Raven's father held over her.

And although she knew after five weeks in his company that Rafael's attitude would never manifest in sexual malice, he was in no way less dangerous to her peace of mind. Truth be told, the more she suffered his blatant sexual taunts, the more certain she was that she wanted to see beneath his outwardly glossy façade.

With every atom of her being, Raven wished she'd known this on his unfortunate race day. But, tormented by her mother's suffering, her control when it came to Rafael had slipped badly. Instead of walking away with dignified indifference, she'd lashed out. Unforgivably—

'So deep in thought. Dare I think those thoughts are about me?' Warm air from warmer lips washed over her right lobe.

'Why would you think that?' she asked, sucking in a deep, sustaining breath before she faced the man who seemed to have set up residence in her thoughts.

'Because I've studied you enough to recognise your frowns. Two lines mean you're unhappy because I'm not listening to you drone on about how many squats or abdominal crunches you expect me to perform. Three lines mean your thoughts are of a personal nature, mostly likely you're in turmoil about our last conversation before my accident.' He held out a glass of champagne, his blue eyes thankfully no longer charged with the frosty fury they'd held at the chapel. 'You're wearing a three-line frown now.'

She took the proffered drink and glanced away, unable quite to meet his gaze. 'You think I'm that easy to read?'

'The fact that you're not denying what I say tells me every-

thing I need to know. Your guilt is eating you alive. Admit it,'
he said conversationally, before taking a sip of his drink. 'And
it kills you even more that I can't remember the accident itself but can remember every single word you said to me only
minutes before it happened, doesn't it?'

Her insides twisted with regret. 'I…Rafael…I'm sorry…'

'As I told you in Barcelona, *I'm sorry* won't quite cut it. I
need a lot more from you than mere words, *mi corazon*.'

Her heart flipped and dived into her stomach. 'And I told
you, I won't debase myself like a cheap paddock bunny just
to prove how sorry I am for what I said.'

'Even though you meant every single word?'

'Look, I know I shouldn't have—'

'You meant them then, and you still believe them now. So
we shall continue as we are. I push, you push back; we both
drown in sexual tension. We'll see who breaks first.'

Her fingers tightened around the cold glass. 'Is this all really a game to you?' The man in turmoil she'd glimpsed at the
chapel seemed very distant now. But she'd seen him, knew
there was something else going on beneath all the sexual gloss.

'Of course it is. How else do you expect me to pass the
time?'

'Your racing career may be stalled for the moment but, for
a man of your wealth and power, there are a thousand ways
you can find fulfilment.'

A dull look entered his eyes but disappeared a split second later. '*Fulfilment*…how New Age. Next you'll be recom-
mending I practise Transcendental Meditation to get in touch
with my chakra.'

'Meditation isn't such a bad thing. I could teach you…'

His mocking laugh stopped her in her tracks. 'Will we
braid each other's hair too? Maybe share a joint or two while
we're at it?'

She tried to hide her irritation and cocked her head. 'You
know something? I have no idea what all those girls see in

you. You're cocky, arrogant and dismissive of things you know nothing about.'

'I don't waste my time learning things that hold no interest for me. Women hold my interest so I make it a point to study them. And I know plenty about women like you.'

She stiffened. 'What do you mean, women like me?'

'You take pleasure in hiding behind affront, you take everything so personally and pretend to get all twisted up by the slightest hint of a challenge. It's obvious you've had a... traumatic experience in the past—'

'That's like a psychic predicting someone's been hurt in the past. By virtue of sheer coincidence and indisputable reality, half of relationships end badly, so it stands to reason that most people have had *traumatic experiences*. If you're thinking of taking up clairvoyance, you'll need to do better than that.'

His bared teeth held the predatory smile of one who knew he had his prey cornered. '*Claro*, let's do it this way. I'll make a *psychic* prediction. If I'm wrong, feel free to throw that glass of vintage champagne in my face.'

'I'd never make a scene like that, especially not at your nephew's christening.'

The reminder of where they were made him stiffen slightly but it didn't stop him moving closer until his broad shoulders and streamlined body blocked out the rest of the party. Breath catching, Raven could see nothing but him, smell nothing but the heady, spicy scent that clung to his skin and seemed to weave around her every time she came within touching distance.

As if he knew his effect on her, his smile widened. 'No one will see my humiliation *if* I get it wrong.'

Afraid of what he'd uncover, she started to shake her head, but Rafael was already speaking.

'You've been hurt by a man, someone you really wanted to depend on, someone you wanted to *be there* for you.' He waited, his eyes moving to the fingers clenched around her glass. When she didn't move he leaned in closer. 'Since that relationship ended, you've decided to take the tired *all men are bastards* route. You'd like nothing more than to find yourself a nice, safe man, someone who *understands* you.' His gaze moved to her face, his incisive stare probing so deep Raven wanted to take a step back. With sheer strength of will, she stood her ground. 'You hate yourself for being attracted to me but, deep inside, you enjoy our little skirmishes because the challenge of sparring with me makes your heart beat just that little bit faster.' His gaze traced her hopefully impassive face down to her throat.

For a blind moment, Raven wished she'd worn her hair down because even she could feel the wild tattoo of her pulse surging underneath the skin at her throat.

She tried to speak but the accuracy of his prediction had frozen her tongue.

'Since my face is still dry, I'll take it Psychic Rafa is accurate on all accounts?'

His arrogance finally loosened her tongue. 'Don't flatter yourself. I told you when you started playing these games that I wouldn't participate. I know you're challenged by any woman who doesn't fall for your charms, but not everyone subscribes to the OMG-Rafael de Cervantes-makes-my-knickers-wet Fan Club.'

Rafael's smile was blinding, but it held a speculation that made her hackles rise. '*Pequeña*, since there's only one way to *test* that you're not a member, I now have something to look forward to. And just like that, my days suddenly seem brighter.'

Heat punched its way through her pelvis but, before Raven could answer, a deep throat cleared behind them.

Marco de Cervantes was as tall as his brother and just as visually stunning to look at but he wore his good looks with a smouldering grace where Rafael wholeheartedly embraced his irreverent playboy status.

Marco nodded to Raven, and glanced at his brother.

'I need to talk to you. You don't mind if I borrow him for five minutes, do you, Raven?'

Relief spiked, headier than the champagne she'd barely drunk. 'Not at all. We weren't discussing anything important.'

Rafael's eyes narrowed at the thin insult, his icy blue eyes promising retribution just before they cleared into their usual deceptively indolent look.

Lifting her glass in a mocking salute, she walked away, piercingly aware that he tracked her every step. Out of his intoxicating, domineering sphere, she heaved in a breath of pure relief and pasted a smile on her face as Sasha beckoned her.

Rafael turned to his brother, mild irritation prickling his skin. 'What's on your mind?' He discarded his champagne and wished he had something stronger.

'You need another hobby besides trying to rile your physiotherapist.'

His irritation grew as Raven disappeared from sight, pulled towards a group of guests by Sasha. 'What's it to you? And why the hell does everyone feel the need to poke their nose into my business?'

Marco shrugged away the question. 'Consider the matter dropped. The old man's been asking for you.' Grey eyes bored sharply into his. 'I think it's time.'

Every bone in his body turned excruciatingly rigid. 'That's for me to decide, surely?' And if he didn't feel he was ready to ask for forgiveness, who was anybody to decide otherwise?

'There's been enough hurt all around, Rafa. It's time to move things forward.'

He spiked tense fingers through his hair. 'You wouldn't be trying to save me again by any chance, would you, brother?'

An impatient look passed through Marco's eyes. 'From the look of things, you don't need saving. Besides, I cut the apron strings when I realised you were driving me so nuts that I was in danger of strangling you with them.'

Rafael beckoned the waiter over and exchanged his untouched champagne for a crystal tumbler of Patrón. 'In that case, we're copacetic. Was there anything else?'

Marco's gaze stayed on him for several seconds before he nodded. 'You sent for the papers for the X1 All-Star event coming up?'

Rafael downed the drink, welcoming the warmth that coursed through his chest. 'Unless I'm mistaken, I'm still the CEO of X1 Premier Management. The events start in three weeks. You delegated some of the event's organisation but it's time for me to take the reins again.'

His brother's gaze probed, worry lurking within. 'Are you sure you don't want to sit this one out—?'

'I'm sure. Don't second-guess me, *mi hermano*. I understand that my racing career may be in question—' He stopped as a chill surged through his veins, obliterating the warmth of moments before. Although he didn't remember his accident, he'd seen pictures of the wreckage in vivid detail. He was very much aware that *lucky to be alive* didn't begin to describe his condition. 'The racing side of my career may be up for debate,' he repeated, beating back the wave of desolation that swelled up inside his chest, 'but my brain still functions perfectly. As for my body...' He looked over as a flash of orange caught his eye. The resulting kick gave him a surge of satisfaction. 'My body will be in top condition before very long.'

Marco nodded. 'I'm happy to hear it. According to Raven, you're on the road to complete recovery.'

'Really?' Rafael made a mental note to have a short, precise conversation with his physio about sharing confidential information.

'...*Dios*, are you listening to me? Never mind, I think it'll be safer for me not to know which part of your anatomy you're thinking with right at this moment. *Bueno*, I'll be in touch later in the week to discuss other business.'

'No need to wait till next week. I can tell you now that I'm back. I own fifty per cent of our business, after all. No reason why you should continue to shoulder my responsibilities.

Come to think of it, you should take a vacation with your family, let me handle things for a while.' He glanced over to where Sasha stood chatting to Raven. As if sensing their attention, both women turned towards them. Marco's face dissolved in a look so cheesy, Rafael barely stopped himself from making retching noises.

'Are you sure?' Marco asked without taking his eyes off his wife. 'Sasha's been on my back about taking some time off. It would be great to take the yacht to the island for a bit.' They joint owned a three-mile island paradise in the Bahamas, a place neither of them had visited in a very long time.

'Great. Do it. I'll handle things here,' Rafael responded.

His brother looked sceptical.

'This is a one-time offer, set to expire in ten seconds,' he pressed as his sister-in-law and his physiotherapist started walking towards them. For the first time he noticed Raven's open-toed high heels and saw the way they made her long legs go on for ever. Sasha said something to her. Her responding smile made his throat dry.

Hell, he had it bad if he was behaving like a hormonal teenager around a woman who clearly had *man issues*.

He barely felt it when Marco slapped his shoulder. 'I'll set things in motion first thing in the morning. I owe you one, brother.'

Rafael nodded, relieved that the disturbing subject of his father had been dropped.

'What are you looking so pleased about?' Sasha asked her husband as they drew level with them.

'I have news that's guaranteed to make you adore me even more than you already do.' He kissed her soundly on the lips before leading her away.

Rafael saw Raven looking after them. 'I do believe if they had a *like* button attached to their backs you would be pressing it right about now?'

Her outraged gasp made him curb a smile. He loved to rile her. Rafael didn't hide from the fact that while he was busy riling Raven Blass, he was busy not thinking about what this place did to him, and that gained him a reprieve from the torment of his memories.

She faced him, bristling with irritation and censure. 'Whereas if you had a *like* button I'd personally start a worldwide petition to have it obliterated and replaced with one that said *loathe*.'

He took her elbow and, despite her resistance, he led her to an exquisitely laid out buffet table. 'We'll discuss my various buttons later. Right now you need to eat something before you wither away. I noticed you didn't eat any breakfast this morning.'

She glared at him. 'I had my usual bowl of muesli and fresh fruit.'

'Was that before or after you spent two hours on my beach contorting yourself in unthinkable shapes in the name of exercise?'

'It's called Krav Maga. It works the mind as well as the body.'

He let his gaze rake her from top to toe. 'I don't dispute the effects on the body. But I don't think it's quite working on the mind.'

He stopped another outraged gasp by stuffing a piece of chicken into her mouth. Her only option, other than spitting it out, was to chew, but that didn't stop her glaring fiercely at him.

Rafael was so busy enjoying the way he got under her skin that he didn't hear the low hum of the electric wheelchair until it was too late.

'*Buenos tardes, mi hijo.* I've been looking for you.' The greeting was low and deep. It didn't hold any censure or hatred or flaying judgement. In fact it sounded just exactly as it would were a loving father greeting his beloved son.

But every nerve of Rafael's being screeched with whitehot pain. His fist clenched around his walking stick until the metal dug excruciatingly into his palm. For the life of him, he couldn't let go. He sucked in a breath as his vision blurred. Before the red haze completely dulled his vision, he saw Raven's concerned look as her eyes darted between him and the wheelchair-bound figure.

'Rafael?'

He couldn't find the words to respond to the greeting. Nor could he find the words to stem Raven's escalating concern.

Dios mio, he couldn't even find the courage to turn around. Because how the hell could he explain to Raven that he and he alone was responsible for making his father a quadriplegic?

CHAPTER THREE

'Do you want to talk about it?'

'The *therapy* in your job title pertains only to my body, not my mind. You'll do well to remember that.'

Raven should've heeded the icy warning, should've just kept her hands on the wheel of the luxury SUV and kept driving towards the stunning glass and steel structure that was Rafael's home on the other side of the de Cervantes estate from his brother's villa.

But her senses jumped at the aura of acute pain that had engulfed Rafael the moment he'd turned around to face the old man in the electric wheelchair. The same pain that surrounded him now. Grey lips were pinched into a thin line, his jaw carved from stone and fingers clamped around his walking stick in a white-knuckled grip. Even his breathing had changed. His broad chest rose and fell in an uncharacteristically shallow rhythm that screamed his agitation.

She pulled over next to a tall acacia tree, one of several hundred that lined the long winding driveway and extended into the exquisitely designed landscape beyond. Behind them, the iron gates, manned by twenty-four-hour security, swung shut.

Narrowed eyes focused with laser-like intensity on her. 'What the hell do you think you're doing?'

'I've stopped because we need to talk about what just happened. Your mental health affects your body's recovery just as much as your physiotherapy regime.'

'Healthy mind, healthy body? That's a piss-poor way of trying to extract the hot gossip, Raven *mia*. You'll need to do much better than that. Why don't you just come out and ask for the juicy details?'

She blew a breath, refusing to rise to the bait. 'Would you tell me if I asked you that?'

'No.'

'Rafael—'

Arctic-chilled eyes narrowed even further. 'In case you didn't already guess, that was my father. Our relationship comes under the subject line of *kryptonite—keep the hell out* to any and all parties.'

'So you can dissect my personal life all you want but yours is off limits?'

His smile was just as icy. 'Certain aspects of my personal life are wide open to you. All you have to do is say the word and I'll be happy to educate you in how we can fully explore it.'

'That is not what I meant.'

'You've taken pains to establish boundaries between us since the moment we met. This is one of *my* boundaries. Attempt to breach it at your peril.'

She frowned. 'Or what? You'll fall back on your default setting of sexual innuendo and taunts? Rafael, I'm only trying to help you.'

His hand slashed through the air in a movement so far removed from his normal laid-back indolence her mouth dropped open. 'I do not need your help unless it's the help I've hired you to provide. Right now I want you to shut up and *drive*.' He clipped out the final word in a hard bite that sent a chill down her spine.

After waiting a minute to steady her own shot nerves, she set the SUV back onto the road, aware of his continued shallow breathing and gritted-jaw iciness. Her fingers clenched over the titanium steering wheel and she practised some nerve-calming breaths of her own.

From the very first, Rafael had known which buttons to push. He'd instinctively known that the subject of sex was anathema to her and had therefore honed in on it with the precision of a laser-guided missile.

Seeing his intense reaction to his father—and she'd known immediately the nearly all-grey-haired man in the wheelchair was his father—had hammered home what she'd been surprised to learn this morning at the chapel, and had somewhat confirmed at Marco's villa: that Rafael, as much as he pretended to be shallow and sex pest-y, had a depth he rarely showed to the world.

Was that why she was so driven to pay penance for the way she'd treated him several months ago—because deep down she thought he was worth saving?

Raven shied away from the probing thought and brought the car to a stop at the end of the driveway.

The wide solid glass door that led into the house swung open and Diego, one of the many staff Rafael employed to run his luxurious home, came down the steps to open her door. In silence, she handed him the car keys and turned to find Rafael rounding the bonnet. The sun glinting off the silver paint cast his face into sharp relief. Her breath snagged in her chest at the masculine, tortured beauty of him. She didn't offer to assist him as he climbed the shallow steps into the house.

In the marble-floored hallway, he shrugged off his suit jacket, handed it to Diego and pulled his shirt tails impatiently from his trousers. At the glimpse of tanned golden flesh a pulse of heat shot through her belly. Sucking in a breath, she looked away, focusing on an abstract painting that took up one entire rectangular pillar in the hallway for an infinitesimal second before she glanced his away again, to find him shoving an agitated hand through his hair.

'Do you need—?' she started.

'Unless I'm growing senile, today's Sunday. Did we not agree we'd give the Florence Nightingale routine a rest on Sundays?'

Annoyance rose to mingle with her concern. 'No, *you* came up with that decree. I never agreed to it.'

Handing his walking stick to a still-hovering Diego, he

started to unbutton his shirt. 'It's a great thing I'm the boss then, isn't it?'

Her mouth dried as several inches of stunning flesh assaulted her senses. When her brain started to short-circuit, she pulled her gaze away. 'Undressing in the hallway, Rafael, really?' She tried to inject as much indifference into her tone as possible but was aware her voice had become unhealthily screechy. 'What do you think—that I'm going to run away in virginal outrage?'

His shameless grin didn't hide the strain and tension beneath. 'At twenty-four, I seriously doubt there's anything virginal about you. No, *mi dulzura,* I'm hoping you'll stay and cheer me on through my striptease.'

The sound that emerged from her throat made his grin widen. 'Don't you want to heal completely? That limp will not go away until you work hard to strengthen your core muscles and realign the bones that were damaged during the accident. If you'd just focus on that we can be rid of each other sooner rather than later.'

Although she thought she saw his shoulders stiffen as he turned to give his shirt to Diego, his grin was still in place when he faced her. 'You're under the impression that I want to be shot of you but you couldn't be further from the truth. I want you right here with me every day.'

'So I can be your whipping girl?'

'I've never been a fan of whips, myself. Handcuffs, blindfolds, the odd paddle, certainly…but whips?' He gave a mock shudder. 'No, not my thing.'

His hand went to the top of his trousers. Deft fingers freed his button, followed by the loud, distinct sound of his zip lowering. She froze. Diego didn't bat an eyelid. 'For goodness' sake, what *are* you doing, Rafael?'

He toed off his shoes and socks. 'I thought it was obvious. I'm going for a swim. Care to join me?'

'I…no, thank you.' The way her temperature had shot up, she'd need a cold shower, not the sultry warmth of Rafael's azure infinity pool. 'But we'll need to talk when you're done. I'll come and find you—' She nearly choked when he dropped his trousers and stepped out of them. The way his designer cotton boxer shorts cupped his impressive man package made all oxygen flee from her lungs. Utterly captivated by the man whose sculpted body, even after the accident that had laid him flat for months, was still the best-looking she'd even seen or worked with, Raven could no more stop herself from staring than she could fly to the moon.

His thighs and legs bore scars from his accident, his calves solid powerful muscle that made the physio in her thrilled to be working with such a manly specimen. Dear Lord, even his feet were sexy, and she'd never been one to pay attention to feet unless they were directly related to her profession.

Helplessly, her gaze travelled back up, past his golden, sculpted chest and wide, athletic shoulders to collide with icy blue eyes.

'My, my, if I didn't enjoy it so much I'd be offended to be treated like a piece of meat.'

She snapped back to her senses to see Diego disappearing up the granite banister-less staircase leading to Rafael's vast first floor suite. The click of his walking stick drew attention back to the man in question. One brow was raised in silent query.

'What do you expect if you insist on making an exhibition of yourself?'

One step brought him within touching distance. 'That's the beauty of free will, *querida*. The ability to walk away when a situation displeases you.'

'If I did that every time you attempted to rile me, I'd never get any work done and you'd still be in the pathetic shape I found you in five weeks ago.'

Another step. Raven breathed in and clenched her fists against the warm, wicked scent that assailed her senses.

'You know what drew me to you when you first joined Team Espíritu?' he breathed.

'I'm sure you're going to enlighten me.'

'Your eyes flash with the deepest hypnotic fire when you're all riled up but your body screams *stay away*. Even the most seductive woman can't pull that off as easily as you can. I'm infinitely fascinated to know what happened to make you this way.'

'Personal subjects are off the table. Besides, I thought you had me all worked out?'

His gaze dropped to her lips. She pressed them together to stop their insane tingling. 'I know the general parameters of your inner angst. But I can't help but feel there's another layer, a deeper reason why you want me with every cell in your body but would chop off your hand before you would even bring yourself to touch me in any but a professional way.'

The ice that encased her soul came from so deep, so dark a place that she'd stopped trying to fathom the depths of it. 'Enjoy your swim, Rafael. I'll come by later to discuss the next steps of your regime.'

'Of course, Mistress Raven. I look forward to the many and varied ways you intend to *whip* me into shape.' With a step sideways that still managed to encroach on her body space and bring even more of his pulsing body heat slapping against her, he adjusted the walking stick and sauntered away in a slow, languid walk.

Hell, even a limping Rafael de Cervantes managed to move with a swagger that made her heart race. Tearing her traitorous gaze away from his tight butt, she hurried up the floating staircase to her room. Gritting her teeth against the firestorm of emotions that threatened to batter her to pieces, she changed into her workout gear. The simple act of donning the familiar attire calmed her jangling nerves.

But she couldn't forget that, once again, Rafael had cut through the outer layer of her defences and almost struck bone, almost peeled back layers she didn't want uncovered.

She pushed the niggling sensation away and shoved her feet into comfortable trainers. After a minute's debate, she

decided on the gym instead of her preferred outdoor regime.
Even though the day was edging towards evening, the Spanish sun blazed far too hot for the gruelling exercise she needed
to restore balance to her equilibrium.

She took the specially installed lift that divided her suite
from Rafael's to the sub-basement level where the state-of-
the-art gym was located. It was the only room in the whole
house that didn't have an exhibitionist's view to the outside.

Rafael's house held no concrete walls, only thick glass in-
terspersed with steel and chrome pillars. At first the feeling of
exposure had preyed on her nerves, but now the beauty of the
architecturally stunning design had won her over. Nevertheless, right this minute she was grateful for the enclosed space
of the gym. Here she didn't need to compose herself, didn't
need to hold back her punches as she slammed her gloved fist
into the punching bag. Pain repeatedly shot up her arms, and
gradually cleared her mind.

She was here to do her job. Which started and ended with
helping Rafael heal properly and regain the utmost mobility. Once she achieved her aim and made peace with her part
in his accident, she could walk away from the crazy, bone-
deep, completely insane attraction she felt for the man who
was in every shape and form the epitome of the man who'd
fathered her.

The man whose playboy lifestyle had mattered to him on
so deep a level he'd turned his back on his parental responsibilities until they'd been forced on him by the authorities.
The same man who'd stood by and barely blinked while his
friends had tried to put their hands on her.

Punch!

Her hand slipped. The bag continued its lethal trajectory
towards her. Only her ingrained training made her sidestep
the heavy-moving bag before it knocked her off her feet. Chest
heaving, she tugged off the gloves and went to the climbing
frame and chalked her hands.

Clamping her lids shut, she regulated her breathing and forced herself to focus.

Rafael would not derail her. She'd made a colossal mistake and vocalised her roiling disgust for his lifestyle at the most inappropriate moment. Whatever the papers had said, Raven knew deep down she was partly, if not wholly, responsible for putting Rafael in the dangerous frame of mind that had caused his accident. She also knew things could've turned out a million times worse than they had. This was her penance. She would help him get back on his feet. Then she would leave and get on with the rest of her life.

Reaching high, she grabbed the first handhold.

By the time she reached the top seven minutes later, her new course of action was clearly formulated.

'I've laid out the itinerary for the next three months. If you cooperate, I'm confident I can get you back to full health and one hundred per cent mobility with little or no after-effects,' she started crisply as she opened the door and entered Rafael's study. She approached his desk, only to stop when she noticed his attention was caught on the papers strewn on his glass-topped desk.

'I'm talking to you, Rafael.'

'I heard you,' he muttered, and held out his hand for the sheet without looking up. After a cursory glance, he started to shake his head. 'This isn't going to work.' He slapped it down and picked up his own papers.

Raven waited a beat. When he didn't look up, she fought a sharp retort. 'May I ask why not?'

'I have several events to host and meetings to attend between now and when the X1 season starts. Your itinerary requires that I stand still.'

She frowned. 'No, it doesn't.'

'It might as well. You've upped the regime from two to three times a day with sports massages thrown in there that would require me to be stationary. And was that *acupuncture*

I saw in there?' His derisive tone made her hackles rise higher. 'I'll be travelling a lot in the next three months. You're sorely mistaken if you think I intend to take time off to sit around being pricked and prodded.'

She watched the light glint off his damp hair. 'What do you mean, you'll be travelling a lot? You're supposed to be recuperating.'

Steely blue eyes met hers and instantly Raven was reminded of the unwavering determination that had seen him win several racing championships since he'd turned professional at nineteen.

'I have a multi-billion-dollar company to run, or have you forgotten?'

'No, I haven't. But wasn't…isn't Marco in charge for the time being? He told me he had everything in hand when we discussed my helping you—'

His eyes narrowed. 'What else did you discuss with my brother?'

Mouth dry, she withstood his stare. 'What do you mean?'

'I expected an element of confidentiality when I hired you…'

'What *exactly* are you accusing me of?'

'You will not discuss details of my health with anyone else but me, is that clear?'

'I didn't—'

'You're glowing.' His gaze raked her face down to her neck and back up again.

'Excuse me?'

'You look…flushed. If I weren't painfully aware of the unlikelihood of it, I'd have said you had just tumbled from a horizontal marathon in a lover's bed. Not quite tumbled to within an inch of your life, more like—'

'Can we get back to this, please?' She waved the sheet in his face then slammed it back in front of him.

He shrugged and sat back in his plush leather chair, the cool, calm businessman back in place. 'Marco has his own company to run…and a new family to attend to. Besides, he's taking a well-earned break, so I'm managing his company as well.'

A wave of shock nearly rendered her speechless. 'And you didn't think to speak to me before you decided all this?'

'I wasn't aware I needed your permission to live my life or run my business.' His voice, a stiletto-thin blade, skimmed close to her skin.

She took a breath and searched for calm, a state which she'd concluded long ago was near on impossible when in Rafael's presence. 'It's part of the contract we agreed. If you're going to take on any substantial amount of work I'll need to know so I can formulate your therapy accordingly. For goodness' sake, you can't go from zero to full-time work in the space of an afternoon. And I really don't know what you were thinking, telling your brother you'd take on this amount of work for the next goodness knows how long!'

Rafael's gaze dropped to her annoyed almost-pout and fought not to continue downward to the agitated heaving of her breasts. Peachy…the smooth skin of her throat glowed a faint golden-pink. He'd long been fascinated by how a woman with jet-black hair such as hers could have skin so pale it was almost translucent. He knew she took care to stay out of the sun and practised her exercises before daybreak.

An image of her, streamlined, sleek and poised upside down in a martial arts pose, slammed into his brain. The groin-hardening effect made him grip his pen harder. His gaze fell once more on her lips and it was all he could do not to round his desk, clasp her face in his hands and taste her. Or maybe coax her round to him, pull down that prim little skirt she'd donned and discover the delights underneath.

Dios, focus!

'Luckily, I don't answer to you, *mi dulzura.*' He certainly had no intention of enlightening her on what he'd been working steadily on for over a month; what he hadn't stopped thinking of since he'd woken from his coma.

Because finding a way to occupy his mind was the only sure way of keeping his many and varied demons at bay.

'…I hope to hell you're not thinking of adding racing to this insane schedule.' She paled a little as she said it and the usual kick of satisfaction surged.

'And what if I am?' He moderated his voice despite the cold fist of pain that lodged in his gut. Unless a miracle happened, his racing career was over. A part of him had accepted that. Deep inside his soul, however, it was another matter.

'I'm hoping it won't come to that. Because you know as well as I do, you're in no shape to get into a racing cockpit.'

He raised an interested brow. 'And how exactly do you intend to stop me?'

Her delectable lips parted but no words emerged, and her eyes took on a haunted look that made him grit his teeth. 'I can't, I suppose. But I think you'll agree you're not in the best shape.'

'Physically or mentally?'

'Only you can judge your mental state but, as your physiotherapist, I'd say you're not ready.'

He finally got his body under enough control to stand. He caught her sharp inhalation when he rounded the desk and perched on the edge next to where she stood. Hazel eyes, wide and spirited, glared at him.

Taking the sheet from her hand, he dropped it on the table, reached across—slowly, so she wouldn't bolt—and traced his forefinger along her jaw. 'Your eyes are so huge right now. You're almost shaking with worry for me. Yet you try and make me think you detest the very ground I walk on.'

Her hand rose to intercept his finger but, instead of pushing it away, she kept a hold of it, imploring eyes boring into his. 'I don't detest you, Rafael. If I did, I wouldn't be here. I'll admit we're…different but—' her shoulders rose and fell under the thin layer of her cotton top '—I'm willing to put aside our differences to help you recuperate properly. And racing before you're ready…come on, you know that's crazy.

Besides, think of your family, of Sasha. Do you think you're being fair to them, putting them through this?'

He froze. 'I've never responded well to emotional black-mail. And leave Sasha out of this. I'll tell you what, if you don't want me to race, you'll have to find other ways to keep me entertained.'

She dropped his hand as if it burned, just like he'd known she would. 'Why does everything always circle back to sex with you?'

'I didn't actually mean that sexually, but what the hell, let's go with it.'

'Stop doing that!'

'Doing what, *mi encantador*?'

'Pretending you're a male bimbo whore.'

'Are you saying I'm not?' He pretended astonishment, the fizz of getting under her skin headier than the most potent wine.

She nodded at the papers on his desk. 'You just reminded me that you run a multi-billion-dollar corporation. I don't care how great you claim to be in bed; you couldn't have made it without using some upstairs skills.'

He leaned back on the table when a twinge of pain shot through his left hip. 'How do you know?'

'You shouldn't sit like that. You're putting too much pres-sure on your hip.'

Annoyance replaced his buzz. He didn't deny that Raven had made much progress where his previous physios had failed. After all, it was the reason Team Espíritu had hired her as his personal therapist last year. She was the best around and got impressive results with her rigorous regime. But she'd always been able to brush him off as if he were a pesky fly.

He remained in his exact position, raising a daring brow when her gaze collided with his. His blood thickened when she took the dare and stepped closer.

Without warning, her hand shot out and grabbed his hip. Her thumb dug into his hipbone where the pain radiated from.

A few rotations of pressure-based massage and he wanted to moan with relief.

'Why do you fight me when you know I'm the best person to help you get better?' she breathed.

'Because my *mamá* told me I never took the easy way out. You will never get me to ask how high when you say jump.'

She paused for a second, then continued to massage his hip. 'You never talk about your mother,' she murmured.

Tension rippled through him. 'I never talk about anyone in my family. The prying all comes from you, *bonita*. You've made it a mission to upturn every single rock in my life.'

'And yet I don't feel in any way enlightened about your life.'

'Maybe because I'm an empty vessel.' He tried damn hard not to let the acid-like guilt bleed through his voice.

'No, you're not. You just like to pretend you are. Have you considered that by pretending to be something you're not, all you're doing is attracting attention to the very thing you wish to avoid?'

'That's deep. And I presume that thought challenges you endlessly?'

Her hand had moved dangerously close to his fly. If she looked down or moved her actions a few inches west, she'd realise that, despite their verbal sparring skimming the murkier waters of his personal life, he was no less excited by her touch.

In fact, he wasn't ashamed to admit that he found the return of his libido exhilarating. For a few weeks after he'd emerged from his coma it'd been touch and go. His doctors had cautioned him that he might not resume complete sexual function. Raven Blass's appearance in his hospital room five weeks ago had blown that misdiagnosis straight out of the water.

'No,' she responded. 'I know better than to issue challenges to you.'

'You're such a buzzkill,' he said, but he felt relieved that she'd decided to leave the matter of his mother alone.

He saw the faintest trace of a smile on her face before it disappeared. Her fingers moved away, rounded his hip and settled into his back. The movement brought her closer still, her chest mere inches from his. Firm, relief-bringing fingers dug into his muscle. Again he suppressed a moan of relief.

'I know. But think how smug I'd feel if you got back into racing before you were ready and reversed your progress. You'd never hear the end of it if you proved me right.'

The sultry movement of her mouth was a siren call he didn't try very hard to resist. His forefinger was gliding over her mouth before he could stop himself. Her fingers stilled before digging painfully into his back. The rush of her breath over his finger sent his pulse thundering.

'Or I could die. And this relentless song and dance could be over between us. Once and for all.'

CHAPTER FOUR

THE CALM DELIVERY of his words, spoken with barely a flicker of those lush jet eyelashes, froze her to the core.

'Is that what you want? To die?' Her words were no more than a whisper, coated with the shock that held her immobile.

'We all have to die some time.'

'But why, Rafael? Why do you wish to hurry the process when every rational human being fights to stay alive?'

'*Mi tesoro*, rational isn't exactly what most people think when they look at me.'

'That's not an answer.' She realised she was hanging on to him with a death claw but, for the life of her, Raven couldn't let go. She feared her legs would fail her if she did. And hell, she wasn't even sure *why* Rafael's explanation was so important to her. For all she knew, it was another statement meant to titillate and shock. But, looking closer, her blood grew colder. Something in his expression wasn't quite right. Or, rather, it was too right, as if he held his statement with some conviction. 'What is it, Rafael? Please tell me why you said that.'

'Quid pro quo, sweetheart. If I bare my soul, will you bear yours?'

'Would that give you something to live for?'

Raven could've sworn she heard the snap of his jaw as he went rigid in her arms. Grasping her by the elbows, he set her away from him and straightened to his impressive six foot three inches. His lids shuttered his expression and he returned to the seat behind his desk.

'The amateur head-shrinking session is over, *chiquita*. Modify your regime to accommodate travel and liaise with Diego if you'll need special equipment for where we'll be travelling. We leave on Wednesday.' He reeled off their intended destinations before picking up a glossy photo of the latest Cervantes sports car.

Knowing she wouldn't make any more headway with him, she turned to leave.

'Oh, and Raven?'

'Yes?'

'We'll be attending several high profile events, so make sure you pack something other than kick-boxing shorts, trainers and tank tops. As delectable as they are, they won't suit.'

Raven fought the need to smash her fist into the nearest priceless vase as she left Rafael's study. Not because he would see her, although the glass walls meant he would, but because *not* losing control was paramount if she wished to maintain her equilibrium.

She'd fought long and hard to channel her tumultuous emotions into useful energy when, at sixteen, she'd realised how very little her father cared for her. For far too long, she'd been so angry with the world for taking her mother away and replacing her with a useless, despicable parent, she'd let her temper get the better of her.

Rafael could do his worst. She would not let him needle her further.

Taking the sheet into the vast living room, she spent the next hour revising Rafael's regime and speaking to Diego about organising the equipment she would need. Again she felt unease and a healthy amount of frustrated anger at Rafael's decision to return to X1 racing. She didn't shy away from the blunt truth that she herself wanted to avoid the inevitable return.

Even though she'd been paid handsomely by Team Espíritu and treated well by the team, she'd always felt ill at ease in that world. She didn't have to dig deep to recognise the reason.

Sexual promiscuity had been almost a given in the paddock. Hell, some even considered it a challenge to sleep with as many bodies as possible during one race season.

She'd received more than her fair share of unwanted male attention and, by the end of her first season, she'd known she was in danger of earning a *frigid* badge. Ironically, it was Sasha Fleming's catapult into the limelight as the team's lead racer that had lessened male interest in her. For the first time, female paddock professionals were seen as more than just the next notch on a bedpost.

'A two-line frown. I don't know whether to be pleased or disappointed.'

She looked up to find Rafael standing a few feet away, two drinks in his hand and his walking stick dangling from his arm. He held one out to her and she accepted and thanked him for the cold lime based cocktail she'd grown to love since coming to Leon.

'I was thinking about how it would be to return to the X1 circuit.'

'Shouldn't that warrant a three-line frown since I feature in there somewhere?'

'Wow, are you really that self-centred? A psychologist would have a field day with you, you know that?'

With a very confident, very careless shrug, he sank into the seat next to her. 'They'd have to fight off hordes of adoring fans first. Not to mention you.'

'Me? Why would I mind?'

'You're very possessive about me. If you had your way, I'd stay right here, doing your every bidding and following you around like a besotted puppy.'

Eternally thankful she'd swallowed her first sip, Raven stared open-mouthed. Several seconds passed before she could close her mouth. 'I'm stunned speechless.'

'Enough for me to sneak a kiss on you?'

Blood rushed to her head and much lower, between her legs, a throbbing started that should've shamed her. Instead, she exhaled and decided to give herself a break. A girl could only withstand so many shocks in one day.

'Earth to Raven. I don't know how to interpret a wish for a kiss when you go into a trance at the thought of one.'

'I…what?'

'I said kiss me.'

'No. I don't think that's a good idea.'

'It's a great idea. Look at me; I can barely walk. *You'd* be taking advantage of *me*.' His smile held a harsh edge that made the Rafael de Cervantes charm even more lethal.

'Whatever. It's not going to happen. Now, is there anything else I can help you with?'

His sigh was heavy and exaggerated. 'Bianca is almost ready to serve dinner. I figure we have twenty minutes to burn. Shall we be very English and talk about the weather before then?'

'The weather is fantastic. Now, let's talk about your return to X1. I don't wish to get personal…'

His low laugh made heat rush into her face.

'What I mean is…you'll have to be careful when it comes to being…um…'

'Just spit it out, Raven.'

'Fine. Sex. You can't have sex.'

He clutched his chest, then tapped carefully on his sculpted muscle. '*Dios*, I think my heart just stopped. You can't *say* things like that.'

'I mean it. The last thing you need to be doing is chasing after paddock bunnies. You could reverse any progress we've made in the last few weeks. Your pelvis needs time to heal properly. You do want to get better, don't you?'

'Yes, but at what cost? My libido could just shrivel away and die,' he returned without the barest hint of shame while she…she'd grown so hot she had to take a hasty sip of her drink.

'It won't.' She set her glass down on the table. 'Not unless you put too much stress on your body by taking on too much. Look, I'm not asking for much. I'm saying keep your…keep it in your pants for just a little bit longer, until you're more fully recovered.'

He opened his mouth but she raised her hand before he could speak. 'And please don't say you need sex to recover. Despite what you want everyone to think, you're not a sex addict. In fact you were one of the most disciplined men I knew when it came to dedication to racing. All I'm saying is apply that same discipline to your…needs, at least for the time being.'

Sensual masculine lips tilted at the corners. 'I think there was a compliment in there somewhere. Fine, I'll take your lecture under advisement.'

'You need to do more than that, Rafael. Your injuries are too serious to take recovery lightly.'

He shoved a hand through his hair. '*Dios*, did I call you a buzzkill earlier?'

'I believe you did.'

'Congratulations, you've just been upgraded to manhood-killer. Ah, here comes Bianca. Let's hope she's got something to revive me after that complete emasculation.'

'Yeah, my heart bleeds.'

Rafael tried to follow what the financial newsreader was saying on the large high definition screen on his plane. He failed.

Opposite him, ensconced in the club chair, Raven twirled a pen between her lips as she read and made notes on a piece of paper. On any other woman he'd have ridiculed such a blatant sexual ploy. But he knew the woman opposite him was unaware of what she was doing. And its totally groin-hardening effect on him.

Giving up on finding out how the Dow-Jones was doing, he turned off the TV and settled back in his seat.

She raised her head and looked at him with those stunning hazel eyes. 'What?'

'How did you get into physiotherapy?'

She regarded him for several seconds before she depressed the top of her pen. 'The random kindness of strangers.'

He raised an eyebrow.

She shrugged. 'A chance meeting with an ex-PE teacher in my local park when I was seventeen changed my life.'

'Was he hot?'

She rolled her eyes. '*She* realised I loved to exercise but I had no interest in being an athlete. We met and talked a few times. About a month later she took me to the local sports centre where professional athletes trained and introduced me to their head coach. By the end of the day I knew what I wanted to be.'

'And she did this all out of the goodness of her heart?'

'She realised I had…anger issues and worked to give me focus. She didn't have to, so yes, I guess she did.'

He held back the need to enlighten her that nothing in life came free; that every deed held a steep price. 'What were you angry about?' he asked instead.

'Life. My lot. What do most teenagers get angry about at that age?'

'I don't know. I was on the brink of realising my dream and getting ready to step into my very first X1 racing car when I seventeen. I was pretty happy with life at that age.' Blissfully ignorant of the consequences fate had in store for him.

'Of course you were. Well, some of us weren't that lucky.'

'Not all luck is good. Some comes from the devil himself, *bonita*. So, you achieved your light bulb moment, then what?'

Her gaze slid from his. He forced himself to remain quiet.

'Although my teacher helped direct my vision, I couldn't really do anything about it. Not at seventeen. I spent most of that year counting the days until my eighteenth birthday.'

'Why?'

He saw her reticence. Wondered why he was probing when he never intended to get as personal himself.

After a minute, she answered. 'Because turning eighteen meant I could make my own decisions, get myself away from…situations I didn't like.'

Rafael knew she wouldn't elaborate more than that. He respected that but it didn't stop him from speculating. And the directions his thoughts led him made his fist tighten on his armchair.

Raven's attitude towards sex and to him in particular had always puzzled him, not because of the women who had fallen over their feet to get to him since he'd shot up and grown broader shoulders at sixteen.

No, what had always intrigued him was the naked attraction he saw in her eyes, coupled with the fortress she put in place to ensure that attraction never got acted upon.

It didn't take a genius to know something had happened to make her that way. Her little morsel of information pointed to something in her childhood. He tensed, suddenly deciding to hell with respecting her boundaries.

'What happened to you? Were you abused?' he rasped, his fingernails digging into the armrest.

She froze. Darkened eyes shot to his before she glanced out of the porthole. When she returned her gaze to his, the haunted look had receded but not altogether disappeared. 'Have you ever heard of the term—the gift of the gab?'

He nodded.

'Well, my father could make the world's most famous orators look like amateurs. His silver tongue could charm an atom into splitting, so the term *abuse* never could stick, especially if the social worker who dealt with any allegation happened to be a woman. So technically, no, I wasn't abused.'

His teeth gritted so hard his jaw ached. Inhaling deeply, he forced himself to relax. 'What the hell did he do to you?'

She blinked, looked around as if realising where they were, or rather *who* she was with. Her features closed into neutral and she snapped the pen back out. Lowering her gaze, she snatched up her papers from her lap and tapped them into a neat sheaf. 'It doesn't matter. I'm no longer in that situation.'

Rafael almost laughed. Almost told her being out of the situation didn't mean she was out of its control. The past had tentacles that stretched to infinity. He was in the prime place to know.

His father...his mother. Not a day went by that the memories didn't burn behind his retinas—a permanent reminder only death would wipe away. They plagued him in his wakeful hours and followed him into his nightmares. He could never get away from what he'd done to them. No matter how far he went, how much he drank or how many women he let use his body.

'I've revised the regime.' Raven interrupted his thoughts, her tone crisp, businesslike. Her lightly glossed lips were set in a firm line and her whole demeanour shrieked step back in a way that made him want to reach across and *ruffle* her.

Grateful for something else to focus on rather than his dark past, he settled deeper into his seat and just watched her.

She flicked a glance at him and returned her gaze to the papers. 'I've ensured that we'll have a clear hour every morning for a thorough physio session. You already know that if you sit or stand for extended periods of time your body will seize up so I'll recommend some simple exercises for when you're in meetings, although the ideal situation would be for you not to *be* in meetings for extended periods.'

'I'll see about scheduling video conferences for some of the meetings.'

Her head snapped up, surprise reflected in her gaze. 'You will?'

'Don't sound so surprised. My boundless vanity draws the line at cutting my nose off to spite my face. You should know that by now.'

'If you can video conference, then why do you need to be there in the first place?'

'Like any other organisation, there's always a hotshot usurper waiting in the wings, ready to push you off into the great abyss at the slightest hint of weakness. I've grown attached to my pedestal.'

'You speak as if you're decrepit.'

'I haven't had sex in months. I *feel* decrepit. And with your decree of no sex, I feel as if my life has no purpose.'

'You mean you miss your fans and just want to resume basking in their admiration?'

'I'm a simple man, Raven. I love feeling wanted.'

Her lips compressed again, although he saw the shadows had faded from beneath her eyes and her colour had returned to her cheeks. He barely stopped himself from feeling inordinately pleased by the achievement.

She stared down again at the sheet in her hand. 'Why Monaco?'

'Why not? It's the glamour capital of motor racing. Most of the current and ex-drivers live there. It affords the best platform for the launch of the All-Star event.'

'Will there be any actual racing?' she asked.

He caught the wariness in her tone and suppressed another smile. Like it or not, Raven Blass was worried about him.

Just like Marco. Just like Sasha... Just like his father. He had no right to that level of concern from them. From anyone.

The tiny fizz of pleasure disappeared.

'There won't be any actual racing until we get to Monza in two weeks' time.' His brisk tone made her eyes widen. Rafael didn't bother to hide his annoyance. 'Racing is my life, Raven. I haven't decided whether or not I'll ever get behind another steering wheel but that decision will be mine to make and mine alone. So stop the mental hand-wringing and concentrate on making me fit again, *si*?'

The large, luxurious private jet banked left and Raven felt her heart lurch with it. Below them, the dazzling vista of the Côte d'Azure glittered in the late winter sunshine. With little over a month before the racing season started, the drivers would be in various stages of pre-season tests in Barcelona.

Which was where Rafael would've been had he not had his accident.

At nearly thirty-one, he'd been in his prime as a racing driver and had commanded respect and admiration all over the world. He still did if the million plus followers he commanded on social media and adoring fans from the racing paddock were anything to go by. But Raven hadn't considered how he must be feeling to be out of the racing circuit for the coming year. And what it would do to him if he could never race again.

'I'm sorry. I didn't mean to make this any harder for you than it already is,' she murmured.

She braced herself for his usual innuendo-laden comeback.

'*Gracias*,' was all he came out with instead. 'I appreciate that.'

Before she could respond, a stewardess emerged from behind a curtain to announce they would be landing in minutes.

'Time for the crazy circus to begin. You ready?' He raised a brow at her.

'Sure. After living with you for five weeks, Rafael, I think I'm ready for anything.'

His deep laugh tugged at a place inside her she'd carefully hidden but he seemed to lay bare with very little effort.

'Let's hope you don't end up eating those words, *querida*.'

'I probably will, but…promise me one thing?'

He stilled and his eyes gleamed dangerously at her from across the marble-topped table between them. Finally he nodded.

'Promise me you'll let me know if it all gets too much. No glib or gloss. I can't do my job properly if you don't tell me what's going on.'

His eyes narrowed. 'This job, it's that important to you?'

'Yes, it is. I…I'm here to make amends. I can't ever take back what I said to you, and you don't remember if what I said played a part in your accident. Your recovery is important to me, yes.'

'Hasn't anyone told you being in a hurry to fall on your sword is an invitation to a shameless opportunist like me?'

'Rafael—'

He made a dismissive gesture. 'You won't need me to report my well-being to you, *querida*. You'll be with me twenty-four seven.'

The plane, lending perfect punctuation to his words, chose that moment to touch down. Rafael was up and heading towards the doors before the jet was fully stationary.

Jumping up, she hurried after him.

And realised—once a thousand flashlights exploded in her face on exit—that he hadn't been joking when he'd referred to the circus.

Monaco in late winter was just as glorious as it was during the summer race weekend but with an added bonus of considerably fewer people. But for the paparazzi dogging their every move, Raven could've convinced herself she was on holiday.

After a series of introductions and short but numerous meetings, they were finally driven higher and higher into the mountains above Monte Carlo. Glancing out at the spectacular view spread beneath them, her senses came alive at the beauty around her. It was different to the rugged gorgeousness of Rafael's estate in León, but breathtaking nonetheless.

'Don't you usually stay at the Hôtel de France?' She referred to the exquisite five-star hotel where all his meetings had taken place with the upper echelons of his X1 Premier Management team.

'I prefer to stay there during the race season. But not this time.'

She wondered at the cryptic remark until they arrived at their destination. Wrought iron gates swung wide to reveal a jaw-droppingly stunning art deco villa. The design wasn't unique to the French Riviera but several marked add-ons—large windows and a hint of steel and chrome here and there—made it stand out from the usual.

'Who lives here?' she asked.

'For the next few days, you and me and the usual number of complementary staff. It used to belong to an Austrian countess. I'm toying with the idea of buying it, making this my permanent base.'

She faced him in surprise. 'You're considering leaving León?'

He shrugged, seeming carefree, but his expression was shuttered. 'I haven't really lived full time in León for a very long time. It won't be a big deal.'

'Have you discussed it with Marco and Sasha? Won't they mind?'

'They'd be relieved not to have an invalid cluttering up the place, I expect.'

She suspected his brother and wife thought nothing of the sort but chose not to express that opinion. 'But…it's your home. Won't you miss it?'

'It's only bricks and mortar, *bonita*.'

Realising he meant it, she frowned. '*Is* there a place you actually call home?'

Raven was unprepared for the darkness that swept over his features. In a blink of an eye it was gone, his face restored to its rugged, breathtaking handsomeness that set so many female hearts aflutter whenever the spectacular Rafael de Cervantes made an appearance.

'Rafael?' she probed when he remained silent.

'A long time ago, I did. But, like everything else in my life, I trashed it completely and utterly. Now—' he pushed the door of the limo open, stepped out and held out a hand for her '—come in and tell me what you think. I read somewhere that a woman's opinion is priceless when choosing a house, especially a woman you're not sleeping with. Personally, I disagree with that assertion but I've been known to be wrong once or twice.'

She managed to hold her tongue until the trio of staff who greeted them at the door had taken up their luggage. The minute they were alone, she faced Rafael in the large open style living room, which had an exquisitely moulded ceiling that extended over two floors. Once again—and she was beginning to notice a pattern—the room consisted mostly of windows, although this villa had a few solid walls.

'What did you mean when you said you've trashed everything in your life?' she asked.

He flung his walking stick into the nearest chair and made his way slowly towards her. Stopping a mere foot away, he glanced down at her.

'I was hoping you'd forgotten that.'

'I haven't, and I don't really think you meant me to.'

His smile was fleeting, poignant, and barely touched his eyes. 'I guess my probing on the plane makes you feel you're entitled to a certain…reciprocity?'

'No, I don't. I shared a little of my past with you because I wanted to. You don't have to feel obliged to return the favour but I'd like to know all the same.'

'Tell me what you think of the villa first.'

Her gaze took in the various OTT abstract art and cutting edge sculptures and high-spec lighting and shrugged. Every item in the room shrieked opulence a little too loudly. 'I like it but I don't love it. I think it's trying too hard to be something it's not. I don't think it suits you.'

He glanced around at the plush leather chairs and carefully placed art and sculptures, the high-tech gadgets and priceless rugs.

'Hmm, you could be right. Although that single armchair looks perfect for…de-stressing.'

'Answer my question, Rafael. Why don't you have a home any more?'

His smile dimmed slowly until only raw, untrammelled pain reflected in his eyes. He held his breath for a long, interminable moment, then he slowly exhaled. 'Because, *querida*, everything that meant a damn to me went up in a ball of flames eight years ago.'

CHAPTER FIVE

THE GLITTERING BALLROOM of the Hôtel de France had been re-designed to look like a car showroom, albeit a very expensive car showroom, complete with elaborately elegant priceless chandeliers.

A vintage Bentley MkVI Donington Special from Rafael's own car collection gleamed beneath a spotlight in the centre of the room.

Raven stood to one side as guests continued to stream in from the Automobile Club de Monaco where the X1 All-Star event had kicked off with an opening by the resident head of the Monégasque royal family.

Glancing at the door, she caught sight of Rafael as he chatted to the head of one of the largest car manufacturers in the world. Dressed in a black tuxedo with the customary studded shirt and bow tie, it was the most formal she'd seen him. The sheer stomach-clenching magnetism he exuded made her clutch her champagne flute harder to stem the fierce reaction that threatened to rock her off her feet.

As she watched he laughed in response to a joke. Looking at him, it was hard to believe he was the same man who, for a minuscule moment in time, had bared a part of his soul to her at the villa three days ago. The moment had been fleeting—as most of those moments were with Rafael. Hell, he hadn't even bothered to elaborate after that one cryptic statement about the ball of flames. But his pain had been unmistakable, visceral in a way that had cut through her defences.

Far from recoiling from the man he'd revealed, she'd wanted to draw closer, ease his pain.

I'm going loopy.

He glanced over suddenly and held up three fingers. Her

fingers flew up her face to touch her forehead before she could stop herself. Feeling a wave of heat creep up at his knowing smile, she flung a vaguely rude sign his way and turned her back on him.

He found her minutes later. 'Are you avoiding me?'

'Nope. You seem to be in your element. How's your hip?'

'Not well enough to attempt a paso doble but I'm holding my own.'

'You never told me what all of this is in aid of.'

'Have you never been to an All-Star event?' he asked.

She shook her head. 'I don't tend to involve myself in out of season activities. I've heard of it, but only in vague terms.'

'So what *do* you do when the season ends?' He latched onto the revelation.

Raven bit the inside of her lip, then decided she had nothing to lose by revealing just a little bit more about her personal life. 'I work with injured soldiers, mostly from Afghanistan and Iraq.'

His eyes narrowed slightly, a solemn look descending over his face. 'This must seem so very pointless and horribly ostentatious to you in comparison.'

'Since I don't know exactly what *this* is, I'm prepared to reserve judgement.'

'*This* is nothing but a huge elaborate scheme to get rich people to preen and back-slap while reaching into their pockets to fund a few charities.'

'Good heavens, in that case I condemn you all to Hades,' she said around the smile she couldn't seem to stop.

'Some of us would feel at home there,' he murmured. The bleakness in his voice made her glance up at him but his features gave nothing away.

Deciding to let it go, she glanced around the glittering ballroom. 'It must be nice to click your fingers and have everything fall into place for you like this.'

'Not quite…everything.' His gaze dropped to her lips before returning to capture hers.

Her pulse kicked hard. She fought to pull her gaze away from his but it only went as far as his mouth. 'Well…consider yourself fortunate, gluttony being a sin and all that.' She attempted another smile. When Rafael's own mouth curved into a smile, her heart did a hugely silly dance then proceeded to bash itself against her ribcage.

He beckoned a waiter, took Raven's champagne and exchanged it for a fresher-looking glass. He stopped her with a restraining hand on her arm when she went to sip it.

'Take it easy. It may look like champagne but it's not.'

She eyed the drink warily. 'What is it?'

'It's called Delirium. Don't worry, it's not as sinister or as sleazy as it sounds. Sip it slowly, tell me what you think.'

She did and nearly choked on the tart, potent taste. Almost immediately, the tartness disappeared to leave her tongue tingling with a thousand sensations that made her eyes widen. 'Oh my goodness, it's incredible. What's in it?'

'Edible gold dust and the tiniest drop of adrenaline.'

'You're kidding!'

'About the adrenaline, *sí*, but not the gold dust. Although, in my opinion, it's wasted in the drink. I can think of much better uses for it.' Again his words held a note quite different from his usual innuendo-laden tone.

The ground didn't quite shift but Raven felt a distinct rumble and decided to proceed with caution. 'You were about to tell me about the All-Star event.'

'It's an event I hold every year to get all the racing drivers across various racing formulas together before the season starts. Here we can be just friends, instead of championship competitors, while raising money. It's also an opportunity for retired motor racers to still feel part of the sport for as long as they want to.'

'How many events are there in total?'

'Six races in six countries.' He waved to a grey-haired man who stood with a towering brunette with the hugest diamond ring Raven had ever seen adorning her finger. When the couple beckoned them over, Rafael sighed and took her elbow.

Raven's irritation at having to share Rafael was absurd considering he was the host. But, short of being rude, she had no choice but to let herself be led to the couple.

'Rafael!' the brunette's husky voice gushed a second before she threw herself into Rafael's arms. Dropping Raven's arm, he deftly caught the woman before she could unbalance him and laughed off her throaty murmurs of apology.

They conversed in fluent French as Raven stood to the side.

'Let me introduce you—Sergey Ivanov and his wife, Chantilly. Sergey owns the Black Rock team.'

'And I own his heart,' Chantilly gushed. But even while she planted an open-mouthed kiss on her husband, her eyes were gobbling up Rafael.

Raven tried not to retch as she murmured what she hoped were appropriate conversational responses. After ten unbearable minutes, she was about to make her excuses and escape to the ladies' room when she saw Chantilly reach into her bag. With her husband deep in conversation with Rafael, neither man noticed as she withdrew an expensive lipstick and pulled closer to Rafael.

Raven barely held back her horrified gasp as she saw what Chantilly was doing.

'Did she write her number on your walking stick?' she asked the moment the couple walked away.

He lifted the stick and peered at it. 'Hmm, I believe she did. Interesting…'

Irrational anger bubbled up through her. 'Excuse me.' She barely spat out the words before marching off to the ladies' room. She forced calming breaths into her lungs, calling on every control-restoring technique she knew to help her regain her equanimity.

But when she couldn't even summon up the will to make conversation on the ride back to the villa, she knew she'd failed.

At the door, she bit out a terse goodnight, nearly tripping over the hem of the black sequined gown she'd hastily shopped for in Monaco that morning. She was unused to such elaborate, expensive outfits, as was her credit card, but as she went up to her room, the slide of the seductive material over her heated skin was unmistakable.

Or was it Rafael's gaze on her bare back that caused sensations to skitter all over her body?

She didn't care. All she cared about was getting away from the man who, in more ways than she was willing to admit, was cut from the same cloth as her father.

'I can feel the volcanic waves rising off your body,' Rafael drawled as they finished the last of his exercises next to the large, sparkling infinity pool the next morning. 'I hope your outrage didn't keep you up all night?' His blatant amusement set her teeth on edge.

She stepped back from the bench she'd set up outside, and especially from the man whose potent sweat-mingled scent made her head swim. Taking a deep breath, she fought the feeling.

'Are you seriously so without a moral compass that you don't see anything wrong with a married woman slipping you her phone number right in front of her husband?' she asked, her insides twisting with raw acid.

'Your claws are showing again, *piqueña*.'

'I don't have claws, certainly not where you're concerned. I'm merely disgusted.'

From his position lying flat on the bench, he rose smoothly into a sitting position. 'But you could be so much more if you'd just say the word.'

Flinging a towel onto a nearby chair, she whirled to face him. She tried to tell herself her heart pumped with outrage but underlying that was another emotion she flatly refused to examine. 'For the thousandth time, I'm here to make sure you heal properly, not be your sex pet!'

He rubbed his chin thoughtfully in the morning light, a smile teasing his lips. 'Sex pet. *Dios*, the sound of that makes my pulse race, especially seeing as you're just the right size and shape for a pet.' He shut his eyes, one long arm lifting to trace the air. 'I can just see my hand gliding over that glorious raven hair, sliding down the side of your elegant neck. Of course, you'd gasp in outrage. That's when I'd slide my finger over your full, sexily kissable mouth. And if you were to nip it with just the right amount of pressure—'

She gulped. 'Dammit, Rafael—'

'Shh! Don't spoil my fantasy. The sweat trickling down your chest now just makes me want to undo those no-nonsense buttons and follow it with my tongue.'

Raven glanced down and, sure enough, a bead of sweat was making its way between her breasts. Heat slammed inside her, setting off trails of fire everywhere it touched as if seeking an outlet. This wasn't good. Fires like this eventually escaped, sought the oxygen they needed to burn. Oxygen that looked temptingly, deliciously like the half-naked man in front of her. She could never let it escape, never let it burn because she had a feeling this particular conflagration would be nearly impossible to put out.

She'd more than learned her lesson. She'd been burned badly. Never again.

'Rafael, unless you want to spend the rest of the morning sitting here burning to a crisp, I suggest you zip it and help me get you indoors.'

With a put-upon sigh, he opened his eyes. His low laugh bounced on the morning air before ricocheting through parts of her she didn't want to think about or even acknowledge. 'All right, sex pet. I'll keep my lustful thoughts to myself. But if at any time you want a demonstration, don't hesitate to ask.'

'I won't.'

His smile grew even more wicked, more dangerous than she felt able to cope with. 'You won't hesitate?'

'I won't ask,' she stated firmly, dragging her eyes from the sweat-sheened torso that gleamed mere feet from her.

For several seconds he held her gaze, challenging her with the unabashed heat in his eyes, as if daring her to refuse him.

Raven stood before him, bracing herself and silently praying he would give up or move. Or something!

Finally, he dropped his gaze and reached for his walking stick. With the other hand he pulled her closer and braced his arm over her waist.

'So, you're concerned about my moral compass?' he asked in a droll voice.

'Don't let it go to your head. Sergey seems like a decent man. Are you not concerned about how he'll feel when he finds out you're intending to call his wife for a tryst?'

His laugh was deep and long.

'A *tryst*? That sounds so…decadent.'

She leaned forward, hoping her hair would hide the renewed flush of her cheeks. 'Don't mock me, Rafael. I can still ensure you never walk again.'

'Spoilsport.' He gave a dramatic sigh. 'Before you unleash your many weapons on me, I have no intention of calling or *trysting* with Chantilly. It's a little dance we do. She slips notes and numbers in my pocket. Sergey and I pretend we don't notice.'

She stopped dead. 'You mean he knows?'

His expression was world-weary and full of cynicism. 'He's old enough to be her grandfather, *bonita*. He knows she's not with him for his virility and good looks. Sorry if that bursts your happy little moral bubble.'

The rest of the slow journey to his study was conducted in silence. Raven concentrated hard on ignoring the relief fizzing through her.

She succeeded only because with every step his body bumped against her, his warm, tensile body making her so hyper-aware of her own increased heartbeat. His scent washed over her. She swallowed, the knowledge that it was wrong to feel this way about her patient doing nothing to stop the arrows of lust shooting into her abdomen.

By the time the reached the long sofa that faced the large floor-to-ceiling window in his study, Raven wasn't sure which one of them was breathing heavier.

Rafael slumped into the seat and rested his head on the back of the sofa. Lines of strain bracketed his mouth. Her heart lurched for him.

'Are you okay?'

'Nothing a new hip won't sort out.'

'I can get you some painkillers to ease the pain?'

His jaw clenched. 'No.' From day one, Rafael had refused pain relief, opting for physical therapy to heal his body.

'You have three meetings tomorrow before we leave. I think you should cancel them. Your pelvis isn't as fluid as it could be…and please, no *double entendre*. I mean it. I…I advise you to rethink and let Marco to take over.'

Every last trace of mirth left his face and eyes. His jaw clenched tight and he speared her with suddenly cold eyes. 'I'm not cancelling anything. And my brother and Sasha will be staying exactly where they are.'

The sudden descent into iciness made her shiver. 'Is it true you tried to break them up?' she blurted before she could stop herself.

His gaze grew colder. 'You're straying into none-of-your-business territory, *chiquita*.'

'I thought we were past that? After all, you seem to feel free to stray into my life whenever you feel like it. I'm merely returning the gesture.'

He locked gazes with her for endless seconds. Then he shrugged. 'Okay. Yes, I tried to break them up.'

'Why?'

'Because it seemed like a great idea at the time. Obviously, it didn't work.'

'It wasn't because you loved her?'

Why was she doing this? Asking questions she was fairly certain she didn't want answers to.

'Love? Yes, love. I did it out of love. Twisted, isn't it? If you had a lover too, I'd probably try to separate you from him.'

She frowned. 'Why would you do that?'

He laughed, a half bitter, half amused sound that chilled her nerves. 'Haven't you noticed yet, Raven? I like chaos. I like to cause as much damage as possible wherever I go. Haven't you learned this of me by now? I'm trouble with a capital T.'

She tried for a shrug. 'Some women go for that sort of thing, I hear.'

'But not you, *si*? You remind me of one of the girls I went to Sunday school with.'

Shock held her rigid. 'You went to Sunday school?'

He nodded, the unholy gleam in his eyes lightening the blue depths. 'Religiously. My mother was very keen I got into heaven.'

She laughed at the very idea. She knew no one more devilish in temperament and looks than Rafael de Cervantes.

His grin widened. 'The idea of me in heaven is laughable?'

'In the extreme. You'd corrupt all the other angels within seconds.'

'And they'd love every minute of it.'

'I bet.'

Laughter faded, slowly replaced by an incisive look that should've been her first warning. 'You hide your pain underneath a veneer of blistering efficiency.'

'While you hide yours under the cover of irreverent, sometimes callous charm.'

He reached out a hand for her, and Raven found herself moving towards him, his aura drawing her in like a moth to a flame.

When he patted the seat next to him, she sat down. 'What a pair we are,' he muttered.

She shrugged. 'I guess we must do what we need to do to protect ourselves.'

'From the outside world, yes. But we know what the other is. So there's no need for pretence with us.'

His smile slowly faded to leave a serious, probing look that made her whole body tingle. Slowly he reached out and clasped his hand around her nape. Effortlessly, he drew her forward. She wet her lips before she could stop herself. His groan echoed the deep, dark one inside her.

'What do you want from me, Rafael?' she muttered, her tongue feeling thick in her mouth.

'Nothing you aren't prepared to give me.'

'Don't pretend you won't take more than your fair share.'

His head dropped an inch closer. 'What can I say, I'm a greedy, greedy bastard.'

'What the hell am I doing?'

'Letting go. Living a little. Just because you were hurt before doesn't mean you have to stop living. Pleasure, in the right circumstances, with the right person, can be the most exhilarating experience in life.'

'But you're the exact opposite of the right person, I can't even see how you can say that with a straight face.'

'*Sí*, I'm the devil. You would never be satisfied with a Normal Norman. You'd be bored rigid in three seconds flat.'

He kissed her before she could countermand his assertion. As first kisses with the devil went, it was soul-stealing and Raven was eternally grateful she was sitting down.

Because Rafael devoured her as if she were his favourite fruit. No millimetre of her mouth went unkissed. When he was done ravaging her lips, he delved between to boldly slide his tongue into her mouth. The toe-curling sensation made her fingers bite hard into his bicep. She needed something solid to hold on to. Unfortunately, Rafael—unyielding, warm— no, hot—heady, sexily irreverent Rafael—was the last anchor she should've been seeking. And yet she couldn't pull away, couldn't summon even the smallest protest as she let him devour her lips.

'*Dios*, you taste even better than I imagined.' He only gave her a chance to snatch a quick breath before he pounced again.

One hand caught her waist, his fingers digging into her flesh to hold her still as he angled his head to go even deeper. Her moan felt ripped from her very soul.

He started to lean her back on the sofa, then he stilled suddenly. Between their lips, the sound of his pained hiss was smothered but Raven recognised it all the same.

Reality came crashing down on her, her dulled brain clamouring to make sense of what she'd let happen. Slowly, painfully, he straightened until he was upright again.

Raven wanted to reach across and help but she was too weak with thwarted lust, too stunned from the realisation that she was still as hopelessly attracted to Rafael as she'd been the first time she was introduced to him as his physiotherapist.

'Shut up,' he ground out hoarsely.

'I didn't say anything.'

'No, but I can hear you thinking. Loudly, noisily. I've never had to compete with a woman mentally working out the Fibonacci Sequence while I was trying to get her naked. And you know what? It's not sexy. It's quite deafeningly unsexy, actually.'

She slid agitated hands into her hair. 'You're being offensive.'

'And you're ruining this electric buzz with all that overthinking. I would much prefer it if you'd shut up and strip for me.'

Her mouth dropped open. Actually dropped opened in a gob-smacked, un-pretty mess that she couldn't stop. 'I really don't know how you managed to snag girlfriend after girlfriend with that insufferable attitude.'

'It's the same way I've snagged you, *piqueña*. It's why you're leaning towards me right now, unable to look away from me as you imagine what it would be like to have me inside you, buried deep, riding us both to ecstasy.'

She jumped back, and her breath whooshed out of her lungs.

'And now you're going to blush.'

As if on cue, heat rose and engulfed her face. 'Crap.'

He laughed, actually laughed at her. Raven had never felt so humiliated. Or so…so hot as he grasped the bottom of his T-shirt.

'Here, I'll go first, shall I? One item of clothing each until we're in flagrante. Deal?'

She wanted to walk out, wanted to tell him what to do with his tight, muscle-packed body and sheer masculine perfection. She wanted to have enough willpower to turn her back on all the things his glinting blue eyes promised. This wasn't her. She wasn't the type of girl who fell casually into sex as if she were choosing the latest hair accessory from a supermarket shelf. So why couldn't she move? Why did every single instinct she had scream at her to move closer to Rafael, to touch, experience the seductive pleasure he promised, instead of running as far as her marathon-trained legs could carry her?

A long-suffering sigh filled with extreme impatience shattered her thoughts. Her gaze sharpened in time to see his hands drop.

'Fine, I get the message. You're about to fall on your puritanical sword, deny yourself pleasure just so you can crawl back into your cold bed and pat yourself on the back. Aren't you?'

'I wasn't…' But she *had* been thinking that, hadn't she? 'Maybe,' she admitted. 'Besides being totally unprofessional, I can't very well advocate no sex for you and then be the one who…who makes you suffer a setback.'

He shook his head, a genuine baffled look on his face. Reaching over carefully, he took her face in his hand. '*Sí*, I get it. More restraint. More suffering for both of us. You're twenty-four so I'm sure you're not a virgin, but are you sure you weren't an inquisitor in a past life?'

Since there was no way she wanted to confirm her virginity, she focused on the second part of his statement. 'I know you don't believe it, but I'm only looking out for you.'

'By torturing me to death? Or is there something else at play here?'

'By making sure you heal as quickly and efficiently as possible.'

He dropped his hand. 'Where's the fun in that?'

Raven kicked herself for immediately missing his touch. 'God, you're unbearable! And what do you mean, "there's something else at play"?'

'Ah. Finally, some fire. Do you have any idea how incredibly hot you look when you're riled?'

Desire dragged low through her abdomen at his heated, husky words. 'You're getting off topic. And that compliment is so clichéd, even a three-year-old wouldn't believe you.'

'Cliché doesn't make it any less true. But yes, I'll get to the point. You like to hide behind a prickly exterior, holding the world at bay because you're afraid.'

'I'm not prickly and I'm most definitely not afraid.'

'You over-think every single move you make.'

'It's called being sensible,' she retorted.

'You're living half a life. Every bone in your body wants to be on the bed with me, yet you're afraid to let yourself just be.'

'Just because I don't put myself about like you doesn't mean I'm not living.'

His lips twisted. 'I wouldn't be this frustrated if I'd been putting it about like you suggest. And don't forget, I was in a coma for several weeks. Have mercy on my poor, withered c—'

'If you finish that sentence I'm walking out of here right now!'

'The C-word offends you?'

'No, your blatant lies do. There's nothing withered or poor about you.'

'*Gracias*...I think.' He tilted his head. 'Now you're about to deflate my ego thoroughly, aren't you?'

'Your ego is Teflon-coated and self-inflating. It doesn't need any help from me.'

He let out an impatient sigh. '*Dios*, Raven, are you going to talk me into another coma or are we going to have a conversation about what's really going on here?'

She shoved her hands onto her hips. 'There's nothing going on. You want to get on with making up for lost time and I happen to be the willing body you've chosen.'

His hands dropped. 'Would it make you feel better if I said yes? It would help you get through the morning-after hand-wringing if you feel righteous anger for being used?'

She gasped. 'I didn't say that.'

He moved further away. 'You didn't have to. *Santa Maria!* We haven't been to bed yet, and already you're seeking excuses to ease your guilt. How long are you going to let your father win?'

Her gasp was a hoarse sound that scraped her throat raw. 'That's low, Rafael.'

'No lower than the way you treat yourself. Have a little pride. You're a beautiful woman, with a powerfully sexual nature you choose to suppress underneath a staid exterior. But, underneath all that togetherness, your true nature is dying to leap out. To be set free.'

'And you're the man to do it? How convenient for you.'

His face remained sober. 'For both of us. I'm willing to rise to the task. I'm very good at it, too. Trust me.'

'Trust you. The self-proclaimed damaged man who is trouble with a capital T?'

'Think of all the experience I'd bring to the task. You couldn't find a better candidate to bed you if you tried.'

She shut her eyes. Despair wove through her because, deep down, she knew he was right. Her body hadn't reacted to anyone this strongly since…heavens, since never! But that was no excuse to throw well-served caution to the wind. 'No. It's not going to happen.'

He was silent for so long her nerves were stretched to the max by the time he spoke. 'What did your father do to you?'

'What makes you think this is about my father, not about an ex?'

'The first cut is the deepest, no?'

She looked around the too posh living room, at the price-less pieces of furniture that most people would give their eye teeth to own.

She didn't belong here. Her presence in Rafael's life was temporary, transient. Baring her soul to a man who didn't possess one was out of the question. Regardless of what she'd told herself she'd seen in his eyes last night, they were nothing more than ships passing in the night.

In a few weeks she would be gone and Rafael would return, healed, to his regular life. 'Yes, the first cut is the deepest, and yes, my father hurt me. Badly. But my scars don't dictate who I am. I am free to choose who to be with, who I have sex with. And I don't want to have it with you.'

CHAPTER SIX

RAFAEL TOOK HER rejection with more grace than she'd given him credit for, especially considering his reaction to her rejection the day of his last X1 race.

Later that day, after shrugging off her terse pronouncement, they strolled into an exclusive rooftop restaurant overlooking Casino Square. Although a whisper of tension flowed between them, Rafael was as charming as ever.

'So, what are your plans after you're done fixing me?' he asked after the first course had been served.

A strange twinge attacked her insides. Pushing it away, she speared her fork through a plump shrimp. 'I'll either get the agency that allocated me the X1 contract to find me another driver to work with, or I'll find one on my own. I could also try the army facility to see if they need a full-time physiotherapist. I have a few possibilities and I figure after you, every other patient would be a breeze to work with.'

Blue eyes gleamed at her across the table. '*Gracias, bonita.*'

She eyed him suspiciously. 'What are you thanking me for, exactly?'

'I've obviously become a yardstick by which you measure your future clients. I consider it an honour.'

She rolled her eyes and found herself grinning when he laughed. Shaking her head, she took another mouthful of her delicious shrimp pasta. 'I knew you were trouble from day one.'

His laughter slowly disappeared. '*Sí,*' he murmured. 'What did you call me? A useless waste of space who was taking up valuable oxygen more worthy human beings were entitled to?'

Her fork clattered onto her plate. 'You remember? Every single word?' she whispered.

His smile was sharp and deadly, the easy camaraderie from moments before completely annihilated as the tension that had lurked solidified into a palpable wall. 'What can I say, *querida*, you cut me to the bone.'

'Was that…was that why…?' She couldn't quite frame the words.

'Why I attempted to turn myself and my car into a Rubik's Cube the next day? Ask me again when I remember anything from the accident.'

She shut her eyes for a brief second, a shudder of guilt and regret raking over her. 'Please believe me, I don't usually lay into anyone quite like that. That day…' She paused, unwilling to bare her whole life to him. But then she realised she owed him an explanation of some sort. 'It was a *very* difficult day.'

'In what way was it difficult?' he probed immediately.

'My mother called me the evening before the race, just before the team dinner where you—'

'When I *dared* to ask you out?' he asked.

Her gaze dropped as she felt a prickle behind her eyelids. 'Her relationship with my father has always been…tempestuous.' That was putting it mildly but she couldn't elaborate any further. 'When she called, she was very upset… She has…moments like that. She wanted to see him. Nothing I said would calm her down. So I called my father—the father I haven't spoken to in years.'

Rafael's brow hitched up a fraction but he didn't interrupt her.

'He wouldn't lift a finger to help. He was too busy, he said. But I could hear the sound of a party in the background. I swallowed my pride and begged him. He refused. When I called my mother to try to explain, her mood…escalated. I was trying to get her some help when you found me and asked me to dinner.'

'So you attempted to slice the skin off my bones because of bad timing?' His words were light but the chilling ice in his eyes told her he hadn't forgiven her. 'What about the dozen times before then?'

She blew out a breath. 'I've just told you the effect my father has on me and on my mother. Do you honestly think I'd ever want to associate myself personally with a man who reminds me of every despicable trait I witnessed growing up?'

'Watch it, *piqueña*,' he murmured softly. 'You didn't think I was despicable when we kissed this morning.'

A wave of heat crept up her face. 'That was a mistake.'

'Also, you may have claws, but I have teeth. Sharp ones and I'm heartless enough to use them.'

She didn't doubt it. For him to have succeeded in securing several championships over the past decade, he had to have a ruthless streak somewhere beneath the indolent playboy demeanour. Certainly, she'd seen his dedication and absolute focus during the racing season.

'I'm sorry, Rafael. But I didn't really understand why you wanted to go out with me. There were dozens more willing girls who would've jumped at the chance to be with you.' If she were being honest, she still didn't understand why he continued to try and goad her into bed. The only thing she could think of was…no, it didn't make sense. 'I'm hardly your Mount Everest.'

'You're not. Been there, done that.'

Her eyes fell to the jagged scar on his forearm. It might have been ugly at one time but now it just blended into the frustratingly captivating masterpiece that was Rafael de Cervantes. 'You've been to a lot of places, done a lot of things.'

'You've been listening to gossip.'

'Before I came to work for you last year, the agency sent me a dossier on you. Is it true that scar on your arm was from a bull goring you?' She pounced on the change of subject all the more because here was her chance to learn more about Rafael.

'*Sí*, and I thanked the bull for the unique, exhilarating experience.'

She suppressed a shudder. 'What is it exactly that you crave? The thrill of the chase? The rush of adrenaline?'

'It's conquering the fear of the unknown.'

His words were so stark, so raw, her breath caught in her lungs.

'What do you mean?'

'I don't like mysteries, *querida*. Take you, for instance. From the moment we met, you held me at arm's length. No woman's ever done that, not effectively anyway, and definitely not for as long as you have, and this isn't arrogance talking. It's just never happened. You were an enigma to me. I wanted to smash aside all your barriers. Instead you built them up higher. You intrigued me to the point I couldn't see anything beyond having you.'

She had never been able to explain the phenomenon of ice and heat that filled her whenever she was in Rafael's presence. She couldn't explain it now the sensation had increased a thousandfold. 'I don't know that I want to be described that way. You make me sound like I'd become your worst nightmare.'

'You had. I wanted to confront it. Turn it into a dream I liked.'

'God, Rafael. Do you hear how twisted that sounds?'

His laugh was nowhere near a normal sound. 'I'm sorry I don't fit your ideal of the right guy.'

'I'm not looking for a right guy. I'm not looking for a guy, period. I just want to do my job.'

'It's not just that though, is it?' He beckoned the waiter and ordered an espresso for himself and a white coffee for her. 'You're here because you want to do penance.'

'And you've been fighting me and trying to drive me away ever since I arrived.'

'If I'd wanted to be rid of you, I would've succeeded.'

'So you want me to stay?'

He shrugged. 'One of the many discoveries I made while stuck in a hospital bed was this—I like being alone. But I don't like being alone in León.'

She sensed the revelation behind the statement. 'Another of your nightmare scenarios?'

He didn't deny it. He just shrugged. 'Tell me more about your mother.'

'Tell me about yours.'

'She's dead.'

In what felt like mere seconds between one and the other, another forceful blow punched through her middle at the stark announcement. 'How—?'

The word stuck in her throat when he shook his head and picked up his newly delivered espresso. 'You're one of a handful of people outside of my family circle I've disclosed that to. It's not a state secret, but it's not a subject I wish to discuss either, so don't ask any more questions. And yes, I know it's hypocritical of me to demand everything from you and give nothing in return, but we both know I do what I like. Your mother?'

She moistened her lips and tried to arrange her thoughts. 'For what it's worth, I'm sorry about your mother.' She sucked in a deep breath and slowly exhaled. All of a sudden, it wasn't so bad to reveal just that little bit more. Because Rafael had shared *something*.

'Mine is alive but barely conscious half the time. You know why? Because she's completely and utterly hung up on a man who can go for months, sometimes years without giving her a single thought. And yet he only has to crook his finger to have her falling into his lap. At least you know your mother loved you. Do you know how devastating it is to find out your own mother would gladly give you away for free if she could have her one true obsession?'

'Is that why you lived with your father?'

'No. Aside from her obsession with my father, she was also diagnosed with severe bipolar disorder when I was seven. For a few years she took the prescribed medication, but as I got older, she would miss a few days here and there. Then days would turn into weeks, then she would stop altogether.'

His frown was thunderous. 'Did you not have any relatives that could step in?'

'None that wanted to add the burden of a pre-teen on top of the responsibilities they already had. And, frankly, I felt I was better off on my own. By ten I could take care of myself. Unfortunately, my mother couldn't. One day she had an episode in a shop. The police were called. Social services got involved. Eventually they tracked down my father and threatened to report him to the authorities when he wouldn't step up.' Bitterness made her throat raw. 'They *made* him take me. And you know what? Every day until I turned eighteen I wished they hadn't.'

'Did he hurt you?' he rasped.

'Not at first. When I initially arrived at his doorstep, he didn't even care enough to resent me for my sudden appearance in his life.' She laughed. 'And he was rich enough that I had my every material need catered for.'

'But?' he demanded.

Ice drenched her skin as the dark memory surged, its oily tentacles reaching for her.

A tinkle of laughter from a table nearby slammed her back into the present. Chilled and exposed, she rubbed her hands over her arms. 'I don't want to relive it, Rafael.'

His jaw tightened. 'It was that bad?'

'Worse.'

His fingers curled around the small, fragile cup in his white knuckled grip before he carefully set it back in its saucer. '*Dios mío*. When did it—?'

'Rafael…please…'

He sucked in a sharp breath, his gaze still fiercely probing as he sat back in his seat. After several seconds, he nodded and pushed back his chair.

Silently he held out his hand. Before the start of the evening she'd have hesitated. But after what she'd shared with him, after seeing his reaction to how she'd grown up, a tiny voice urged her to trust him a little.

She placed her hand in his and let him help her up. 'I should be helping you, not the other way round.'

'Let's forget we're patient and specialist, just for a few hours, *sí*?' The low, rough demand made her breath snag in her throat.

When she glanced up at him, he watched her with hooded eyes that held no hint of their usual teasing. Swallowing, she nodded.

They walked in the unseasonably warm evening along the dock that held some of the world's most extravagant and elegant yachts. Or they tried to walk. Rafael was stopped several times along the way by wealthy Monégasques and visiting celebrities. Again and again, Raven tried not to be enthralled by the sight of his breathtaking smile and easy charm. Even when a paparazzo's camera lens flashed nearby he didn't seem to care. But then she caught the clenched fist around his walking stick. She wasn't surprised when he signalled his driver a few moments later.

When she glanced at him, he merely shrugged. 'We have an early flight in the morning. Don't want you to accuse me of depriving you of your beauty sleep.'

She waited until they were in the car, leaving the bright lights of Monte Carlo behind. 'You strive to put a brave face on it all, don't you?'

'A brave face?'

'I saw how the paparazzi affected you just now. And even though you stopped to speak to people, you didn't really want to be there.'

He tilted his head. 'Your powers of deduction are astounding.'

'Don't dismiss me like that, Rafael,' she murmured. 'You've changed.'

Although his expression didn't alter, she saw his shoulders stiffen beneath his expensive cotton shirt.

'Of course I have, *querida*. My hip no longer works and I carry a walking stick.'

'I don't mean physically. You turned away from the cameras at the airport too. You answer their questions but you no longer bask in the limelight. Oh, the playboy is very much a part of your DNA, probably always will be, but...something's changed.'

'*Sí*, I've turned into a decrepit recluse who's been banned from having a bed partner.'

She ignored the quip. 'I bet you're not going to buy that villa, are you?'

The corner of his mouth lifted in a mirthless smile. 'You assume correctly,' he replied, his gaze steady on her face. 'You were right, it's a little too...stalker-ish for me. I think the owner studied what I liked and tried to replicate it without taking the location into consideration. It's slightly creepy, actually. Besides that, Monaco is great for a visit but not somewhere I prefer to live. But then neither is León.'

'Why?'

'Too many bad memories,' he stated.

Somewhere inside, Raven reeled at the easy access he seemed to be giving her. A strong need to know the man made her probe further. 'Your father?'

He paled a little beneath his tan, but he nodded after several seconds. '*Sí*. Amongst other things. He moved to Barcelona after...for a while, but he's back in León now. Seeing him there reminds me of what a disappointment I've been to my family.'

She gasped. 'A disappointment? How...why? You've won eight world championships and ten Constructors' Championships for Team Espíritu. How in the world can that be termed a failure?'

'Those are just trophies, *querida*.'

'Trophies coveted by the some of the world's most disciplined athletes.'

'Why, Raven, I almost think you're trying to make me feel better about myself.'

'You've achieved a lot in your life. Self-deprecation is one thing. Dismissing your achievements out of hand is an insult to the team that has always supported you. Now, if you're talking about your private life…'

'What if I said I was?'

'I've met your father, albeit very briefly. I saw no trace of disappointment when he tried to talk to you. And, as far as I can see, Marco and Sasha worship the ground you walk on, despite you saying you tried to break them up.'

He lifted a hand, his knuckles brushing her cheeks before she knew what he was doing. 'That may have been an over-exaggeration. Was I annoyed when I woke up from my coma to find my best friend had fallen for my brother? *Si*. But I'm a big boy, I'll learn to adapt. As for worshipping the ground I walk on—appearances can be deceptive. I've done things— things I'm not proud of; things that haunt me in the middle of the night, or in the middle of the day when I smile and shake hands with people who think I'm their golden boy. They don't know what I've done.'

'What have you done, Rafael? Tell me.'

He shook his head, a bleak expression stamped on his face that sent a bolt of apprehension through her.

'Did you notice the condition my father is in?'

She frowned. 'You mean his wheelchair? Of course I did.'

'What if I told you I put him in that wheelchair?'

Rafael looked into her face, trying to read her reaction while at the same time trying to decipher exactly why he was spilling his guts when he never, ever talked about what he'd done eight years ago.

The car passed under a streetlamp and illuminated for a moment her pale, shocked face. 'H…How did you put him in the wheelchair?'

A deep tremor went through him, signalling the rise of the blistering pain that seemed to live just below his skin. 'Take a wild guess.'

'A car accident?'

He nodded, his peculiar fascination with her escalating

when she made a move as if to touch him. At the last moment, she dropped her hand.

'Where did it happen?'

'On the racing track in León. Eight years ago. I walked away unscathed. My father has never walked since.'

This time when she lifted her hand he caught it before she could lower it and twined his around her slender fingers. The surge of pain diminished a little when her fingers tightened.

'I'm so sorry,' she murmured.

His smile felt broken. 'You don't want to know whose fault it was?'

'I'm not going to force you to relive the emotional pain, Rafael. Like you said, I'm not that type of therapist. But one thing I do know is that, contrary to what you might think, your family...your father, from what I saw, is more forgiving than you realise.'

His father might be forgiving of Rafael's role in making him wheelchair-bound, but the other, darker reason would be more unthinkable to forgive. Hell, he hadn't even dreamed of seeking forgiveness. He deserved every baptism of hellfire he lived through every morning when he opened his eyes. 'That's the problem with family. Forgiveness may be readily provided but the crime is never forgotten.'

'Unfortunately, I wouldn't know. Dysfunctional doesn't even apply to me because I had two people who were connected to me by genetics but who were never family.'

The car was drawing up to the villa when he lifted their entwined fingers to his lips. A soft gasp escaped her when he kissed her knuckles. 'Then count yourself lucky.'

Two hours later, Rafael stretched and held in a grimace of pain when he tried to rise from his chair. He eyed the walking stick leaning against his desk and with an impatient hand he reached for it.

Pelvis, fractured in three places...broken leg...multiple cracked ribs...severe brain swelling...lucky to be alive.

The doctor's recital of his injuries when he'd woken from his coma should've shocked him. It hadn't. He'd known for as long as he could remember that he had the luck of the devil. He'd exploited that trait mercilessly when he was younger, and then honed it into becoming the best racing driver around when he was older. No matter how many hairy situations he put himself in, he seemed to come out, if not completely whole, then alive.

Recalling his conversation earlier with Raven, he paused in the hallway. *I'm not going to force you to relive the emotional pain.*

Little did she know that he relived it every waking moment and most nights in his vivid nightmares. He might have cheated death countless times, but his penance was to relive the devastation he'd brought to his family over and over again.

His phone pinged and before he glanced at it he knew who it was.

His father…

He deleted the message, unread. *Dios*, even if they wanted to grant it, who was he to accept their forgiveness—?

The sound in the library next to his study attracted his attention.

Raven's lusciously heady perfume drew him to the room before he could stop himself. 'It's almost midnight. What are you doing up?'

'I was looking for something to read. The only reading material I have upstairs is boring clinical stuff, and my tablet is charging, so…'

He glanced down at the papers in his hand. He had no idea what he was doing, no idea where this project would take him but… He debated for a few seconds and made up his mind. Closing the distance between them, he stopped in front of her.

'Here.' He tossed a bound sheaf of papers at her, which she managed to catch before they spilled everywhere.

'What is this?'

One corner of his mouth lifted in a dangerous little half-smile that always made her forget to breathe. 'Two articles for *X1 Magazine*…and something new I'm working on.'

'Something new? I didn't know you wrote outside of your monthly *CEO's Snippets.*'

He shrugged. 'Three months ago—while I was trussed up like a turkey in a hospital bed—I was approached by a couple of publishing houses to write my memoirs.' He laughed. 'I guess they figured a has-been like me would jump at the chance to lay it all out there before the moths set in.'

She glanced down at the thick inch of paper between her fingers. 'And you agreed?' she asked as she started to leaf through the pages.

'I said I'd think about it. I had time on my hands after all.'

She read, then read some more. On the third page, she looked up. 'This isn't your memoirs, unless you were a girl who grew up in Valencia in the late forties.'

'*Bonita*, you're getting ahead of yourself. *Por favor*, contain yourself and let me finish.'

She stared up at him. Rafael gave himself a mental slap against the need to keep staring into those mesmerising eyes. 'I started writing and realised fiction suited me much better than non-fiction. I told them no to the memoir.'

'And?' she prompted when he lapsed into silence. 'You told them about this?'

'No. I've told no one about this. Except you.'

Surprise registered in her eyes before she glanced back down at the papers. 'Are you sure you want me to read it?'

'It's pure fiction. No deep, dark secrets in there for you to hold over my head.'

Wide hazel eyes, alluring and daring at the same time, rose to lock on his. 'Are you sure?'

'If you're thinking of flipping through the pages for X-rated material, I'm afraid you'll be disappointed.'

Her blush was a slow wave of heat that he wanted to trace with his fingers. For a woman so fierce in her dedication to her craft and so determined to succeed despite her past, she blushed with an innocence that made him painfully erect. Despite his intense discomfort, he wanted to continue to bait her so she blushed for him again.

Unable to help himself, he lowered his gaze to the shallow rise and fall of her chest.

When she cleared her throat delicately, he forced his gaze upwards. 'So what are you looking for—an honest critique? I'm sure I can read whatever it is you've written and give an honest view, if that's what you want?'

He smiled at her prim tone and forced himself to step back before he gave in to the need to kiss her. Their kiss had only opened up a craving to experience the heady sensation again. But, aside from the insane physical attraction, he was feeling a peculiar pull to Raven Blass he wasn't completely comfortable with.

Keeping his distance from her was impossible considering her role in his life, but he wasn't a hormonal teenager any longer and he refused to make any move towards her that reminded her of her sleazebag father.

If anything was going to happen between them, Raven had to make the first move…or indicate in clear and precise terms that she wanted him to.

'*Gracias*, it is. I await your thoughts on my efforts with bated breath.'

CHAPTER SEVEN

THEIR EARLY MORNING departure to Italy, accompanied by Rafael's executive assistant and a trio of ex-racers, meant that Raven had no chance to discuss Rafael's manuscript with him at any point. A fact for which she was more than thankful.

The story of the young girl was both uplifting and heartbreaking. Rafael's language was lyrical and poignant, clever and funny in a way that had made her feel each and every word, every expression.

Reading his work, she'd felt just that little bit closer to him. Raven wasn't sure if she was more frightened or insane for feeling like that. It was that floundering feeling that had made her take a seat as far away from Rafael as possible.

But even though she made the right noises with the guy next to her—whose name she couldn't immediately remember—she couldn't get Rafael's story out of her head.

Nor could she deny his talent. She'd learned very early on, after reading an unauthorised biography on him before accepting the job as his physiotherapist last year, that Rafael had a magic touch in most endeavours he undertook in his life. That he'd dedicated his life to racing had only meant that the sport had benefited endlessly.

His regular contribution to X1 Premier Management's monthly magazine already garnered a subscription said to be in the millions. If he chose to dedicate his life to writing fiction his fan base would become insane.

And you would probably be his adoring number one fan.

Without warning, Rafael's gaze swung towards her. The sizzling *knowledge* in that look sent sharp arrows of need racing to her pelvis. Her pulse hammered at her throat, her skin tingling with the chemistry of what she felt for Rafael.

'…you ever been to Monza?' The German ex-racer seated next to her—Axel Jung, she remembered his name now—stared at her with blatant interest.

She shook her head but couldn't tear her gaze away from the formidable, intensely charismatic man whose gaze held her prisoner from across the aisle. 'Um, no, I was Rafael's physio last year but Monza wasn't on the race calendar so I missed it.'

'You're in for a treat. It's one of the best racetracks in the world.'

She swallowed and tried to dismiss the intensity of Rafael's stare. 'Yes, so I've been told. The old track was even more spectacular, from the pictures I've seen of it.'

Axel's chuckle helped her break eye contact with Rafael but not before she saw his gaze swing to Axel and back to her.

'If you liked danger with your spectacular view, that was the track to race on,' Axel said.

She made an effort to turn her attention to him and almost regretted it when she glimpsed his deepening interest. 'I suspect that's why it's a thrill for most drivers?' she ventured.

He nodded eagerly. 'I don't know a driver who hasn't dreamt of driving at Monza, either on the old or the new track. The tickets for Monza's All-Star event sold out within minutes of going online.'

Raven had a feeling it had something to do with Rafael's presence, this being one of his first public appearances since his accident. 'That's great for the charity, then?'

'Yes, it is. I'd be honoured if you'll permit me to show you around Monza.' He drew closer. His smile widened, lending his blond-haired, blue-eyed features a boyish charm.

'I'm there to work, I'm afraid. And you'll be driving I expect?'

Axel, a two-time world champion twenty-five years ago, nodded. 'Rafael and I have a friendly rivalry that seems to draw the crowd.' He laughed. The fondness in his voice was clear. 'He's a special one, that one. The playboy thing is just a front. Don't let it fool you. Deep down, there beats the heart of a genius forged in steel. A fierce leader who would fight to the death for what he believes in.'

Having her instincts confirmed that there was more to Rafael than met the eye made her slow to respond. A quick glance at him showed him in deep conversation with a member of his All-Star team. 'I…'

'He single-handedly brought the board members to his way of thinking two years ago when they tried to put off new safety measures for drivers,' Axel said.

'*Safety?*' Raven asked in surprise. 'But I thought…'

'You think because we love speed and hurtle around racetracks at two hundred and fifty miles per hour we think less of safety? Ask any driver. The opposite is true. We manage to take the risks we do *because* of people like Rafael and the work they do to ensure drivers' safety.'

Feeling wave after wave of astonishment roll through her, she glanced again at Rafael, only to find his attention fixed on her, his blue eyes narrowed to speculative slits. He glanced away again and resumed his conversation.

The floundering feeling escalated. 'Excuse me,' she murmured to Axel when the stewardess entered to take drinks orders. Standing, she made her way towards the large bedroom and the en suite bathroom.

After splashing water on her wrists, she re-knotted her hair in a secure bun and left the bathroom, only to stumble to a halt.

Rafael stood, back braced solidly against the bedroom door. His presence in the enclosed space, larger than life and equally as imposing, dried her mouth.

Heart hammering, she stayed where she was, away from the danger radiating from him. 'I…is there something you need?'

He folded his arms and angled his head. '*Need?* No.' He remained in front of the door.

Raven licked her lips and immediately regretted it. 'Can we return to the cabin, then?'

'Not just yet,' he rasped, then just stood there, watching her with a predatory gleam that made her nape tighten.

Silence stretched for several minutes as he stayed put, seemingly in no hurry to go anywhere, or speak, for that matter.

She searched her mind for what he could possibly want, and felt her heart lurch with disappointment. 'You're not in here because you want to make sure your playboy status is intact, are you?'

'What was Axel saying to you?'

She waved him away. 'Nothing for you to worry about.' He remained in place, that infuriatingly well-defined eyebrow arched. 'Okay, if you must know, he told me that beneath all that lady-killer persona, you're really a Boy Scout. Oh, and he also offered to show me Monza.'

He glanced away but she saw his jaw tighten. 'I hope you told him no?'

'Maybe.' She started to move towards him in the hope that he'd get the hint and move. He remained, rock-still and immovable.

'Stay away from him,' he said, his voice low but no less forcefully lethal.

Her pulse spiked higher. 'Sexually, socially or just for the hell of it?'

With a swiftness she wouldn't have attributed to him considering his injuries, he reached forward, grabbed her arms, whirled her round and reversed their position. Her lungs expended their oxygen supply as she found herself trapped between the hard, polished wood and Rafael's equally hard, warm body.

One hand gripped her nape while the other settled firmly on her waist. Heat ratcheted several notches. Inhaling only made matters worse because Rafael's scent, potent and delicious, attacked her senses with rabid fervour.

'He was looking at you as if he wanted to serve you up on his sauerkraut.'

'And what, you're jealous?'

'Not if you tell me you're not thinking of falling into the clutches of an ex-racer more than twice your age.'

'Axel's only in his mid-forties. And I'm touched you're looking out for me.'

Blue eyes deepened by his blue long-sleeved shirt and navy jeans narrowed even further. 'And he also likes to think he's slick with the ladies.'

'Scared of the competition?'

'Scared I'm going to have to toss his ass out of the plane without a parachute if you don't tell me you'll stay away from him.' Without warning, one thigh wedged between hers. The heat emanating from him made her whole body feel as if it were on fire. Second by inexorable second, he pressed closer against her. His hard chest brushed against hers, stinging sensitive nipples to life. Raven fought a moan and tried to decide whether defiance or acquiescence was her best path.

'Is this what it means to be caught between a rock and a hard place?' she asked, unable to resist baiting him just a little.

His laugh sent a skitter of pleasure through her. 'You're making jokes, *querida*?'

'You're laughing, aren't you?'

'*Sí*,' he agreed. The hand on her waist moved a fraction higher, dug deeper in an almost possessive hold on her ribcage. 'But I'm still waiting for an answer.'

A small voice cautioned her against throwing more fuel onto the flames.

'I spoke to him for fifteen minutes, but I barely remember what he looks like,' she whispered against seriously tempting lips a hair's breadth from hers. 'But why do you care? Really?'

'You were the first person I told about my father outside my family. You haven't condemned me…yet. In my own small way, I'm trying to return the favour by saving you from a potentially unfortunate situation.'

'By trapping me here and threatening to toss a man out of the plane?'

'It's my Latin blood, *piqueña*. It takes me from zero to

growly in less than five seconds.' He closed the gap between their lips and their bodies.

A fervid moan rose from her chest as sensation crashed over her head. Her knees turned liquid and she would've lost her balance had she not been trapped so powerfully against a towering pile of formidable maleness. As they were, with his thigh wedged so firmly between hers, she felt the heat from his leg caress her intimately. Friction, urgent and undeniable, made her pulse race faster. Even more when his tongue delved between her lips. Like the first time they'd kissed, Rafael seemed bent on devouring her. Although she'd been kissed, she'd never been kissed quite like this, with a dedication so intense she felt as if she were being consumed.

When he finally let her up for air, it was to allow her a single breath before he pounced again. Her hands, which had miraculously risen to glide over his shoulders, finally found the wherewithal to push him away.

'Rafael…'

'No, not yet.' His lips swooped, but she managed to turn her head just in time. He settled for nibbling the corner of her mouth, a caress so erotic she throbbed low down with the sensation.

'We need to stop. Everyone out there will think we're in here…doing…having…'

'*Sex*…saying it doesn't make you a dirty, dirty girl, Raven.' His thigh moved, inserting itself even more firmly between hers. Again friction caused sensation to explode in her belly.

She flushed. 'I know that.'

'Then say it,' he commanded, pulling back to stare into her eyes.

Defiance surged back on a wave of desperation. 'Sex. Sex, sex, *sex*—'

He kissed her silent, and damn, but did she enjoy it. When he finally raised his head she was thoroughly and dangerously breathless. 'It's okay, you've made your point. Although I can't say that'll dissuade our fellow travellers from thinking we've joined the Mile High Club.'

A growl of frustration rumbled out before she could stop it. 'Why couldn't you leave this alone until we landed?'

'The same reason you're still caressing my shoulders even though you're protesting my presence here with you.'

She dropped her hands and swore she could feel her skin tingling in protest.

'I...this is crazy,' she muttered under her breath.

'*Sí*, but we can't help ourselves where the other is concerned. Are you ready to go back?'

A shaky nod was all she could manage before he withdrew his thigh from between hers. The loss of his support and heat made her want to cry out in protest. She stopped herself in time and checked to see if her buttons had come undone.

With a sigh of relief, she stepped away from the door.

Rafael was very close behind her when they exited the bedroom. 'You didn't tell me what you thought of the story.'

She looked over her shoulder. 'I thought it was incredible.'

He stilled, an arrested look on his face. 'You enjoyed it?'

'Very much. The girl has an amazing spirit. I can't wait to find out more about her journey.' She glanced at him. 'That is if you intend to continue with it?'

A look passed over his face, gone too quickly before she could decipher it. 'With such a rousing endorsement, how could I not? As it happens, I have a few more chapters.'

Pleasure fizzed through her. 'Will you let me read it?'

He smiled. 'You mean you want to read more, despite the lack of X-rated material?'

She huffed in irritation. 'Why did I think a lovely conversation with you would last more than five seconds?'

His low laugh curled around her senses. She was so lost in it, she didn't realise he had led her away from Axel until he pushed her into the seat next to his.

The Monza circuit, perched on the outskirts of the small namesake town, was situated north of Milan. The view from above as Rafael's helicopter pilot flew over the racetrack was spectacular.

A riot of colour from the different sponsor logos and team colours defied the late winter greyness. She felt the palpable excitement from small teams readying the race cars before they landed.

Casting a glance at Rafael, she couldn't immediately see his reaction due to wraparound shades and noise-cancelling headphones, but his shoulders, the same ones she'd caressed barely ninety minutes ago, tensed the closer they got to the landing pad. If they'd been alone she would've placed her hand on his—an incredible development considering this time last week the thought of touching him set her teeth on edge—but she didn't want to attract undue attention. The paddock would supply enough gossip to fuel this event and the rest of the X1 season as it was.

Cameras flashed as soon as the helicopter touched down and demanding questions were lobbed towards them the moment the doors opened.

Are you returning to racing, Rafael?

Will you be officially announcing your retirement today or is this the start of your comeback?

Is it true you're suffering from post-traumatic stress disorder?

His jaw was set in concrete even though his lips were curved in a smile as he stepped out of the helicopter and waved a lazy hand at the cameras.

A luxurious four-by-four was parked a few feet away. He held the door open for Raven and slid in after her.

'I don't know how you can stand them without wanting to punch someone in the face,' Raven found herself murmuring as she watched a particularly ambitious paparazzo hop onto the back of a scooter and race after them.

'They help raise the profile of the sport. They're a necessary evil.'

'Even when they're intrusive to the point of personal violation?'

'When I engage them, I engage them on my terms. It's a skill I learned early.'

With a surprise, she realised that everything the press knew about Rafael was something he'd chosen to share with them, not some sleazy gossip they'd dug up. To the common spectator, Rafael lived his life in the public eye but in the past few weeks she'd discovered he had secrets…secrets he shared with no one, not even his family.

'You give them just enough to keep them interested and to keep them from prying deeper.'

Stunning blue eyes returned her stare with amusement and a hint of respect. 'That is just so, my clever Raven.'

'So, what pierces that armour, Rafael?'

His smile dimmed. 'I could tell you but I'd have to sleep with you.'

Raven's heart lurched and then sped up when, for a single second, she found herself contemplating if that was a barter worth considering. *Sleeping with Rafael…*

A tiny electric shock that zapped her system left her speechless.

'Since you're not slapping my face in outrage, dare I hope the suggestion isn't as repulsive as you found it previously?'

'I…I never thought you were repulsive,' she replied. 'You may have been a little too intense with your interest, that's all.'

'You dislike my intensity?'

She opened her mouth to say *yes,* and found herself pausing. 'I wasn't used to it. And I didn't like that you had everyone falling over themselves for you and yet you weren't satisfied.'

'But now we've spent some time together you think you *understand* me?' His tone held a hint of derision that chilled her a little.

'I don't claim to understand you but I think I know you a little better, yes.'

The warmth slowly left his eyes to be replaced by a look so neutral he seemed like a total stranger.

Their vehicle pulled up in front of the expansive, stunning motor home that had been set up to accommodate the Italian All-Star event. Several dignitaries from the sports world waited to greet Rafael. He reached for the door handle and turned to her before alighting.

'Don't let that knowledge go to your head, *querida*. I'd hate for you to be disappointed once you realise I won't hesitate to take advantage of that little chink in your armour. Underneath all this, there is only a core of nothingness that will stun you to your soul.'

He got out before she could respond. Before she drew another breath, he'd transformed into Rafael de Cervantes, world champion and charm aficionado. She watched women and *men* fall over themselves to be in his company. Basking in the adoration, he disappeared into the motor home without a backward glance.

Rafael waved away yet another offer of vintage champagne and cast his gaze around for Raven.

He'd been too harsh, he knew. Had he—finally—scared her away for good? The thought didn't please him as it should have.

But she'd strayed far too close, encroaching on a deep dark place he liked to keep to himself. He hadn't been joking when he'd warned her about the core of nothingness. How could he? What would be the point in revealing that grotesque, unthinkable secret?

She would hate you, and you don't want that.

His gut tightened but he pushed the thought away.

No one could hate him more than he hated himself. It was better that he ensured Raven harboured no illusions. Although she'd probably claim not to be, she was the type to see the good in everyone. If she didn't she wouldn't have asked for help from a deplorable father who had subjected her to *dios* knew what to save her mother. He suspected that, deep down, she'd hoped her father would reveal himself to be something other than he was.

Rafael wasn't and would never be a knight in shining armour. Not to her and not to any other woman. He took what he wanted and he didn't give a damn.

Above the heads of the two men he was talking to, he saw Chantilly enter the room on her husband's arm. She zeroed in on him with an openly predatory look, her heavily made-up eyes promising filthy decadence.

Rafael felt nothing. Or rather he felt…different. On further examining his reaction, he realised the sensation he was feeling wasn't the cheap thrill of playing games with Sergey's wife. It was self-loathing for having played it in the first place.

He looked away without acknowledging her look and cast his gaze around the room one more time. Realising he still searched for Raven—where the hell was she?—he made a sound of impatience under his breath.

'Is everything all right?' the chairman of the All-Star event asked him.

'The old racetrack has been carefully inspected as I requested?'

The white-haired man nodded. 'Of course. Every single inch of it. You still haven't told us whether you'll be participating.'

Tightness seized his chest. He forced himself to take a breath and smile. 'The event is only beginning, Adriano. I'll let you old folks have some fun first.'

'Less of the old, if you please.'

The laughter smoothed over his non-answer but the tightness didn't decrease. Nor did his temper when he looked up a third time and found Raven standing at the far end of the room with Axel.

She'd changed from jeans into yet another pair of trousers, made of a faintly shimmery material, and a black clingy top that threw her gym-fit body into relief when she moved.

The sound of a nearby engine revving provided the perfect excuse for Axel to lean in closer to whisper into her ear. Whatever the German was saying to her had her smiling and nodding. Obviously encouraged, her companion moved even closer, one hand brushing her shoulder as he spoke.

Rafael moved without recognising an intention to do so, a feat in itself considering his hip was growing stiffer from standing for too long. 'Raven, there you are.'

She turned to him. 'Did you want me?' she asked, then flushed slightly.

'Of course I want you,' he replied. 'Why else are you here, if not to come when I want you?'

A spurt of anger entered her eyes. 'What can I do for you?'

'I need your physio services. What else?'

She frowned. 'According to your itinerary, you're working until ten o'clock tonight. Which is why I scheduled a swim therapy for you afterwards and a proper physio session in the morning.'

His eyes stayed on hers. 'My schedule is fluid and right now I need you.'

'Ah, actually, I'm glad you're here, Rafael,' Axel said.

'Really? And why's that, Jung?'

The other man cleared his throat. 'I was hoping to convince you to let my team borrow Raven's services for a few hours. Our regular physiotherapist came down with a stomach bug and had to stay at the hotel.'

'Out of the question,' Rafael replied without a single glance in his direction.

'Rafael!'

'Need I remind you what your contract states?' he asked her.

'I don't need reminding, but surely—'

He shifted sideways deliberately in a move to get her attention. And succeeded immediately. 'What happened?' she demanded, her keen eyes trailing down his body, making a visual inspection.

'You were right. This whole thing has simply worn me out. I think I'll have an early night.' He turned towards the door. 'Are you coming?'

'I...yes, of course.' Concern was etched into her face. Rafael wanted to reassure her that his hip wasn't painful enough to warrant that level of worry.

But he didn't because he couldn't guarantee that she wouldn't wish to stay, return to Axel. The disconcerting feeling unsettled him further.

'I was away for just over an hour. Please tell me you didn't try and do anything foolish to your body in that time.'

'Where were you, exactly?'

'Excuse me?'

'Were you with Jung all that time?' he asked, an unfamiliar feeling in his chest.

'Are we seriously doing this again?'

'How else would he have got it into his mind to poach you?'

'He wasn't...isn't trying to poach me. He was telling the truth. His team's physio was sent back to his hotel because he fell ill. But they think it's just a twenty-four hour virus. I didn't see the harm in agreeing to give my professional opinion.'

'You should've spoken to me first.'

'In the mood you were in? You bit my head off because I got too close again. I won't be your personal punchbag for whenever you feel the need to strike out.'

He sucked in a weary breath and Raven forced herself to look at him properly for the first time. Not that it was a hardship.

It was clear he was in pain. His skin was slightly clammy and stress lines flared from his eyes. 'What the hell did you do to yourself?' she asked softly.

'You should've stuck around if you were concerned.'

She didn't get the opportunity to answer as they'd arrived at the helipad. The blades were already whirring when she took her seat beside Rafael for the short trip to their hotel in Milan.

As they exited the lift towards their exclusive penthouse suite, she turned to him. 'Lean on me.'

When he didn't argue or make a suggestive comment, she knew he was suffering. Raven was thankful she'd had the forethought to ring ahead to make sure the equipment she needed had been set up.

Back in their hotel, after Rafael stripped to his boxers, she started with a firm sports massage to relax his limbs before she went to work on the strained hip muscles.

By the time she was done, a fine sheen of sweat had broken over his face. Pouring a glass of water, she handed it to him.

He drank and handed the glass back to her.

'I don't like seeing you with other men. It drives me slightly nuts,' he said abruptly.

She stilled in the act of putting away a weighted leg brace. 'You can't have all the toys in the playground, Rafael.'

'I just want one toy. The one sitting on top of the tree that everyone says I can't have.'

'What you can't do is to keep shaking the tree in the hope that the toy will fall into your lap. That's cheating.'

'It's not cheating; it's taking the initiative. Anyway, you can't be with Axel.'

She stopped, head tilted to the side, before she tucked a strand of hair behind one ear. 'Okay, I'll play. Why can't I be with him?'

He gave a pained grimace. 'He has a ridiculous name, for a start. Think how ridiculous your future kids would find you. Raven and Axel Jung. Doesn't rhyme.'

'And I have to have a man whose name rhymes with mine, why?'

'Synergy in all things. Take you and me.'

'You and me?' she parroted.

'*Sí*. Rafa and Raven rolls right off the tongue. It was meant to be.'

She passed him a towel. 'I'd suspect you were on some sort

of high, but you didn't touch a drop of alcohol at the mixer and you've refused any pain medication.'

'I'm completely rational. And completely right.'

'It must be hunger making you delirious then.' She handed him the walking stick and walked beside him to the living room. 'Room service?'

With a sigh, he sank into the nearest wide velvet sofa, nodded and put his head back on the chair.

'What would you like?' she asked.

'You choose.'

'Would you like me to spoon-feed you when it arrives, too?'

His grin was a study in mind-melting hotness and unashamed sexual arrogance. 'You're not the first to offer, *querida*. But I may just make you the first to succeed in that task.'

Rolling her eyes, she ordered two steaks with a green salad for them. Then, on impulse, she ordered a Côte du Rhone.

The wine wouldn't exactly lay him flat but it might let him relax enough to get a good night's sleep, especially since he refused to take any medication.

After she'd placed the order, she set the phone down and approached the seating area.

Rafael patted the space beside him.

Very deliberately, and sensibly, she thought, she chose the seat furthest from him and ignored his low mocking laugh.

'So, care to tell me what happened today?'

He stilled, then his eyes grew hooded. 'First day back on the job. Everyone was clamouring for the boss.'

Raven got the feeling it was a little bit more than that but she wisely kept it to herself. 'What are the races in aid of this year?' she asked, changing the subject.

He tensed further, wrong-footing her assumption that this was a safe subject.

For the longest time, she thought he wouldn't answer. 'XPM started a foundation five years ago for the victims of road accidents and their families. But we soon realised that giving away money doesn't really help. Educating about safety was a better route to go. So we've extended the programme to testing road and vehicle safety, with special concentration on young drivers.'

'Was…was it because of what happened with your father?'

His eyes darkened. 'Surprisingly, no. It was because a boy racer wiped out a family of six because he wasn't aware of how powerful the machine underneath him really was. I knew exactly how powerful the car I drove was so my transgression didn't come from ignorance.'

'Where did it come from?'

'Arrogance. Pride. I owned the world and could do as I pleased, including ignoring signs of danger.' His face remained impassive, this slightly self-loathing playboy who wore his faults freely on his chest and dared the world to judge him. His phone rang just then. He checked the screen, tensed and pressed the off button. 'Speak of the devil and he appears,' he murmured. His voice was low and pensive with an unmistakable thread of pain.

Raven frowned. 'That was your father?'

'*Sí*,' he replied simply.

'And you didn't answer.'

The eyes he raised to her were dark and stormy. 'I didn't want to interrupt our stimulating conversation. You were saying…?'

She searched her memory banks and tried to pull together the threads of what they'd been talking about. 'You used the past tense when you said you owned the world? You no longer think that?'

'World domination is overrated. Mo' power mo' problems.' Although he smiled, the tortured pain remained.

'Is that why you won't forgive yourself? Because you think you should've known better.'

'My, my, is it Psychology 101?'

She pressed her lips together. 'It is, isn't it?'

'If I said yes, would you make it all better?'

'If you said yes you would feel better all on your own.' The doorbell rang and she looked towards the door. 'Think about that while I serve our feast.'

The emotions raging within him didn't disappear from his eyes as she went to the door to let the waiter in.

By unspoken agreement they stuck to safer subjects as they ate—once again, Rafael taking her refusal to feed him with equanimity.

When she refused a second glass of wine, he set the bottle down and twirled his glass, his gaze focused on the contents.

'So where is this island of yours that Marco and Sasha have gone to?'

'There are a string of islands near Great Exuma. We own one of them.'

'Wow, what does it feel like to own your own island?'

'Much like it feels to own a car, or a handbag, or a pen. They're all just possessions.'

'Possessions most people spend their lives dreaming about.'

'Are you one of those people? Do you dream of finding a man to take you from your everyday drudgery to a life filled with luxury?'

'First of all, I don't consider what I do drudgery. Secondly, while I think dreams are worth having, I set more store by the hard work that *propels* the achievement of that dream.'

'So I can't sway you with the promise of a private island of your very own?'

'Nah, I have a thing about private islands.'

His brow rose. 'A *thing*?'

She nodded. 'I saw a TV show once where a group of people crashed onto one and spent a hellishly long time trying to get off the damned rock.' Her mock shudder made him grin. 'A concrete jungle and the promise of a mocha latte every morning suits me just fine.'

He raised his glass. 'To concrete jungles and the euphoria of wall-to-wall coffee shops.'

'Indeed.' She clinked glasses with him. Then it dawned

on her how easy the atmosphere had become between them; how much more she wanted to stay where she was, getting to know this compelling man who spelled trouble for her. The thought forced her to push her chair back. 'I think I'll head to bed now. Goodnight, Rafael.'

If he noticed the sudden chill in her voice, he didn't react to it. 'Before you go, I have something for you,' he said, pointing to the elegant console table that stood outside the suite's study.

Seeing the neat stack of papers, Raven felt a leap of pleasure. Going to the table, she picked up the papers and, sure enough, it was the continuation of Ana's story.

'Did you write all of this last night?' she asked him.

He shrugged. 'The muse struck when I was awake. No big deal.' But she could tell it was. His gaze was hooded and his smile a little tight. It was almost…almost as if he was nervous about her reading it.

'Thanks for trusting me with this, Rafael.'

He looked startled for a moment, then he nodded. '*De nada. Buenas noches, bonita*,' he replied simply.

The distinct lack of *naughty* left her floundering for a moment. Then she forced herself to walk towards her suite.

'Raven?' His voice stopped her beside the wide, elegant double doors leading into the hallway. When she turned, his gaze had dropped to assess the contents of his wine glass.

'Yes?'

'Don't flirt with Jung.'

Her pulse raced. Later, when she was safely in her cool bed, she tried to convince herself it was the effects of the wine that made her say, 'Quid pro quo, my friend. If I'm not allowed to flirt, then no more numbers on your walking stick. Agreed?'

Blue eyes lifted, regarded her steadily, their brilliance and intensity as unnerving as they'd been the very first time she'd looked into them. After a full minute, he nodded. 'Agreed.'

CHAPTER EIGHT

SHE FOUND HIM in the penthouse pool the next morning. She stood, awestruck, as Rafael cleaved the water in rapid, powerful strokes, his sleek muscles moving in perfect symmetry. He turned his head just before he dived under and executed a turn and, for a split second, Raven became the focus of piercing blue eyes.

One length, two lengths…three.

After completing the fourth, he stopped at the far end, flipped onto this back and swam lazily towards her. 'Are you going to stand there all day or are you going to join in? We leave for the racetrack in half an hour.'

'I'm not coming in, thank you. We were supposed to have a full physio session this morning.'

'I was up and raring to go, *bonita*. You were not.'

It was the first time ever that Raven had overslept or been late for an appointment. She couldn't stem the heat that crawled up into her face as she recalled the reason why. When she'd found herself unable to sleep, she'd opened up Rafael's manuscript and delved back between the pages. If anything, the story had been even better the second time round, renewed fascination with Ana, the heroine, keeping her awake.

'I was only ten minutes late.'

He stopped on the step just beneath where she stood and sluiced a hand through his hair. 'Ten throwaway minutes to you is a lifetime to me.' He hauled himself out of the pool. Raven couldn't stop herself from ogling extremely well-toned biceps and a tight, streamlined body. Even the scars he'd sustained on his legs and especially his hip were filled with character that made her want to trace her fingers over it, test his skin's texture for herself.

She forced herself to look away before the fierce flames rising could totally engulf her. He grabbed the towel she tossed to him and rubbed it lazily over his body.

'Well, since you had the full therapy session last night, I don't see the harm in reversing the regime.'

He glanced over and winked. 'My thoughts exactly.'

Suspicion skittered along her spine. 'You're surprisingly chipper this morning.' Looking closer, she saw that his face had lost its strained edge, and when he turned to toss the towel aside, his movement had lost last night's stiffness.

'It's amazing what a good night's sleep can do. I feel as if I have a new lease of life.' He picked up his walking stick and came towards her, a sexy, melt-your-panties-off grin firmly in place. 'Come, we'll have breakfast and I can tell you how to make your tardiness up to me.'

'Anything less than a pound of flesh and I'll probably die of shock,' she muttered.

He laughed. The sound floated along her skin then sank in with pleasure-giving intensity. 'You wound me. I was thinking more along the lines of your thoughts on the manuscript.'

She didn't answer immediately. She was too caught up in watching the ripple of muscle as he sauntered out of the pool area—and through his bedroom, where discarded clothes and twisted sheets made her temperature rise higher—towards the sun-dappled balcony where their breakfast had been laid out.

Goodness knew how she managed not to stare like some hormonal schoolgirl.

'Wow, should I take your silence to mean it was sheer dross?'

Focus! She sat down at the table, snapped out her napkin and laid it over her lap, wishing she could throw a blanket over her erotic thoughts just as easily.

He poured her coffee—mocha latte—and added a dash of cinnamon, just the way she liked it. Raven decided she was *not* going to read anything into Rafael's intimate knowledge of how she took her caffeine. But inside she felt a long held-in tightness spring free, accompanied by the faintest spark of fear.

'It wasn't dross. I'm sure you know that. I love Ana's transition from girl into woman. And that first meeting with Carlos was what every girl dreams of. I'm happy she's putting her dark past behind her...'

'But?' He scythed through her ambivalence.

'But I think Carlos is coming on too strong, too fast. He risks overwhelming Ana just a little bit.'

He picked up his own coffee and eyed her over the rim. 'But I think she has a backbone of steel. Do you not think she has what it takes to stay?'

Raven nodded. 'I think she does. She sees him as a challenge...welcomes it to some extent, but I'm still a little scared for her.'

'You're invested in her. Which is what a writer wants, isn't it? Maybe she needs to be pushed out of her comfort zone to see what she really wants.'

'I notice she likes racing, just like Carlos.'

He stilled. '*Sí*. It is a racing thriller, after all.'

Raven carefully set her cup down and picked up a slice of toast. 'She wouldn't, by chance, be modelled on your sister-in-law, would she?' she asked, keeping her voice level.

He shrugged. 'Sasha is one of the best female drivers I've known. What's your point?'

She didn't know how to articulate what it made her feel. Hell, she couldn't grasp the roiling feelings herself. All she knew was that she didn't want Rafael to be thinking of a specific woman when he wrote the story.

'I just think you would appeal to a wider audience if the character wasn't so...specific.'

'You mean, it would appeal to you?'

The toast fell from her hand. 'I don't know what you mean.'

'Are you going to play this game? Really?'

The words, so similar to those she'd thrown at him, made heat crawl up her face. 'Fine. Touché.' She hardened her spine and forced out the next words. 'But you know what I'm trying to say.'

'Are we still talking about my manuscript?' he asked, a trace of a smile on his lips.

'We've taken a slight detour.'

'A detour that touches on our…friendship and the adjustments I need to make in order for it to advance?'

Her hands shook at how quickly they'd strayed into dangerous territory. She couldn't look into his probing gaze so she studiously buttered her toast. 'Y…yes.'

He stayed silent for so long she was forced to glance up. Blue eyes pinned her to her chair. 'Don't expect me to turn into something I'm not, *querida*.'

'Take a first step. You might surprise yourself.'

'And you, *pequeña*, how are you surprising yourself?'

The question, unexpected and lightning-quick, sent a bolt of shock through her. She floundered, unsure of what to say. 'I…I'm not sure…'

'Well, make sure. If I'm to bend over backwards to accommodate you, you have to give something back, *sí*?'

That pulse of fear intensified. Opening up to Rafael in Monaco, telling him things she'd never told another human soul, had left her feeling raw and exposed.

Now, by daring her in his oh-so-sexy way to open up even more, he threatened to take it a whole lot further, luring her with a promise she knew deep down he wouldn't keep. That was the essence of playboys. They exuded charisma, invited confidences until they had you in their grasp.

And yet the rare glimpses she'd caught of Rafael threatened that long-held belief. He was alluding to the fact that playboys could have hearts of gold. Raven wasn't sure she was ready to handle that nugget of information.

For years, her mother had believed it—believed it still—and look where it'd got her. If she let Rafael in and he did a number on her, she wasn't sure who she would hate more—Rafael…or herself.

'You don't have to turn into something else. All I ask is to see a little bit more, make my choice with a clear, if not total, view of the facts. Because I can't have sex with you for the sake of it. I would hate myself and I would hate you.'

'Ah, but we're already having sex, *mi amor*. All that's left is for our bodies to catch up.'

Of course, she could *really* have done without that thought in her head. Because, suddenly, it was all she could think about.

She walked beside Rafael along the long paddock an hour later, watching as he stopped at every single All-Star garage to greet and exchange info with the crew. From her stint as his physio last year, Raven knew just how meticulous a driver he was. He understood the minutiae of racing to the last detail and could probably recite the inner workings of a turbo engine in his sleep.

Which was why his accident, judged to be the result of human error—his—had stunned everyone. Some had speculated that it had been the effects of partying hard that had finally done him in. But, in the last few weeks, she'd caught occasional glimpses of the man underneath and knew Rafael de Cervantes wasn't all gloss. He rarely drank more than a glass of champagne at any event and she knew he'd banned smoking in the paddock a few years back.

What she didn't know was how deep the Rafael de Cervantes well ran, or how monstrous the demons were that chased him. It was clear he was haunted by something in his past. At first she'd thought it was his father. But even though that particular revelation had been painful to him, it had been when she'd mentioned his mother that the real pain had surfaced, just for a moment.

She glanced at him, a little overwhelmed by the many facets she had previously been too riled up to see. Rafael had traits she abhorred, traits that reminded her of the man whose DNA ran through her veins.

But he was also so much more.

'I can hear you thinking again.'

'Unfortunately, my active brain cells refuse to subside into bimbo mode just because I'm in your presence.' She cast a telling glance at a groupie who'd just obtained an autograph and was squealing in delight as she ran to her friends.

'You can wow me with your superior intelligence later,' he said as they approached the last garage in the paddock.

The first thing she noticed was the age group of this particular crew. Aside from two older supervisors, everyone else ranged from early to late teens. The other thing that struck her was their synchronicity and clear pride in what they were doing.

When Rafael greeted them, they responded as if he were their supreme deity come to life. She wasn't surprised by their reaction. What surprised her was Rafael's almost bashful response as they gathered around him. Then it all disappeared as he started to speak. Started to teach.

They hung on his every word, and took turns asking him challenging questions, which he threw right back to them. Respect shone from their eyes and the depth of understanding he'd managed to impart in the space of the hour before the race started left Raven reeling.

'Close your mouth, *piqueña*. You'll catch flies,' he quipped as he led her away from the garage towards the VIP Paddock Club.

Her mouth snapped shut. 'That was incredible, the way you got them to listen, got them to apply knowledge they'd forgotten they had.'

'They're a talented bunch. And they love racing. All there is to learn is a respect for speed.' He shrugged. 'It wasn't hard.'

'No. You're a natural teacher.'

'I learned from the best.'

'Marco?'

He shook his head and held the door open to let her into the lift that whisked them up to the top floor VIP lounge. From there they had a panoramic view over the entire race circuit.

Rafael bypassed several A-listers who'd paid thousands of euros to attend this exclusive event and led her into a private roped-off area. He held out a chair for her then sat down opposite her. 'My father. He gave me my first go-kart when I was five. There's nothing about engines that he doesn't know. By the time I was nine, I could dismantle and reassemble a carburetor without assistance.'

'I didn't know your father raced.'

'He didn't. My grandfather had a small hotel business and wanted my father to study business so he could help him run it. But he never lost his love of racing. The moment his business grew successful enough, he enrolled Marco, then me in learning the sport. And he took us to all the European races, much to my mother's distress.'

The pang of envy for what she'd never had made her feel small so she pushed it away. Especially given what she knew of the strain between father and son now.

'That sounds just like what happened to Carlos in your story.'

He glanced at her with a tense smile. 'Does it?'

'Yes.' When he just shrugged, she decided not to pursue the subject of his story. 'So your father took you to all the races? Sounds like an idyllic childhood.'

'Sure, if you're prepared to forgive the fact that back then I was so intent on winning I didn't feel any compunction in crashing into every single car in front of me just to put them out of business. I was disqualified more times than I actually won races.'

'But I'm guessing your father persevered. He saw the raw talent and did everything he could to nurture it.' Something her own father hadn't even come close to attempting with her.

'*Sí*, he showed me the difference between winning at all costs and winning with integrity. And I repaid that by making sure he would never be able to drive a car again.' His face was taut with pain, his eyes bleak with a haunting expression that cracked across her heart.

'I saw how things were between you two at Jack's christening, but have you spoken to him at all since the accident?'

He tensed, waited for the waiter who'd brought their drinks to leave before he answered. 'Of course I have.'

'I mean about what happened.'

'What would be the point?'

'To find out how he feels about it?'

'How he *feels*? Trust me, I have a fair idea.'

Recalling the look on his father's face, she shook her head. 'Maybe you don't. Perhaps you should talk to him again. Or maybe let *him* talk to you. He could have something to say to you instead of you thinking it only works the other way round.'

He frowned suddenly. 'You're head shrinking me again. And how the hell did we get onto this subject anyway? It's boring me.'

'Don't,' she said softly.

A glaze of ice sharpened his blue eyes. 'Don't what?'

'Don't trivialise it. You'll have to tackle it sooner or later.'

'Like you have tackled your father?'

Her breath shut off in her chest. 'This is different.'

'How?' He had to raise his voice to be heard over the sound of engines leaving the garages to line up on the racetrack. Rafael barely glanced at them, his attention riveted on her face.

'Despite everything that's happened, your father loves you enough to want to connect with you. My father doesn't care if I'm alive or dead. He never has, and he never will.'

Rafael saw the depth of pain that slashed across her features before she turned to watch the action unfolding on the racetrack. He wanted to say something, but found he had no words of wisdom or of comfort to give her.

Because he didn't agree with the redeeming quality she seemed to want to find in him. He had no doubt that if she knew the extent of his sins, she wouldn't be so quick to offer her comfort.

An icy vice threatened to crush his chest, just as it did every time he thought of his mother. He'd awoken this morning with her screams ringing in his ears, the image of her lifeless eyes imprinted on his retinas.

No, he had no words of comfort. He'd trashed everything good in his life, and had come close to dismantling his relationship with his brother last year. The last thing he wanted to do was admit to Raven that part of his refusal to speak to his father was because he didn't want to discover whether he was irredeemably trashed in his father's eyes too.

His gaze flicked to the cars lining up on the track. Unlike the normal grand prix races when the cars lined up according to their qualifying time, the six All-Star cars were lined up side by side.

Team El Camino's red and black racer, driven by the young driver he'd been working with, was the first off the mark. Rafael felt a spurt of pride, which he immediately doused.

He had no right to feel pride. All he'd done was take what his father had taught him and passed it on. His father deserved the credit here, not him.

'Don't be so hard on yourself.'

Irrational anger sprang up within him. The fact that she seemed so determined to make him feel better when she was content to wallow in her own *daddy issues* filled him with anger. The fact that he was sexually frustrated—heck, he was going on eight months without having had sex—was setting his teeth on edge. The fact that he was up here, cooling his heels when he wanted more than anything to be down there… behind the wheel of a racing car—

Ice chilled his veins as he acknowledged the full extent of what he was feeling.

'Rafael?'

He didn't respond or turn towards her. Instead he watched the screen as Axel Jung threatened to take the lead from the young driver.

'Rafael, are you okay?'

'Do me a favour, *querida*, and stop talking. You're holding a mirror up to my numerous flaws. There's only so much I can take before I have to revert to type. And since you don't want that, I suggest you let me absorb a few of them and concentrate on enjoying this race, *si*?'

Far from doing what he expected of her, which was to retreat into sullen silence or—from experience with other women—flounce off in feminine affront, she merely picked up the remote that operated the giant screen in their section and turned it on. Then she picked up the menu, asked him what he wanted for lunch, then ordered it for them, her face set in smooth, neutral lines.

He waited several minutes, despising the emotion that ate away his insides like acid on metal. Guilt. An emotion he didn't like to acknowledge.

Guilt for upsetting her. 'I'm sorry,' he said.

A shapely eyebrow lifted in his direction, then she nodded. 'It's okay. I don't like dredging up my past either. I guess I should learn to respect yours.'

'But I seem to invite you to dig, which is very unlike me.' He frowned.

A tiny, perfect smile played around lips he remembered tasting. A craving such as he'd never known punched through him. Right in that moment, all he wanted to do was taste her again. Keep on tasting her until there were no clothes between them. Then he would taste her in the most elemental way possible. Right between her legs.

He would so enjoy watching her come. Again and again. And again.

Normally, he would have been thrilled by the natural path of his thoughts, but Rafael admitted his need held a previously unknown edge to it…an almost desperate craving he'd never experienced before. He wanted Raven. And yet a part of him was terrified by the depth of his need.

Forcing himself not to analyse it too closely, he returned

his attention to the track and felt a further spurt of discontentment when he saw Axel Jung had taken the lead.

Lunch was delivered and they ate in truce-like silence.

When Axel Jung took the race by a half second, Rafael tried to force back his black mood. As the CEO of the company organising the event, he had to step up to the podium and say a few words.

'If your jaw tightens any further, you'll do yourself an injury,' Raven murmured next to him.

'I'm smiling, *querida*, like the great racer slash CEO that I am,' he muttered back, turning towards her.

This close, her perfume filled his nostrils and invaded his senses. She gave a laugh and raised a sceptical brow. 'We both know you want to throw your toys out of the pram because the team you silently support came second. You're supposed to be unbiased, remember?'

He moved closer to her, felt the brush of her arm against his side and the depth of need intensified. 'I am unbiased. I just wanted my young driver to win, that's all,' he said, unrepentant.

Her teasing laugh and the way she bumped his shoulder in playful admonition unravelled him further. He glanced down into her face and his breath strangled at her breathtaking beauty.

A shout made him turn. Axel had stepped off the podium and was making his way towards them. Or Raven in particular, if the interest in his eyes was anything to go by.

Before conscious thought formed, Rafael moved, deliberately blocking the German from accessing the woman beside him. *His woman.*

'Congratulations, Jung. I think the press want their interview now.' He deftly turned the German towards the waiting paparazzi. As moves went, Rafael thought it was supremely smooth, but Raven's gasp told him the grace had been lost on her.

'Did you just do what I think you did?'

'That depends. Did you want him to come over here and slobber all over you?'

She shuddered. 'No, but I'm not sure I wanted a blatant territory-marking from you either.'

He wanted to tell her that he wished the whole paddock knew to keep away from her. But he knew it wouldn't go down well. It would also point out just how much he detested the idea of Raven with any other man. 'Point taken.'

Her eyes widened. 'Wow, I'm not sure whether to feel suspicious or special that you've conceded a point to me.'

'You should feel special.' His gaze trapped and held hers. 'Very special.'

Raven returned his stare, trying to summon a tiny bit of ire beneath all the high octane, breath-stealing emotions coursing through her. But the excitement licking along her nerve endings put the effort to shame.

Something of her feelings must have shown on her face because his eyes darkened dramatically. His gaze dropped to her lips, the heated pulse beating a wild rhythm in her neck, then back to her face.

Calmly, he breathed out and gave her a slow, electrifying smile. Eyes still locked on hers, he pulled out his phone and spoke in clear tones. Unfortunately, Spanish wasn't her forte so she had no clue what he was saying. But she made out the word *avión,* which made her even more curious.

'What was that about?' she asked when he hung up.

'I've arranged for our things to be packed. I thought we might head to Mexico a couple of days earlier than the rest of the racers.'

'Won't you be needed?'

'Possibly, but for the next two days I'm taking your advice and delegating. Does this make you happy?'

There was a deeper question beneath the stated one, a hungry gleam in his eyes that boldly proclaimed his intention should she agree to what he was proposing.

In a single heartbeat, Raven accepted it. 'Yes.'

It was almost a relief to let go of the angst and the rigid control. At least for a while. She knew without a shadow of a doubt that it would return a hundredfold soon enough.

CHAPTER NINE

SHE WAS GOING to take a lover. She was going to lose her virginity to the very man she'd run a mile from last year. The man who would most likely break her heart into a tiny million pieces long before this thing between them was over.

Nerves threatened to eat her up as their tiny seaplane banked and headed towards the private beachfront of the stunning villa Rafael owned in Los Cabos, Mexico. By now she knew all about the eighteen-bedroom villa, the lower level sauna and steam room, the two swimming pools and the names of every member of the construction crew who'd built the villa to Rafael's exact specification three years ago.

Because she'd needed to babble, to fill her head with white noise to distract her from the urge to spill the fact that she hadn't done this before. The closer they drew to their destination, the higher panic had flared beneath the surface of her outward calm.

Rafael's experience with women was world-renowned. What if she made a spectacular fool of herself? What if he was so put off by her inexperience he recoiled from her? To silence the voices, she babbled some more, found out that he had a staff of five who managed the villa and that he practised his handicap on the legendary golf course nearby when the occasion suited him.

In direct contrast to her nervous chirping, Rafael had been circumspect, his watchful silence unlike anything she'd ever known. Although he'd answered her questions with inexhaustible patience, his eyes had remained riveted on her the whole time, occasionally dropping to her lips as if he couldn't wait to taste, to devour.

They touched down on the water and powered to a stop next

to a large wooden jetty. After alighting, they headed towards an open-topped jeep for the short drive to the villa.

Even though she felt as if she knew the property inside and out, Raven wasn't prepared for the sheer, jaw-dropping beauty of the adobe white-washed walls, the highly polished exposed beams and almost ever-present sea views from the windows of the mission-style villa. Spanish-influenced paintings adorned the walls, lending a rich tapestry to the luxurious interior.

In her bedroom, rich fabrics in earthy colours formed the backdrop to a mostly white theme set against warm terracotta floors. But one item drew her attention.

'What's this for?' She touched the black high-powered telescope that stood before one large window.

He came and stood behind her, bringing that warm, evocative scent that she'd come to associate with him and only him. It took an insane amount of willpower not to lean back into his hard-packed body.

'The waters around here are well-known grounds for sperm whales. They tend to come closer to shore first thing in the morning. If you're lucky you'll spot a few while we're here.'

Again the sombre, almost guarded response caught her off-guard. She glanced at him over her shoulder. He returned her stare with an intensity that made her breath catch. After a full minute, he lifted his hand and drifted warm fingers down her cheek in a soothing, belly-melting gesture.

'You're nervous, *bonita*. Don't be. I promise it will be good.'

Her laugh was aimed at herself as much as at him. 'That's easy for you to say.'

His finger touched and stayed on the pulse jumping in her throat. 'It isn't. I haven't done this for a long time, too. Hell, I don't know if the equipment works.'

He gave a wry smile when her brows shot up. 'You don't?'

'You will be the first since a while before the accident.'

'But I felt…I know you…'

'Can get a hard-on? *Sí*, but I'm yet to test the practical integrity of the machinery.'

'Oh, so I'm to be your guinea pig?' she teased, a little appeased that she wasn't the only one climbing walls about the prospect of them together.

'Guinea pigs don't have mouths like yours, or eyes the colour of a desert oasis. Or breasts that cry out to be suckled. Or the most perfect heart-shaped ass that makes me want to put you face down and straddle—'

'Okay, I get it. I'm hotter than a Greek furnace.' Her eyes strayed to the perfectly made up bed, her imagination running wild. She swallowed. 'I…I'd like a tour of the outside now, if you don't mind.'

His finger drifted up to the corner of her mouth, pressed gently before he put his finger to his own lips and groaned.

'If that's what you want.'

She nodded.

He didn't heed her request right away. He leaned down, placed his lips at the juncture between her neck and shoulder and ran his tongue over her thundering pulse. He answered her groan with one of his own, then he reluctantly stepped back. Raven was glad when he offered his arm because her legs had grown decidedly shaky.

The heeled leather boots she'd worn with her jeans and black-edged white shirt clicked alongside his heavier tread as they went outside.

On one side, an extensive stretch of grass led to a large thatched poolside bar surrounded by potted palm trees.

Beside it, an area clearly designated for relaxing featured a hot tub under long bales of white linen that had been intertwined to form a stunning canopy that offered shade. After the chill of Europe, it was a balm to feel the sun on her face.

'Come, there's something I want to show you.' There was heated anticipation in the low rumble that fluttered over her skin, feeding her own sizzling emotions.

Rafael led her across the grass and down shallow steps to

the private, secluded beach. All through the tour, his hand had been drifting up and down her back, stealing her thoughts and playing havoc with her pulse.

Which meant that she was totally unprepared for the sight that confronted her when he led her round a rock-sheltered cove.

The thick timber four-poster canopy had been erected right on the shore, with a massive day bed suspended by thick intertwined ropes. The sight was so vividly breathtaking, and so unexpectedly raw and pagan, she stopped in her tracks.

There was only one reason for the bed.

Sex. Outdoor sex.

Heat engulfed her whole body as Rafael's gaze met and trapped hers.

'The high rocks shield even the most determined lenses. And see those?' He indicated three discreetly placed floodlights pointing out towards the water. 'They come on at night and send a glare out to sea so any cunning paparazzi out there get nothing but glare when they try and get pictures of the villa.'

She swallowed hard. 'Even so, I can't imagine doing…it so blatantly.'

He caught her hand in his and kissed her palm. 'Never say never. Now, I believe we have a therapy session to work through?'

The fact that she'd forgotten her main reason for being there made her uncomfortable.

She hastened to cover it up. 'Yes, and don't hate me, but we'll need to step things up a bit.'

'Do with me what you will, *querida*. I'm but putty in your hands.'

He led the way back into the villa and into his bedroom. The setting sun threw orange shades across the king-size wooden-framed bed that seemed to dominate the room. When he threw his walking stick on the exquisitely designed recliner facing the double doors leading to a large balcony, she was reminded again why she was here with Rafael in the first place.

She'd cautioned him against sex only a handful of days ago, and yet here she was, unable to think beyond the raging need to strip every piece of clothing from his body.

Guilt ate away inside her.

'I can hear you thinking again. And I don't feel warm and fuzzy about the direction of your thoughts.' He started to unbutton his shirt.

She tried and failed not to let her eyes linger over his muscular chest and down over his washboard stomach, following the faint line of hair that disappeared beneath his jeans.

'Is this where we hold hands and pray about whether we should have sex or not?'

He was back. The irreverent, sexy, endlessly charismatic man who had women the world over falling at his feet.

Or was he?

A careful look into his eyes showed not the gleam of irreverence but a quietly speculative look beneath his words. 'Are you afraid you'll hate sex with me? Or afraid you'll love it so much you'll beg to become a groupie?'

She shook her head. 'As much as I want it to be easy, I've never taken a decision lightly. And I don't think you should either. It's not just me I'm thinking about here, Rafael. What if all this turns around on you? What if we do this and you get even more damaged?'

'Then I'll learn to live with it. Come here,' he said, holding out his hand. Although his mouth was smiling, his eyes held a very firm command.

She had to dig her toes in to stay put. 'You'll live with it because you think you deserve all the bad things that happen to you?'

His smile slowly eroded until only a trace remained. 'Raven, it's time to stop being my therapist and just be my lover.'

'Rafael...'

'Come. Here.'

He held still, hands outstretched. Almost against her will, she found herself moving forward. He waited until she was within touching distance. Then he lunged for her, sliding his fingers between hers to entrap her.

With his other hand he pulled her close, his fingers spreading over her bottom. Moving forward, he backed her against the wall, enclosing her thighs between his. 'I've got you now. No escape. Now, are you going to undress or do you need help?'

She gnawed on her lower lip, rioting emotions tearing her apart. 'I was so sure I wanted this, Rafael, but I'll never forgive myself if I make things worse for you—'

He growled, 'Damn it, just get naked, will you?'

When she remained still, he took the task into his own hands. For a man who hadn't slept with a woman for almost a year, he didn't seem to lack the skill needed to undress her.

She was down to her bra and knickers within seconds. One deft flick of his fingers disposed of her bra. Slowly he took one step back, then another.

'*Dios*, I knew you would be worth it,' he rasped, his fiercely intent gaze making her skin heat up and pucker in all the right places. Grabbing her by the waist, he reversed their positions and walked her back towards the bed. At the back of her mind she knew she needed to tell him about her lack of experience. But words were in short supply when confronted with the perfection that was Rafael's muscled torso.

With one firm push, she lay sprawled on the bed. He placed one knee on the bed, pushed forward, then winced as he positioned himself over her.

Her concerned gasp drowned beneath his kiss. The kiss that rocked her to her very soul. His tongue pushed inside, warm, insistent and pulse-melting as he showed her the extent of his mastery. Unable to bear the torrent of sensation, she jerked, her hands flailing as she tried to find purchase. He moved over her, pinned her more firmly to the bed with his hips flush against her. When he winced again, she wrenched her mouth from his.

'Before you say it, I'm fine. Dampen the mood with another virtuous monologue and I will spank you. Hard.'

She flushed deep and fierce, but it didn't keep her silent. 'I can't…I can't stop caring about your well-being just because it's inconvenient for you. Just tell me if you're okay.'

'I'm okay. But if I had to, I'd cut off my arm just to be inside you, to feel you close around me like you'd never let me go.'

'Bloody hell, do you practice those lines or do they really just fall off your lips?'

'If I plan to relaunch myself as a multimillion euro best-selling writer, *bonita*, then a way with words is a must.' He sobered. 'But that doesn't mean I don't mean them. I mean every single word I say to you.'

Her heart stuttered, then thundered wildly. 'Rafael…' Her eyes drifted shut.

'I'm lethal. I know.' He settled himself more firmly until she felt his rigid size against the fabric of her knickers. He rocked forward and the relentless pressure on her clitoris made a few dozen stars explode behind her closed eyelids.

'You're beyond lethal,' she breathed shakily. 'You're everything I should be running away from.'

His mouth drifted down her cheek to her jaw and back again. He pressed another kiss to the corner of her mouth, then she felt him move away. 'Hey, open your eyes.'

Reluctantly, she obeyed, already missing his mouth on her.

His gaze was solemn. 'Don't run, Raven. I'm broken and cannot chase after you. Not just yet.'

Her breath caught. 'Would you really? Chase after me?'

'Most definitely. Because I get extremely grumpy when I'm cheated out of an orgasm.'

The slap she aimed at his arm was half-hearted because his mouth was descending to wreak havoc on hers once more. When he finally allowed her to breathe, she was mindless with pleasure.

'I've wanted you for so long, I can't remember when I didn't want you.'

'But…why? Because I was the only paddock bunny who wouldn't fall into your bed?'

She expected a clever quip about his irresistibility. Instead, his gaze turned serious. 'Because within that tainted, false existence, you managed to remain pure. Nothing touched you. I craved that purity. I wanted to touch it, to see what it felt like. But you wouldn't even give me the time of day.'

'Because you had enough groupies hanging around you. I…I also thought you were with Sasha.'

He groaned. 'I guess I played the playboy game a little too well.'

'You mean you weren't?'

'I grew jaded a long time ago but some cloaks are more difficult to cast off than others.'

At her half-snort, he laughed. 'Do you know this is the longest I've been in a bedroom with a woman without one of us halfway to an orgasm?'

She knew that he meant the woman, not him. 'How trying for you.'

He pushed against her once more, his erection a fierce, rigid presence. '*Sí*. It's very trying. You should do something about it before my poor body gives out.' He trailed his mouth over hers before planting a row of kisses along her jaw.

'You really are incorrigible,' she gasped.

'Yes, I am,' he murmured, slowly licking his way down her neck to her pulse. 'I am incorrigible. And I deserve to be punished. Mercilessly.' He slid a hand to caress her belly, then lower to boldly cup her. 'Show me who's boss, my stern, sensible Raven. Give me the punishment I deserve.'

Her breath snagged in her chest. The same chest where her heart hammered like a piston about to burst its casing.

His fingers pressed harder, rhythmic, unrelenting. This time the explosion of heat stemmed from her very core and radiated throughout her body. Her legs parted wider, inviting him to embed himself even deeper. Her restless fingers traced the line of his jeans and found firm skin. Her fingers slipped an inch beneath and he moaned. The sound vibrated along her nerves as heat oozed between her legs.

Her hips undulated in sync with the movement of his fingers, and in that moment, Raven felt as if she were melting from the inside out. She moaned at the intensity of it.

'That's it, *precioso*, give it up for me,' he murmured in her ear, then bit on her lobe. Her cry echoed in the room, the sound as alien to her as the feelings coursing through her body. When his hot mouth trailed down her neck, over her shoulder blades, she held her breath, at once dreading and anticipating the sensation of his stubble roughness on her breast.

With a hungry lunge, he sucked one nipple into his mouth and drew hard on it. At the same time, one firm finger pressed on her most sensitive spot.

'Oh God!' Pleasure exploded in a fiery sensation that made her hips buck straight off the bed. She felt Rafael move off her and alongside her, but the pressure of his fingers and mouth didn't abate. Her climax dragged out until she feared she would expire from it. When her tremors subsided, he left her breasts to plant a forceful kiss on her lips. She fought to breathe.

Heavens, he was too much.

She opened her eyes to find his gaze on hers, intense and purposeful. 'If you're thinking of concocting a means of escape now you've come, know now I have no intention of letting that happen.'

'Why would I want to escape? Unless I'm mistaken, the best is yet to come. Yes?'

The relieved exhalation made her guess he'd suspected she was feeling overwhelmed. 'You have no idea. Kiss me.'

Raven's fingers curled into his nape, glorying in the luxurious heat of his skin as she complied with the heated request.

No, she didn't want to escape. Touching him felt so good, so incredibly pleasurable, that fleeing was the last thing on her mind. The thought surprised her, almost tripping out of her mouth. She curbed it in time. Rafael's head was already swollen by the thought that he could turn her on. Admitting how totally enthralled she was by him would make him even more insufferable. Although, the way she was feeling right now, she wouldn't be surprised if his sharp intellect worked it out before long—

'You're thinking again.'

She stared into blue eyes filled with raw hunger and masculine affront. Slowly she let her fingers drift through his hair, experiencing a keen sense of feminine satisfaction when he groaned. 'What are you going to do about it?'

His lips parted in a feral smile. 'Don't challenge a man on the knife-edge of need, sweetheart. You might regret it. If you survive the consequences.'

Without giving her time to answer, he pulled her down on top of him, both hands imprisoning her to his body as he fell back on the bed. Unerringly, his mouth found hers.

Raven stopped thinking.

And gave herself over to sensation. Rafael's pelvic bone might have been broken and pieced back together but there was nothing wrong with his arms. He lifted her above him and held her in place while he feasted on her breasts. When he was done, he lifted even higher. 'Take off your panties for me.'

With shaky fingers she drew them off, experienced a momentary stab of self-consciousness, which was promptly washed away when he positioned her legs on either side of him and looked up at her.

'You might want to hold onto something,' he murmured huskily, taking a sharp bite of the tender skin of her inner thigh.

The statement wasn't a casual boast. At the first brush of his tongue on her sex, her whole body arched and shook. She would've catapulted off him had he not been holding her hips in an iron grip.

Pain shot through fingers which had grasped the wooden

headboard at his warning. He licked, sucked and tortured her with a skill that left her reeling and hanging on for dear life.

When she tumbled headlong into another firestorm, he caught her in his arms and caressed her body until she could breathe again. Then he left her for a moment.

The sound of foil ripping drew her hazy gaze to him. The sight of his erection in his fist made her sex swell all over again.

He caught her stare and sent her a lethal smile. 'Next time, you get to do it.'

Raven didn't know what to do with that. Nor did she know how to find the correct words to tell him she'd never done it before. In the end, they just spilled out.

'Rafael, I'm a virgin.'

He stilled, shock darkening his eyes. A look flitted through his eyes a second before he shut them. The hand he raked through his hair was decidedly shaky.

He sucked in a long harsh breath, then opened his eyes. The raw hunger hadn't abated but the fisted, white-knuckled hand on his thigh showed he was making an inhuman effort to contain it. 'Do you want to stop?' he rasped, jaw clenched as he fought for control.

The thought of stopping made her insides scream in rejection. 'No. I don't. But I wanted you to know before…before it happened.'

He exhaled slowly. His hand unclenched, then clenched again as his gaze slid hungrily over her. 'I can guess your reasons for remaining celibate. What happened to you would make anyone swear off sex. I know the chemistry between us is insane, but you need to be sure you want to do this now, with me.'

'Would you rather I do it with someone else?' she quipped lightly, although the very thought of anyone but Rafael touching her made her shudder in rejection.

He lunged for her, firm hands grasping her shoulders in a rigid hold before she could take another breath.

'Not unless that *someone else* wishes to get his throat ripped out,' he bit out. He pinned her to the bed and devoured her with an anger-tinged, lethally aroused intensity that made fire roar through her body.

By the time he parted her legs and looked deep into her eyes, she was almost lost.

'I'd planned for you to be on top our first time. But I think this will be easier on you.'

His bent arms caged her as he probed her entrance, his gaze searching hers with every inch he slid inside her. The momentary tightening that made her breath catch stilled his forward momentum.

'Raven?' he croaked, tension screaming through his body as he framed her face in gentle hands.

'I'm okay.'

'That makes one of us.'

Her fingers tried to smooth back his hair but the silky strands refused to stay in place. 'I...can I do anything?'

His laugh was tinged with pain. '*Sí*, you could stop being so damned sexy.' He pushed another fraction and her breath hitched again. '*Dios*, I'm sorry,' he murmured, bending to place a reverent kiss on her lips.

Raven didn't know what was in store for her but she knew her body was screaming with the need to find out. With a deep breath—because, hell, no pain no gain—she pushed her hip upward. His cursed groan met her hiss of pain, which quickly disappeared to be replaced by a feeling so phenomenal words failed her.

'Raven!' Rafael's response was half praise, half reproach.

Tentatively, she moved again.

He growled. 'Damn it, woman. *Stay still.*'

'Why?'

'Because this will be over sooner than you'd like if you don't.'

Heart hammering, she inhaled and gasped when the tips

of her breasts brushed his sweat-filmed chest. 'But at least we know the equipment is working, right?'

He pushed the last few inches until he was firmly seated inside her. Sensation as she'd never known flooded her. At her cry of delight, he pulled out slowly and repeated the thrust. Her head slammed back against the pillow, her fingers clenching hard in his hair as she held on for mercy.

Yep, there was nothing faulty in Rafael's equipment.

With another hungry groan, he increased the tempo, murmuring hot, erotic encouragement in her ear as she started to meet his hips with tiny thrusts of her own.

This time when she came the explosion was so forceful, so completely annihilating, she wasn't sure whether she would ever recover.

Rafael plucked her hands from his hair and pinned them on the bed, then proceeded to dominate her senses once more until she was orgasming again and again.

When she heard his final guttural groan of release, she was sure she'd gone insane with pleasure overload.

'*Dios...*' His voice was rough. Mildly shocked. 'This must be what heaven feels like.'

A bolt of pleasure, pure and true, went through her.

Don't get carried away, Raven.

To bring herself down to earth, she searched her mind for something innocuous to say.

'If you break out into *At Last*, I'll personally make sure you never walk again.'

His laugh was deep, full and extremely contagious. She found herself joining in as he collapsed onto his side and pulled her body into his.

They laughed until they were both out of breath. Then he fisted a hand through her hair and tugged her face up to his. After kissing her breathless, he released her.

'I was thinking more along the lines of *Again and Again and Again*. If there's a song like that, I'll need to learn the lyrics. If there isn't I might need to write one.' He cupped her nape and pulled her down for another unending kiss that left her breathless and seriously afraid for her sanity. 'I love kissing you,' he rasped.

A bolt of something strong and unfamiliar went through her, followed swiftly by a threat of apprehension. Steadying a hand on his chest, she pulled herself up.

'Where do you think you're going?' he asked.

She averted her gaze from his and fought to find reason in all this madness. 'I need to get up.'

'No. You need to look after me, and my needs demand that, after what you've just done to me, I stay in this bed. Which means you have to stay too.'

Unable to resist, she glanced down his body and swallowed the hungry need that coursed through her. It was unthinkable that she would want him again, so voraciously, so soon. But she did.

'If you carry on licking your lips and eyeing me like that, I'll have to teach you this lesson all over again.'

She blinked. 'I can't…we can't…it's too soon.'

'As you rightly noted, the equipment works so I most certainly can, *pequeña*.' He moved and she saw his fleeting grimace. 'But maybe you need to go on top this time.' He held out his hand and she swayed towards him.

'This is crazy, Rafael,' she protested feebly, even as she let him arrange her over him.

'But crazy good, no?'

She melted into his arms. 'Crazy good, yes.'

'Tell me what really happened with your father. What did he do to make you yearn for your eighteenth birthday?'

Rafael couldn't believe the words tumbling out of his mouth. But then again, he couldn't believe a lot that had happened in the last twenty-four hours. From the moment he'd placed the phone call to set things in motion to fly them to Mexico, he'd felt control and reason slipping out of his grasp.

Not that he'd had much in the way of control when it came

to the woman drifting in and out of sleep only a heartbeat away. Sure, he used the Los Cabos villa for entertaining. But it was mostly on business, never for pleasure. And he'd never let a woman stay over. Until now.

Her raven-black hair spread over his arm and he couldn't resist putting his nose to the silky strands, inhaling the peach-scented shampoo as he waited for the answer to the question that invited shared confidences he wasn't sure he wanted to reciprocate. But what the hell? She'd pried more information out of him in the last few weeks than he'd ever released in years.

A little reciprocity didn't hurt.

She turned towards him and spoke in a low, quiet voice. 'Remember I told you he barely acknowledged my existence at first?'

He nodded.

'Over time, as I got older, that began to change. I noticed from the way he looked at me. I thought I was imagining it. Then I overheard the housekeeper saying something to my father's driver.'

'What did she say?'

'That my father didn't really believe I was his daughter. I couldn't be because I looked nothing like him—he has ash-blond hair and blue eyes. I inherited my mother's colouring. Between fourteen and fifteen, I shot up in height and grew breasts. I tried not to link that and the fact that he'd started entertaining more and more at his house instead of at his private club.'

Rafael's hand tightened into a fist out of her sight and he fought to maintain a regular breathing pattern as she continued.

'He encouraged me to stay up at the weekend, help him *host* his parties. When I refused, he got angry, but he didn't take his anger out on me. The housekeeper's son, who was the general handyman, got fired when my father saw me talking to him, then the gardener went, then his driver of fifteen years. I got the hint and decided to do as I was told. By the time I turned sixteen, he was entertaining a few nights during the week and most weekends, and the outfits he wanted me to wear to those parties got…skimpier.'

Rafael's sucked-in breath made her glance up, her eyes wary. Swiftly he kissed her and nudged her nose with his to continue. But the white-hot rage inside him blazed higher.

'I knew I had to do something. I asked for the housekeeper's help, even though I knew I was putting her livelihood in jeopardy. Luckily, she was willing to help. We forged my father's signature and got a DNA test done. When the results came I showed them to him. He was angry, of course, but he couldn't refute the evidence any longer.'

'And did things get better?'

She shrugged but Rafael knew the gesture was anything but uncaring. 'For a time, he reverted to his old, cold indifference. I was hoping he'd take his partying out of the house but they continued…'

Her lids descended and he saw her lips tremble. Spearing his fingers in her hair, he tilted her face until she was forced to look at him. Haunting memory lurked in the green depths. 'Raven, what happened?'

'His…his male friends began to take notice of me.'

'*Que diablos!*' He could no longer stem the tide of anger. Right that moment, he wanted nothing more than to track down her bastard of a father and drive his fist into the man's face. 'They didn't take it further than just noticing, did they?'

The longer she stayed silent, the harder his breathing got.

Ignoring the pain throbbing in his groin and hip, he hauled himself against the headboard and dragged her up. Tilting her jaw, he forced her to look into his eyes. 'Did they?'

Her lower lip trembled. 'One of them did. One day after a party, I thought everyone had left. He…he came into my room and tried to force himself on me. I'd started training at the gym so I knew a few moves. I managed to struggle free and kicked him where it hurt most.'

He passed his thumb over her lips until they stopped trembling. '*Bueno*. Good girl.'

'I ran out of my room. My father was waiting in the hallway. I thought he was coming to help me because he'd heard me scream. But he wasn't…'

Rafael's blood ran cold. 'What was he doing?'

'He knew exactly why his friend had come to my room. In fact, I don't think his friend could've found my room without help.' She shuddered and goose bumps raced over her arms. He pulled her close and wrapped his arms around her.

'Did you report it to the authorities?' he asked.

She shook her head. 'I'd reported him a few times in the past and been ignored. I knew once again it would be his word against mine. I bought a baseball bat and slept with it under my pillow instead and I moved out on my eighteenth birthday.'

'Where is he now?' He entertained thoughts of tracking down the bastard, wielding his own baseball bat.

'I hadn't spoken to him until I called him last year to help my mother but, the last I heard, he'd lost all his money in some Ponzi scheme and is living with his mistress somewhere in Scotland.'

Rafael filed that piece of information away. When she gave another shudder, he kissed her again, a little deeper this time. He made sure when she shuddered again minutes later it was with a different reaction, one that set his blood singing again.

On impulse, he got out of bed and tugged her upright.

'What are you doing?' she asked.

He went into his dressing room and came out with a dark blue T-shirt. 'Put that on.'

'Why? Where are we going?'

'You'll find out in a minute.' He pulled on his shorts and grabbed her hand.

Five minutes later, she pulled at his grip. 'No, I'm not going on there.' She dug her feet into the sand when he would've tumbled her onto the wide beach bed.

'Of course you are. You've been dying to try it since we

got here.' He set down the vintage champagne and flutes he'd grabbed from the kitchen.

'Rafael, it's the middle of the night,' she protested, although her glance slid to the white-canopied bed that gleamed under the moon and starlit night.

'Where's your sense of adventure?'

'Back upstairs, where it doesn't run the risk of being eaten by sharks.'

He let go of her hand and started uncorking the champagne. 'Unless sharks have developed a way of walking on sand, you'll have to come up with a better excuse.'

'I'm not wearing any knickers. I don't want to catch cold.'

His grin was utterly shameless. 'That's a very good reason.' He popped the cork, poured out a glass of golden liquid and handed it to her. Setting the bottle down, he shucked off his shorts and got onto the bed. Casting her a hot glance, he patted the space beside him. 'I'll be your body blanket. If I fail completely in my task you'll be free to return to the safety of my bed.'

He saw her battle for a response. But his insistent patting finally won through. The mixture of hunger, innocence and vulnerability on her face touched a part of him he'd long thought dead. When she set her glass down and slid into his arms, Rafael swore to make her forget everything about her bastard of a father. If only for a few hours.

Why taking on that task meant so much to him, he refused to consider.

He made love to her with a slow, leisurely tempo even though everything inside him clamoured for quick, fiery satisfaction.

When she came apart in his arms, he let himself be swept away into his own release. Sleep wasn't far behind and, gathering her close, he kissed her temple and pulled the cashmere blanket over them.

CHAPTER TEN

THE INTRUSION OF light behind her eyelids came with firm, warm lips brushing her jaw.

'Wake up, *querida*…'

'Hmm, no…don't want to…'

A soft deep laugh. 'Come on, wake up or you'll miss the sunrise.'

'Sun…no…' She wanted to stay just as she was, suspended between dream and reality, entranced by the sultry air on her face and hard, firm…aroused male curved around her.

'Open your eyes. I promise you, it's spectacular.'

She opened her eyes, simply because she couldn't resist him, and found herself gazing into deep blue eyes. Eyes she'd looked into many times. But still her heart caught as if it'd been tugged by a powerful string.

'*Buenos días*,' Rafael murmured. 'Look.' He nodded beyond the canopy to the east. She followed his gaze and froze at the sheer beauty of the gathering sunrise. Orange, yellow and blue where the light faded, it was nature at its most spectacular and she lay there, enfolded in Rafael's arms, silent and in complete awe as the sun spread its stunning rays across the sky.

'Wow,' she whispered.

'Indeed. Does that win me Brownie points?' he whispered hotly into her ear.

Turning from the sight, she looked again into mesmerising eyes. And once again she felt her heart stutter in awe.

'It depends what you intend to use the points for.'

'To get you to come yachting with me today. My yacht is moored at the Marina. We can take her out for the day.'

More alone time with Rafael. *Too much…too much…*

She should've heeded the screeching voice of caution. But

Raven had a feeling she was already too far gone. 'I'd love to. On one condition.'

He mock frowned. '*Condition*…my second least favourite word.'

'What's your least favourite?'

'*No.*'

She laughed. 'That figures. Well, I need to exercise. Then *you* need to have your session. Then we'll go yachting.'

With a quick, hard kiss, he released her and sat back. 'You can do your exercise right here on the beach.'

She felt heat rise. 'While you watch?'

'I'm a harmless audience. Besides, I want to see if this Krav Maga is worth all the hype.'

She bit her lip and hesitated.

'What?' he demanded.

'I…I'm not wearing any knickers, remember?'

His laugh was shameless and filled with predatory anticipation. 'Kinky Krav Maga…sounds even better.' He lounged back against the plump pillows, folded golden muscled arms and waited.

It was the hottest, most erotic exercise routine Raven had ever performed.

The rest of the day went like a dream. Rafael's yacht was the last word in luxury. With a crew of four, they sailed around the Los Cabos islands, stopped at a seafront restaurant for a lunch of cerviche and sweet potato fries, then sunbathed on the twenty-foot deck until it got too hot. Then he encouraged her to join him in the shower below deck.

She clung to him in the aftermath of another pulse-destroying orgasm.

'Hmm…I have a feeling you won't be needing my services for much longer.'

He raised his head from where he'd been kissing her damp shoulder and stared deep into her eyes. 'What makes you say that?'

'You haven't used your cane all day, and your…um…stamina seems to be endless.'

His frown was immediate, edged with tension that seeped into the atmosphere. 'You're signed on for another three months. Don't make any plans to break the contract just yet.' He moved away and grabbed two towels. He handed her one and wrapped the other around her waist, his movements jerky.

'I wasn't making plans. I was just commenting that your movements are a little more fluid. And you haven't used the cane all day today. I think it's a great sign. You should be pleased.'

'Should I?'

His icy tone made alarm skitter over her. 'What's the matter?'

He smoothed a hand over the steamed up mirror and met her gaze over his shoulder. 'Why should anything be wrong?'

'I've just given you the equivalent of an almost clean bill of health. You're reacting as if I've just told you your puppy has died.'

He whirled to face her. 'This clean bill of health, will it pass the X1 training board and see me reinstated as a race driver?'

Her breath caught. 'You're thinking of going back to racing?'

'You sound surprised.'

She licked her lips. 'Well, I am. I thought since Marco had sold the team, and Sasha had quit—'

'What are you saying, that I should follow the family tradition and quit while I'm ahead?'

'No…but—'

'You don't think I can hack it?'

'Stop putting words in my mouth, Rafael. You're almost done with phase three of the physio regime. I'm just trying to find out what your plans are so I can work with you to achieve them.'

He stalked to where she stood and gripped her nape in a

firm hold. His kiss was hot, ravaging and rage-tinged. 'Right now, my only plan is to be inside you again.'

She barely stopped herself from dissolving into a puddle of need. 'And afterwards? We can't stay here indefinitely, indulging in wall-to-wall shagging.'

His eyes narrowed, his grip tightening. 'Are you trying to set a time limit on what's happening between us? Is that what all this is about?'

The shard of steel that lodged in her chest made her breath catch. 'I don't know what you mean.'

'Don't you? From the start you've tried to manage what was happening between us, tried to define it into something you can deal with. Now you want to set a time limit on it so you can walk away once the time comes, *si*?'

'Are you saying you're not? Am I not just one more challenge to you? Can we please not delude ourselves into thinking this is anything more than sex?'

He sucked in a breath as if he'd been punched. Stepping back, he dropped his hand and left the bathroom.

Raven trailed after him into the large, exquisite gold and cream cabin. He was pulling on a pair of boxers, which he followed with cargo shorts and a white T-shirt.

Feeling exposed, she slipped on her underwear and the lilac flowered slip dress she'd worn to go sailing. 'I'm not sure what's going on here, Rafael. Or why you're annoyed with me. I may not know the rules of this sleeping together thing but even I know there is a time limit when it comes to your affairs—'

'*Affairs*? Is that what we're doing, having an affair?' he asked with a cocked eyebrow. 'How quaint.'

'Will you please stop mocking me and tell me what's really bothering you?'

He slammed the drawer he'd just opened none too gently. 'I don't like time limits. I don't being head-shrunk. And I don't like the woman I'm sleeping with hinting that she'll be leaving me the day after we start sleeping together. There, does that sum things up for you?'

'So you want to be the one to call the shots? To dictate when this aff…*liaison* starts and ends?'

He dragged a hand through his damp hair and glared at her. '*Santo cielo*, why are we even having this argument?' he shouted.

'I have no idea but you started it!' she yelled back.

His eyes widened at her tone, then he sighed. 'Forgive me, I'm used to having things my way, *pequeña*. You have every right to shout at me when I step out of line.'

'Thanks, I will.'

He laughed, and just like that the tension broke. Striding to her, he tugged her into his arms and proceeded to kiss the fight out of both of them. They sailed back to the villa shortly after and, once again, she let him coax her into spending part of the night on the beach bed.

They were halfway through their breakfast when the delivery arrived.

'What is it?'

'I've got something for you.' The gleam in his eyes was pure wickedness. Her heartbeat escalated as she eyed the large gold-ribboned package sitting on the floor beside their breakfast table.

'Don't worry, you'll enjoy it,' he promised with a smile so sexy, and so deliciously decadent, her toes curled.

Even though the subject quickly changed to their plans for the rest of the day, Raven's gaze strayed time and again to the package. But Rafael, as she'd discovered in the past two nights, was skilled in delayed gratification. He was also skilled in being the perfect host. She was stunned when she discovered how many details he'd picked up through their conversation. When he shepherded her towards the SUV mid-morning, she gaped in surprise when she found out he'd organised the hang-gliding trip she'd casually mentioned was on her list of things to do.

She'd barely descended from that high when he whisked her by helicopter to the Mayan encampment she'd been dying to explore.

'You're seriously scaring me now by how utterly close I am to adoring you for this,' she said in hushed tones as they were ushered into the hallowed grounds of the ancient burial site.

His breath hissed out. When she glanced at him, he'd paled a little.

'Rafael? Are you in pain?' He'd left his walking stick back at the villa and nothing from his gait told her he'd suffered a mishap. All the same…

He shook his head. A second later the look had disappeared. 'It's nothing.'

She stopped as the full import of her words struck her. Wide-eyed, she turned to him. 'No, I didn't mean…I was only joking…'

'Were you?' The intensity of his gaze pinned her where she stood.

'Yes! Ignore me, I'm babbling because you've made two dreams come true today.'

'So you don't adore me?'

She opened her mouth to refute the comment and found she couldn't speak. Because she realised she did adore him, and more than a little. The Rafael she'd come to know in the past few weeks had a depth she'd never got the chance to explore last year. She felt a connection to this Rafael, and not just because he'd been her first lover.

The depth of the feeling rampaging through her made her shake her head.

One corner of his mouth lifted in a mirthless smile. Then he nodded to the tour guide looking their way.

'Now that we've established that you *don't* adore me, I think you need to go see your artefacts.'

She felt a stab of disappointment. 'Aren't you coming?'

'Been there, done that.' He pulled the phone from his pocket. 'The drivers and cars arrive this afternoon. I need to return a few calls.' He walked away before she could reply.

Disappointment morphed into something else. Something she couldn't put her finger on but which confused the hell out of her. The more she tried to grasp it, the further away it slithered from her.

He was waiting when she finally emerged. Back in the helicopter, he pulled her close and sealed his lips over hers, his mouth hungry and demanding.

She was breathless when he finally pulled away. 'What was that for?' she asked huskily.

His lids swept down over his eyes. 'Maybe I want you to adore me, just a little.'

Rafael watched her breath catch all over again and wondered just what the hell he was doing. Why he was letting the angst riding underneath his skin get to him.

So she didn't adore him. Big deal. There were thousands of women out there who were more than willing to fall into his bed should he wish them to.

But none like the woman in his arms. None like the woman who refused to mould into a being he understood, could predict. Most women would be halfway to falling in love with him by now; would be secretly or not so secretly making plans on how to prolong their presence in his life.

When he wasn't kissing her breathless—a diversionary tactic he'd grown to enjoy immensely—Raven seemed to be counting the days, hell, the minutes until she could walk away from him.

The notion unsettled him enough to make him want to probe, to find an answer.

Had she glimpsed the darkness in his soul? Had opening up to her in Monaco and again in Monza made him into a man she could sleep with but not a man she wanted in her life for the long-term?

The long-term? Santa María. Had he finally lost all common sense? Certainly, reality had slid back these past two days. Being with her had been like living some sort of dream. A dream where he could look at himself in the mirror without being revolted by what stared back at him.

A dream where he could continue the secret writing project he'd started before his accident without feeling as if he was tainting the very memory he wanted to preserve.

He stared down into her face, a face flushed with pleasure from the activities of the day or, he thought semi-cockily, from kissing him. All at once he wanted to blurt his very innermost secret to her.

He stopped himself just in time.

Permanent wasn't part of his vocabulary. He wasn't about to seek it out now. And, really, he should thank his lucky stars because Raven knew his flaws and had adequately cautioned herself against getting too close.

So why did the thought not please him?

His phone rang and he happily abandoned the questions that threatened to flood him. But he didn't abandon his hold on the soft body of the woman next to him. Delight curled in his chest when she slid closer.

'De Cervantes,' he answered.

The conversation was short and succinct. And it raised every single hair on his nape to full, electrifying attention. Feeling slightly numb, he ended the call.

'What's happened?' she asked.

'One of the drivers has pulled out of the remaining races.'

'Can they do that, pull out without warning?'

He shook his head. 'I've never had a driver pull out before. Normally I have them begging to race.' She didn't miss the frown in his voice. 'But he's just been offered a race seat for the coming season and it's an opportunity of a lifetime. I recognise how important that is to a young driver.'

'So what does that mean for your event?' she asked, pulling back to stare up into his face.

He looked down but didn't really see her. The thoughts tumbling through his head both terrified and excited him at the same time.

'They can find a replacement if they search hard enough…'

Raven pulled away further. He wanted to tug her back but he couldn't seem to summon the strength it took because of the feelings rushing through him.

'Or?'

'Or…the general consensus is that I should step in.'

'No,' she said. Naked fear pulsed through the single word.

He finally focused on her, felt a burn in his stomach from the impact of her searing look. 'No?'

'You're not ready.'

'Shouldn't *I* be the judge of that? And didn't you say yourself I was almost healed?' he asked.

'Yes, *almost!* As your physiotherapist, I strongly do not recommend it. You could reverse everything you've achieved in the last several weeks…'

'If I crash?'

She paled a little, and he felt a tug of guilt for pushing her. 'I won't answer that. What I will say is that you're the head of X1 Premier Management. All you need to do is make a single phone call and any one of dozens of drivers will fly out and take your driver's place. You don't have to do this. *Please don't do it.*'

The naked plea in her eyes struck deep. The unsettling angst of a moment before subsided as he traced his finger down her face.

'Dare I believe that you care about me, just a little bit?' He couldn't stop the question from spilling out. But, once it was out there, he *needed* to know.

'I care, Rafael. More than a little bit, I think.' The naked truth struck them both. Their eyes met, locked.

Breaths held until the banking helicopter jolted them. The sight of the villa sprawled beneath them made Rafael want to swear. Instead he activated his phone again.

'Angelo—' he addressed his second-in-command '—call around the teams, find out if there's any driver who isn't testing and offer them a place on the newly available seat on the All-Star event. You know which guys I rate the most. Tell them they're guaranteed a spread in the next issue of *X1 Magazine* and my personal endorsement of whatever charity they choose. Oh, and I want a driver on his way to the racetrack in Los Cabos by the end of the day.' He ended the call and looked down at her.

'Now what?' he asked softly as the helicopter blades slowed to a halt.

Her smile held such radiance he found it hard to breathe. 'Now, I may let myself adore you a little bit more…see where it takes me.'

He regretted that he wasn't healed enough to swing her into his arms and carry her off to his lair. But he was well enough to drag her from the helicopter to his bedroom. And he made sure he kept her fully occupied until neither of them could move.

'You never told me what was in the package,' Raven murmured, drifting somewhere between *I-can't-move* satiation and a drugging need to experience that mind-bending pleasure all over again.

The wicked grin he sent her way made her heart pound all over again. He left the bed and she could no more help herself from visually devouring him than she could stop breathing.

He picked up the package from the foot of the bed and returned it to her. 'This may just buy me a few more Brownie points.'

That got her attention. She dragged herself up to lean on one elbow. The sight of his naked chest threatened to fry her brain cells. 'What is it?' Her mind whirled with the possibilities, then latched onto what she wanted it to be. Could it be the rest of his manuscript?

Her senses now on a high, she stared down at the box,

feeling like a kid on Christmas morning. 'What's in the box, Rafael?'

He lifted the lid. All she could see were sheaves of wrapping paper. 'See for yourself.'

Carefully, she lifted the sheer paper. The first items made her heart knock in her chest. And not in a good way. Praying she was dreaming, she nudged the material aside with her finger and looked underneath. Each layer held more of the same.

'Naughty underwear? *That's* what you got me?' Raven let the garments drop back into the box, unable to stem the cold wave of hurt that washed over her. She wasn't even sure why it hurt so much. But it felt as if she'd climbed a mountain only to look back and find out that she'd only taken a few steps.

He looked genuinely stunned. 'You don't like it?'

'What's wrong with my own underwear?'

His perplexed look deepened. For the first time, Rafael looked seriously nonplussed. It would have been funny had it not been so far from funny.

'I didn't…I just wanted to…' He stopped, a flush lighting his high cheekbones.

If someone had told her as little as a week ago that she'd be sitting in bed discussing naughty lingerie with Rafael, she'd have laughed herself blind.

Now, she forced herself to glance at the lacy silks and delicate satin bows that didn't seem as if they would stand up to any overt pressure.

'That's not even my size, Rafael. I'm a size twelve, remember?'

His flush deepened. 'I have a feeling you'll punch me when I tell you I don't have a clue what size underwear you wear or what yours look like. By the time I get to your panties, I'm nearly insane with lust. Damn it. I've got it spectacularly wrong, haven't I?'

'Not all wrong. You got my favourite colours right.'

He picked up the package and flung it across the room.

Then he tugged her close. 'Is there any way I can make you forget the last ten minutes?'

Against her will and certainly against her better judgement, she glanced at the lilac silk material caught over a chair back. It seemed so delicate and forlorn.

'I don't need expensive lingerie to feel sexy. If you don't want me as I am—'

He caught her chin between his fingers. 'I do,' he breathed. 'Let me prove it…' His head started to descend.

Raven's gaze swung once more to the basque. Pulling herself from his arms, she walked, naked, to the garment and plucked it off the chair. Carefully, she rubbed the material between her fingers and turned. Rafael's breath caught as she slowly traced the warm silk over her body.

A glance from beneath her lashes showed a definite effect on him.

Pure feminine power washed away her misgivings. With a wanton smile she'd never have believed herself capable of, she sauntered back towards him.

'You need to understand one thing, Rafael.'

He nodded but his eyes were riveted on her breasts. '*Si*?'

'You promise never to buy me lingerie again as long as we're together. I choose my own underwear.'

He swallowed and nodded.

Raven glanced down at the panties and shook her head. 'I can't believe you thought I was a size eight,' she muttered.

'*Por favor!* Forgive me.' He wet his lips in such a blatantly sexual way, a blush suffused her whole body.

'You're just saying that so I hurry back to bed.'

'*Si*. And you can forget the lingerie if you wish.'

'And give up the chance to see you sweat. No can do.' She slowly, deliberately swept her hair to one side before sliding the lace-trimmed garment over her head.

She nearly bottled it then, but the scorching intensity in his eyes had the direct effect of firing up her courage. The soft lilac tulle basque hugged her breasts in such a blatant caress, she bit her lower lip to stop a moan of excitement. She turned, then glanced back over her shoulder.

'Are you going to help me with the laces?' she rasped.

'*Dios mío*, what are you trying to do?'

'Teach you a lesson.'

He got off the bed, almost a little too eager for his punishment. 'Turn around,' he instructed.

She did, and heard him hiss out a breath as he pulled the delicate laces and tied it.

'Once again, I have no knickers.'

His moan was a heartfelt balm to her soul.

Turning, she placed her hands on her hips, feminine power fuelling her desire as she saw her effect on him.

When he stumbled back and sank onto the side of the bed, she laughed. 'Hoisted by your own petard, Rafael?'

She took a step towards him and gloried in the slide of the silk on her skin. She would never don anything like this again. Naughty lingerie wasn't really her style but, just for tonight, she would allow herself this experience.

His face was strained like the steely erection that jutted from between his legs. Heat oozed between her thighs, made her movements slow as the magnetic force between them pulled her inexorably into his orbit.

When she reached him, she raked her fingers down his chest. 'You won't see me like this again, Rafael, so look your fill.'

His features altered, a look of regret passing through his eyes that made her stomach hollow out. 'You're breathtaking without it, Raven. How can I make this up to you?'

Her heart thundered at the sincerity in his voice. 'You don't need to. Just see me as I am.'

He inhaled, long and deep, and dropped his head between her breasts. For a long moment, Raven held him close. Then his breathing altered. Hers followed as lust sizzled, rose to the fore once more.

She pushed him back on the bed and climbed on top of him. By the time he donned the condom, they were both nearly insane with need. She'd barely positioned her thighs on either side of him when he thrust hard and deep inside her. Raven lost all coherent thought.

In the sizzling, excruciatingly heady aftermath, she curled into him but found she couldn't breathe, even after his deft fingers pulled the basque from her body and flung it away. She'd always known that Rafael's dominance was larger than life. But she'd trusted herself not to get pulled into his devastating, fast-spinning orbit. Her emotions were fast skittering out of control. How long had she watched her mother experience the same devastation over and over? Now she was running the same risk—

'What is it?' he demanded, his intuitiveness almost scary.

'Nothing…' she started to say, then stopped. 'How many times have you done this?' she blurted.

'I think I definitely need a definition of *this,* otherwise I'll have to plead the fifth.'

'Bought risqué underwear for a woman?'

His lids dropped for a second before rising to spear her with that intense blue. 'Never.'

Her snort was borne of disbelief and a sharp pang she didn't want to touch with a dozen bargepoles. She shook her head and started to move away.

He caught her back easily. A shiver ran through her when his finger slid under her chin and tilted her head up. Almost afraid, she looked into his eyes.

'I've never lied to you, Raven. I'm skilled in evading subjects I don't wish to discuss, but I have never and will never lie to you. Understood?'

She was stunned by how much she wanted to believe him, how much she wanted to be the first at something in his life. 'Why haven't you done this before?'

Surprise flared in his eyes. 'You're asking me why I haven't bought lingerie for a woman before?'

She pursed her lips. 'It seems the kind of thing ruthless playboys specialise in.'

His own lips flattened at the label, then he shrugged and relaxed onto the pillows. 'Not specialise. I have knowledge of it because I'm always the recipient. The assumption has always been that I would prefer the bedroom unveiling to be a knock-my-brains-out surprise, not a joint enterprise. I haven't felt the inclination to alter that assumption.'

A small fizz of pleasure started in her belly. Which was really foolish because she knew this particular experiment had been a means to an end for him.

Unwilling to face up to what all this meant, she buried her face in his neck. 'I'm glad.'

'Enough to forgive my grievous error?'

'That depends.'

'On?'

'On whether you'll give me what I expected to find in the box when I opened it.' She told him.

Another peculiar look crossed his face. 'The story has reached a crossroads.'

'Are you saying I did all of that for nothing?'

He pushed her firmly onto her back and leaned his powerful, endlessly intoxicating body over hers. Unable to resist, she let her hands wander at will over smooth muscle.

'For nothing? No, *bonita*, it was most definitely not for nothing. I think you could be the key to unlocking everything.'

Although she went into his arms at his urging, Raven sensed he wasn't as in control as he made out. She'd heard a different note in his voice—part vulnerability, part bravado. She slid her hand up and down his back in a strong need to comfort him. The persistent voice that had cautioned against getting too deep was receding—almost as if it knew the path she'd chosen. She would live in this fantasy now.

This magic, this overwhelming sense that she was exactly

where she wanted to be, was too great to deny. Reality would encroach soon enough.

So where was the harm in experiencing it for a little while longer?

CHAPTER ELEVEN

IT TURNED OUT a little while was all she would get.

Things started to go wrong the moment the helicopter touched down at the Autódromo Hermanos Rodríguez in Mexico City the next morning. The replacement driver Angelo had lined up didn't turn up. As the day went on with no immediate solution, Raven felt the pressure mount as everyone turned to Rafael for a solution.

Even though this was primarily a charity event, high profile sponsors had channelled millions of euros into it in the hope of gaining maximum exposure, courtesy of the sold-out events. Racing five cars instead of the usual six would make the headlines and throw negative publicity on the event—something X1 Premier Management and Rafael in particular couldn't afford to let happen.

Already the paparazzi, sensing blood in the water, were sniffing around, cameras and microphones poised to capture any salacious gossip.

She recalled how they'd decimated Sasha de Cervantes and her gut churned at the thought of what that type of publicity could do to Rafael.

As if she'd conjured him up, Rafael walked past the window, his pace carrying him from one end of the air-conditioned VIP lounge to the other, his gait remarkably improved despite the physical stress she'd put on his body in the last three days.

Feeling a blush creep up her face, she glanced away before he or any of the other management team hastily assembled for the meeting could guess at her thoughts.

Angelo, Rafael's assistant, approached him, a phone in his

hand. Rafael listened for several seconds, his tension increasing with each breath he took.

'Tell him if he threatens me with a lawsuit one more time, I'll personally see to it that his brand of vodka never leaves the icy wilderness of Siberia...*bueno*, I'm pleased you're finally seeing things my way. We will find a driver, and your logo will be emblazoned on the side pod just as we agreed.'

He hung up, glanced around the room and caught a few nervous gazes. 'They want to play dirty; I'm more than happy to oblige.'

A three-time world champion, now in his early sixties, cleared his throat. 'The race starts in three hours. I don't see that we have much of a choice here. You all but agreed to step in two days ago when we were a driver short. I'm not sure what changed your mind but perhaps you'd revisit the idea of racing?'

Raven half rose out of her seat, the scrape of her chair on the tiled floor drawing attention from the rest of the room.

She collapsed back into her seat when Rafael's fierce gaze settled on her. When the quick shake of her head didn't seem to register, she cleared her throat.

His eyes narrowed. Then he turned, slowly, deliberately away from her.

A block of ice wedged in her chest and her stomach hollowed out. From very far away, she heard him address the race coordinator and chief engineer of the driverless team.

'I have a couple of spare seats around here somewhere. Angelo will arrange to supply you with one to fit into the car. I'll be along in ten minutes to go over race strategy with you.' He looked around the room, the devil's own grin spreading over his face. 'Gentlemen, let's go racing.'

The explosion of excitement that burst through the room drowned out her horrified gasp. Manly slaps of his shoulder and offers of congratulations echoed through her numb senses.

When someone suggested a quick press conference, Raven

finally found the strength to stand and approach him as the room emptied.

'R...Rafael, can I talk to you?'

'Now is not a good time, *bonita*.' His voice was brusque to the point of rudeness.

The endearment she was beginning to adore suddenly grated. But she refused to be dismissed. 'I think this is a bad idea.'

'*Sí*, I knew you would think so. But I can't help what you think. Needs must and I stand to become embroiled in all sorts of legal wrangling if this isn't sorted out.'

She frowned. 'But it was the driver who broke the contract. Isn't he liable?'

'No, he isn't. XPM is staging this event, so I'm responsible. I should've taken more time to ensure contingencies were in place before we arrived. Everyone here knows someone's dropped the ball. Unfortunately, they're looking at me to pick it up and run with it.' He was the hard businessman, the ruthless racer who'd held a finite edge over his competitors for years.

He was certainly nothing like the lover who'd taken her to the heights of ecstasy.

She fought to regain her own professionalism, to put aside the hurt splintering her insides. 'As your physiotherapist, I'll have to recommend that you don't race.'

'Your recommendation is duly noted. Is that all?'

Her fists clenched in futile anger. Anger she wanted to let loose but couldn't. Her days of lashing out were far, far behind her. 'No, that's not all! This is crazy. You're risking your health, not to mention your life, Rafael.'

His smile was tight and tension-filled. 'And *you* are running the risk of overstepping, *querida*. I won't be tacky enough to point out just what your role is in my life considering the lines have been blurred somewhat, but I expect you to recognise the proper time and place for voicing disagreement.'

The blunt words hit her like a slap in the face. Regret momentarily tightened his face, then it smoothed once again into the outward mask of almost bored indifference.

It took every ounce of self-control to contain her composure. 'No, you're right. Pardon me for thinking of your health first.' She indicated the frenzy outside, the racetrack and the baking heat under which the cars gleamed. 'Off you go, then. And good luck.'

He reached forward and grabbed her arm when she'd have turned away.

'Aren't you forgetting something?'

'What?' She made herself look into his eyes, determined not to be cowed by the storm of fear rolling through her gut. He returned her look with one that momentarily confused her. Had her thoughts been clearer, Raven would've sworn Rafael was scared out of his wits.

'As my physio, you need to come with me, attend to my needs until I'm in the cockpit. Have you forgotten your role already?'

She had. Whether intentionally or through mental blockage, she'd tried to put her role eight months ago as Rafael's race physio out of her mind. Because every time she thought of it, she remembered their last row. Her rash, heated words; the stunned look on his face as he'd absorbed her bone-stripping insults before he'd walked out to his car. They'd been in a situation like this, momentarily alone in a place that buzzed with suppressed energy. His race suit had been open and around his neck she'd spied his customary chain with the cross on it. The cross he kissed before each race.

In the months since, she'd remembered vividly that Rafael hadn't kissed his cross that day...

Now, Raven was in favour of forgetting all about it. All she wanted to do right now was find a dark corner, stay there and not come out until the blasted race was over. Watching his crash that day had been one of the most heart-wrenching experiences of her life. She would give anything not to be put in that position again.

But she had a job to do. Sucking a sustaining breath, she nodded. 'Of course, whatever you need.' Pulling herself from his grasp, she walked towards the bar and picked up two bottles of mineral water. She handed him one. 'We're a little late off the mark in trying to hydrate you sufficiently so I'd suggest you get as much liquid in as possible.'

He took the bottle from her but made no move to drink the water.

'You think I'm making the wrong decision.' It wasn't a question.

'What I think is no longer relevant, remember?' Her gaze dropped meaningfully to the bottle.

He uncapped it and drank without taking his gaze off her face. She felt the heavy force of his stare but studiously avoided eye contact. When he finished and tossed the empty bottle aside, she handed him the second bottle.

'Drink this one in about ten minutes.' She started to walk towards the door, eager to get away from the clamouring need to throw herself in his path, to stop him putting himself in any danger.

Too late, she realised the media had camped outside the door, eager to jump on the latest news of Rafael's return.

Is this the start of your comeback?

Are you sure you can take the pressure?

Which team will you be driving for when the X1 season starts next month?

Rafael fielded their questions without breaking a sweat, all the while keeping a firm hold on her elbow. Every time she tried to free herself, he held on tighter.

Raven spotted the keen reporter from the corner of her eye.

Is there a new woman in your life?

Without the barest hint of affront, he smiled. 'If I told you that you'd stop hounding me, then my life would no longer be worth living, would it?'

The paparazzi, normally a vicious thrill-seeking lot, actually laughed. Raven marvelled at the spectacle. Then berated herself for failing to realise the obvious. Sooner or later, everyone, man, woman or child, fell under Rafael's uniquely enthralling spell.

She'd fooled herself into believing she could fall only a little, that she could go only so far before, wisely and safely, she pulled back from the dizzying precipice.

How wrong she'd been. Wasn't she right now experiencing the very depths of hell because she couldn't stand the thought of him being hurt again?

Hadn't she spent half the night awake, her stomach tied in knots as she'd wondered why so beautiful a man suffered tortured dreams because of his choices and his determination to shut everyone out?

She hadn't missed the phone calls from his father that he'd avoided, or the one from Marco yesterday that he'd swiftly ended when she entered the room.

Pain stabbed deep as she acknowledged that she'd come to adore him just a little bit more than she'd planned to. She'd probably started adoring him the moment he'd answered her call and agreed to see her in Barcelona seven weeks ago.

Because by allowing her in just that little bit meant he didn't hate her as much as he should. Or maybe he didn't hate her at all.

Or maybe she was deluding herself.

'A three-line frown. Stop it or I'll have to do something drastic, like confirm to them just who the new woman in my life is. Personally, I don't mind drastic but I have a feeling you wouldn't enjoy being eaten alive by the paparazzi.'

She'd been walking alongside him without conscious thought as to where they were going. The sound of the engine revving made her jump. 'No, I wouldn't.'

'*Bueno*, then behave.'

They'd arrived at the garage of the defected racer. Rafael grabbed the nearest sound-cancelling headphones and passed them to her.

She was about to put them on when she spotted Chantilly,

lounging with a bored look on her face on the other side of the garage. The second she spotted Rafael, she came to vivacious life.

'Damn it, your frown just deepened. What did I say about behaving?'

'What's she doing here? In this garage, I mean?'

Rafael followed her gaze to Chantilly, then glanced back at her. 'Her husband owns this team.'

The single swear word escaped before she could stop it. A slow grin spread over Rafael's face but it didn't pack the same charismatic punch as it usually did. Examining him closer, she noted the lines of strain around his mouth.

'Sheath your claws, *chiquita*. I told you, I have no interest in her. Not after discovering the delights of fresh English roses.' A pulse of heat from his eyes calmed her somewhat but it was gone far too quickly for her to feel its warmth.

The chief engineer called out for Rafael and, with another haunted look down at her, he went over to discuss telemetry reports with the team.

The ninety minutes before the race passed with excruciating slowness. With every second that counted down, Raven's insides knotted harder. The walk across the sun-baked pit lane into the race lane felt like walking the most terrifying gauntlet.

She hitched the emergency bag higher on her shoulder and took her place beside Rafael's car, making sure to keep the umbrella above his head to protect his suit-clad body from overheating. She ignored the sweat trickling down her own back to check for signs of distress on him.

'If you feel your hip tightening, try those pelvic rotations we practised by flexing your spine. I know you don't have much room in the cockpit but give it a try anyway,' she said, trying desperately to hang on to a modicum of professionalism.

He nodded but didn't look up. His attention was fixed on the dials on his steering wheel. When the first red light flashed on, signalling it was time to clear the track, Raven opened her mouth to say something...anything, but her throat had closed up.

She took one step back, and another.

'Rafael...' she whispered.

His head swung towards her, ice-blue eyes capturing hers for a single naked second.

The stark emptiness in his eyes made her heart freeze over.

Rafael fought to regulate his breathing. Shards of memories pierced his mind, drenching his spine and palms in cold sweat.

His fight with Marco the night before the Hungary race...

You're dishonouring Mamá's memory by continuing with this reckless behaviour...

Sasha's voice joined the clamouring...*it's not okay for you to let everyone think you're a bastard.*

And Raven's condemning truth...*you're a useless waste of space...who cares about nothing but himself and his own vacuous pleasures...*

He tried to clear his mind but he knew it wouldn't be that easy. Those words had carried him into that near fatal corner that day in Hungary because he'd known they all spoke the truth. What they hadn't known was that the day had held another meaning for him. It was emblazoned into his memory like a hot iron brand.

That day in Hungary had been exactly eight years to the day he'd charmed his mother into the ride that had ended her life...the day he'd let partying too hard snuff out a life he'd now happily give his own to have returned.

Looking into Raven's eyes just now, he'd known she was recalling her words, too; he'd seen the naked fear and remorse in her eyes. But he hadn't been able to offer reassurance.

How could he, when he knew deep down she was right? Since his mother's death, he'd lived in the special place in hell he'd reserved for himself. That *no trespassing* place where no one and nothing was allowed to touch him.

It was a place he planned on staying...

No matter how horrifyingly lonely…

His gaze darted to the lights as they lit up. Jaw tight, he tried to empty his mind of all thought, but her face kept intruding…her pleading eyes boring into his ravaged soul despite every effort to block her out.

Que diablos!

He stepped on the accelerator a touch later than he'd planned and cursed again as Axel Jung and Matteo, the teenage driver, shot past him on either side. Even in a showcase event like this one, a fraction of a second was all it took to fall behind.

Adrenaline and age-old reflexes kicked in but Rafael knew he was already at a disadvantage. He eyed the gap to the right on the second corner, and calculated that he could slot himself in there if he was quick enough. He pressed his foot down and felt his pulse jump when Axel, in a bid to cut him off, positioned himself in front of him.

In a move he'd perfected long before he'd been tall enough to fit into an X1 cockpit, he flicked his wrist and dashed down the left side of the track. Too late, Axel tried to cover his mistake but Rafael was already a nose ahead of the German. From the corner of his eye, he saw the other driver flick him a dirty gesture.

Where normally he'd have grinned with delight behind his helmet, Rafael merely gestured back and pressed down even harder on the accelerator, desperately trying to outrun his demons the way he had that day in Hungary.

You're not all bad…

Yes, he was. Even his father looked at him with pity and sadness.

His father…the man he'd put in a wheelchair. The man who kept calling and leaving him messages because Rafael was too afraid…too ashamed to talk to him.

The car shot forward faster. Inside his helmet, his race engineer's voice cautioned him on the upcoming bend. The words barely registered before disappearing under the heavy weight of his thoughts. He took the bend without lifting off the throttle or easing back on his speed.

He heard the muted roar of the appreciative crowd but the spark of excitement he'd expected from the recognition that he was still in fine racing form, that his accident hadn't made him lose what was most important to him, didn't manifest.

That was when the panic started.

For as long as he could recall, that excitement had been present. No matter what else was going on in his life, racing was the one thing that had always...*always* given him a thrill, given him a reason to push forward.

Fear clutched his chest as he searched for and found only emptiness. In front of him, Matteo had made a mistake that had cost him a few milliseconds, bringing Rafael into passing distance of him.

He could pass him, using the same move he'd used in Hungary. He had nothing to lose. The grin that spread over his face felt alien yet oddly calming, as did the black haze that started to wash over his eyes.

He had nothing to lose...

'Rafael, your liquid level readings show you haven't taken a drink in the last thirty minutes.'

Her voice...husky, low, and filled with fearful apprehension, shot into his head with the power of a thunderclap. He gasped as he felt himself yanked back from the edge, from the dark abyss he'd been staring into.

For a single second, he hated her for intruding.

'Rafael?'

Sucking in a breath, he glanced up and realised Matteo had regained his speed and was streaking ahead. And still, Rafael felt...nothing.

'Rafael, please respond.' A shaky plea.

He didn't, because he couldn't speak, but he took a drink and kept his foot on the pedal until the race was over.

The shoulder slaps of congratulations for coming in second washed right over him. On the podium, he smiled, congratulated Axel and even felt a little spurt of pride when Matteo took the top step, but all through it he was numb.

The moment he stepped off the podium, he ripped off his race suit. He brushed away the engineer's request for a post race analysis, his every sense shrieking warning of imminent disaster.

He rushed out of the garage, for the first time in his life ignoring the media pen, the paparazzi and news anchors who raced after him for a sound bite.

Relief rushed through him as he entered his motor home and slammed the door shut behind him.

'Rafael?'

Dios mío. Had he lost it so completely he was now hearing her voice in his head? Bile surged through his stomach and leapt into his throat. He barely made it to the bathroom before he retched with a violence that made his eyes water.

For several minutes he hunched over the bowl, feelings coursing through him that he couldn't name. No…he knew what those feelings were, it was just that he'd never allowed them room in his life.

He was a racing driver. Racing was his lifeblood. Therefore he had no room for despair or fear. He was used to success, to adrenaline-fuelled excitement. To pride and satisfaction in what he did. So why the hell was he puking his guts out while fear churned through his veins?

Because, *diablo*, he *had* finally parted ways with reality.

With a stark laugh and a shake of his head, he cleaned up after himself, rinsed his mouth thoroughly…

And turned to find Raven in the doorway, her face deathly pale and her gorgeous eyes wide with panic.

'*Madre de dios.* What the hell are you doing here?'

CHAPTER TWELVE

'ARE YOU ALL right?' Raven asked, making a small movement forward.

Rafael instinctively stepped back from her. If she touched him, she would know. And whatever else he was...*or wasn't*, the last thing he wanted Raven Blass, this infuriatingly bright, mind-bendingly sexy woman, to see was his fear.

He took another step back, feeling more exposed than he'd ever felt in his life.

The water he'd splashed over his face chilled his skin. 'Am I all right? Sure. I puke my guts out after every race. Didn't you know that?'

'No you don't.' She took another step closer and, instantly, another more urgent need surged to the fore. The need to grab her, plaster her warm, giving body against his, use her to stem the tide of icy numbness spreading over him.

Use her...

Bile threatened to rise again and he swallowed hard. He stepped past her, entered the bedroom and started to undress.

'Tell me what's wrong.'

Rafael glanced down at his hands and realised they were shaking. The realisation stunned him so completely, his whole body shuddered before he could control himself. The idea that he was losing control so completely, so unstoppably, made irrational anger whip up inside him.

'Stop it, Raven. Stop trying to save me. You've done your penance.'

'Excuse me?' Her voice was hushed but strong.

'That's what you've wanted since you phoned me up two months ago, isn't it? To hear that I forgive you for what you think you did to cause my accident?'

'What I think…' She sucked in a sharp breath. 'Are you saying you remember why you crashed?'

He firmed his lips. *Brava*, Rafael. 'Perhaps I do. Or perhaps I'm just tired of watching you fall on your sword over and over again. I wouldn't be surprised if that was why you gave me your virginity, considering you didn't like me much before then.'

He felt like the lowest form of life when her colour receded completely. But, *dios*, admiringly she rallied.

'You're trying to push me away by being hateful. But I won't leave until you tell me what happened out there today.'

'What do you mean, what happened? I raced. I came second. Considering I've been out of the game for nearly a year, I think that's a commendable start, don't you?'

He shucked his suit and peeled off the fire-retardant long-sleeved gear. Her eyes darkened but she didn't lose her determination.

'Aside from the fact that you didn't hydrate nearly enough, why did you not pass Matteo the half a dozen times you had the chance?'

'What are you talking about? After he recovered his mistake in Sector 4 there was never a chance to pass Matteo…'

'Of course there was. He damaged his front wing when he went too close to the pit wall on his exit but you stayed behind him when you could've passed. And many times you came close to passing him but you pulled back every time. Your race engineer tried to talk to you but you didn't respond.'

He froze, scrambled around to supply the adequate information to refute her words and came up blank. Panic cloaked his skin, sank its claws deeper into him.

'Are you saying you don't remember?' she almost whispered, her voice thick with emotion.

Rafael couldn't breathe. 'I…no, I don't remember.'

The black haze crowded his mind, encroaching rapidly with each excruciating second. He knew he was in deep trouble when he didn't stop her from touching him, from pulling him down to sit on the king-sized bed.

'Rafael, you're freezing. And you're shaking!'

His laugh was hollow. '*Sí.* In case you haven't guessed yet, *querida*, I'm a hot mess right now.'

'Oh God!' She threw her arms around him, her warm hands pressing into his skin.

Another series of shudders raked through him, setting his teeth chattering. Her fingers speared through his hair, pulling him down into the crook of her neck. He wanted to move, *needed* to move. But he stayed right where he was, selfishly absorbing her warmth, her heady scent, inhaling her very essence as if that would save him. But nothing could save him. He was beyond redemption in more ways than he could count.

Blanking out behind the wheel had cemented the realisation.

And still he found himself leaning into her, his lips finding that soft, sweet spot below her ear lobe where he knew she loved to be kissed. He kissed it, felt her try to shift away, and trapped her in his arms.

'Rafael…'

He trailed his mouth down her neck, to the pulse that jumped when he flicked his tongue against it.

The shaking receded a little, the numbness fading under the pulse of seductive heat that was all Raven. Greedily, he tried to grab onto it, to delay the encroaching darkness beneath the bliss of her touch. With a deep groan, he moved to cup her breasts.

Only to fall into a deeper hell when she pulled away and rushed to her feet.

'Sex isn't going to make this problem go away.'

Darkness prowled closer. 'I know, but a guy can still dream, can't he?'

'No, it's time for reality. We need to discuss what happened. When I saw you throwing up, I thought it was a panic attack. But I think it's more than that,' she said.

Ice snapped through him, freezing him once more to the soul. 'Leave it, Raven.'

'No, you need help, Rafael.'

He couldn't hold her gaze—she saw far too much—so he concentrated on his clenched fists. 'And you think you're the one to offer that help?'

He knew his tone was unduly harsh but he had gone beyond remorse. He was in his special frozen place.

'What happened?' Her voice pleaded for understanding.

Since he was at a loss himself, he contemplated silence. Then he contemplated seduction. When bile threatened, he contemplated pleading for mercy.

Through frozen lips, he found himself speaking. 'I remembered everything about the race in Hungary.'

He looked up to see her hands fly to her lips. He gave a grim smile and stared back down at his hands. Hands that shook uncontrollably.

'You know what I remember most about it?'

She shook her head.

'As I went to the wall, I knew, no matter what happened, no matter how hard I tried, I wasn't going to die.'

'You mean you...*wanted* to die?' Horror coated her words.

He shrugged. 'It doesn't matter what I wanted. I knew it wasn't going to happen. My expertise lies in many other areas. Killing myself isn't one of them.'

'I don't... Explain, please.'

He raised his head, took in her tall, proud figure and felt a moment of regret that he'd messed this up too. She was one thing he'd have fought to hang on to, if it hadn't been too late for him.

'I've been dicing with death since I was old enough to walk. If a situation has an element of danger, I'm there. Being born with racing imprinted into my DNA was just a bonus.'

'Even if it ends up consuming you so thoroughly it kills you?'

The look that came over his face was so gut-wrenchingly

stark she felt pain resonate inside her. 'Sorry, I didn't mean it like that—'

He shook his head. 'I won't die from racing.'

'Are you retiring?'

He dashed the hope in her question. 'No. Regardless of everything that's happened, I still crave it. I've been spared death so far. It seems I'm destined for other things.'

A frown formed. 'What do you mean?'

'Haven't you guessed it yet? My skill lies in killing everything I come into contact with. If you haven't woken to the fact that all I'll bring to your doorstep is utter chaos then you're not as bright as I thought.'

'That sounds like…are you trying to warn me off you?'

He laughed. '*Sí*, I am. Which in itself is strange. Normally, I just take what I want and leave the husk behind.'

Pain darkened her eyes. 'Why are you doing this?'

'Doing what, *querida*?'

'Trying to belittle what we have, and don't use that endearment any more. It's a beautiful word you've made tacky because you don't really mean it. You're trying to paint yourself in a vile light, trying to put me off you so I'll walk away.'

'I'm not *trying*. I'm telling you I'm not a great bet for you. I always escape unscathed but everyone I come into contact with sooner or later suffers for it.'

'You make yourself sound as if you've got a contagious disease. Stop it. And no one suffered today. You still need to address exactly what happened during the race but no one had an accident.'

'That's where you're wrong. At the start, when I realised I was getting squeezed out, I contemplated a move that would've taken Matteo out. For a moment, I forgot that I was supposed to be his teacher. I forgot the reason I'm staging the All-Star event in the first place. In that cockpit, I was just a racer, programmed to win.'

'But isn't that what racers do?'

'He's only nineteen, Raven! And I came within a whisker

of taking him out. Do you know his mother is here today? Can you imagine how devastated she'd have been if I'd crossed that line?'

'But you didn't cross it. You pulled back before you did any damage.'

'Yeah, and you know how I felt? Nothing. No remorse, no victory, no sympathy. I felt nothing.'

'Because there was something else going on. You say you remembered your crash in Hungary but then you blanked out the rest of the race. That could be a form of PTSD.'

He raked a hand through his hair. '*Santo cielo!* Stop trying to make excuses for me. Stop trying to make me the sort of man you'll fall for. There is nothing beneath this shell.'

Raven's heart lurched, then thundered so hard she was surprised it didn't burst out of her chest. Surprised she managed to keep breathing, to keep standing upright despite the knee-weakening realisation that it was too late.

She had fallen hard. So very, very hard for Rafael.

'And if I don't fall in with your plan to drive me away? You know me well enough by now to know I'm no pushover.'

He speared her with a vicious look meant to flay the skin from her flesh, and maybe a few weeks ago she'd have heeded the warning, but she'd found, when it came to Rafael, she was made of sterner stuff than that.

'No, but I'm a complete bastard when I'm pushed to the edge, *chiquita*. Are you prepared for that?' he parried.

'You'll have to do more than throw words at me. I *know* you, Rafael. I see beyond your so-called shell. And I know, despite what you say, you love your family and would do anything for them. I also know that you're pissed off right now because you're terrified of what's happening with you. But I'm not walking away, no matter how much you try to push me. I won't let you.'

Anger hissed through his teeth. Rising from the bed, he stalked, albeit with a barely visible limp, to the drawer that held his clothes and pulled it open. 'A few days ago, you were counting the days until this thing between us ended. Now I'm trying to end it and you've suddenly gone ostrich on me?' He returned with a handful of clothes.

'I'm not burying my head in the sand—far from it. I'm trying to understand. What have you done that's so viciously cruel that you think I'll walk away from you?'

He froze before her, his whole body stiffening into marble stillness. Only his lips moved, but even then no words emerged.

A chord of fear struck her. 'Rafael?'

'What does your mother mean to you?' he rasped.

Although she wondered at the change of subject, her answer was immediate. 'Everything. She's the only family I have. She may think I'm her enemy half the time because she doesn't want to be where she is, and she may blame me some of the time, imagining I'm the reason my father doesn't want her, but the times she's lucid, she's a wonderful human being and I love her unconditionally, regardless of what persona she is on any given day. The thought of her, safe and a phone call away, makes me happy. I'll do anything for her…' Her words drifted to nothing when she saw the look on his face. He'd grown paler with each word she'd uttered, the jeans he'd pulled from the drawer crushed in his vice-like grip. His face, hewn from a mask of pain so visceral, made her step towards him.

He stepped back swiftly, evoking a vivid image of carrying the contagion she'd accused him of seconds ago.

'Well, stay away from me, then, and enjoy that luxury. Because once you have me in your life, you may not have her for long.' His voice came from far away, as if from the shell he'd referred to moments ago.

'What on earth are you talking about?'

'You know I put my father in a wheelchair eight years ago. But, even before that, my life was on a slippery downward slope.'

'You've let yourself suffer enough. You have to learn to forgive yourself, Rafael.'

His head went back as if she'd struck him. 'Forgive myself? For not only crippling my own father but for taking away the one person he treasured the most?'

'What did you do?'

'*I killed my mother*, Raven. I put her in my car, drove too fast into a sharp corner and executed a perfect somersault that snuffed her out within minutes.'

The horror that engulfed her had nothing to do with his emotionless recounting of events. No, the dismay that rocked through her stemmed from knowing just how much more he'd suffered, how he'd buried it all under the perfect front.

His laugh was a harsh, cruel sound. 'Now that's more like it. That look of horror is what I expect. Maybe now you'll listen to me when I suggest you stay away from me.'

He pulled on his jeans, fished out a black polo shirt and shrugged into it.

Reeling as she was from the news he'd delivered, it took her a moment to realise what he was saying into his phone.

'You're leaving Mexico?' she asked when he hung up.

'The race is over. The next one isn't for another four days.'

She started in surprise. 'Where are you going?'

He gave her a grim smile. 'No. The twenty questions is over, *quer*—' He stopped, looked around, then shoved more things into the large bag he'd placed on the bed.

Scrambling wildly, she said, 'What about your physio sessions?'

'I've just endured a two-hour race. I hardly think I'm going to crumble into a million little pieces if I go without a session for a few days.'

Her lips firmed but the questions hammered in her mind. 'No, you won't. As long as you're not attempting to skydive over any volcanoes?'

'Been there, done that.'

His phone rang. He stared at it for several seconds, pain rippling in tides over his face. Finally, sucking in a deep breath, he answered it.

'*Sí*, Papá?' he rasped.

Raven's heart caught. The faint hope that help for Rafael would come from another angle was stymied when the conversation grew heated with bursts of staccato responses.

Rafael grew tenser with each passing moment until his body was as taut as a bow.

The moment he hung up, he reached for his bag. The action held an air of permanence about it that terrified her.

'So, I'll see you at the track in Rio?' she asked, hating herself for the desperation in her voice.

He gave her a smile that didn't reach his eyes. He started to answer but his phone rang again. He stared into her eyes, his expression inscrutable save for the tinge of relief she glimpsed before he masked it.

'No, you won't. *Adios, bonita.*'

He pressed the *answer* button, raised the phone to his ear and walked out of the door.

Rafael told himself to keep moving. To walk away before he brought chaos to her life. Time was running out for him.

He knew he wasn't ready to give up racing. Just as he knew it was his guilt that was causing the feelings rushing through him. For him to hang onto the only thing that kept him sane, he had to try to make amends.

No, racing wasn't the only thing that kept him sane. If he admitted nothing else, he would admit that.

Raven Blass kept him sane, made him laugh, made him feel things he hadn't felt in a long time. But for her sake he had to walk away. Keep walking away. He was toxic in this state.

He couldn't allow himself to be swayed into thinking he was anything else but what she'd first thought him to be.

As for what he planned to do… His father had summoned him.

Since he had nothing to lose, he saw no reason to refuse the summons. Just as he saw no reason to examine why his heart felt as if it would burst out of his chest with every step he took away from her.

Gritting his teeth, he walked out, threw a *'no comment'* to a stunned media before he stepped up in his helicopter and buckled himself in. He had no heart. So he had nothing to worry about.

Raven got the email an hour later. She'd been fired. Rafael de Cervantes no longer needed her services. She would be paid her full contract fee and an insanely hefty bonus for her inconvenience. Et cetera…et cetera…

Thing was, she wasn't surprised. Or even hurt. The man she'd fallen in love with was in full retreat mode because she'd got under his skin, had glimpsed the ravaged soul of the outwardly irreverent but desperately lonely playboy who had been grappling with monstrous demons.

She could've fought to stay, cited contract clauses and notice periods, but she knew first-hand how intransigent Rafael could be. And she knew offering her help when it was unwelcome would only set back the progress she'd made.

So she sent an email response. She would leave on one condition. That he let her recommend a physio who could help.

His curt text message agreeing to the condition made her heart contract painfully. Her next request was flatly refused.

No, Rafael stated, he had no wish to see her. But he wished her good luck with her future endeavours.

Raven watched the remaining All-Star events like most people did around the world—from the comfort of her couch. Except she had an extra reason to watch. She told herself she was making sure Rafael's new physio was doing a good enough job. It only took a glimpse of Rafael walking down the paddock en route to his car at the Montreal race to know that he hadn't suffered any setbacks.

At least not physically.

His haggard features told a different story. That and his studious avoidance of the media.

Her heart clenched as she devoured images of him; called herself ten kinds of fool when she froze his latest image and let her gaze settle on his hauntingly beautiful face.

The icy blue eyes staring into the camera still held the hint of devilish irreverence that was never far away but a raw desperation lurked there too, one that made tears prick her eyes. With a shaky hand, she pressed the release button and sat, numb, as the rest of the race unfolded.

Whatever Rafael had been running from still chased him with vicious relentlessness. The thought made her heart ache so painfully, she was halfway to picking up the phone when she stopped herself.

What would she say to him that she hadn't said before? He'd made it painfully clear he didn't want her interfering in his life. Like all his relationships, she'd been a means to an end, a sexual panacea to make him forget. She had no choice but to accept it was over.

She needed to put the past in the past and move on.

Which was why she nearly binned the invitation that arrived a week later.

The All-Star event's last race was taking place in Monaco. To be followed by an All-Star gala in honour of the drivers who'd given up their time to raise money for the road safety programme.

The only thing that stopped her from throwing the invitation away was the hand-written note from Sasha de Cervantes on behalf of her and her husband.

Sasha had been a good friend to her when she'd first joined the X1 Premier. Raven knew she'd put her friendship with Rafael on the line because of her and it had almost caused an irreparable rift between them. Certainly, she knew that not admitting Raven's role in Rafael's accident was what had caused the initial friction between Sasha and Marco.

So although attending the gala would mean she ran the risk of coming face to face with Rafael, Raven slid the invitation and the accompanying first class aeroplane ticket into her bag, then spent the next three days desperately trying to stop her heart from beating itself into exhaustion every time she thought of returning to Monaco.

Rafael stood before the door leading to the study at Casa León, where his father waited. Contrary to his intentions when he'd left Mexico two weeks ago, he hadn't made the trip to León. The indescribable need that had assailed him as he'd lifted off the racetrack in Mexico had led him down another path. A path which had brought him an infinitesimal amount of comfort. Comfort and the courage to grasp the door before him…and open it.

His father was seated behind his ancient desk in the room that seemed to have fallen into a time warp décor-wise.

'*Buenos tardes,* Papá.'

'*Mi hijo,*' his father replied. My son. 'It's good to see you.'

Guilt and sadness welled in Rafael's chest as he let his gaze rest properly on his father for the first time in eight years. His hair had turned almost completely grey and his limbs, paralysed thanks to Rafael, appeared shrunken. But his eyes, grey and sharp like Marco's, sparked with keen intellect and an expression Rafael thought he'd never see again. Or maybe it was just wishful thinking. 'Is it?' he asked, his throat tight with all the emotions he held within.

'It's always good to see you. I've missed you. I miss you every day.'

Rafael advanced into the room on shaky legs, inhaling an even shakier breath. 'How can you say that after all I've done?'

'What exactly do you think you've done, Rafa?'

He let out a harsh laugh and speared a hand through his hair. '*Por favor*, Papá. Condemn me to hell. It's where I belong, after all.'

'I think you've done a good job all by yourself. Now it's time to end this.'

'End this?'

His father nodded to a file on his desk. 'Sit down and read that.'

The hand he reached across the desk felt as feeble as a newborn's. The file contained a three-page report, one he read with growing disbelief.

'What is this?' he rasped through numb lips.

'It's the truth of what happened to your car that day, Rafael. You're not responsible for your mother's death.'

Shock hollowed his stomach. 'No…it can't be. Please tell me you're not making this up in some attempt to make me feel less guilty.'

'As your father, it's my duty to comfort you when you feel bad. It's also my duty to make you see the truth in front of your own eyes. You've been so bent on punishing yourself you've failed to listen to reason or contemplate the evidence. You told me when you first drove the car that you felt something wasn't right. That's what made your brother decide to investigate further. It turned out your hunch was right.'

'It says here all fifteen models of that car have been recalled for the same error. But it doesn't excuse the fact that I was running on fumes that day, high from partying even though my body was exhausted from being up almost twenty-four hours straight.'

'All things you'd been doing since you hit late puberty. All those things combined, while it gave me nightmares as a father, didn't make me think for a second that you would be dangerous behind a steering wheel or I wouldn't have bought you such a powerful machine, and I certainly wouldn't have allowed my beloved Ana in the car with you.'

The pure truth behind his father's words hit him square in the solar plexus. He stumbled backward and sagged onto the ancient leather armchair.

'I can't…I don't know what to say.' His head dropped into his hands and he felt tears prick his eyes.

'Let it go, Rafa. You've punished yourself enough over this. Your mamá wouldn't want this for you.'

The sob choked him, hot and tight and cathartic. Once it started, he couldn't seem to make it stop. He didn't even have the strength to lift his head when he heard the haunting whine of his father's wheelchair.

'Enough, son…enough.'

He looked up through a mist of tears. 'Forgive me, Papá.'

His father's smile touched him in a way that went beyond the physical. 'There's nothing to forgive. There never was.'

Footsteps sounded and Marco walked in, cradling his son, with Sasha right behind him.

She stopped dead when she saw him, her eyes widening in disbelief. 'Good grief, I never thought I'd live to see the day you'd be reduced to tears, Rafa. Quick, Marco, activate your phone's camera. We'll make a killing on YouTube.'

Marco laughed, their father snorted, even baby Jack chimed in with a hearty gurgle.

'So, we're all good here?' Marco asked several minutes later, his grey eyes probing as they darted between his father and his brother.

Rafael's gaze met his father's and the unconditional love he saw made the tightness in his chest give way just a tiny bit further. 'We're getting there.'

He had a feeling he'd never get there completely. Not while he felt a part of himself still missing.

'Pacing a crater through that carpet won't make the next few hours of your life any easier. You're screwed ten ways to Sunday. Accept that now and you'll be fine.'

Rafael glared at the amusement on his brother's face and clenched his fist. 'Don't you have an adoring wife somewhere who's waiting for you to swoon over her?' He walked over to the balcony overlooking the immense ballroom and scoured the crowd again, his stomach clenching when he didn't spot the figure he sought.

'Sí,' Marco replied smugly. 'But watching you twist yourself into knots is fun, too.'

'Keep it up and I'll be twisting my fist into your face.'

Marco grinned, an expression that had been rare in the years after his own personal tragedy of losing his unborn child. Sasha had brought the smile back to his brother's face. A smile that was now rubbing him a dozen different wrong ways.

As if he knew he was skating close to the edge, Marco sobered. 'If it helps, I messed up with Sasha, too.'

'It doesn't. Sasha is a soft touch. I'm not surprised she was fooled by those puppy-dog eyes of yours.'

Marco laughed. 'You're in more trouble than I thought if you're that deluded.' When his brother tapped him on the shoulder, Rafael was ready with a pithy response. Instead he saw Marco nod over his shoulder.

'Your Armageddon is here. I'd wish you luck but I've always thought you were dealt more than your fair share at birth. So I'll just suggest you don't balls it up…'

Rafael had stopped listening. His attention, his whole being was focused on the figure framed in the double doors of the ballroom.

Her black silky hair was caught up in a high, elaborate bun that made her sleek neck seem longer. And her dress, a simple but classy white gown threaded with gold sequined lines, followed her curves in a loving caress that made his mouth dry.

The vision of her, so stunning, so held together while he was falling apart inside, made his fingers tighten over the banister railing.

He watched Sasha approach and hug her. Her smile made his breath catch and, once again, Rafael felt a bolt of dismay at the thought of what he'd thrown away.

A waiter offered her a glass of champagne. She was about to take a sip when her gaze rose and collided with his.

The force of emotion that shot through him galvanised his frozen feet. He was moving along the balcony and the stairs before he'd taken a full breath.

Sasha saw him approach, gave him a stern *don't-mess-this-up-or-I'll-castrate-you* look and melted away into the crowd. Raven made no move to walk away, and he wasn't sure whether he was relieved or disturbed because her face gave nothing away.

No pleasure. No censure. Just a careful social mask that made his heart twist.

'You're late.' Ah, *brava*, Rafa. *Brava*.

'My flight out of London was delayed due to fog. I explained to Sasha. She's forgiven me.'

The not-so-subtle barb found its mark. *I'm not here for you.*

He wanted to touch, wanted to feel the warmth of her skin so badly, he had to swallow several times before he could speak.

'I need to talk to you.'

Her eyes widened. 'Why? I thought you said all you had to say in Mexico.'

He tried for a careless shrug. 'Perhaps I have a few more things to say.'

She glanced away and gave her still-full glass to a passing waiter. 'I don't want to hear it. We were never friends, not really. And you fired me from being your physio. That leaves us nothing in common.'

'I'm seeing a therapist,' he blurted out.

Shocked eyes returned to his. 'You are?'

His smile felt false and painful. 'Yes, I figured I must be the only high-profile figure without the requisite head-shrinker as an accessory. Now I'm a fully fledged, card-carrying whack-job. But I still want to talk to you.'

She pressed lightly glossed lips together and shook her head. 'I don't think it's a good idea.'

Feeling the ground rock under him, he reached out and captured her wrist. 'You were right.'

Her breath caught. 'About what?' she whispered.

He started to answer but a burst of laughter from nearby guests stopped him. 'Not here.' He pulled her towards the doors and breathed in relief when she didn't resist. The lift ride up to his VIP suite was made in silence. After shutting the door, he threw his key card on a nearby table and shrugged off his tuxedo jacket.

'You were right about everything.'

She turned from the window overlooking the stunning marina. Her gaze slid over him, a hasty assessment which nevertheless made the blood thrum in his veins.

'Even I can't take responsibility for *everything*.'

'According to my shrink, I'm suffering from a combination of survivor's guilt and PTSD. Together, they make for one sexy but volatile cocktail of emotions.'

She licked her lips then curved them into a quick smile. An impersonal smile. She started to move towards the door. 'Well, I'm happy that you're getting some help. If that's all, I'll return downstairs. I don't wish to be rude to Sasha—'

'I also spoke to my father.'

She froze. He took advantage of her hesitation and stalked after her. Catching her around the waist, he pulled her body into his. She gave the tiniest gasp but didn't fight to get away.

Rafael took that as a good sign. 'I finally flew to León and spoke to my father.' He gave her the gist of their family meeting.

'Why are you telling me all this, Rafael?' she whispered.

He pulled her closer until he felt the sweet curve of her bottom against his groin. For a quick second, he lost himself in her scent, breathed her in and let her warm his frozen soul. The past three weeks had shown him there was an even worse hell than the one he'd previously inhabited. Because in that one he'd lost Raven.

Hell without Raven was a whole new reality. One he was desperate to escape.

'You made me face up to my flaws, to seek help before I hurt anyone else.' He couldn't stop himself from brushing his lips against her nape.

Her delicate shudder gave him hope but her next words dashed them completely. 'So you wanted to thank me? I accept your gratitude. Let me go, please.'

He held on tight. 'I'm seeking help, Raven, learning to change. But I need you. Without you, all this will be for nothing.'

She finally turned in his arms. The look on her face threatened to stop his breath. 'You can't do this because of me. You should want to seek help for yourself.'

'*Sí*, even I get that. But nothing I do will have any meaning unless you're part of that change.'

'What exactly are you saying?' she whispered.

Go for broke, Rafa. Hell, there was nothing left to lose. No, scratch that. There was everything to lose. Without her, his life had no meaning. So he took the biggest gamble he'd ever taken.

'*Lo siento.* I got it horribly wrong. I'm sorry.'

'What did you get wrong?'

'Not seeing the treasure I had in you until it was too late.'

She shook her head and grimaced. 'I'm no treasure, Rafael. I am just as damaged as you. I fooled myself into thinking a half-life was better than letting myself feel. You made me see that I'd let my father's treatment of me cloud my judgement so I pushed everyone away.'

His hand tightened on her waist. 'You know what I want to do?'

She shook her head.

'I want to track him down and ram my fist so far down his throat, he'll never speak again.'

'Don't let your shrink hear you say that.'

His smile felt grim and tight. 'I said I was trying to change. I never said I was aiming for saint of the year.' He sobered. 'I'm disgusted that my behaviour brought up what happened to you when you lived with him.'

'That's just it. Deep down I knew you were nothing like him but I'd programmed myself so thoroughly I let myself grasp the excuse when everyone told me you were nothing but a ruthless playboy.'

'And of course I went out of my way to prove them right.'

'If you were, you'd never have agreed to stop flirting with other women. Never have refused Chantilly's blatant invitation.'

Raven saw the flash of self-disgust and pain in his eyes.

'There was a time when I wouldn't have.'

'Past tense. You're a better man now. A better person.'

'Because of you.' His knuckle brushed down her cheek in a gesture so soft and gentle, tears threatened.

Despite the foolish hope that threatened, Raven's heart remained frozen. She couldn't remain here. If she did, she'd end up making a total fool of herself.

'I have to go—'

'I love you,' he rasped in a whisper so fierce it sizzled around the room.

'I...*what?*'

His heartbreakingly beautiful face contorted in a grimace. 'I'm still broken, *querida*, not so much on the outside any more, but I'm a long way from being perfect. And I know it's selfish of me but I want you so very desperately that I have to ask you to consider taking a chance on me, flawed and hideous as I am.' Acute vulnerability shone from his eyes and, when he grasped her arms, Raven felt the tremor in his fingers.

'You love me?'

'I have no right to, and I can't promise that I won't be a complete bastard on occasion, but *si*, I love you. And I'll do anything to make you agree to hitch a ride with this broken wagon.'

'Rafael...'

He kissed her silent, as if he was afraid of what she'd say. She kissed him back, infusing every single drop of what she felt into the act. Somehow, he got the message.

He pulled back sharply, the question blazing its intensity in his eyes.

'Yes, my gorgeous man. I love you too.'

A frenzied tearing of clothes followed that sweet, soul-shaking confession. They made love right there in the living room, on the plush, expensive rug helpfully supplied by the five-star hotel.

She held her breath as Rafael slid on the sheath and prowled his naked body over hers. Hardly believing that this beautiful man was hers, she caressed her fingers down his firm cheek. He turned his head and kissed her palm, then, being the shameless opportunist he was, he kissed his way down her arm to her shoulder, then over her chest to capture one rigid nipple in his mouth.

At the same time, he parted her thighs with his and entered her in one bold thrust. Their coupling was fast, furious, their need for each other a raging fire that swiftly burned out of control.

When they'd caught their breaths, Rafael moved, picked her up and walked her into the bedroom.

'Should you be doing that?' she asked.

'I'm a renewed man. I can move mountains.' He let go of her and she tumbled onto the bed. Before she got totally lost in the effortlessly skilled seduction she knew he was aiming her way, she placed a hand on his lips.

'We haven't talked about your racing.'

His settled his long frame next to hers, his eyes serious. 'I think I need to concentrate on getting myself mentally in shape before I get behind the wheel. I've turned down a seat for this season.'

Knowing what it must have taken for him to turn down what he loved doing, her heart swelled. 'You take care of the mental aspect. I'll make sure your body is whipped into shape in time for next year's season.'

He grinned and tugged her close. 'I'd expect no less from my take-no-prisoners future wife.'

Her breath stalled. 'Is that a proposal, Rafael?'

'It's whatever you want it to be. If you don't think I'll make a good enough husband, you can take me as your sex slave. Or your boy toy. Or your f—'

She stopped him with a kiss before he finished. His incorrigible laugh promised retribution. And, for the life of her, Raven couldn't think of a better way to be punished.

'Sasha is going to hate me for disappearing from her gala,' she said an hour later.

'No, she's not. I begged her to send you the invitation. We both agreed I owe her big.'

She mock glared at him. 'You're right, you haven't changed one little bit.'

He laughed, a rich sound that made her soul sing. When he stared deep into her eyes her heart turned over. 'I have something to show you.'

Curious, she watched him reach into his drawer and pull out a sheaf of papers.

'You finished it?'

'Yes,' he answered. There was no laughter in his voice, no shameless lust monster lurking behind the stunning blue eyes.

There was only a careful, almost painfully hopeful expectancy.

She took the papers from him. Seeing the one word title, her heart caught—*Mamá*.

'I knew it. I knew Ana and Carlos were your parents.'

Two hours later, she looked up, tears streaming down her face. He'd sat with her back tucked against his front, in watchful silence while she read, all the while knowing he'd been reading his words alongside her.

The sheen of tears in his eyes rocked her soul.

'It's beautiful, Rafael.'

'*Gracias*. I hope, wherever she is, she forgives me for what I did.'

'She's your mother. That's what mothers do. And I promise to remind you of that whenever the nightmares threaten.'

The look in his eyes made hers fill all over again. '*Mi corazon*. I don't deserve you.'

Her smile was watery. 'No, you don't. But I'll let you have me anyway.'

EPILOGUE

'So what do I get for winning the bet?' Raven asked as they stood in another luxurious room, surrounded by well-heeled guests, the very best vintage champagne and excellent food.

'What more could you possibly want, *mi amor*? You have my slavish adoration by day and my hot body by night.'

'Yes, but do you know how draining it's been to reassure you every day for the last three months that your book will be a smashing success? That more than one person will turn up at this launch?'

Rafael mock frowned. 'Have I been that needy?'

'Yes, you have, but don't think I wasn't fooled by what that neediness got you. You owe me big.'

'I seem to owe everyone big. Okay, how about...' He whispered a very hot, very dirty suggestion of payment. She was still blushing several minutes later when they both heard the whine of an electric wheelchair.

Rafael's father stopped beside them. An electronic copy of Rafael's book had been programmed into a tablet on his wheelchair, and the front page showed a picture of Rafael's mother, her face creased in a stunning smile as she laughed into the camera.

Rafael told her he'd taken that picture the year before she died.

'Carlos, please tell your son to stop worrying about his book. He thinks one of us has been bribing the critics to give it rave reviews.'

Carlos smiled and glanced at his son. Then he started to speak to him in Spanish. Slowly, Rafael's smile disappeared until his face was transformed into a look of intense love and gratitude. With a shaky hand, he touched his father's shoulder, then bent forward and kissed both his cheeks.

'*Gracias,* Papá.' His voice was rough as he straightened.

Carlos nodded, his own eyes holding a sheen of tears as he rolled his chair away.

'What did he say?'

'He's proud of me. And my mother would be too if she were here.'

As hard as she blinked, the tears welled. 'Damn it, you de Cervantes men sure know how to ruin a girl's make up.'

He caught her around the waist and pulled her close into his hard body.

'You're now a de Cervantes too. You can't take back your vows.'

She gave a mock grimace. She was still getting used to her new name, just as she was getting used to wearing the exquisite engagement and wedding ring set that had belonged to Rafael's mother. 'Raven de Cervantes is such a mouthful.'

'Hmm…' He nuzzled her neck, instantly melting her insides. 'We could shorten it.'

'You mean like just initials or a symbol like that rock star?'

'Not quite.'

'What have you in mind?' she asked, her fingers toying with buttons she couldn't wait to undo later. The promise of exploring the flesh underneath made her hot.

He worked along her jaw until he reached the side of her mouth. With a whisper-soft kiss, he raised his head and looked directly into her eyes. 'How about just…*amor querida*?'

Her heart, her soul and the rest of her body melted into him. When his thumb brushed her cheek, she blinked back tears.

'That works. That works very well for me.'

* * * * *

BOUND BY
A CHILD

BY
KATHERINE GARBERA

Katherine Garbera is a *USA TODAY* bestselling author of more than forty books who has always believed in happy endings. She lives in England with her husband, children and their pampered pet, Godiva. Visit Katherine on the web at www.katherinegarbera.com, or catch up with her on Facebook and Twitter.

Huge thanks to all of the readers who chat with me on my Facebook page, especially Danny Bruggemann, Jean Gordon, Barbara Padlo, Angie Floris Thompson and Amelia Hernanadez, who suggested names for the hurricane in this book. I ended up choosing Pandora since it sort of fitted my story. :-)

Plus a shout-out to my UK writing buddies Celia Anderson and Lucy Felthouse. Thanks for talking books, hotties and UK phrases with me. Writing is a hard, lonely job and I have to thank my darling husband and kiddos for their support. And as always thanks to my editor, Charles, for his insight.

One

Allan McKinney might look like a Hollywood hottie with his lean, made-for-sin body, neatly styled dark brown hair and piercing silver eyes that could make a woman forget to think. But Jessi Chandler knew he was the devil in disguise.

He was the bad guy and always had been. More tempting than sin itself as he rode in at the last minute to ruin everything. Knowing him the way she did, she couldn't imagine he had come to her table in the corner of Little Bar here in the Wilshire/La Brea area of Los Angeles for any other reason than to crow about his latest victory.

It had been only three weeks since he and his vengeful cousins at Playtone Games had taken over her family's company, Infinity Games, bringing their longtime rivalry to a vicious climax.

She'd just come from a meeting at Playtone Games where she'd made a proposal to try to save her job. The most humiliating thing about this merger was having to grovel in front of Allan. She was a damned fine director of marketing, but instead of being able to continue

in her role and just get on with the work that needed to
be done, she had to trek into the city from Malibu once
a week and prove to the Montrose cousins that she was
earning her paycheck.

He slid into the booth across from her, his long legs
brushing against hers. He acted as if he owned this
place and the world. There was something about his
arrogance that had always made her want to take him
down a notch or two.

It was 5:00 p.m., and the bar was just beginning to
get busy with the after-work crowd. She was anonymous
here and could just let her guard down for a minute, but
now that Allan was sitting across from her, messing
with her mojo, that wasn't going to happen.

"Are you here to rub it in?" she asked at last. It fit
with the man she believed him to be and with the little
competition they'd had going since the moment they'd
met. "Seems like a Montrose-McKinney thing to do."

Her father had been adamant about staying away
from Thomas Montrose's grandsons due to the bad
blood between their families. She got that, but even
before the takeover, she'd had no choice but to deal with
Allan when her best friend, Patti, had fallen in love with
and married his best friend.

"Not quite. I'm here to make you an offer," he said,
signaling the waitress and ordering a Glenlivet neat.

"Thanks, but I don't need your kind of help," she
said. She'd probably find herself out of a job quicker
with him on her side.

He ran his hand over the top of his short hair, narrowed his eyes and looked at her in a way that made her
sit up straighter in her chair. "Do you get off on pushing me to the edge?"

"Sort of," she said. She did take a certain joy in sparring with him. And she kept score of who won and who lost.

"Why?" he asked, pulling out his iPhone and setting it on the table next to him. He glanced down at the screen and then brought his electric gaze back to her.

"Concentrating on your phone and not on the person you're with is one reason," she answered. It irked her when anyone did that, but bothered her even more when the person was Allan. "Besides, I like getting to see the chinks in your perfect facade when you can't hide the real Allan."

The waitress delivered his drink. He leaned forward on his elbows. The woman was thin and pretty and wore a pair of large black glasses that were clearly a personality statement and went well with her pixie haircut. Allan smiled at her, and the waitress blushed, which made Jessi roll her eyes.

"What did I do to make you so adversarial toward me?" he asked, turning back to her as the waitress left.

"Why do you care?"

"I'm tired of always arguing with you. In fact, that brings me back to my reason for tracking you down," he said.

"What reason?"

"I'd like to buy you out. Your shares in Infinity Games are now worth a lot of money, and we both know you don't want to work for my cousin Kell or me. I'll make you a fair offer."

She sat there in shock as his words sank in. Did he think her family heritage meant so little to her? When she thought of how her dad and grandfather had always been so busy at work that they'd never been around…

well, hell, no, she wasn't selling. Especially not to a Montrose heir. "Never. I'd give them away before I sold to you."

He shrugged. "I just thought I'd save all of us a lot of frustration. You don't seem to be really interested in working for the merged company."

"I'm not selling," she said one more time, just in case he had any illusion that she was going to walk away easily. "I'm planning to keep my job and make you and your cousins eat your words."

"What words?"

"That Emma and I are expendable. Don't deny that you believe it."

She and her older sister still had to prove themselves if they wanted to keep their jobs. Sure, they were shareholders, so they'd always have an ownership stake in the company, but their actual jobs were on the line. Their younger sister, Cari, had already jumped through hoops for the Montrose cousins and had ended up keeping her position and falling in love with one of them.

Declan Montrose was now engaged to her, though three months ago he'd arrived at Infinity Games to manage the merger of the two companies, which meant he was there to fire the Chandler sisters. But Cari had turned the tables on him, revealing that he was the father of her eighteen-month-old son as a result of a brief affair they'd had. This had been a big surprise to everyone on both sides of the merger. It had been an interesting time, to say the least, but in the end she and Dec had fallen in love and Cari had managed to save her job at the newly merged Playtone-Infinity Games.

"I wasn't going to deny it," Allan said. "The situation with both you and Emma is different than the one with

Cari. When she approached Dec and I with her ideas for saving the staff at Infinity Games she was happy to listen to our ideas, as well."

His words hurt; Jessi wasn't going to lie about that. But Cari was known for being the caring sister, and Jessi, well, she'd always been the rebel, the ballbuster. But that didn't mean she was emotionless. She wanted to see her family's legacy in video games continue; after all, Gregory Chandler had been a pioneer in the industry in the seventies and eighties. "I have a few ideas that I've been working on."

"Share them with me," Allan invited, glancing again at his phone.

"Why?" she asked.

"To see if you're sincere about wanting to keep your position. No more lame ideas like sending out Infinity-Playtone game characters to make appearances at malls. You're head of marketing and we expect more than that."

"It wasn't—" she said, but in her heart she knew it sort of was. She didn't want Playtone-Infinity to be successful so she'd...shot herself in the foot. "Okay, maybe it was a little lame."

"What else do you have in mind? You're too smart not to have something big," he said, staring at her with that intense gaze of his.

"Was that actually a compliment?"

"Don't act so surprised. You're very good at your job and we both know you know it. Talk to me, Jessi."

She hesitated. She *was* good, and she wasn't ever as tentative as she felt right now. It was just that she'd been beaten and felt like it today. "I don't... What can you do?"

"Decide if it's worth my time to help you," he said at last.

"Why?"

"Our best friends are married and we're their daughter's godparents. I can't just let Kell fire you without at least making some sort of effort to help," he said. "Patti and John would never forgive me."

"Then why offer to buy me out?"

"It would solve the problem and we'd both be able to walk away from this."

"It would," Jessi said. "But that's not happening."

She rubbed the back of her neck. She didn't like anything about this merger but she also didn't relish the idea of being fired. "I'm one person who wouldn't be swayed by your bank account."

He shrugged off her comment and for a moment looked pensive.

"It bothers you that I sent the jet to pick you and Patti up that first time we met, doesn't it?" he asked, leaning back and glancing at his iPhone, but quickly looking back at Jessi, which earned him a few more points toward being a good guy.

She took a swallow of her gin and tonic. "Yes. It felt like you were trying too hard. I mean, offering your private jet to fly us to Paris…that was showing off."

"Maybe I just wanted Patti to have a proposal she'd always remember. You and I both know that John doesn't earn what I earn. I was just helping my friend out."

"I know. It was romantic. I admit I didn't behave as well as I could have…. I guess I can be a bit of a brat."

"Well, you certainly were that weekend," he said,

leaning in so that she caught a whiff of his spicy aftershave.

She closed her eyes for a minute and acknowledged that if she didn't keep Allan in the adversary category, there was a part of her that would be attracted to him. He was the only person—man or woman—she'd ever met whom she could go head-to-head with and still talk to the next day. He understood that winning was important to her and didn't get mad when she won. He just got even, which, to be fair, appealed to her as much as it irritated her.

"But that's in the past. Let's work together. I think you and Emma probably have a lot to contribute to the newly merged company."

"Probably? Jeez, that sounds encouraging," she said, taking another sip of her drink.

"I'm trying here," he said.

"Well, I've got a few feelers out in the movie industry. There are three new action movies coming next summer that I think are good matches for the type of games that we develop, which might be enough lead time to get a really good game out." Given that the merged company was not only a prime video game developer for consoles like Xbox and PlayStation, but also had a thriving app business for smartphones and tablets, making games with movie tie-ins was a naturally good idea. Infinity Games had never pursued this line of business before, but since the takeover, Jessi and her sisters had been thinking outside the box.

"That's a great idea. I have some contacts in that area if you'd like me to use them," Allan offered.

"Really?"

"Yes," he said. "It's in my best interest to help you."

"Is it?"

"I'm the CFO, Jessi. Anything that affects the bottom line concerns me."

"Of course it does," she said.

She was torn. A part of her wanted to accept his help, but this was Allan McKinney, and she didn't trust him. It wasn't just that he'd thrown around his money as if the stuff grew on trees; it was also that she hadn't been able to find out much about him from her private investigator, whom she'd hired to check out John when Patti had first met him. What the detective had turned up about Allan…well, frankly, it had all seemed too good to be true.

No one had the kind of happy, pampered existence the P.I. had found when he dug into Allan's past. It was too clean, too…perfect. There was something he'd been hiding, but none of that had mattered at the time, since John McCoy was the main subject of the investigation and he'd turned out to be a good guy.

Maybe Jessi should ask Orly, her P.I., to start digging again. When it came to Allan, there had been too few leads and many closed doors the first time around. Given what had happened with Playtone and Infinity, and that she'd recently had Allan's cousin Dec investigated, too, maybe it was time to ask Orly to find out what more he could about Allan.

"Sure, I'd love your help," she said.

"You sound sarcastic," Allan commented, glancing down at his mobile phone yet again.

"It's the best I can do," she said.

"Excuse me for a moment. I keep getting a call from a number I don't know," he told her.

He picked up his phone and answered. After a moment, his brow furrowed, and he hunched back in his chair. "Oh, God, no," he muttered.

"What?" she asked. She grabbed her Kate Spade bag and started to slide off the bench, until Allan grabbed her hand.

She shook her head but waited as he listened, and then his face went ashen. He turned away from her.

"How?" he asked, his voice gruff.

She could only stare at him as he shook his head and rasped, "The baby?" After a pause he murmured, "Okay, I will be there on Friday." He disconnected the call and turned to her. "John and Patti are dead."

Jessi wanted to believe he was lying, but his face was pale and there was none of that arrogant charm she always associated with him. She pulled her phone out and saw that she, too, had received several calls from an unknown number.

"I can't believe it. Are you sure?"

He gave her a look that was so lost and wounded, she knew the truth.

"No," she said, wrapping her arm around her waist. *God, no.*

Allan was shaken to his core. He'd lost his parents at a rather young age, which was part of the reason he and John had bonded, but this was…wrong. It was just wrong that someone so young and with so much to live for had died.

Jessi's hands were shaking, and he glanced over at her, only to find everything he was feeling inside was there on her face. The woman who always looked so tough and in control was suddenly small and fragile.

He got up and moved around to her side, putting his

arm around her shoulder and drawing her into the curve of his body. She resisted for the merest of seconds before she turned her face into his chest, and he felt the humid warmth of her tears as they soaked into his shirt.

She was silent as she cried, which was nothing more than he'd expect from someone as in control as Jessi always was. By focusing on her pain and her tears he was able to bury his own feelings. A world without his best friend wasn't one he wanted to dwell on. John balanced him out. Reminded Allan of all the reasons why life was good. But now—

"How?" she asked, pushing back from him and grabbing a cocktail napkin to wipe her face and then blow her nose.

Her face was splotchy, red from the tears, and she took a shuddering breath as she tried to speak again. The tears were at odds with her rebel-without-a-care look. She wore her version of business attire, a short black skirt that ended at her thighs, a tight green jacket that had bright shiny zippers and a little shell camisole that revealed the upper curves of her breasts and her tattoo.

His chest was too tight for words. He didn't really know how to talk through the grief. But as he stared into those warm brown eyes of Jessi's—one of the very first things he'd noticed about her when they'd met—he realized that he could do this. He would pull himself together and do this for her.

"Car accident," he said.

"John is an excellent driver, as is Patti—oh, God, is Hannah okay?"

"Yes. She wasn't with them. Another driver hit them

head-on as they were coming home from a Chamber of Commerce meeting."

Allan was John's next-of-kin contact, which was why he'd gotten the call. "Let's get out of here."

She nodded. He could tell she was in no shape to drive, and steered her toward his Jaguar XF. She got into the passenger seat and then slumped forward, putting her hands over her face as her shoulders shook.

Never in his life had Allan felt this powerless, and he hated it. He stood outside the car and tipped his head back, staring up into the fading fall sunset. He felt tears burning in his own eyes and used his thumbs to press them back. He pushed hard on his eye sockets until he was able to staunch the flow, and then walked around the car and got inside.

Jessi sat there silently next to him, looking over at him with those wet, wounded eyes, and for the first time he saw the woman beneath the brashness. He saw someone who needed him.

"What is Hannah going to do? Patti's mom has Alzheimer's and there's no other close family."

"I don't know," he admitted. "John has some family but not really anyone close. Just a couple of cousins. We'll figure it out."

"Together," she said, meeting his gaze. "Oh, God. I can't believe I just said that."

"Me, either. But it only makes sense now."

"It does. Plus John and Patti would want us to do it together," Jessi said.

"Yes, they would," he said.

The little girl would never know her parents, but Allan decided he'd do everything in his power to ensure that she wouldn't grow up alone.

He took Jessi's hand in his. "Let's call their attorney back and find out the answers we both need."

She linked her fingers with his as he made the call and waited to be connected.

When he was put through, he said, "This is Allan McKinney again. You and I were just discussing John McCoy. Do you mind if I put you on speaker? I'm with Jessi Chandler. She is Hannah's other godparent."

"Not at all." Allan put the phone on speaker. "Go ahead."

"This is Reggie Blythe, Ms. Chandler. I'm the attorney for the McCoys."

"Hello, Mr. Blythe. What can you tell us?"

"Please call me Reggie. I don't have all the details as to what happened, but John and Patti were on their way back from a Chamber of Commerce dinner and were involved in a fatal accident. Miss Hannah was at home with a sitter—" they heard the rustling of papers "—Emily Duchamp. Emily has agreed to stay overnight with the baby. Hannah will be placed in a temporary foster situation in the morning."

Jessi's grip on Allan tightened. "Patti would hate that. Is there any way you can keep Hannah in her home?"

"Actually, as cogodparents, you have certain rights, but you will need to get here as soon as possible to avoid her being placed in the state's care."

State care. Allan knew that John never would have wanted Hannah to end up there. And there was no need for it. Didn't John have distant cousins and a great-aunt on his dad's side? "I believe John had a cousin who lives nearby."

"I don't think it's best to go into this over the phone. When can you both get to North Carolina?"

"As soon as humanly possible."

"Good," Reggie said. "I'll be in my office all day tomorrow. Please let me know when you two will get here."

"Oh, we're not together," Jessi said.

"Aren't you? You called me together, and given the terms of the will—never mind. We will sort it all out when you get to my office," Reggie said.

"Why did you think we were together?" Allan asked.

"John and Patti indicated in their will that they wanted guardianship to be given to the two of you."

"We figured as much," Jessi said. "We can come up with some sort of schedule."

"In the eyes of the courts," Reggie said, "the best arrangement is to provide a stable home for the child. But again, we can talk more about this when you get here."

When Allan disconnected the call, he dropped Jessi's hand, and she looked at him as if he'd grown two heads. "We fight all the time."

"We do," he said, before turning away and trying to think. It was almost too much to process.

His best friend was dead. Allan was a committed bachelor who had been named coguardian of a tiny baby with the one woman on the planet who aggravated him the most. He looked at her again. She seemed as upset by the tragedy as he was. But he knew they'd both do whatever they could to make the situation work. It didn't matter that they were enemies; from this moment forward they were bound together by baby Hannah.

"You and me…" she said.

"And baby makes three."

Two

Allan dropped Jessi off at her place in Echo Park. She looked small and lost and so unlike the indomitable woman he usually knew her to be that he didn't know how to handle her.

She didn't turn and wave as she entered her house, and he hadn't expected her to. He knew in time she'd get back to herself, but then he wondered if that were true. How could either of them ever be the same again?

Traffic was heavy, and it took him forty minutes to get to his home in Beverly Hills. He'd purchased the mansion after Playtone had made him a millionaire. John had actually helped him build the pergola and brick backyard eating area and barbecue. As he pulled into his circle drive, he was haunted by memories of his friend on his last visit to California.

Allan dropped his head forward on the steering wheel, but tears didn't come. Inside, he was cold and felt alone. And he realized that the last person he cared about was gone. He'd loved his parents, really loved them. They'd been a close family unit—just the three of them. Allan's grandfather had disowned his daughter when she'd refused to marry a wealthy heir he'd picked out for her, intending to funnel that money into his revenge against the Chandlers. It had only been after his grandfather's death when Kell had come to Allan and invited him to be a part of Playtone that he'd joined the company and put his penchant for managing money to good use.

She'd married instead for love, and they'd lived a quiet little life in the Temecula Valley—two hours away from Los Angeles, but really a world apart.

Allan heard a rap on the window of his Jaguar XF and looked up to see his butler, Michael Fawkes, standing there. The fifty-seven-year-old former middleweight boxer had been in his employ since he'd inked his first multimillion-dollar deal for Playtone. Fawkes was a great guy and looked a little bit like Mickey Rourke.

"Are you okay, sir?"

Allan took his keys from the ignition and climbed out of the car. "Yes, Fawkes, I am. But John McCoy was killed in a car accident. I'm leaving tomorrow to fly to the Outer Banks to help make funeral arrangements and see to his daughter."

"My condolences, sir. I liked Mr. McCoy," Fawkes said.

"Everyone liked him," Allan said.

"Shall I accompany you?" Fawkes asked.

"Yes. I need you to make sure we have accommodation in Hatteras. I think we should be able to stay at the B and B that John and Patti own…owned," he said, turning away from Fawkes. "Give me a minute."

Jessi would probably have a hard time booking a flight to North Carolina at this hour, and it wasn't a big town they were flying into. For a moment he rejected the idea of making an offer to let her fly with him. But then he knew he had to at least reach out to her. She was truly the only other person who felt the way he did right now.

As much as she irritated him, and though it irked him to admit it, he needed her. She made him feel as if he wasn't dealing with John's death alone.

"Please include Ms. Chandler in our arrangements," Allan said.

"Really?" Fawkes asked in a surprised tone of voice. Jessi did her best to rattle the butler whenever they came into contact.

"Yes. I was with her when she got the news. She's as affected by this as we both are."

Allan pulled his iPhone out of his pocket and texted her.

I'm taking the jet to North Carolina in the morning. Want a lift?

Jessi's response was immediate. Thanks. I'd appreciate that. Are you leaving tonight? I've made arrangements with the funeral home to talk about Patti's service in the morning. If we go tonight I can talk to them in person.

I had thought to leave tomorrow but given that we are going to lose three hours perhaps tonight is best.

I thought so.

Can you be packed and ready in two hours?

Of course. TTYL

"Very well, sir. I shall make all the arrangements," Fawkes said when he learned of the plan. "When are we leaving?"

"Two hours," Allan said.

He left his assistant and headed to his den, where he poured himself a stiff Scotch and then went over to his recliner to call his cousins. But there was a knock on the door before he could dial.

"Come in," he called.

Kell and Dec entered the room. They looked somber, and he realized that though John was his best friend, both his cousins had counted John as their friend, as well.

"We came as soon as we heard," Dec said. He stood in the doorway looking awkward.

"Thanks. I'm leaving tonight. I don't expect the trip to take more than a week. Jessi is coming with me, Kell. I think we might have to adjust some of her deadlines," Allan said. Even if she was his most irritating adversary, he had to help her out now. He'd seen her broken and he shared her pain.

"We can discuss business later. When will the funeral be?"

"I don't know. I have to talk to the funeral home once we get to North Carolina. John only had a few distant cousins. I won't know what kind of arrangements they might have already made until I'm on the ground there. I might end up in charge of the planning. And then there is Patti to consider. I know that Jessi is arranging her service."

"Just let us know and we'll fly out for it," Dec said. "Do you need anything?"

He shook his head. What could he say? For once he was at a loss for words. "I've got this," he finally said.

"Of course you do, but he was our friend, too," Dec said. Allan saw a quiet understanding in his cousin's eyes as he looked over at him.

Falling in love had changed the other man. He wasn't as distant as he'd always been.

"I don't know how else to handle this except to plan and take control," Allan admitted.

"That's the only way," Kell said. "We'll leave you to it."

Dec glanced quickly at him again as he followed Kell out. When his cousins were gone, Allan fell back on the large, battered brown sofa that didn't quite fit with the decor in the elegant and luxuriously appointed room. The couch had major sentimental value—John and Allan had purchased this piece at a garage sale for their first college apartment.

He put the heels of his hands over his eyes, pushing as hard as he could until he saw stars and there were no more tears.

"Another Scotch, sir?"

Allan dropped his hands and glanced up at his butler. Fawkes was standing there with a glass in one hand. "No. I'm going to pack and then get ready to head to the airport."

"Yes, sir," Fawkes said. "I have already arranged the accommodations. I've been tracking the weather, as well…. There might be a situation."

"What kind of situation?"

"Tropical storm in the Atlantic, but it's not predicted to head toward North Carolina. Just keeping my eye on it."

"Thanks, Fawkes."

Allan walked away and forced his mind to the task at hand. There was no reason why he couldn't get through his best friend's death the way he handled everything else. He'd manage and take control of the situation.

For once, Jessi's sharp tongue was dulled by Allan's generous offer to let her ride on his jet to the Outer Banks with him. Or maybe it was all the talk of funerals making her numb. As soon as she finished texting, she turned to put her phone on the hall table and found herself staring at a photo of Patti on the wall.

Jessi's heart hurt and she started to cry. She missed Patti. She missed the talks they wouldn't have. She longed to be able to pick up the phone and call her again. But that couldn't happen.

She sank to the floor, wrapped her arms around her waist and just sat there, trying to pretend that the news wasn't true. She didn't want to imagine her world without Patti. Granted, she had her sisters, but Patti was the person who knew her best. They'd gotten into trouble together since the second grade. What was she going to do now?

There was a knock on the door and she stared at it before forcing herself to her feet and wiping her face on her sleeve. Then she took a quick look at herself in the mirror.

Pitiful. Suck it, up, Jess. No one likes a crybaby.

"Coming," she called, but took a moment to wipe off the smudges that the combination of her tears and her heavy eyeliner had made on her face.

"We came as soon as we heard," Emma said when Jessi answered the ringing doorbell. Their youngest sister was there, too. Both women had their children with them. Emma's three-year-old Sam was holding his mother's hand, and twenty-one-month-old D.J. was sleeping quietly in Cari's arms.

"I didn't think you guys would get here so fast," Jessi said.

"Dec heard about it from Allan," Cari said, crossing the threshold and giving Jessi a one-armed hug. Jessi wrapped her own arms around her sister and nephew and held them close. Emma shut the door and joined the group hug.

Jessi felt the sting of tears once more, but choked them back. Though it was okay to let loose with her sisters, she didn't want to start crying again. Tears weren't going to bring Patti and John back. Tears weren't going to do anything helpful.

"What can we do?" Emma asked.

"I'm not sure. The funeral will have to be arranged, and then there is Hannah…."

"What about her?"

"Allan and I are her godparents. I agreed to it because Patti asked. But I'm not good with babies. You both know this. I'm just—" Jessi abruptly stopped talking. She wasn't going to admit to her sisters that she had no idea what to do next. For only the second time in her life she was lost. Lost. It was a place she'd vowed to never let herself be again.

Emma wrapped her arms around her again and for a minute Jessi was seven and her big sister's hug could fix all her problems. She hugged her sister back and took comfort from her before gathering herself and stepping away.

"I'm okay."

Cari looked skeptical, but was too nice to say anything. Emma just watched her, and finally Jessi turned on her heel and walked toward her bedroom. She could tell one of her sisters was following her, but didn't turn around to see who. If it was Cari, that would be fine. Cari would just accept whatever Jessi said and leave it be. But Em. Em had seen her share of heartbreak and had dealt with grief when she'd lost her young husband. Emma would be harder to keep her true feelings from.

"What bag are you taking?" Cari asked as she entered the bedroom without D.J.

Jessi breathed a sigh of relief and pretended it wasn't tinged with disappointment. She could have used a little of Emma's meddling right now. Something to rebel against instead of Cari's kindness.

"I don't know how long we'll be gone," Jessi said. "I need to leave some notes for my assistant, Marcel. My job is still on the line."

"Even Kell can't be that heartless. He'll give you some more time," Cari said. "I'll talk to him about it."

She nodded at her sister, but at this moment was too numb to get worked up about it. Patti was dead. That dominated every thought Jessi had.

"How about if I pack for you," Cari said. "You go talk to Marcel. Get everything sorted out before you leave."

"Thanks, Cari."

Her pretty blonde sister looked as if she was going to cry. For a minute, as Jessi gazed at her, with her neat preppy skirt, her tucked-in blouse and her hair in that high ponytail, she envied her. Cari had seen some rough times—giving birth to her son on her own after the father had abandoned her—but she'd found her own strength. That was what Jessi needed right now.

Work wasn't a solace for her the way that it had been for Emma when her husband died. And Jessi's personal life… Well, without Patti she didn't know what she was going to do.

She left her bedroom without another word, avoiding the living room, where she heard Emma talking to Sam and D.J. After listening a moment, Jessi made her way to her home office.

It was decorated with sleek modern furniture in bright primary colors. She sat down on her desk chair and opened her laptop to start sending emails.

As her system loaded messages and sorted them into different folders, she noticed the file labeled Patti had a new message. For some reason it hadn't downloaded to her phone, maybe because she'd turned off email during her meeting at the Playtone offices earlier in the day. As she reached for her phone and adjusted the settings, she started to cry. This would be the last message from Patti.

Jessi looked back at her laptop screen and hovered the cursor over the folder, afraid to open it. But after taking a deep breath, she clicked her mouse and read the email.

Can't wait to see you in two weeks. Here's a quick picture of Hannah. She's teething and that means her first tooth! And you, dear godmother, have to buy her a pair of shoes—according to my great-aunt Berthe. Hope everything is ok at work. I just know that you will figure it all out. Call me later.
Take care,
Patti

A photo of Hannah's little face filled the bottom of the screen. She had her fist in her mouth, there was a drool on her lips and she looked out from the picture with Patti's eyes. Jessi's heart clenched and her stomach roiled as she realized that her dear friend wasn't going to see that first tooth come in.

Since her door was closed and no one could witness it, she leaned her head on the desk and let herself cry.

As the plane lifted off, Allan watched Jessi put her earbuds in and turn away from him toward the window. To say that she wasn't herself was an absolute understatement. The woman who'd always irritated him was positively subdued. A shadow of her normal self. He saw her wipe away a tear in the reflection from the glass.

He knew it was none of his business. He owed Jessi next to nothing, and she was entitled to her grief. In fact, he understood completely how she felt, but a part of him wanted to needle her. Wanted to jar her and force her out of her funk so she could irritate him and he'd be able to forget. The last thing he wanted to do was spend a cross-country flight with his own thoughts.

Not right now when he was wondering why a confirmed bachelor was still alive and a family man with everything to live for was dead. God knew that Allan wasn't religious, and something like this just reinforced his belief that there definitely wasn't a higher force in the world. There was no fairness to John dying when he had so much to live for.

Allan looked around the cabin. He'd bought the G6 jet when Playtone had signed their first multibillion-dollar contract, and he didn't regret it. If there was one thing he prized in this life it was his own comfort. The cream-colored leather chairs had more than enough room for him to stretch out his six-foot, five-inch frame. He did so now, deliberately knocking over Jessi's expensive-looking leather bag in the process.

She glanced at him with one eyebrow arched and picked up the bag without removing her earbuds. She leaned her head back against the seat and a lock of her short ebony hair slid down over her eye. He had touched her hair once. It was cool and soft. He'd tangled his hand in it as he'd kissed her at John and Patti's wedding, behind the balustrade, out of the way of prying eyes.

Like everything between the two of them, he'd meant the kiss to be a game of one-upmanship, to shock her, but it hadn't worked. It had rocked *him* to his foundations, because there'd been a spark of something more in that one kiss. How was it that his archnemesis could turn him on like no other woman could?

He nudged her bag and she took her earbuds off as she turned to him and stared. Her gaze was glacial, as if he wasn't worth her attention.

"What's your problem?" she asked.

"Can't get comfortable," he said.

She glanced around at the six other empty seats before turning her chocolate-brown eyes back at him. "Really? Looks like you could stretch out and not bother me if you wanted to. So I ask again, what's your problem?"

"Maybe I want to bother you."

"Of course you do. What's the matter, Allan, finally found the one thing your money can't buy?" she asked.

"And what would that be?" he retorted. In his experience there wasn't much money couldn't afford him. Granted, it wasn't going to bring John back, but there was nothing that could stop death. And hadn't he learned that at an early age, anyway, when his mother had been the victim of a botched surgery?

"Peace of mind," Jessi said, swiveling her chair to face him and leaning forward so that the material of her blouse gaped and afforded him a glimpse of her cleavage.

She said something else, but all he could concentrate on was her body. Though she dressed in that funky style of hers she always looked well put together and feminine. And he couldn't help but recall the way she'd felt in his arms at John and Patti's wedding.

Dammit, man, enough. She's the enemy and it's just grief making her seem irresistible.

"I'll grant you that. Though I do find that my peace of mind is enhanced by the things I buy," he said.

"Me, too," she admitted.

"What do you want to buy right now?" he asked. He had already decided to order himself a Harley-Davidson, which he and John had been talking about buying when they turned thirty-five. Now that John was gone, Allan wasn't going to wait any longer. Life was too short.

"Nothing," she said. "I usually splurge on travel, and Patti was my…" She turned her chair to face forward.

"Not talking about her isn't going to make your grief any easier," he said softly.

She shrugged. "You're right. Maybe tomorrow I'll be able to think about this rationally, but tonight…I can't."

"Why?"

She turned to give him one of her you're-an-idiot-glares. "Seriously?"

"I don't want to sit in silence for the next few hours.

I keep thinking about John and Patti and how the last time I saw them both…"

"Me, too," Jessi said. "I can't stop. I remember how you and I were fighting, and Patti asked me to try to get along."

She stopped talking and turned away again to wipe a tear from her eye.

"John said the same thing to me. He even went so far as to mention that you weren't too bad," Allan said.

She shook her head. "I liked him. He was good for Patti and he loved her, you know?"

"He certainly seemed to." John had spent a lot of time talking about Patti, and Allan believed his friend loved her. But Allan had never experienced any emotions like that so it was a little hard to believe love existed.

"Seemed to? Don't you believe he loved her?" Jessi asked.

"I think he thought he did. But I'm not sure that love is real. I think it's something we all come up with to assure ourselves we're not alone."

She turned in her seat and arched both eyebrows as she leaned forward. "Even you can't be that cynical."

He shrugged. He didn't get the love thing between a man and a woman. He'd seen people do a lot of things out of "love" and not one of them had been altruistic or all that great. And his own experiences with the emotion had been haphazard at best.

Especially since he'd become a very wealthy man. Women seemed to fall for him instantly, and as Jessi would be the first to point out, he wasn't that charming. It made it very hard for him to trust them. But to be honest he'd always had trust issues. How could you believe in love when so many people did things for love that weren't all that nice?

"But you're always dating," she said. "Why do that if you don't believe in love and finding the one to spend the rest of your life with?"

"Sex," he said bluntly.

"How clichéd," she replied. "And typically male."

"Like your attitude isn't typically female? It's true I like women for sex. And companionship. I enjoy having them around, but love? That's never entered into the picture," he said.

"Maybe because you'd have to put someone else first," she suggested.

"I'm capable of doing that," he said, thinking of his friendship with John, but also his relationship with his cousins. He would go to them in the middle of the night if they called. Hence this cross-country red-eye to settle John's affairs. "What about you? You don't really strike me as a romantic."

"I'm not," she said. "But I do believe in love. I've got the heartbreak to prove that falling in love is real."

"Who broke your heart?" he asked. It was the first time in the five years he'd known her that she'd admitted to anything this personal. And he found himself unable to look away. Unable to stop the tide of emotions running through him as he stared at her. Who had hurt her and why did it suddenly matter to him?

"Some dick," she said.

He almost smiled because she sounded more angry than brokenhearted. "Tell me more."

"That's none of your business, Allan. Just trust me. If you ever let yourself be real instead of throwing around money and buying yourself trophy girlfriends, you'd find love."

He doubted it. "You think so? Is that how it happened for you?"

"Nah, I was too young and thought lust was love," she said. "Happy?"

"Not really," he said. "If you haven't experienced real love why are you so convinced it exists?"

"John and Patti. I've never met two people more in love. And as much as it pains me to admit it, your cousin Dec seems to be in love with my sister."

"They are borderline cutesy with all that hand-holding and kissing."

And just like that, she'd turned the tables and made him realize the truth of what she was saying. John was one of the few people he'd genuinely cared for, but they'd been friends for a long time, way before Allan had made his fortune and started running with the mon-eyed crowd. He didn't want to admit that maybe Jessi was right, but a part of him knew she was.

Three

She'd turned away after that conversation and he'd let her. Really talking about love with Allan wasn't something Jessi was truly interested in. The music on her iPod wasn't loud or angry—in fact, she was listening to the boy band 'N Sync. She and Patti had listened to their music endlessly when they were teens, and now the songs brought her some comfort. However, when "Bye Bye Bye" almost made her cry, she pulled her earbuds out of her ears and turned her attention to Allan.

He was restlessly pacing the length of the cabin and talking on the phone. She thought she heard him saying something about Jack White. She currently had a lead on the famous Hollywood director-producer and was trying to book a meeting with him later this month to discuss developing some of his summer blockbusters into games. It would be a coup if she could do a deal with Jack, and it would guarantee her job at Playtone-Infinity.

Allan glanced over and caught her staring.

"I'll have to call you back when we land."

He disconnected the call and pocketed his iPhone.

"We're playing for the same team now," she said. "You don't have to hide your business."

"You're on probation," he reminded her. "I'm not sure you'll make it past the ninety days."

"Really? I'm pretty sure I will. Have you ever known me to fail?"

He turned the leather chair in front of her to face her, and fell down into it. "Not without a hell of a fight."

She smiled. It almost felt like old times. They were finally finding their way back to their normal bickering, but she had the feeling they were both playing a role. Hell, she was. She was trying to be "normal" when everything inside of her was chaos.

"True dat."

"With all that's going on, we haven't had a chance to talk about my offer to buy you out," he reminded her. "I'm still willing to do that."

"I thought we'd already taken care of that. My answer remains no. I'm sorry if I've given you the impression that I'm someone who walks away from a difficult situation."

"Okay, okay. So what are you going to do to convince the Playtone board of directors to keep you on?"

Aside from doing a deal with Jack White, which was a long shot, she had no idea. Her plans for her future at the merged company were vague. It wasn't like her to be so wishy-washy, but she was tired of the entire family feud thing and was beginning to wonder if she even liked video games. She'd never admit that particular fact to a living soul. There were parts of the company that she loved, but right now she couldn't name them. There had been so much contention lately with the Montrose heirs that she hadn't been able to enjoy going to work.

"I am working on a push for Cari's holiday game. It will launch in two weeks' time and my team is working to make sure it's a hit."

Her sister and the development team had come up with an idea for a game app for the holidays that enabled players to decorate houses and Christmas trees, and then post screen shots to the online game center to try to get the most votes for their decor. The leaderboard was updated every day. The project had used existing assets at the company, so had a really low cost, and Emma believed it was that kind of out-of-the-box thinking that had saved Cari's job. It wasn't that there weren't other holiday apps; it was more the fact that Infinity Games had never done one before and that practically every component of the game was pure profit.

"That's good, but it won't be enough to save your job," he said.

She wished there was something easy or magical she could do to get herself out of this situation. But it was hard enough to be in this position, let alone having to come up with something so revolutionary it would impress the board at Playtone. It was going to take a lot to do that. Kell, Dec and Allan hated her grandfather and Infinity Games for what they'd done to old Thomas Montrose, and they wanted her to fail.

She held back a sigh—she'd never let Allan see that kind of weakness from her. "I'm not about to let you win. I don't care if I have to work 24/7 when we get back from taking care of this business on the East Coast. That's what I'll do."

He gave her that cocky half grin of his. "I expected a fight. Glad to hear you will be delivering one."

"Really?"

"Yes," he said. "I like our skirmishes."

"Is that all our encounters are to you?" she asked, thinking of that one kiss they'd shared. There was something weird about kissing your enemy and finding some attraction there.

"Are you asking about the night of Patti and John's wedding?"

"Yes. Seemed like we weren't at war that night."

"Well, we were, but we got distracted," he said.

"Until someone prettier came along," she said, remembering watching another bridesmaid, Camille Bolls, walk out of Allan's hotel room the morning after.

He shook his head. "There is no one who can compare to you."

"Ah, I've looked in the mirror. I'm not a classic beauty," Jessi admitted. And clearly not his type. It didn't bother her. Really, it didn't. She had chosen her look a long time ago and had done it deliberately. Most people saw her modern punk exterior and decided she was hard as nails. Exactly what she'd intended when she'd had her nose pierced and a small tattoo done on her collarbone near the hollow of her throat. It was discreet and could be covered with the collar of most blouses.

"No, but there is still…something about you that makes it hard to look away," he said.

"You must have an iron will because you don't have any problems doing it," she said.

He leaned forward, his arms resting on his knees and his expression more sincere than she'd seen in a while. "That's because I'm not a sap. I know better than to let you think there is anything between us. You'd use it, and me, to get whatever you wanted."

She shrugged. It would be nice to believe she had that kind of power over him. "Good thing I stopped believing in fairy tales a long time ago."

"Sometimes I don't know whether to arm wrestle you or kiss you."

"Kiss me? That didn't really get us anywhere the last time," she said.

"I was hesitant because of business complications, but now Playtone has the upper hand with Infinity and there is nothing stopping me from taking what I want."

"Except me," she said softly.

She looked over at him to gauge his reaction, and it was clear that he took it as a challenge. Suddenly, she was able to let herself forget about everything else that had happened today. Forget about the mess that her life was at this moment and remember that Allan McKinney was the one man who'd always been a worthy opponent.

"Except you," he said, "But I have a feeling you want to know if that one kiss was a fluke, as well."

"I have a feeling you're nothing but ego," she countered, refusing to let him see that she was intrigued. She'd never admit it out loud, but she'd had more than one hot fantasy about him.

She didn't really want to do this now, didn't want to have some kind of intense physical attraction to Allan McKinney. But there was no denying that she'd thought about that embrace more times than she'd wanted to over the past year and a half. She'd thought about *him* more than she'd wanted to. And those thoughts hadn't always involved fantasies of seeing him roasted over a pit.

She had to admit that in her musings he was usually shirtless, and most times they were both overheated. But that was her secret desire, and no way was she letting anything like that out in the open.

She looked so determined and at the same time so adorable.... What was wrong with him? Had he really become so bored with life that the only time he felt truly engaged was when he was going toe-to-toe with this woman? He could deny it all he wanted, but he knew the truth. There was something about Jessi that turned him on.

They were alone in the jet and would be for the entirety of the flight. Fawkes rode up front in the cockpit and functioned as copilot.

Allan had thought of Jessi as steel-hearted before today. She'd always seemed sort of a ballbuster until he'd seen the cracks and chinks in her tough-girl facade. Even when she'd hired that P.I. to investigate John before he'd married Patti, Allan hadn't realized that she'd done it because of her deep emotional attachments, not just to be a bitch. Because she cared about her friend... maybe even loved her. He'd never suspected that the woman who needled him the way she did could be as soft as he was beginning to suspect she was.

"I think I might be able to persuade you to come around to my way of thinking about sex instead of love," he said. He needed to change the dynamic between them. Get them back to the familiar footing they'd always been on.

"That's putting a lot of pressure on your charm and sex appeal," she said with a wry grin.

"Trying to take potshots at my ego?" He put his hand over his heart. "Hoping to see if you can deflate me?"

"Sort of. Is it working?"

"Nah, I still know I'm all that and a bag of doughnuts," he said.

She laughed, but it sounded a little forced to him, and he realized she was on edge, too. Maybe because she'd felt something for him that one night, or maybe it still had to do with John's and Patti's deaths. Allan had no idea, and if he were honest, he didn't care at this moment. Thinking about Jessi, sparring with her, kept him from remembering his best friend was dead.

"You're some piece of work," she said. "Let's see what you're bringing to the game, big boy. How are you going to tempt me?"

"I thought I'd make it into a challenge," he said.

"What kind?"

She seemed intrigued, and he had to wonder if maybe she needed a distraction, the way he did. They'd always made bets over outrageous things and always honored them. In fact, if she weren't so…well, if she weren't *Jessi,* he'd actually like her. But she was Jessi. A Chandler. A prickly, ornery woman with as much cuddliness as a porcupine.

"One you won't want to lose," he said.

"I'm listening."

"I'm betting that you're attracted to me and that you can't control yourself better than I can when we put each other to the test," he said. It was a calculated risk. A chance to prove to himself that his iron willpower over his body and his sexual prowess were still intact. Because there was something very different about Jessi, something that he didn't entirely know how to deal with.

"I know I can," she said. "So what's in it for me?"

He thought about it for a few long minutes, shifting back in the chair. Just thinking of kissing her made him stir, so he stretched his long legs out in front of him to relieve the pressure on his groin.

"If you win I'll help you keep your job at the newly merged Playtone-Infinity Games," he said.

A light went out of her eyes and he saw her nibble on her lower lip. He didn't know what he'd said to cause that reaction, and made a mental note to pursue the question at another time.

"And if you win?" she asked.

"You let me buy you out," he said. "You walk away from gaming a wealthy woman."

"If you agree to help me, can you guarantee that I won't be axed?" she asked. "Because I don't think Kell is going to be that impressed with you saying that you lost a kissing contest with me and that's why you have to keep me on."

"Oh, Jess, I'm not going to lose," Allan said. "But if I do, I will help you by making my network of contacts available to you. I have a feeling that with those connections you'd be unstoppable."

"Why not just do that anyway?" she asked.

"We're enemies, remember? From the first moment we met you knew I was a Montrose cousin and I knew you were a Chandler sister."

"True. The family feud will always be there, won't it? Even though Cari and Dec have a son and are planning to get married…there's still bad blood between our families in your eyes."

"It's hard to just dismiss it," he said. "So do we have a deal?"

She crossed her arms under her breasts while she leaned back in her chair, then crossed her slim legs. She wore boots that would look ridiculous on anyone else, combat boots with a thick, three-inch heel that gave her added height. Tight-fitting leather pants and a loose, sheer black blouse completed the outfit. But it wasn't inappropriate, given that it was Jessi. He could tell by her all-black outfit that she was mourning.

"All I have to do to win is make sure you are more affected by one kiss than I am?" she asked.

"That's it. Keep in mind in certain circles I'm known as—"

"The man with a big mouth and bigger ego?" she taunted.

"You're going down, Chandler," he said.

"Only if I agree to your deal. And given how hard you're pushing for me to accept it, I'd say I'm destined to win."

"There was something destined to happen," he said, leaning forward in his chair and putting his hands on the armrests on either side of her. "Stop baiting me and make your choice."

"Am I baiting you?" she asked, shifting closer to him and tilting her head to one side as she stared at his mouth.

"You know you are," he said, trying to ignore the tingling of his lips. He was in control here.

"Well, then I guess I'm going to have to accept your wager. Prepare to lose, McKinney," she said.

Jessi came over to him and straddled his lap. Slowly, she eased forward and brought her mouth down on his. Her only thought was to do this and win, and then she'd focus on keeping her job. But the moment her mouth met his something changed.

It had been easy to tell herself that her memory of

what had happened between them at the wedding wasn't
accurate, or that everything had been due to the champagne she'd drunk that night. But now, in the cold reality at thirty-five thousand feet in the air, there was
no denying that the attraction she felt for him was real.

His mouth was firm against hers and his lips were
soft. He was letting her be the aggressor, and she took
full advantage of that, running her tongue over the seam
where his lips met. He tasted minty and fresh, and she
pulled back, but felt his hand on her head, keeping her
in place.

His tongue traced her lips, as well, and she wondered
if he'd like the flavor of her strawberry lip gloss or if it
would be too sweet for him. But he didn't say anything,
only kept coming back to taste more of it and of her.

She opened her mouth and felt the brush of his
tongue over hers. She wanted to moan, but kept that
sound locked away. She struggled to remember she
was competing here. And suddenly it seemed stupid
to her that the first man she'd kissed in a long time—
and wanted to keep on kissing—was playing a game
with her.

She closed her eyes and let herself experience the
embrace of a man who made her want to forget she was
a Chandler, and just enjoy being a woman.

His mouth was warm, and he tasted good. So good
she never wanted the kiss to end. She shifted to get
closer to him, but he kept the distance between them
and she realized she was in danger of losing this bet.
She hadn't anticipated having to fight her own urges
while she kissed him.

She tried to think of Allan, tried to stem the need
welling up inside her to feel his solid chest pressed

against hers. Tried to forget that she'd seen him shirtless enough times to know that he had solid pecs and a well-developed six-pack. Tried to forget that the man was seriously ripped.

She was losing it and losing the challenge. But then she felt the barest movement of his fingers against her neck. The tracing of a pattern that sent shivers down her spine and electric tingles through her entire body. *Dammit,* she thought, as every nerve ending started to pulse in time with her heartbeat.

She reached for his head. Tunneled her fingers through his thick hair and pulled him closer. She thrust her tongue deep into his mouth and forced him to take her. Reminded him that she was in control of this desire and this embrace.

But then he answered back and she was once again adrift. Forced to forget about wagers and feuds and every single thing except the way his mouth felt against hers and the way he made her wish this kiss would never end.

She rubbed her thumb against the base of his neck in a small circle and felt his heartbeat quicken. She took her time spreading her fingers out and enjoying the feel of his scalp under her hand, until she shifted forward and forced his head to the side, where she could take more control of their embrace.

But it was no longer about power or winning. Now she was kissing him because the taste of him was addictive. She'd never forget this one moment for years to come; she knew it with bone-deep certainty. The way he felt with just her hands in his hair and her lips on his. The way his tongue felt deep in her mouth as the smell of his aftershave surrounded her.

The dreams and desires she'd forced aside for too long came rushing up to her and she saw a chance to have everything she'd ever wanted. A man who could make her feel real desire and an out to walk away from the gaming world once and for all. All she'd have to do was give up everything she'd made herself into as an adult.

She'd have to lose to Allan. She'd have to show him that she could be vulnerable, and she'd have to admit it all out loud.

She sucked his lower lip into her mouth and bit down, and then rubbed her tongue over it to soothe it. She didn't think she could do that. But when she felt his hands tightening in her hair for a moment and a low groan issued from the back of his throat, she realized she might not have to.

He pulled his mouth from hers. She opened her eyes to look up into his intense gaze, and shook from what she saw there. He might want to pretend that she was nothing more than an old enemy to him, but the truth was there in those dilated pupils and in the flush across his cheekbones.

She almost cursed out loud as she realized there was no winner in this. No outcome that could be decided other than the truth. She was attracted to him. And though she'd hoped that maybe kissing him would distract her from the lonely feeling in her soul, it hadn't worked. In fact, she really wanted to just curl up next to him and forget about challenges and the world outside, and take some comfort in his arms.

If he hadn't made this a contest and if she'd been a different sort of woman—the kind who was okay being emotional and needy—then she'd be able to just rest her head on his shoulder and admit that she hadn't ever felt this scared and alone before.

"So…" he said. "That was more than I expected."

"Me, too," she admitted. "I guess we underestimated how much we'd enjoy each other."

"I sure did. Tonight especially, I…I enjoyed kissing you, Jessi."

"Me, too, Allan. I don't think you're my archnemesis anymore."

"That's good. So what are we going to do about this? Is it just grief? Did we turn to each other because our friends are gone?"

She shrugged. A part of her wanted to say yes and make this about the tragedy that had brought them both together. But she knew that would be a lie. And lying even to herself was something she didn't like to do.

"I really don't know," she admitted.

"Me, either. I have always been able to… Never mind. The real question is what are we going to do about it?"

She didn't have an answer. There wasn't a clear solution. He had surprised her and made her realize that there was more to this man than she'd previously thought. Because if he'd been all ego, then he would have swaggered away from her. But he was sitting across from her, looking just as perplexed as she was.

Four

It was humid and breezy as they stepped off the plane at the Dare County Airport in Manteo, North Carolina. Unlike the Los Angeles area, where everything was either developed or part of the desert, North Carolina—and especially the Outer Banks—was made up of small villages surrounded by state-owned land that had been preserved to keep this part of the world wild.

As the breeze flattened her shirt to her breasts, Allan was transfixed for a second by the sheer beauty of Jessi. Who'd have guessed that she would be a femme fatale without even trying? He fiddled with the strap on his overnight bag to distract himself.

But there was no distraction from Jessi. Her perfume danced on the wind and wrapped around his senses as he stood there in the eerie predawn light.

"Thanks for the lift," she said in that smart-ass way of hers that signaled the truce they'd sort of reached on the plane was over.

"You're welcome. It was an enjoyable flight," he said.

"Whatever. I figured I'd stay at Patti and John's bed-and-breakfast until we go home," she said.

"Fawkes has taken care of all the arrangements. The staff has canceled new arrivals, and when I spoke to the caretaker, he said there were only two couples left at the resort and that they would be leaving today."

"I guess that's one less thing to worry about," she said. "I'm more than ready to talk to their attorney and do whatever we need to do. Patti's mother isn't going to be much help…since she's ill."

Allan understood that Patti's mom, Amelia Pearson, was in the second stage of Alzheimer's-related dementia, but John had told him to keep it quiet, since Patti hadn't wanted anyone to know. He saw how thinking about Amelia's condition affected Jessi. Her shoulders were stooped for a second and he imagined it was from the burden of knowing that your best friend's own mother might not be able to mourn her.

"As soon as we see the attorney this morning we'll know more," he said. It wasn't something he was looking forward to, but at least Allan already knew a lot about John's wishes for the future. His friend had always been very loquacious and liked to share his dreams once he'd met and married Patti.

"I don't get why they wanted to live here," Jessi said. She glanced around the small airport. "I mean, it's nice enough to get away from the bustle of L.A. once in a while, but all the time? I don't think I could do it," she said. "It's going to take us over an hour to get to their place on Hatteras."

"I know, and my cell phone signal stinks. I think Kell is probably going to disown me if I don't check in, and I've only got one bar," Allan said.

Jessi pulled her iPhone out of her pocket and glanced

at the screen. "I've got almost two bars…want to use mine?"

He looked at her. As an olive branch gesture it was almost remarkable. She'd never offered him anything before. He tucked that fact away in the back of his mind to analyze later as he nodded at her.

"I have his number preprogrammed. He's listed under Darth Sucks-A-Lot," Jessi said as she handed the phone over.

Allan turned away to keep her from seeing the smile that spread across his face. He couldn't wait to tell Dec, who would think Jessi's tag for Kell was funny. "Don't let him see that. He hates *Star Wars*."

"Who hates *Star Wars*? Just another thing that proves your cousin is an alien cyborg," Jessi said. "Do you need privacy to talk to him?"

"Yes, if you don't mind."

"No problem. I'll go check with Fawkes about the car."

"Sounds good. Will you need to call your sisters?" he asked.

"Not at this time of the night. They both have little kids and will probably be sleeping," she said. "Are you sure Kell will be up at 4:00 a.m.?"

"Yes. He only needs four hours of sleep a night. Plus he'll be waiting for me to check in," Allan said.

"Of course, since he's some kind of future-engineered, high-performing robot," she said, walking away.

Allan watched her leave, as he had many times before, but now he noticed how her entire body moved. The swish of her hips in those skintight leather pants, the way the heels on her boots canted her hips forward and made her legs seem miles long. The way the tail of her blousy shirt curved around her ass.

He appreciated her as a woman, and despite how chaotic things were inside him right now, watching her walk was like a balm. It reminded him that he was still alive.

He hit the auto dial for Kell and waited three rings until his cousin picked up.

"Montrose here."

"It's Allan."

"What number are you calling me from?" he asked. "I had this down as someone else's."

"It's Jessi's phone. Mine isn't working right and I couldn't get a signal, but hers did. I wanted to check in and see if I missed anything last night."

"Not much. I sent you an email that details everything I need done today. Will you have reception later?" Kell asked.

Allan felt as if he had to defend the fact that the cell towers in this part of the world weren't thick on the ground. But he knew Kell wasn't irritated with him per se, but more with anything that interrupted the normal flow of business. "I don't know. John has Wi-Fi at his place so once I get there we should be good to go. I'm going to be busy this morning with the attorney and the funeral arrangements, but I'll get everything back to you today."

"That's what I was hoping you'd say. It's not much, but I need you to run some figures on a pro forma that Emma submitted. Also, I've talked to Dec, and unless Jessi pulls out something spectacular we're in favor of offering her a package and cutting her from the company. I need you to work on that today."

"Can't you cut me a little slack? I get that this is business, but we're dealing with the loss of our best friends," he said.

There was silence on the other end of the phone, and Allan wondered if he'd pushed Kell too far.

"You're right. I can give you both a few extra days. How are you holding up?"

"Fine," Allan said. "You know me."

"I do, which is why I don't buy that B.S. answer. You and John were like brothers."

"It's hard, Kell," Allan said. "But I can't talk about it."

"Fair enough. I'm here if you need me," he stated.

Allan knew that his older cousin would be there for him. Despite how cold he seemed in the office and how single-minded he could be in his quest for revenge against the Chandlers, Kell had a very strong sense of loyalty to both his cousins.

"I'll call when I know something more. I'm going to have to reboot my phone, so until I notify you, call me on this number."

He clicked off and thought about his cousin's hard-line attitude. Kell was determined to let Jessi go, and there was nothing Allan could do to save her. And a part of him was very glad about that, because she was the kind of complication he didn't need in his life for the long term, even though he knew that she was in it for the foreseeable future.

The Land Rover Fawkes had arranged for them to use was a new model. It was spacious and comfortable and had four-wheel drive, something that seemed important out here in the wilderness of North Carolina.

Fawkes had stowed their bags in the back of the vehicle and then opened the door to the backseat for Jessi. She stood for a minute as the warm breeze stirred around her. The sun was rising and for a minute she enjoyed the view of the sun coming up over the ocean instead of her normal view of it sinking down into it.

"Thanks," she said, climbing in.

"You're welcome, Ms. Jessi."

"You can just call me Jessi, you know."

"Very well," Fawkes said.

Allan didn't say anything as he got into the passenger seat in the front, which suited Jessi just fine. She put her earbuds in her ears and pretended to disappear. She loved the fact that it was acceptable by society to do so, even though a part of her felt a bit rude. But right now she couldn't talk to anyone.

She didn't want to talk to anyone. Being here made Patti's death more real. Jessi watched as they left the small barrier island where the airport was located and crossed the bridge to another small strip of land. The Outer Banks were really just tiny bits of land that barely kept the sea at bay.

Once again she pondered Patti's choice in making her home here on the edge of the wilderness. It was pretty, though, she thought, as the sun continued to rise over the ocean. They turned right at Whale Bone Junction Information Station and followed NC 12 south, crossing the Oregon Inlet Bridge. She took her earbuds out when Allan gestured toward her.

"Yes?"

"Seems like the end of the world, doesn't it?" he asked.

She nodded, a bit unnerved that they were thinking

along the same lines. Was it also occurring to him that if Patti and John hadn't moved out here maybe they'd still be alive?

"I think that's why Patti liked it," she said at last, unwilling to voice her real thoughts.

"I agree. No rat race here. Especially now that it's the off-season," Allan said. "Fawkes was just mentioning that the man at the desk in the airport warned him that that tropical storm in the Atlantic is now predicted to strengthen into a hurricane, and one of the projected paths has it coming straight toward Hatteras, where the B and B is located."

"Really?"

"Yes, ma'am—Jessi," Fawkes said. "I didn't think it would be a concern, but seeing these roads, I thought it best to mention it. Any kind of surge in the tide would wipe some of this out."

"I agree," Allan said. "Fawkes is going to keep an eye on the situation while we're taking care of the funerals and other arrangements. But if need be we should be ready for a quick escape."

"I always am," Jessi said.

"That's right, you are," he agreed. "So am I. But escaping a tricky personal situation and escaping Mother Nature are two different things."

She nodded. She put her earbuds back in as the conversation lagged. She was listening to Pink's latest and enjoying the mix of raw emotion and anger that Pink was always able to capture in her songs.

Twenty or so minutes into their drive, she noticed skid marks on the road. She pulled her earbuds from her ears as Fawkes slowed the Land Rover to a stop.

"Is this…?"

"I think so," Allan said, opening his door before Fawkes had the car in Park.

Jessi sat where she was, looking at the crushed grass, the wreckage from the other car and the remains of Patti's sweet little Miata, which still was there. Upside down and impossibly mangled.

Her heart started beating fast, and in her mind she heard screams. But she knew that was only her imagination. She got out of the vehicle and walked over to the side of the road. This was it, she thought.

Oh, God. This was it. This was how Patti and John had died, and it was worse than anything Jessi could have pictured in her head.

Car accident. Those words could mean anything, and the reality was so much harder to stomach than anything she'd imagined.

Staring at the wreckage, she heard the far-off sound of someone sobbing, and realized it was her. She turned away, not wanting Allan or even Fawkes to see her like this. But then she felt a hand on her shoulder.

When she turned back around, she didn't look up, but just moved forward, wrapping her arms around Allan's waist and burying her face in his chest. He held her tightly as she let loose the emotions she'd tried so unsuccessfully to tamp down.

She wanted to pretend that none of this had happened. But she had never been one for running away from the truth. And in this moment she knew she no longer could keep alive the very small hope that the authorities here had gotten it wrong. That Patti and John were still somehow alive.

No one had walked away from this scene. She knew it and accepted it. But the pain of losing her friend felt fresh and new, and so sharp that she couldn't breathe. Allan's hands moved up and down her back and she felt him shudder in her arms. Tipping her head back, she looked at the underside of his stubbled jaw.

When she noticed a thin line of tears running down his neck, she turned her head into the curve of his shoulder and held him as tightly as he held her.

She'd always seen him as her enemy. Even the ride out here and that kiss they'd shared on the plane hadn't really changed her perception—not at a gut-deep level. But in this moment, as she held on to the only other person in the world who understood her grief, she realized that he'd ceased being her rival.

Somehow in the past twenty-four hours he'd started to become simply Allan. Her Allan.

It was safe to assume he'd never felt this way before, and if he was completely honest, he never wanted to feel this way again. Losing John was making Allan question so many things, but most importantly, as he held Jessi in his arms, he wondered why he'd waited until his friend was gone to finally listen to him.

John had claimed from the beginning that he'd observed Allan and Jessi checking each other out when they thought no one was looking. And now, holding her in his arms, letting the tears he couldn't contain fall, Allan admitted that once again his friend had been right.

He felt a heavy hand on his shoulder and knew that Fawkes had joined them. The three of them, who'd never gotten along, were now united in grief.

And Allan had to wonder how much of what he felt at this moment was simply the need to feel the loss. The need to ensure that the empty part of his soul was filled with something…someone. He didn't want to be alone and didn't want to lose the memories he had of John, and whether he liked it or not…well, right now he'd be lying if he said he didn't like the fact that Jessi was here with him. She was the one he wanted to be with.

"I didn't think I'd fall apart like that," she said.

Pulling away, Fawkes walked closer to the wreckage, leaving the two of them alone. The breeze off the Atlantic was warm and strong, and for a minute Allan wished it could carry them away from here.

But that was only because he had no idea how to handle his grief. He turned his head away from Jessi and wiped his eyes before turning back.

"I saw you cry," she said, her tone kind and the look in her eyes one of the softest he'd ever seen. Her short punky hair was flying about in the wind, and her eye makeup had run from her tears, leaving dark tracks down her face.

"I saw *you* cry," he said, trying hard for a teasing note he just didn't feel.

"I guess we're even then," she said at last. "You know what?"

"What?" he asked. He wasn't sure he wanted to keep talking when every word she said made him feel raw and exposed.

"I'd be happy to lose to you now if it meant Patti and John were still here."

One of the things Allan had always respected about Jessi was her honesty, even when it would serve her better to lie. At first he'd thought her bluntness was just another tool she used to keep him disarmed, but then he'd realized that she had no barriers.

It had been his first clue that the girl who looked as if she'd take on hell with a bucket of water was actually vulnerable. He didn't need to be reminded of that right now. He needed her fierce and prickly, needed her to be his enemy. But he feared that ship had sailed. He was never going to look at Jessi the same way again.

"Me, too," he admitted.

"What the hell happened out here?" Jessi asked. "I know they were hit and then drove into the tree, but really, who would be driving that fast on this kind of road?"

"An idiot," Allan said. Inside, he felt some of that rage, as well. But his modus operandi was to channel it into graciousness and fake ennui. "I hope I never meet the guy," he added.

"Same here. I don't think it would be easy to have to see the person who caused this and… It would just be too much, you know?"

"I do know," he said as she looked up at him with that gaze of hers that cut through a man and made him feel he was completely exposed from the inside out. God, Allan hated that. He didn't want Jessi to see him—really see him.

She started laughing, and he glanced at her to see if she was okay or if she was truly losing it.

She shook her head. "Sorry. I was just thinking that we're finally getting along. Patti would be giving me an I-told-you-so look if she were alive at this moment."

"John would, too," Allan said. He couldn't count the number of times his buddy had taken him to one side and asked him to give Jessi a chance. To stop baiting Patti's best friend and just let her into that protected inner circle of trust that Allan fiercely guarded.

"Why didn't we?" she asked. "Why didn't we do this before they were gone? They were our dearest friends. All they wanted was for us to get along, and we could never be anything but enemies."

"We are 'enemies' because there's something very similar in both of us, and we were raised to distrust each other's families. We like to win, we like to protect our friends, and mostly, we don't like it when anyone notices that we aren't invincible," he said.

She crossed her arms over her chest, and then with a sigh uncrossed them and turned to face him. "I don't want to admit this, but there is a small kernel of truth in what you just said."

He felt the band of tension inside of him loosen.

"I was right?" he asked. Those were words he'd been positive that Jessi Chandler would never utter in his presence.

"Don't let it go to your head," she said, putting her arms around her waist and turning to walk back toward the Land Rover. "I'm pretty sure that it won't happen again."

For the first time since he'd gotten the awful news that John was dead, Allan felt something. He wanted to pretend it was lust, because just looking at Jessi made him want her. Or maybe he could explain it away as shared grief. But the truth of the matter was much harder to accept.

He liked her. He liked being with her. And he'd have to say, in all honesty, that he wanted this new feeling to grow.

Five

Jessi sat next to Allan in the attorney's office, trying to let the newest shock sink in.

Reggie Blythe was a tall, thin African American man who looked to be in his mid-fifties. He had a little gray at his temples and a wiry look that said he spent more time at work than at home. Jessi thought that his office had a charming Old South feel to it, but freely admitted to herself that the impression came from images she'd seen in Hollywood movies.

She felt nervous and unsure. She didn't know how to handle this meeting or Allan.

Actually, it was only Allan who was shaking her up right now. She could handle attorneys. But Allan was something else.

Reggie had been giving them a rundown on John and Patti's will and their hopes for Hannah's upbringing. But Jessi was busy looking at Allan and remembering that moment when they'd stopped by the accident scene and he'd held her in his arms. He had just offered comfort, and been so damned human that she'd had to rethink everything.

Not just what she'd thought about him, but also what she'd always believed about herself.

"I don't understand. Is that even legal?" Allan asked.

Damn. She needed to pay better attention. What had he said?

"It's highly unusual for joint custody to be given to two people who aren't married, but it's not illegal," Reggie said.

"Why would they do this?" Jessi asked. It was slowly sinking in that Patti and John had left custody of Hannah to her and Allan, even though they'd known that she and Allan didn't really like each other.

"I suspect they didn't anticipate dying so young," Reggie said with a wry note in his voice. "Also that they wanted to ensure Hannah had influences from both sides of her parents' lives."

"Of course. Where is Hannah now?" Allan asked.

"She's in state custody now. We couldn't keep her with her babysitter, but we'll be turning her over to you both as soon as this meeting is finished," Reggie said, glancing at his watch.

"And that's it? We can just go back to L.A.?" Jessi asked.

"No. A judge will be reviewing the case, and once you are both approved as joint guardians, then you can return to California. Patti and John have already paid me to serve as your legal counsel in the proceedings, unless you have objections and would like your own attorney."

"What if one of us isn't interested in being a guardian?" Allan asked.

"Is that the case?" Reggie asked, his kind brown eyes meeting Allan's gaze first before shifting to Jessi.

Allan didn't say anything else. Jessi was worried. She knew nothing about raising a baby—in fact, she'd already decided she wasn't ever having kids. But this was Patti's final request, and she found that she couldn't deny her friend.

"Can we have a moment alone to discuss this?" Jessi asked.

"Of course. You may use my office," he said, getting up to leave the room. When the door closed behind him she turned to Allan.

He stood and paced to the window, pausing with the sun behind him, which made it very difficult for her to see his expression. He didn't seem like the Allan who'd held her so tenderly and shared her grief. He seemed like the old Allan, maneuvering around while trying to figure out the best position to be in.

She didn't like it. Which man was the real one? She wanted him to be…something she suspected he couldn't be. But maybe she should give him the benefit of the doubt. He was in the same situation she was. Just as blown away by the fact that they were going to be raising a little girl.

Or were they? Would he stand by her and help her or was she going to be doing this on her own?

"Do you not want to be a guardian?" she asked bluntly.

"Of course I do. She's John's daughter and he was closer to me than a brother. I only voiced that option in case you wanted an out but were too timid to ask," he said.

"Are you kidding me? I don't do timid," she said. "You know that. So what's this all about?"

Allan walked toward her. As he moved closer, she

could see for the first time since she'd met him a very sincere look on his face. He wasn't doing the fake charming thing or acting as if he could buy his way out of this.

"I don't walk away from commitments," he said. "John and Patti must have had their reasons for appointing both of us. I don't know what they were, but today I started to see a glimpse of it. I'm just not sure if you did."

"I did," she admitted. "But is this real?"

"We won't know until we get Hannah and return to the West Coast."

"I agree. I can't say no to this," Jessi said.

"Me, either."

The atmosphere in the room was becoming too heavy, the situation too real, and she didn't like it. She needed time to process the fact that Allan was going to be in her life for the rest of it. She started doing the logistics. "So what are we going to do?" she asked. "I mean, from a practical standpoint. I live in Malibu."

"I'm in Beverly Hills," Allan said.

"Well, we can hand her off to each other at work," Jessi said. "I'm not as familiar with the Playtone Games campus, but if we use the facility at Infinity, they have a first-rate day care center where Hannah can stay during our working hours. Then we can divide up her nights."

"I like that plan, but we should have a contingency in case your probation doesn't work out," Allan said.

She made a face at him. Of course he'd bring that up. "I'm not going to lose my job. I've already told you I have some new ideas."

"I'm just saying we should figure out some more options," he said. "I like to plan for every eventuality."

She wondered if she'd ever really know what he was thinking. Then she shook her head. She had other things to worry about than that. Hannah, her future, dealing with Allan every day from now on. It was a big responsibility and one Jessi wouldn't shirk. She'd figure out a way to make this work.

"I guess it's decided then," she said.

"Yes, I'll go and get Reggie."

She sat back in the leather chair and tried to relax, but she couldn't. Every time she thought she'd adjusted to losing Patti there was something new that surprised her. Jessi ran her hands through her short hair and realized it was getting easier to think about her friend being gone. Not *easier;* that wasn't the right word. She just could do it without crying, which was a relief.

She'd always hated the fact that she couldn't control her tears. In general, she didn't cry unless she was mad, but this kind of grief, well, she supposed there was only one way for it to be expressed.

She heard the door open and turned to see Allan striding in with Reggie. Allan was a bit taller than the attorney and had his head bent to listen intently to what Reggie was saying. For all the world they looked as if they'd known each other for years. Typical of Allan, she thought. The man never met a stranger.

"Allan has told me the good news that you both will share guardianship. I can't tell you how happy that would have made Patti and John. They were adamant that they wanted their best friends to raise their daughter," Reggie said.

"Well, we really want to honor their wishes," Jessi answered.

"Good. I've got some paperwork for you to fill out,

and then I'll drive you over to get Hannah. The authority from the state wants to check you both out and ask you a few questions before she's released to you temporarily. I've already got a call in to the judge's office for scheduling."

"How long do you think this entire process will take?" Allan asked. "I'm— We're both needed back in L.A."

"I don't think it will take too long—maybe a week to ten days."

A week was definitely too long to Jessi's way of thinking. Hell, the plane flight with Allan had seemed endless. Sure, she knew there was no speeding this type of thing up, and there shouldn't be. She wanted the state officials to do their job and ensure that Hannah was going to be well cared for.

But staying in Hatteras with the man who was turning out to be her Achilles' heel didn't sound ideal. And she needed to think of the future. When it was just her it wouldn't have mattered if she lost her job at Playtone-Infinity Games. But now that she was going to be an example to Hannah...

Dammit, Jessi was going to have to rethink everything she'd thought she knew about herself, and reorder her priorities for Hannah's sake.

And that meant trying to get along with Mr. Allan McKinney, not liking him more than she already did, and most importantly, staying out of his bed.

When Reggie drove them to the foster home where Hannah was being kept, Jessi realized she was glad they'd gotten to Hatteras when they did. The home was nice enough from the outside, but the people inside were strangers to the baby girl. The sooner she was set up in a more permanent custody arrangement, the better.

"Hi there, I'm Di, and this my husband, Mick. We own a local restaurant and knew John and Patti," the foster mother said as they entered the house.

"This is Allan McKinney and Jessi Chandler, Hannah's guardians," Reggie replied.

"I'll go get her," Di said, as Mick led them into the living room.

Jessi was too nervous to really pay attention to the conversation. Inside, she was a quivering mess, because she knew next to nothing about babies. She always avoided holding her sisters' kids because she was afraid of dropping them or breaking them in some way. And she hadn't held Hannah for more than five minutes in her short life. Jessi figured she didn't have a maternal bone in her body. "Here she is," Di said, returning with a sleepy-looking Hannah.

Jessi went over and held her arms out, and Di handed her the baby. Jessi felt awkward and unsure until she looked down into those eyes that were so similar to Patti's.

This was Patti's daughter, Jessi thought. She held her closer and had a moment's horror as she realized she was about to start crying. She tried to turn away, but then Allan was there by her side. He didn't say anything, just wrapped his arm around her and looked over her shoulder at the baby.

Jessi didn't feel as overwhelmed when he was touching her. She wasn't alone. It didn't matter that there were still big issues between the two of them; they were united in this and right now that was all that mattered.

"I guess John and Patti's instincts were correct,"

Reggie said. "You two are going to make good guardians of their little girl."

"We will do our best," Allan said, looking Jessi straight in the eye.

It felt as if he was making a promise to her, and she couldn't help but feel as if together they would make this work. But she wondered how her sisters and his cousins would react to the news that she and Allan were going to be raising a child together.

She felt a twinge as she imagined the look on Darth-Sucks-A-Lot's face when he heard that another one of his cousins was so closely involved with a Chandler sister. But that little bit of mirth didn't change the fact that she and Allan were going to have to figure out how to be friends, because they were going to be the closest thing to parents that Hannah had.

"We can't screw this up," Jessi said.

"We won't," Allan answered. "We both are very good at making things happen the way we want them to."

Allan poured himself two fingers of Scotch and put his feet up on the railing as the sun set over Pamlico Sound. He was making promises he had no business making, he thought. But being here in John's old home, he found it hard not to feel the man he was in L.A. slipping away. The water was still and calm, and there was a soothing element to sitting here and forgetting about the long forty-eight hours he'd just lived through. Today had seemed endless, and he was more than ready for it to be over.

They'd finished making the funeral arrangements. In the end it had made more sense to have a joint ceremony, and Jessi had been very efficient at managing the little details.

Seeing that side of her had made him realize why she was so good at her job. He'd seen the reports on the interviews that Dec had conducted with the employees at Infinity Games. They'd all said that Jessi was singularly organized and always successfully launched their games.

Allan rubbed the back of his neck. He was square in the middle of it right now. Kell's hatred… Was it really just Kell who resented the Chandlers anymore? Allan knew that he'd started out with just as much anger toward them, but right now it was hard not to see the Chandlers, especially Jessi, as real people.

People who weren't part of the long-ago feud.

Jessi had volunteered to give little Hannah a bath after dinner, and he'd let her. He knew that she was tired, too, and maybe he should have been gentlemanly and stepped in to do it, but he wasn't ready to deal with a child yet.

He decided to text his cousin Dec, who was the father of a toddler himself. Of course, Dec had just met his son for the first time a few months earlier, but that made his perspective perfect for Allan. He needed some info, and quick, if he was going to do what he always did—make life look effortless. Because the baby was already throwing him off.

She'd cried and then spit up on his shirt, and he hadn't been too successful at diaper changing, either. He'd have to fix this situation. He didn't allow anything to get the better of him and he certainly didn't intend to start now.

He'd managed to reboot his phone so that he had cell coverage now. He messaged Dec.

Help. How do you deal with a baby?

The phone immediately rang and he answered it. "McKinney here."

"I love it. The great Allan McKinney doesn't know what to do," Dec said.

"I doubt you knew what to do the first time you held D.J."

"True. I didn't. Do you want me to ask Cari for advice?"

"No. Don't you dare. Just wanted to know how you handled it when you met D.J."

"I was afraid I'd break him. I kind of held him at arm's length. But then after I started spending time with him, I realized two things—one, it didn't matter what I said if I talked in a quiet, kind tone, and two, everyone screws up with kids. Even Cari, though she'll deny it."

"Thanks for that. Hannah's a little girl, Dec. I don't know anything about girls. I mean, we were all boys…."

Dec laughed. "You seem to do okay with women."

"Hannah's not a woman. This is different. I can't be charming or do all the things I know women expect a man to do. I have to be—"

"Real," Dec said. "It's that way with D.J. for me. I can't just phone it in. Kids require more. Hannah's a baby, and she's new to this situation just like you are. You'll figure it out."

"I hope so. I've downloaded a few books about child rearing on my Kindle app. But I needed to talk to someone who's actually done this."

"Well, that's all I got without asking my woman," Dec said.

"I'd rather you didn't, since she'd probably tell her sister," Allan said.

"How's that situation?"

He had no idea how to answer his cousin. The truth was, Jessi irritated him more now than she had two days ago. But she also fascinated him more. And he was obsessed with her, spending his time thinking about how soft her skin was and how much he liked her perfume.

Finally, he just said, "Good. We're both making the best of it. The funeral is going to be in four days' time. Are you coming? I can send the jet back for you."

"Yes. That would be great. I know that Cari and Emma are both interested in attending. Kell doesn't want to travel with them. In fact, he said he might not come at all."

"I'm worried about him. He has too much hatred toward the Chandlers," Allan said.

"Me, too. But what can we do? Hey, do you want to go with me when the Lakers play the Mavs in two weeks? Cari has to work," Dec asked.

Allan smiled to himself. He and Dec had grown closer since Dec had come back from Australia and found himself a family.

"Love to. Later, dude."

"Later," Dec said, disconnecting the call.

Allan skimmed the first book he'd downloaded on his phone, and felt a lot better about the next few days than he had before. After a while, he put his Scotch aside and got up to go find Jessi.

He wasn't too confident that their child-sharing plan was going to be successful. Even though Hannah was tiny she seemed to require a lot of attention, and two heads were better than one.

He wondered… Should he suggest that the three of them live together? It might cause less disruption for Hannah and help them both out. But he didn't know if his self-control was up to having Jessi in the same house. Already just the thought of her sleeping down the hall was enough to make him contemplate things he knew he shouldn't.

He heard the sound of singing and went to investigate. As he got closer, he realized that Jessi was singing Pink's "Blow Me" to Hannah as she dressed the baby.

Not exactly Brahms, he thought as he stood in the door of the nursery. But he saw that Hannah seemed to like it; she was slapping her hands and staring up at Jessi.

When Jessi finished singing the song, she said, "That was Pink. Your mom and I saw her in concert about eight times. For a while we both had our hair cut real short like Pink's. And your mom…"

All of a sudden Jessi's voice broke and she leaned in close, lifting Hannah off the changing table and into her arms, burying her head on top of the baby's. Allan started to back away. This moment was between the two of them, and he knew he'd be intruding.

Suddenly, that song seemed entirely right for her to sing to the baby. It was something that Patti and Jessi had shared. This was why their friends had named them coguardians. So that their daughter would never forget either one of them.

It also underscored why Jessi and Allan couldn't live together, ever. The more times he saw her looking like a real woman—not a punk pain-in-his-ass, but a real human being—the harder it would be for him to help Kell fire her.

And he knew that he was going to have to do that. His cousin had better appreciate the situation that Allan was in right now. It was hard enough to fire someone he knew casually. But to do it to a woman he was starting to like and respect and—ah, hell—really care for... There was no way he was going to be able to do it and not lose a little part of himself.

Six

Jessi had thought everything was going well with Hannah until she and Allan were watching *The Daily Show* and the baby started crying. Jessi tried to comfort the little girl, but nothing seemed to work. Singing had calmed Hannah down earlier, but no way was she going to sing in front of Allan.

"Your turn," she said, picking the baby up and taking her over to Allan.

"Gladly. Why don't you go and get yourself a drink?" he suggested.

Though she'd been planning to do just that, she decided not to. She didn't want to let the dynamic between the two of them change now. It would be too easy to fall into the pattern of roommates…and much more. And she'd already promised herself that what had happened on the flight out here wouldn't happen again.

Kissing him had been a mistake, and given that they were now alone together, with Fawkes mostly out of the way in the guest quarters, she had to be especially careful to keep her sexual urges firmly under control. But even though she had about a million other things on her mind, the images of kissing Allan kept cropping up.

Right now she hoped that Hannah would settle down and go to sleep early, because tomorrow they had a lot of stuff to do, including going to visit Hannah's grandmother. It was a visit that Jessi wasn't looking forward to, but she knew it had to be done.

She had talked privately to Reggie Blythe and knew that the care home had been notified of Patti's death. But Jessi wouldn't feel right unless she went and visited Amelia herself.

She noticed that Allan was walking around the room with Hannah. The little girl had her binky in her mouth and was now sleeping. Jessi told herself it was just beginner's luck, but a part of her was jealous that he'd been able to get the baby to sleep when she hadn't.

"I'll go put her down," he said in a very quiet voice.

She nodded.

As soon as he left the room she stretched her legs out on the couch, put her head back against the armrest and stared at the ceiling. They were in the back of the bed-and-breakfast in the suite of rooms that John and Patti had lived in. It was small compared to her place in Malibu, but so homey. Everywhere Jessi looked she saw her friend's touch, and it made her miss Patti that much more.

She rubbed her forehead, thinking that she'd better get started on a decent marketing plan tonight. She'd already had one email from Kell telling her that her deadlines for delivering her items hadn't been changed.

She felt torn. It went against her nature to back down, but this time she just didn't feel like the fight was worth it. Even Allan, who didn't hate her as much as Kell did, had intimated that she was probably not going to be keeping her role at the end of her probationary period. Should she put in the effort?

It was just one more thing she had to contemplate. A part of her liked the thought of her, Allan and Hannah all spending the day in the same place. And that made Jessi contemplate a future for herself that she'd never wanted. For a minute she felt like a little girl. The little girl she'd been before reality had intruded and taught her that things like perfect families didn't happen all the time the way they did in TV sitcoms.

She was okay with that. She prided herself on being a realist, but now that she'd had a glimpse of domesticity she'd be lying if she said she didn't want it for herself. A part of her did want to be part of a family unit.

But that was a pipe dream, probably brought on by Patti's death. Hell, it wasn't even Jessi's dream. She'd never wanted a husband to tell her what to do, the way her father had dominated her mother's life and her choices. Never wanted a child who could be used as a pawn in that relationship.

She sat up and leaned forward, putting her elbows on her knees. She had to fight for her job at the newly merged Playtone-Infinity Games. And then she had to do her best to raise Hannah to be strong, but also open to love, the way Patti had been. Jessi sensed that had been why her friend had wanted her to be coguardian. Because Allan would never let the little girl want for anything material. But there were things a man—a father—wouldn't understand about a daughter.

"Are you sure you don't want a drink? I'm getting myself one," Allan said from the doorway. He'd changed out of his suit and had on a pair of basketball shorts that rode low on his hips and a loose-fitting Lakers tank top.

She couldn't speak as she stared at his chest. He was lean and tan—not like some gym-crazed guy, just fit. Damn, she didn't need a reminder of just how good-looking he was. Or how much she still wanted him.

She had to ignore her baser instincts....

"Do you want a drink?" he repeated.

"Yes, please," she said at last, and then realized it had to have been obvious to him that she'd been staring at him. "Are you getting them?"

"I was planning on it," Allan said.

"I wasn't sure you could function without your butler, and since Fawkes is staying in the guest quarters..."

"I think I can manage to get us both a beer. Then I'm hoping to catch a little of the Lakers game," he said. "Want to watch it with me?"

"Yes, but I have work to do. And you mentioned giving me some contacts," she said.

"I believe our contest ended in a draw."

"It did. But Kell isn't budging on his deadlines and I could really use some help."

"I'll email the information over to you," he said. "But I'd rather you stay and watch the game with me."

"Why?" she asked. "I know you don't think I can pull it off, but I'm intent on saving my job."

"I'm sure you'll do it. I've seen you in action before. But for tonight I'd rather just enjoy some time with the one person who must feel the emptiness in this room as keenly as I do."

Jessi swallowed hard, surprised he'd mentioned what they'd both been avoiding: that without John and Patti, being here felt wrong somehow.

* * *

"I've got an idea," Allan said as he came back into the room with two beers.

"For what?"

"To distract us," he said.

"We need distracting?"

"I do, Jess. I'm on the edge here and I don't like it."

"What don't you like?" she asked, in that way of hers that made him want to just bare his soul and stop pretending that he wasn't attracted to her.

No matter what had happened in the past two days, she'd made adjustments and seemed to be dealing with everything okay. And he wanted to know how she did it. On the outside, sure, he looked like a guy who was holding it together, but on the inside…he was a hot mess. And he hated that.

Emotions made a man sloppy, and made Allan in particular realize how often he'd pushed them aside to keep focused on the path ahead. But being here in John's living room with his baby sleeping down the hall, and knowing that he was going to be raising her with this woman had shaken him to his core.

"Emotions," he admitted. "I need something to take my mind off things."

"And the basketball game can't do that?"

"Not when you are sitting there looking sexy," he said.

"I look sexy?" she asked. "I'm wearing a button-down shirt and a denim skirt. Not exactly femme fatale gear."

"It is on you," he said. "All evening long I've been sitting here watching you and thinking about that kiss on the plane. The one we both meant to be a competition that turned into something else entirely."

Suddenly, she didn't look smug or aloof. She looked intrigued and vulnerable. The way he felt inside.

"So what's your solution?"

"The way I see it," he said, moving into the room and handing her the beer he'd poured for her, "we've got two choices."

"Two?" she asked, and he noticed that when he sat down right next to her on the couch, she didn't scoot over. In fact, she sort of leaned a little bit toward him.

He nodded and took a sip of his beer before he said, "We could always ignore this and hope that it goes away. But to be honest, I'm not that good at ignoring a beautiful woman."

"Don't lie to me," she said.

"I'm not."

"Really? I know I'm not beautiful," she declared. "I'm cute and sexy, but beautiful—not so much."

"We'll have to agree to disagree on this," he said. He didn't know how she defined beauty, but for him she was the embodiment of everything female. She was strong enough to know who she was, bold enough to go after what she wanted, and also smart enough to admit when she needed someone. Earlier, she'd needed him, and that had awakened something inside Allan that he didn't know how to control.

"You were saying?"

"We can either ignore the attraction between us or face it, decide to have an affair and see where it leads," he said.

"Are you trying to shock me?" she asked.

"Nah, I do say things sometimes to throw you off.

Mainly to see if you react. But seriously, those are our only choices, ya know?"

"Ignoring it doesn't seem like it's going to work," she said slowly. "Right now you are the only person I can turn to. And I haven't been able to stop thinking about that kiss, either."

"What have you been thinking?" he asked.

She tipped her head to the side and took a slow sip of her beer. "Are you sure you want me to be honest?"

"Hell, yeah. I'm laying it all on the line here," he said.

"I liked it better when you were just my enemy…that douche, Allan. I don't want to think of you as the guy who makes me hot and wet."

Her words were evocative and made him harden in his pants. He wanted to say screw it, then take her hand and lead her to the bedroom. But what he wanted was physical, not emotional.

Liar, he thought. But he really wanted to keep the two things separate if he could.

And he wanted to keep her hot and wet.

"You said be honest," she said. "Did I shock you?"

"A little, but I shouldn't be. You've never been shy about speaking your mind."

"True. Plus I wanted to see if you were as horny as I am."

"Stop. We can't have a logical discussion if you keep talking like that."

"Why not?"

"Keep pushing me, Jessi, and I'll prove to you that you've barely seen hot and wet."

"I'm tempted to," she said.

"Why?"

"If I keep pushing and you react, then neither of us is responsible. We can blame hormones."

"But neither of us would believe that," he said, watching as she took another delicate sip of her beer.

She tossed her head and then leaned forward to set her glass on the coffee table. "I'm tempted, Allan. But I can't do it. Emma would kill me if I hooked up with you and screwed up something at Infinity for her."

"This has nothing to do with our families."

"Sure, we can say that now, but we both know it would impact them," she said. "Emma is already struggling, and with Dec and Cari…it just makes things difficult at times."

Allan understood what she meant. Kell was difficult. He still hated the Chandlers. Allan had been trying to stay neutral as Dec tried to influence them to go easier on the Chandler sisters.

"So we're still at a crossroads," he said. He'd always been very good at reading people, but Jessi had never been easy for him. Yet he had a hunch that giving in to the attraction might be a solution for them. But it would mean mixing together the two separate areas of his life, something he'd never done before. And it would mean showing Jessi a part of himself he preferred to keep private. Yet at the same time it could be the answer to this entire sexual tension thing that was going on between them.

"I'm okay with ignoring it until we get back from North Carolina, but I don't know how successful I'll be. I'm not handling Patti's death as well as I wish I was. I can't be philosophical about it."

"I'm not handling it well, either," he said, still searching for the words that would give them both what they needed. "That's why I brought this up."

He put his free hand on the back of the sofa and touched the skin at the base of her neck. Jessi flinched, spilling some of her beer on him. Her eyes were glassy and he didn't have to be Sherlock Holmes to guess that thinking of Patti was going to make her cry.

"Sorry about that," she said.

"Sorry is not enough," he said.

"It's not? That was just a drop of beer."

He arched one eyebrow at her. And she reached for his thigh, rubbing her finger over the spot the beer had left.

"What do you think I should do about it?" she asked.

"Clean it up," he said.

She leaned back and crossed her arms over her chest. "You surprise me, Allan. You know I'm not the type of woman to take orders from a man."

He shouldn't be surprised. Jessi had been making him uncomfortable since they met. Unlike most of the women he dealt with, she hadn't been wowed by his charm or money. He'd put that down to their family rivalry, but it was more than that.

"There is a lot about me you don't know," he said at last. "And I think there's a lot about you I haven't seen yet, either. I'm willing to bet that you take orders when it suits you."

"Maybe. It depends on the man," she said in that quiet way of hers, watching him with that gaze that was almost too serious. She shook her head and he thought that would be the end of it.

"I'm the right man," he said. "And I'm waiting."

* * *

Jessi hated to admit it, but she was intrigued. He was flirting around with something that had always been a secret fantasy of hers. She was so bold in life that most men expected her to be the aggressor once they got to the bedroom. But Allan didn't.

She wondered if she could actually do it, even though the thought of giving over control of her body to a man had always been a turn-on. She wasn't sure that giving up control to Allan was something she could embrace, but she'd always been a never-say-never type girl. "I don't know. I'm leaning more toward just handing you a towel and letting you dry your shorts," she said.

He shrugged, and she watched his body movements with different eyes now. What did it say about the outwardly effusive man that he liked his sex controlled and with limits? She didn't want to know. Really, she didn't. She liked keeping Allan in the jerk category. It made life easier when he didn't seem multidimensional. She could just not like him and move on.

But now…now he was starting to seem human and real to her. She groaned.

"What?" he asked. "What are you afraid of?"

"Not you," she said hastily, and then realized she probably had given away the fact that he did unnerve her. "I don't want to make things awkward between us."

"When hasn't it been?" he asked. "Listen, we're attracted to each other whether we like it or not. Our lives are forcing us to be with each other. So we can either let this thing control us or—"

"We can control it," she said. She leaned back on the cushions of the couch and looked at him. Taking her time and letting her gaze start at his feet and move slowly up to his waist and his chest, to his face.

He was good-looking but he wasn't classically handsome. Though there was something in the blunt cut of his lips that made it hard for her not to lick her own at the thought of his mouth against hers again.

He sat there, all arrogant male, and then did the one thing that tipped things in his favor. He held his hand out to her.

He hesitated for a second and then closed the gap between them. He took the back of her head in his hand, his grip on her firm but not forceful, and brought his mouth down hard on hers.

If their last kiss was exploratory and new, this one was about domination, and left no doubts in her. He wanted her. She knew that whether she wanted to admit it or not, she was going to end up in Allan's bed.

Allan McKinney. *Dammit,* she thought. *Why him?* Why did he have to be the man to make her feel like this?

But then she stopped thinking as his mouth moved over hers. His tongue plunged deep inside and she shifted, trying to get closer to him. She opened her mouth wider and sucked on his tongue, but that still didn't bring the relief she sought. She tried to lean in closer to him. Wanted to feel his body wrapped around hers, but he lifted his head and eased away from her.

His lips were swollen and wet from kissing her, his face flushed with desire. His silver eyes narrowed as his kept his gaze fixed on her, and she shivered with awareness, but also anticipation.

She did want what he was offering. The attraction to him was more powerful than she wanted it to be, but she wasn't about to lie to herself. It existed and she wasn't going to be happy until she had him in her bed.

She leaned toward him, but he held up a hand to stop her. "No. That was just a sample of what I can offer you, but there is no halfway. If you want this take my hand."

She wasn't entirely clear what he was offering, but at this point, with her pulse racing and every nerve in her body crying out for more, she really wasn't going to turn away. If one kiss could do that to her…she had to find out what else was in store.

It had been too long since she'd had really good sex. The trouble with the takeover and her general dissatisfaction with her career had conspired to keep her from focusing on her needs. And now Allan was offering her a solution to that situation.

She lifted her hand and saw how small it looked when he clasped it in his. His nails were square and blunt, his fingers large, his palm warm. There was strength and control in his grasp.

She nibbled at her bottom lip as he drew her close, until barely an inch of space separated them. He put his forefinger under her chin and tipped her head back, making her look up at him. He didn't say anything, just let his gaze move over her face.

She noticed he paused as he took in the small diamond in the side of her nose, and then his hand moved down her neck to trace the pattern of her tattoo. The small raven was her reminder not to let herself be swept away, and for the first time since she'd made the decision to get the tattoo, at age eighteen, she realized she was in very real danger of not heeding its warning.

Seven

Jessi felt small under his hands. He used his touch on her back to turn her and draw her toward him.

Seeming eager for his kiss, she lifted her face toward his, so he nipped her lower lip. Her tongue darted out and tangled with his, and he hardened.

He pulled her onto his lap. He took her hands and held them loosely behind her back, in the grip of one of his. She raised an eyebrow at him.

"We can't both be in control," he said.

"Why not?"

"That's not how I like things," he said. Then he brought his free hand up between them and ran his finger down the length of her neck. He liked touching her. Her skin was soft and the scent of it…peaches on a summer day.

"This doesn't work for me," she said. "I want to touch you. I don't want to be at your mercy."

"You already are," he said with confidence. She wasn't trying to get her hands free. She was sitting there waiting to see what he'd do next. He reached for the tasseled gold cord holding the decorative curtain in place and used it to bind her hands together behind her back. The cord was thick and didn't have much give. When he was done tying it, he reached for the buttons that ran down the front of her shirt.

She watched him with an unreadable gaze, but her breathing became more rapid, pushing her breasts against the fabric of her shirt. As the cloth fell away to reveal her cleavage, he paused to take a deep breath and admire her.

She was small but not tiny, her breasts full and suited to her frame. She wore a plain cotton bra, which surprised him. For a minute he'd expected a corset or something else punk. But he realized that the inner woman was very different from the outer one.

He ran his finger along the top curve of her breasts. "Do you like this?"

She shrugged, which pushed her breasts forward, and he reached beneath the fabric of her bra to caress one nipple. "It's different. There is something tantalizing about watching your reaction to my body."

"What do you see?"

"That you like touching me," she said. "You also like just looking at me. When you think I'm not watching, your eyes narrow and you stare at my breasts. What are you thinking?"

"I'm wondering what you'll look like naked."

"Why not find out?" she asked.

"I intend to, but in my own time," he said. Caressing her narrow waist, he ran his finger around her belly button. She shivered, and her stomach clenched. She liked being touched as much as he needed to touch her.

He reached behind her and undid the clasp of her bra and then pulled the straps forward on her arms until the fabric fell away, framing her breasts. Her nipples were a rosy-pink color and he cupped both breasts in his hands, rubbing his palm over them until they were hard. He leaned in to delicately lick at first one and then the other.

Jessi's hips moved against his erection, and he shifted his legs to get into a more comfortable position.

"Untie me," she said.

"Are you uncomfortable?" he asked.

"No," she said. "But my shirt is open…."

"I will untie you if you insist, but I like you this way and I think you do, as well," he said.

He leaned down to capture one nipple in his mouth. He suckled her and ran his tongue around it before biting lightly. "I like you this way!" he repeated

"I'm still deciding if I like you or not," she said.

Inside, he smiled. He wasn't too sure how much longer he could wait, but the knife's edge of anticipation made him feel…alive. And he knew that he'd keep this going for as long as he could.

He dipped his finger into his beer and rubbed it against her nipple, watching it tighten, before licking her slowly and then moving up her chest to taste her mouth with long, slow kisses. The saltiness of the beer and the taste of Jessi blended together, and he felt something clench deep inside him.

He was about to give in to the desire, free himself and take her. He knew it was time, knew he was hanging on to control by a thread. So he reached behind her to undo her hands and then set her next to him on the couch, tipping his head back to stare at the ceiling.

Jessi had never felt so sexually charged or as unnerved as she did at this moment. And she didn't like it. In fact, she'd rather just have a quickie than this.

The true problem was that it felt as if he was playing mind games. Her body was so turned on, but Allan was just sitting there, looking cool as could be. It was like their kiss on the airplane. A test to see who could hide their reactions the longest.

Right now she felt like the loser. Except…well not entirely. "I'm not sure this is the wisest bargain I've ever entered into with you."

He gave her one of his wry, knowing looks, and she shivered a little as she realized that he wasn't as unaffected as he wanted to be by their exchange.

"Nothing involving the opposite sex ever is," he said.

"Is that your motto?"

"No, actually, it was Grandfather's. But I have to admit the old bastard was right."

"What was he like?" Jessi asked to distract herself. She didn't really know that much about old Thomas Montrose. Unlike Allan and his cousins, who'd been taught to see the Chandlers as the enemy, she and her sisters hadn't really been raised to hate the Montrose family. As a matter of fact, a portrait of old Thomas had hung in the lobby of Infinity Games for as long as she could remember.

"He was bitter and thought only of revenge. That kind of attitude really taints a man's perspective."

"Yours?" she asked. As they talked, she almost forgot that her shirt was unbuttoned and her breasts were exposed, that there was nothing normal about the conversation they were having.

"No, Kell's. I don't think he's ever going to accept Cari as part of the merged company, and he really doesn't want you or Emma to come on board."

"What about you?" she asked.

"I'd rather buy you out, as well. But it's really hard to think about that stuff when you're sitting here like this," he admitted.

She breathed a little easier at his admission. "For me, too. But I'm sort of getting used to it."

"You are?"

"Now that I know it's distracting you," she said with a smile. Patti had always said there was more to Allan than the antagonist she knew.

"Still feel like backing down?" he asked.

"Never. I'm wondering if you are interested in me or if this is all a game to you?"

He stood up and took her wrist, drawing her hand to his crotch. "What do you think?"

She ran her palm over the heavy ridge of his erection. She stroked him through his shorts, wondering what he'd feel like naked in her grip. She used her forefinger to trace the line of his erection and heard his quick intake of breath.

She took hold of the waistband of his shorts and tugged it down slightly. But then stopped.

"What are you waiting for?" he asked.

"I thought you liked taking things slow," she said.

"Only if you are under me…taking me," he answered. She felt herself moisten and realized that this had long ago ceased being a game. Allan was the one man who could make her feel this way right now. She wasn't entirely sure she liked it, but she knew she wasn't going to walk away from him.

Their lives were entwined now and it was silly to pretend that they weren't.

"That doesn't sound like it's completely by the rules," she said.

"Nothing with you ever is," he said, picking her up in his arms and walking toward the bedroom at the back of the house.

She wrapped her arm around his shoulders and studied his face as he moved. There was a flush to his skin, which she put down to desire. There was a birthmark behind his left ear that she'd never noticed before. She traced the small kidney-shaped mark with her finger and he shivered and turned to face her, his silver eyes intense and sexual.

He definitely wasn't in the mood for games now and she was glad. She'd never been the kind of woman who liked to play around in the bedroom. She tried very hard not to equate sex with emotion, and instead tried in her own way to keep the two things separate, since she'd learned early in her dating life that most men did that.

"I like the way your hands feel on me," he said.

"Good, because I plan to put them all over you," she said.

He set her down on her feet next to the bed, put the baby monitor on the dresser and nudged the door closed with his hip. He kept his hands on her waist and they both just stood there for a long moment. In her mind this was the quiet before the storm. The moment when they both waited to see who would break first.

He lifted his hand and she felt his touch on her tattoo once again. He traced the shape of the raven over and over, and she felt shivers of intense pleasure move down her body from that one point of contact. She stood there watching the intensity on his face as he touched her.

It would be impossible to ever believe after this moment that she left him unaffected. She saw the proof of how much she turned him on in the narrowing of his eyes as he lowered his head toward hers, then felt it in the heat of his kiss.

His mouth moved over hers with surety and strength. He claimed her in that kiss. This was not the same way he'd teased and tempted from the first moment that they'd met. Now he was intent on leaving his mark on her, and as she reached for him and tried to draw their bodies together, she admitted to herself that she wanted nothing more than this.

For this moment it was enough to have him physically. She understood this wasn't her wisest decision and that there would be consequences, but she just didn't care.

She wanted him and she was determined to have him. She sucked his tongue deeper into her mouth, and as he held her by the waist with one hand to keep her from brushing her aching breasts against his chest, she reached between their bodies and stroked his erection.

His other hand moved from her neck, tracing a path straight down her ribs to her belly button. She'd had it pierced a few years ago, but had let the hole close up. Feeling the way he toyed with her navel made her wish she still had the piercing. His touch seemed too knowing and too intense for her, and she shifted a little, pulling her head back to look at him.

His eyes were half-closed, but she still felt the intensity of his gaze. He pushed her backward until her thighs hit the edge of the bed, and she sat down. He smiled at her as he pushed her shirt down her shoulders and off. She shrugged out of her bra and reached for his shorts. She didn't want to be the only one exposed.

She felt vulnerable and needed to keep the scales balanced between the two of them. If it had been any other man she would have changed positions, pushed him down on the bed and taken control. But with Allan everything was different—and it always had been.

In a moment of clarity, she admitted that from the first moment they'd met she'd felt a zing of attraction.

He grasped her hands to keep her from taking off his shorts. "Not yet."

"Yes," she said.

"No. Put your hands on the bed by your hips," he ordered. His voice was forceful and commanding, sending a pulse of liquid heat straight through her loins. She almost did it, but then stopped herself.

"You're not in charge anymore," she said.

"Oh, I think I am," he said, kneeling down and bringing her hands together behind her back. His face was close to her breasts, and she couldn't help arching her spine and thrusting them forward. He dropped soft kisses along the pale white globes and then tongued his way around the areolas.

She shuddered and shivered, shifting on the bed to try to relieve the ache between her legs. She parted her thighs, and he maneuvered himself forward between them. She felt completely dominated by him physically. He held her hands behind her, forcing her thighs apart with his body as he buried his head between her breasts.

Though she was clearly not in a position of power, his shuddering breath and the way he held her let her know that he was enthralled with her. Her body, which had never seemed to her to be the ideal of beauty, made her proud now. That she could literally bring this strong, domineering man to his knees made her sit a little taller.

She leaned forward and rested her head on top of his, rubbing her cheek against the thickness of his hair as he suckled one of her nipples. She stretched her legs farther apart and then canted her hips forward until she rubbed her center over his erection.

He lifted his head and shifted his body back from hers. Still holding her wrists with one hand, he pushed her skirt to her waist, and she felt him pause as he realized she wore thigh-high hose. He groaned. And then stood up, drawing her to her feet with him.

"Indulge me?" he asked.

"How?" she asked.

"Take off everything," he said.

"What are you going to take off?"

"Nothing."

"That hardly seems fair."

"Sex isn't about fair, it's about what turns us on. And I have a feeling that having me fully dressed while you're bare naked will be a big turn-on for you," he said.

He was right, but that didn't mean she would admit it. It scared her a little how well he seemed to know what she wanted sexually. "I'll do it, but only if you take your shirt off."

"Done," he said, quickly pulling the tank top over his head and then moving to sit in the armchair next to the bed.

He had a lean chest, his well-defined pecs covered with a light dusting of hair. She liked the way he looked, and stood there for a minute drinking him in.

Slowly, keeping her gaze on his, she reached for the zipper at the back of her skirt and tugged it down.

"Is this what you wanted?" she asked.

The skirt slipped lower on her hips, but she kept her stance wide enough that it didn't fall all the way off. Then, when she'd made him wait long enough, she shook her hips and slowly let the skirt fall to the floor.

"Pick up your skirt," he said, not answering her question.

She turned away from him and slowly bent down, watching him over her shoulder as she did so. His eyes narrowed as she reached for the garment and slowly picked it up before tossing it on the bed next to her bra and her shirt.

She shivered a little at the look in his eyes. She slowly pushed her panties down her legs and once again bent to remove them over her boots. He was suddenly there behind her, his hands on her waist and his body bent over hers. She felt the heat of his erection against her buttocks as he pulled her back into the cradle of his hips.

She put her hand out for balance as he rubbed himself against her. He was long and thick and hot. She felt branded by him, and empty as she waited for him to enter her. She was wet and had never been more willing for sex. Ready for him to take her. *And like this,* she thought. She didn't want to have to guard her reactions. She just wanted to let go and enjoy this without worrying if she seemed too vulnerable.

He leaned over her and whispered dark, sexy words into her ear, things that made her even wetter. He told her what he was going to do to her and how deep he was going to take her. She canted her hips back and rubbed herself against him. He took her hands in his and guided them to the footboard, and with their hands joined, she felt him shifting behind her and the tip of him poised to enter him.

"Dammit, give me a second," he said.

He turned away, and she stayed exactly where she was as she heard him open his shaving kit on the nightstand. She glanced over at him to see him opening a condom and putting it on. Later, it would bother her that he had planned for sex, but right now she was grateful.

He was back behind her again, his palms on her waist and his mouth on the back of her neck. He nibbled his way down her spine as he held her still. His hands shifted up to cup her breasts, his fingers pinching lightly at her nipples as he positioned himself behind her again. She felt him shifting between her legs, and one hand lowered to her feminine mound. His finger circled her clit, rubbing lightly. She shifted her hips and moved to where she needed his touch. Then he pulled his hand away, after tapping her lightly with one finger, which made her moan out loud.

She felt him at her entrance again. He teased her with the tip of his erection, and she enjoyed the sensation of his body pressed to hers for a little while, but then the wanting was too much. She arched her back and tried to take him into her body. But he shifted away from her, and she moaned again.

Then he leaned over her, whispering into her ear, "Do you want me?"

"Yes," she said, hating the breathy quality of her own voice. "Dammit, Allan, I need you now. Enough of the games."

"But waiting is the best part," he said, rubbing himself over her again.

"Taking is the best part," she countered.

She heard him groan, and then he plunged into her body in one long, hard stroke that sent the first shivers of orgasm through her. But then he stopped and when she tried to take in more of him, or force him to move, he didn't. He just stayed buried in her body as he kissed her neck and caressed her skin.

But it was too much. She needed him slamming into her and driving her over the edge. She didn't like the feathery sensations that were making the hairs on the back of her neck stand up and shivers course through her.

"Enough waiting," she said. "Take me."

"Not yet." It sounded as if he spoke through gritted teeth.

She tightened herself around him and heard him groan yet again, and then he started moving. His hips rocked with so much force that each thrust drove her forward. She held on tighter to the footboard as he continued moving in and out of her body. Oh, he felt good, she thought as he reached the right spot inside her.

She arched her back to take more of him and keep him hitting her in that delicious spot, as she was so desperate to get to her climax. His breath was hot against her neck and his body warm and sweaty as he moved faster and faster, until she felt the first pulse of her own orgasm. Then he called her name and thrust into her hard for three long strokes, before leaning forward and resting his head between her shoulder blades.

He dropped a kiss on her skin, one so gentle and

tender it made her heart clench. He was supposed to be the arrogant playboy. He wasn't supposed to kiss her like that. He wasn't supposed to be gentle with her. He was supposed to be…well, the Allan she'd always thought him to be.

She shook her head and tried to pretend this orgasm was like any other she'd had, but she knew it was different. She wanted to be a guy about it. To just make some sort of remark about scratching an itch, though inside she knew that this had changed everything between them.

She hated that very fact. Why was it that Allan McKinney, the man she'd always thought of as the devil incarnate, had just made her come harder than anyone else? Or actually made sex seem fun and—

He pulled out of her body, interrupting her thoughts. Unsure what to say, she stood up and looked over at him. They'd just been closer than she'd ever thought they would be, but they were still enemies, she figured. Nothing had changed, yet at the same time everything had.

Allan cursed under his breath and then drew her into his arms, pushing her head down on his shoulder as he hugged her close.

"What are you doing?" she asked.

"Hiding," he said.

"What are you hiding from?"

"You," he said. "You have a way of looking at me that makes me feel like I don't measure up."

His words were a tonic for her weary soul and she struggled to let herself take them at face value. She refused to believe that he'd glimpsed her vulnerability, but at the same time she knew he had, and that there was no way she was going to be able to keep fighting with him and pretending that she loathed him.

The truth was finally forced into the light, she thought. Allan McKinney wasn't her bitter enemy, he was a man. A man she found sexy as hell—and that unnerved her more than she wanted to admit.

Eight

Jessi was jerked awake by the sound of a baby crying. She lay in bed in Allan's arms, not recognizing the strange room for a split second, before she jumped to her feet, grabbed the closest piece of clothing she could find—Allan's shirt—and pulled it on as she ran through the door down the hall to the nursery. Allan was hot on her heels, pulling on his shorts.

They both continued into the nursery, where in the glow of the soft night-light they found Hannah on her back, crying. All her limbs where flailing as she sobbed for all she was worth. They both reached for the baby, but Allan let Jessi pick her up.

She cradled little Hannah against her chest and looked helplessly up at him. "What do you think she needs?"

"I think she might need a bottle. I'll go and warm up the formula while you change her diaper," Allan said.

He left before she could respond. She carried the baby to the table and changed her wet diaper. It bothered Jessi a little that Allan was right. He was probably spot-on about the bottle, too. How was it that he knew more about kids than she did?

She knew he hadn't visited their friends since Hannah was born. They'd both flown out to be there for the birth—and they'd kind of called a truce that day, as well. She remembered how they'd looked at each other in the hospital waiting room when they'd gotten the news about Hannah. They'd almost hugged, but then John was standing there and it had just seemed so awkward.

But for a few moments when they'd been focused on John and Patti, they had sort of gotten along. And then there was little Hannah to hold. And their friends to congratulate.

Hannah was still crying now, and Jessi leaned over the baby. She hummed a tune she'd heard playing earlier on the mobile over Hannah's crib, and then slowly sang words she made up.

"Stop crying, little Hannah. Soon Allan will bring your bottle and you'll go to sleep."

"Here it is," Allan said as he rushed back into the room. "I checked the temperature of the formula on my wrist so I know it's safe for her."

"Great thinking," Jessi said. "I didn't consider that it might be too hot."

He shrugged. "I'm thorough like that. Do you want to feed her or do you want me to?"

"You can do it," she told him.

He came over and scooped the baby up, placing the bottle in her mouth. He stood there next to Jessi while the baby drank eagerly. She brought her little hands up and touched Allan's finger as he held it.

Both adults stared down at Hannah, and Jessi for

her part again felt the heavy loss of John and Patti. "I wonder how often they both stood here like this?" she murmured.

"I was thinking the same thing," Allan said. "It's a sin that we're here and they aren't."

She agreed. Not that she wanted to be dead, but it made no sense that John and Patti had been killed when they had so much to live for. Jessi reached down and touched Hannah's cheek as her little eyes drifted closed, even while she kept drinking her bottle.

"She's so sweet," Jessi said softly. "I'm never going to let anything happen to her."

"Me, either," Allan stated.

She glanced over and noted that he was looking at Hannah as intensely as she was. "You really mean that."

"Of course I do. I gave my word to take care of her," he said.

"Sometimes girls need things that men don't understand," Jessi commented.

He glanced back at her, and she realized too late that she'd revealed something she hadn't intended. "Is that why you're so prickly?"

She smiled a little at the way he said it. "I'm not. I simply get that no one is going to fight my battles for me. At least not the ones that matter to me. And I'm going to make sure that little Hannah here knows she's always got me in her corner. No matter what."

"What battle did you have to fight for yourself?" Allan asked.

"All of them," she said. "But then I'm a bit argumentative, as I'm sure you've noticed."

"With your dad?" he pressed.

"And Granddad. They both had certain ideas about

how a Chandler woman should behave and what she should do."

"Go into gaming and ruin all the Montrose men?" Allan suggested.

Jessi thought about it and wondered if that was the motivation behind her grandfather's desire for her to be so proper. But in the end her family just hadn't worried too much about Thomas Montrose or his heirs. "We didn't really talk about your family that much."

Allan's face tightened. "My grandfather was road-kill to yours, and he never looked back to see the consequences, did he?"

Jessi had never thought of the ousting of Thomas Montrose from the gaming company he'd cofounded with her grandfather that way before, but she could see a certain truth to what Allan said. Gregory Chandler had really cared about only one person and that had been himself. Something he'd passed along to her father.

"Grandfather really wasn't very good at relating to people," Jessi said. "I guess you could say the same about me."

"Nah." Allan walked over to the crib to put the sleeping Hannah down. Jessi joined him as he removed the bottle, and they both sort of held their breath to see if she'd stay asleep.

She did.

Allan looked up at Jessi and smiled, and she smiled back. They had averted a middle-of-the-night crisis. When they got out into the hallway, she started to walk back to her room, but Allan stopped her with a hand on her elbow.

"You're nothing like your grandfather," he said.

"How do you know?"

"By all reports he was a driven man who cared about nothing but the bottom line. Who thought that the people who worked for him were nothing but cogs that kept the machine going. But you aren't like that, Jess. You care about the people around you—I've seen you passionately defend them."

"Yes, you have. I'm amazed John could forgive me for what I did. I did have the best of intentions when I hired that P.I. to investigate his past," Jessi said, trying not to feel all bubbly and warm inside that Allan had called her Jess, an intimate nickname that only her true friends ever used. Maybe it meant nothing, though. It probably was just a slip of the tongue.

"John told me that he couldn't do anything other than forgive you, because you'd been the one to keep Patti safe until he could find her and take over the job. And he said if he'd been anything other than honest with Patti, he wouldn't have deserved to marry her."

"He was truly a great man. Patti was lucky to have fallen in love with him." Jessi felt a lump of emotion in her throat and turned away, but Allan noticed and drew her into his arms, hugging her close. And for the first time since she'd known him she felt a moment's peace in his presence as he eased the ache in her heart.

Allan loosely held the bottle in one hand as he hugged Jessi with his other arm. No matter how hard he tried, it was impossible to keep his distance. They kept having little moments like this one where he couldn't help but see her as a woman. Not his enemy. Not the granddaughter of a man who'd ruined his grandfather's life. Just a girl who'd been wounded, as well.

This was dangerous, he thought. Sex was one thing,

but emotions… He couldn't allow himself to start caring for her. That was when he'd lose the steely grip he'd always had on his control. And he couldn't do that.

Not just because of the situation with Kell and work, but also because of Hannah. If he and Jessi had an affair that involved more than sex, it would end. Everything did. Allan knew this to be the one certainty of his life. And then they'd have to see each other at every important event in Hannah's life.

It would be difficult. More difficult than when their best friends had married and he and Jessi couldn't stand each other. He knew this, yet he also loved the smell of her perfume as she was nestled against his chest. With her head pressed over his heart, for this one second it was easy to forget she was Jessi. Yet at the same time he knew exactly who she was. It was that juxtaposition that made the moment that much more untenable for him. Made it that much harder to drop his arm and move away—something he knew he should do.

Yet he didn't do it. Instead, he let the bottle drop to the floor, so he could wrap both arms around her as she tipped her head back and looked up at him. He saw the same questions in her eyes that were echoing inside him. This was a mistake; they both knew it, yet couldn't stop.

He closed his eyes, trying to remember all the reasons why he needed to let her go, and then he felt the one thing that made it impossible: her lips brushing lightly against his.

"Thanks for being almost human," she said, so softly he had to strain to hear her.

"You're welcome," he said with a chuckle as he opened his eyes and looked at her.

Her gray eyes were cloudy, and for a minute he almost wished he was a different kind of man. One who would know how to soothe the savageness he saw there.

Despite that knowledge of his shortcomings, he hugged her close. "I'm always that way."

She shook her head and put her hand on his shoulder, just a soft light touch as she stayed on her tiptoes, staring into his eyes. He knew she was searching for something—probably answers to the questions that lingered in her own mind—but he had no idea if she'd find them. He wasn't even sure he knew what the answers were.

She opened her mouth, and he put his fingers over her lips. "Don't. We're not going to change this."

She nodded and took his hand in hers and turned to lead him down the hallway in the direction of the room she was using. He followed her even though he knew it wasn't smart. This wasn't a controlled sexual encounter. She was emotional, and he'd be lying if he said he wasn't, too. He already knew there was something else going on inside him. Maybe it was just losing his best friend. Maybe it was—

Who cared? He wasn't going to deny himself Jessi, and he'd figure out everything else later.

She paused on the threshold of her room, turning back to look over her shoulder at him. He realized how irresistible she was with her spiky pixie haircut and that oversize T-shirt that fell to the tops of her thighs.

"Dammit, woman, you're sexy as hell," he said, tracing the hem of the shirt.

"I'm not wearing silk or lace," she said.

"That's probably part of the reason why I find you so hot," he admitted. "It's my shirt."

"This doesn't change anything," she said a warning in her voice.

It changed everything, and she knew it. But by denying it, she was sending him a message that tomorrow they'd be back to acting like the only reason why they were together was because of the their friends' deaths. But last night had changed all that. And there was no going back, no matter what she said now.

He just nodded and picked her up, carrying her into the bedroom and dropping her in the center of the bed. She bounced lightly and arched one eyebrow at him.

"That's not very smooth," she said.

"I'm not smooth or romantic. You know that," he said. He needed to make sure she understood who he was. At heart, he wasn't polished or sophisticated. It didn't matter that he had money and could buy whatever and whoever he wanted. He needed Jessi to understand that growing up in the shadow of hatred had forged him into the kind of man who wasn't gentlemanly. He was a man who'd fought for everything he had, and he doubted if there was a force on earth that could change him.

Not even Jessi Chandler, with her spicy-hot kisses, smooth, pale thighs or strong arms that pulled him closer to her. He knew that she was running from something and using him, but that suited him just fine, because it made it easier to lie to himself and pretend he was using her, too.

Jessi had given in a long time ago to the fact that she often did things that others might deem stupid, such as what she was about to do tonight. But this behavior made her feel alive and distracted her from things that really scared her.

Like how tender Allan had looked holding little Hannah.

Jessi wanted that image out of her head. She wanted him to be a quick lay, and as he stood next to the bed, shoving his shorts down his legs, the last thing she was thinking of was sappy emotional stuff.

She hadn't gotten a chance to really see him when they'd had sex earlier, and as he started to move over her, with one knee on the bed, she reached out to touch his thigh.

She traced the hard muscles with her fingertip, trying to concentrate on that instead of his sex, which jutted toward her. But when she turned her head to look at it, she drew in her breath at the size of him. A shiver of sexual desire coursed through her, making every nerve ending come to attention.

She lifted her hand and wrapped it around the length of his shaft, stroking him up and down until he moved forward to straddle her waist. Then she let go of his sex and raised her hands to his chest.

He was warm, and the light dusting of hair there tickled her fingers as she caressed him. His hands were busy finding the hem of her shirt and tugging it up over her head. He tossed it aside and then looked down at her. He didn't say anything, but leaned forward and slowly swept his hands over her torso to her waist and then lower to her hips, where he squeezed her and held on to her as he rolled to his side and kept her there, pressed against him.

They were both completely naked, and she didn't want to admit it, but they felt right pressed together.

Their bodies just naturally fit, as if they were meant for each other.

He thrust one thigh between her legs and used his hands on her hips to draw her forward. As the ridge of his shaft rubbed all along her feminine core, she shuddered.

She tipped her head back, and he lowered his mouth to hers as she did so. His kisses were long and languid and left no room for thoughts of anything but where his next touch would fall on her body and how long she could wait before she reached between them and forced him to enter her.

She swept her hand down his back. It was wide and smooth, and when she reached lower to cup his buttocks and draw him forward, he groaned her name. She flexed her fingers, letting him feel the bite of her nails as she rocked her hips against him.

He shuddered in her arms, and she felt a wave of feminine power washing over her. She exploited it, claimed it as her own by pushing him onto his back and climbing onto his lap, lifting her mouth from his.

He smiled up at her in an expression she'd never seen on his face before. Then his hands were on her breasts as she shifted until the tip of his erection was at the entrance of her body. It was the feel of his naked flesh that jarred her and made her realize she was about to have unprotected sex with him.

She cursed and drew back.

"What's wrong? Oh, the condom."

"I don't have any," she said.

"I do. But I don't want to leave your bed," he said.

She understood that, and she'd always lived with no regrets. But the impact of the past few hours and realizing that she wasn't ready to have a child with this man made her extra cautious. "Well, you're going to have to."

He sighed and rolled out from underneath her. He returned in a quick second with the condom already in place. He climbed into bed and drew her back over his lap. He didn't say anything, just tangled his hands in her short hair and drew her mouth down to his for a passionate kiss that left no doubt that he was still very much turned on.

She put her hands on his shoulders and watched him carefully as she lowered herself onto his shaft and took him completely. His eyes were closed and his neck arched back, and she leaned forward, drawing his head to hers and thrusting her tongue into his mouth as she rode him.

His hands caressed her back, cupping her butt and urging her to quicken her pace, and she did, driving them both toward climax, which she reached instantly. She felt him keep thrusting inside her, and he tore his mouth from hers and leaned down to catch her nipple in his mouth, sucking strongly on it until his hips jerked upward. He gripped her hips, drawing her down hard as he groaned her name.

He turned his face to the side, and she collapsed against him as he held her to his chest, rubbing his palms up and down her back.

She wanted to pretend that nothing had changed, just as she'd said earlier. But as she lay there in his arms and felt the fingers of sleep drawing her in, she realized that everything had changed. She was no longer sure that running away from her emotions was a viable option, because somehow when she hadn't been expecting it, Allan had slipped past her guard.

Nine

Allan woke up with the sun streaming in the windows of an empty bedroom. He knew where he was and remembered clearly holding Jessi in his arms through the night. But she was nowhere to be found this morning.

Neither was Hannah, he discovered after he put on his basketball shorts and checked the nursery. A quick trip to the kitchen revealed Fawkes sipping coffee and doing the *USA TODAY* crossword puzzle on his iPad.

"Good morning, sir. Would you like breakfast?" the butler asked. "Ms. Jessi left a note for you. It's on the counter."

"Coffee's fine," Allan said, waving to Fawkes to keep his seat while he poured his own coffee, which he drank black. "I need to go to John's office this morning and also speak to the funeral home to make sure we're all set for Saturday."

"I have the car ready to go. Ms. Jessi asked me to pick her up at Hatteras Island Care Home at noon. Will that accommodate your plans?" Fawkes asked.

Allan nodded. Well, that explained where Jessi was.

She must have taken Hannah to see her grandmother. "I'm going to shower and then we can leave."

"Yes, sir."

Allan took the note and his coffee mug back to the bedroom he was using. He settled onto the edge of his bed and unfolded the piece of paper.

Allan,

I took Hannah to visit Amelia at the Hatteras Group Care Home. I'm not sure she'll recognize us, but I wanted to go and chat with her to see if I could make her understand Patti is gone. I hope you don't mind, but I asked Fawkes to drive us there and pick us up. The man was just sitting around waiting for you to wake up.

The letter was signed with a big *J*.

Just as he'd expected, there was nothing about last night. Underneath their obvious differences, they were very similar, he thought as he gathered his clothes and showered and shaved. They both ignored anything that might make them seem weak. And emotions were definitely something that could do that.

He checked his email and saw that Jessi had been busy sending in a revised promotion plan. He'd been cc'd on one of the exchanges between her and Kell that mentioned three meetings she'd set up via Skype to talk to a production company in Hollywood who were producing a new movie franchise based on a string of very popular books. She'd also managed to arrange a meeting with Jack White, one of the hottest producer-directors in town.

He admired her initiative and wondered when she'd

had time to do all that work. While he'd been sleeping? It bothered him that she might have seen him so relaxed in her arms. Because he knew that it had been a long time since he'd felt that laid-back and had slept so soundly.

He pushed that thought to the back of his mind and instead read the emails that Kell had sent privately to Dec and him.

If she can pull this off we will have to reevaluate our plan to end her employment. Keep me posted, Allan. I need to know about all developments.

Kell didn't seem happy, but at the end of the day he was a fair man, and if Jessi met the terms they'd laid out for her, then Kell would honor his end of the bargain. Allan emailed his cousins back and then got down to business, really analyzing Jessi's plan. He saw that she'd obviously given it some thought. It was almost as if someone different had come up with the plan compared to her offering of a few days ago.

The other proposal had shown someone who didn't really care, but this new plan had innovation and real drive behind it. He'd be lying if he said he wasn't impressed. What had made her change her mind?

And it was clear to him that something had. But he didn't have time to dwell on it. Instead, he left for John's storage unit in town to start sorting through a lifetime's worth of stuff his friend had kept there. John and Patti had left behind high-powered careers to open the bed-and-breakfast, Patti as a highly sought after interior designer and John as a corporate lawyer.

When Allan got to the facility and started sorting

through boxes from his friend's life and career, he realized that he finally got why John had left it all behind.

If his friend had still been living in L.A. and hadn't married Patti, these boxes would be all that he'd left behind. Things that had been generated by long hours spent working for someone else. A life lived on someone else's terms.

Mostly it was John's private notes on his clients. Stuff that wasn't part of his official work files. Things about their habits and how they liked to have their paperwork prepared.

Allan shook his head, surprised that John's death was making him reevaluate his own life and choices. But there was one key difference between his friend and him, and that was Patti. John had found his soul mate, a woman who shared his vision of the future and what life should look like. Allan hadn't found anyone like that and doubted he ever would.

He liked being just a little bit selfish and answering to no one save himself when he wanted to do something. It was an attitude he doubted he'd ever lose.

He rubbed the back of his neck as he got a text message from Fawkes informing him that he was going to have to leave to go and pick up Jessi and Hannah. Suddenly, Allan didn't want to keep sorting through files. He wanted to see Jessi and ascertain for himself if she had changed.

There was something different about her note and emails from this morning, and he was curious as to what it was. He told himself it was important that he figure it out so he could advise Kell and keep Playtone Games on top, but he knew that wasn't the only reason he wanted to see her.

He missed her. He hated that he'd woken up alone, and he wanted to see if she was running from him. It could be construed as cowardly, but to him it had seemed as if Jessi had beat a strategic retreat to regroup and refocus.

He wondered why she'd done it. One thing was certain—if it was a calculated move, she'd been successful, because all he'd done this morning was think about her.

Jessi had been running on adrenaline and nerves all morning.

The house where Amelia lived looked from the outside like another bed-and-breakfast, but as soon as she stepped inside, the smell of antiseptic let her know it was a nursing home.

"Hello," the duty nurse said in greeting as she came inside.

Jessi carefully shifted Hannah so she could reach out to shake the nurse's hand. "Hi, I'm Jessi Chandler. Patti McCoy was my best friend and I'm here with her daughter, Hannah, to visit Amelia Pearson."

"Have a seat over there and I'll call for Sophie, Mrs. Pearson's care nurse."

Jessi took a seat and five minutes later a woman wearing crepe-soled shoes and a floral dress came over to her. "Hi, I'm Sophie. I understand you're here to see Mrs. Pearson."

"Yes. Would that be okay?"

"Let's go into my office and talk. There are some things you should know. Who is this little cutie?"

"This is Hannah. She's Amelia's granddaughter," Jessi said.

Hannah made a sweet little coo as Sophie tickled

her chin. Then the nurse led the way into her office. "Please have a seat."

Jessi did. "I don't want to create a problem, but I would feel better if I could talk to Amelia myself and make sure she understands about Patti."

"We've already let Mrs. Pearson know about her daughter's death."

"I figured you had, but I wouldn't feel right if I didn't talk to her myself."

"She's having a good day, so I think we can arrange it. The most important thing for you to do is not agitate her. I'm going to give you a pamphlet to read over while I go and see if she'd like to have visitors."

Jessi read the pamphlet and felt a knot tighten in the pit of her stomach. It made her sad to think that the woman who'd always been so kind to her and treated her like a second daughter was lost in a world that was so confusing.

"Okay, we're all set. She remembers you and is looking forward to talking to you," Sophie said.

"Great," Jessi said, following the nurse into the solarium, where Mrs. Pearson was already seated in a fan-backed rattan chair.

"Jessi. How wonderful to see you," Amelia said as soon as she walked in. The older woman stood up to hug her.

"Look at this baby. Is it yours?" Amelia asked.

"No, she's Patti's daughter," Jessi said, careful to keep her tone quiet and calm, as the brochure had recommended.

Sophie stood in the corner observing them, which made the situation all the more surreal.

"May I hold your baby?" Amelia asked.

Sophie nodded, so Jessi got up and handed the baby to her grandmother. What was truly surprising was how she reached for Hannah and then held the baby so tenderly.

Jessi took her iPhone out of her pocket while Amelia was staring down at the baby and talking to herself, and after making sure it was on silent, took a quick picture, knowing that Hannah might want to see this someday.

Jessi carefully sat back down, and Amelia looked over at her. "Patti is the best baby. Her father's gone a lot but she never fusses."

Jessi glanced over at Sophie in confusion, but then remembered how the brochure had said to restate facts but not to argue. "Patti was a great a baby. This is her daughter, Hannah. She's a little bit of a stinker sometimes, but also a great baby."

"Hannah? My best friend growing up was Anna. I haven't talked to her in years," Amelia said.

"That happens as we get older," Jessi said. "You know Patti was my best friend, right?"

"Yes, I do. Patti is so lucky to have found you as her friend. I remember the first time you came to our home, when you two were in elementary school. You'd been in a fight."

Jessi nodded. She'd been a mess back then. She'd been defending Cari from some boys who used to pull on her long blond ringlets. Jessi had torn her shirt and knew she'd get in trouble at home if she came in looking like that, so Patti had brought her to her house instead. "You were very kind to me, Mrs. Pearson. You fixed my blouse and gave me cookies and promised not to tell my dad I'd been in a fight."

"Well, I could see you needed some love."

Jessi swallowed hard. She had just needed to feel accepted for herself instead of always being the middle Chandler girl, part of a unit instead of an individual. And Patti's mom had done just that.

"Patti is sleeping a lot today. She won't sleep tonight," Amelia said.

"It's okay if *Hannah* sleeps a lot, Amelia. I'm sure she'll sleep tonight."

"No, she won't," Amelia said. "Derek will be mad if the baby cries at night. He needs his sleep."

"It's okay. This is Hannah, not Patti," Jessi said again, seeing Sophie move quickly toward them as Amelia started shaking Hannah.

Jessi jumped up and took Hannah from her grandmother as the baby started crying. Sophie rushed over and tried to calm Amelia, who was now agitated by the baby's cries. Jessi tucked little Hannah against her shoulder and rubbed her back, trying to soothe her.

"It's okay, Amelia," the care nurse was saying. "Ms. Chandler, why don't you step outside? One of the staff will take you to see the doctor on duty."

Jessi went into the hall and found a nurse waiting there, along with two technicians, who went into the solarium to help subdue Amelia. Jessi's heart ached as she watched the woman who'd once taken such good care of her falling to pieces.

Hannah was still crying, and Jessi reached into the Vera Bradley diaper bag and found her pacifier, which the baby latched on to as soon as it was in her mouth.

"I think I'd better have a doctor check Hannah out. Amelia shook her," Jessi said to the nurse.

"I'll take you to him. Are you okay?"

"Yes. But I didn't get to tell her that Patti is dead. I don't think she understands that."

"We've informed her, and her care nurse will keep reminding her of those things when it's needed."

Jessi knew there was nothing more she could do. But seeing Mrs. Pearson in such a state made her glad her own mother's struggle with cancer had ended quickly. Jessi would have hated to see her suffering the way Amelia was.

The doctor on duty was a GP.

"I'm Dr. Gold," he said when he entered. "I heard you had a little incident?"

"Yes," Jessi said. "Hannah was shaken and I just want to make sure she's okay."

"I can check her out. Put her on the bed over there, but keep holding her little hands."

He examined Hannah, making comments to the baby as he worked. Then he looked over at Jessi. "She's going to be just fine."

"Thank you, Doctor."

Jessi had already texted Fawkes to come and pick them up, but he wasn't there when she stepped out into the sunny October day. She tipped her face to the sun and held the baby.

When the car pulled up about five minutes later, she almost groaned as she noted that Fawkes wasn't at the wheel. It was Allan. He got out and pushed his sunglasses up on his head.

"You okay?"

"Yes. Amelia had an episode, so we had to end our visit early," Jessi said. She couldn't recount any more of it since she was still shaken by what had happened.

"What kind of episode?" Allan asked, opening the door to the backseat and reaching for Hannah.

Jessi passed the baby to him and noticed that he dropped a quick kiss on her forehead before putting her into the car seat, fastening her in and then tucking her stuffed frog next to her cheek.

"What kind of episode, Jessi?" Allan asked again as he closed the door.

Jessi realized she'd been staring at him. She didn't like that he kept her off-kilter all the time lately. She mentally gave herself a slap, the type Cher gave herself in *Moonstruck,* and told herself to snap out of it.

"She was worried the baby was sleeping too much and shook her awake. Then she got really agitated when I took the baby and Hannah kept crying. I had to leave so the nurse and some technicians could calm her down," Jessi said.

"She shook Hannah?" Allan asked.

"Yes, but the doctor on duty checked her out, and she's fine. I also was informed before I left that Amelia has been sedated and is sleeping now."

Allan held her door open for her, and Jessi seated herself. She watched him walk around to the driver's side and get behind the wheel. He started the engine and then turned to her.

"It had to be difficult to see that happening with Patti's mom."

"It was, but it just underscored that we're all the family Hannah has now. Amelia will never be a grandmother to her," Jessi said.

"We'll be good to Hannah," Allan said. "Together we will make sure she has all the family she needs."

He'd made them a team, a family, and Jessi didn't

know what to say. She was silent as he drove down the little two-lane road back to the bed-and-breakfast. She really didn't know how she felt about being linked to Allan McKinney for the rest of her life. The part that was upsetting was that it didn't bother her as much as she would have thought it should.

While Jessi put Hannah down for a nap, Allan took some iced tea that Fawkes had made to the porch and then quickly read another chapter in one of the baby care books he'd downloaded to his phone.

"Whatcha reading?" Jessi asked as she came and sat next to him on one of the large pine rockers.

"Uh, nothing," he said. "I saw your aggressive plan to win over some business with the producer Jack White."

"I know it's bold, but, hey, that's my style. He was more than happy to take the appointment when I appealed to his sense of fairness."

"How did you do that?"

"I simply reminded him that at one time he was making small, independent films and he'd had to rely on bigger names to help him along. One of them was my grandfather, who invested a lot of money in what he called *Project 17* back then."

"I didn't know your grandfather did that," Allan said. The Montroses had focused a lot of time on studying the ins and outs of Gregory Chandler's business, but only his gaming stuff. Allan supposed his grandfather hadn't been interested in anything but that. However, this was key information they should have had.

"Well, he did. *Project 17* went on to become his first blockbuster, *Cowboys from Space*...so I appealed to his sense of fair play and asked for a meeting."

"And you got it. I like that you didn't hesitate to go after it, but I'm curious about something," Allan said. He glanced over at her. She was wearing a pair of white shorts that hit her midthigh and a sleeveless top that was fitted over her breasts and then fell loosely around her stomach. She'd put on a denim jacket to combat the breeze. Her sandals had a slight heel. For once, she didn't look all rocker chick, but instead looked like any other woman on the island.

He felt as if something was changing in Jessi and he wondered what, exactly, it was and how he could use it to his own advantage. Because no matter what changed, his reflex was to assume that they were still at war and always would be. Or were they? Had last night changed her enough to call a real truce?

He had woken up with the feeling that something was different in himself, but then when he'd found her gone... Dammit, he hated when he got petty, but had just realized he was bothered by the fact that she'd left him alone in her bed.

"What?"

"Well, two things," he said.

She arched her eyebrows and gave him a look that said to get on with it. He realized she hadn't changed as much as he'd previously thought and wondered again if the change was in him and not her. He hoped not.

"What caused your new attitude toward Playtone-Infinity Games? Don't deny something has changed— last week you didn't use your old contact with Jack White. So why now?" he asked.

"Hannah," she said. "I'm going to be her mother fig-ure now, and I know that kids get a lot more from what we do than from what we say we do. So if I told her to always do her best, no matter what the situation, but she knew that I'd sort of phoned it in at the end and let myself be fired…well, I just don't want her thinking that."

"How would she ever know about this? She's only three months old," Allan said, pushing his sunglasses up on his forehead and turning to face Jessi.

"I figured you'd mention it. I just didn't want it to be an issue. What was your second question?" she asked, leaning back in the chair and looking out toward the Pamlico Sound.

"I'm not ready to let you change the conversation," he said.

"Too bad," she replied. "Do you have another question or not?"

"Actually, I do. Why didn't you wake me up this morning?"

She sat up slowly, nibbling her bottom lip for a second before she seemed to realize what she was doing. She straightened her shoulders and looked at him. "You don't seem like the type of guy who wants a clingy woman, and goodness knows I don't cling."

"Liar," he said. He could hear the bravado and the challenge in her voice.

"Why did you come to my bed last night?" she asked. "And don't say it was just physical."

Allan knew there were two ways he could play this. One was blustery and posturing, and the other was… honest.

He reached out and took her hand in his. "Because I couldn't help myself. I don't know what it is about you, Jessi Chandler, but you always cause me to act in a way… Let's just say you make me forget myself."

"I do? I don't believe that," she said. "I think you get

a wild feeling and just can't resist following it to see what happens."

"I'm not that unpredictable," he said. "Most of the time when it comes to you I just won't back down, because I know you'd see it as a sign of weakness. And like you said earlier, actions speak way louder than words."

"I never see you as weak," she admitted, her voice a little bit softer, all that challenge and bravado ebbing away.

But it wasn't entirely gone, and he realized then something about Jessi that had been abundantly clear from the first moment he'd met her, even though he'd never taken notice of it before. She was always on the edge and ready to jump off. And now he had to decide if he was going to let go and watch or join her for the crazy ride.

Ten

They fell into a sort of rhythm over the days after the funeral. Kell hadn't come but Dec, Cari and Emma all had. It was very somber, and she had been glad to have her sisters there, but their stay had been too brief—they flew in and out on the same day.

She'd hoped that Reggie would have the custody all wrapped up so they could go back to L.A. by now, but the judge didn't move quickly. And then there was the storm in the Atlantic to contend with. First the predictions had the storm going toward Florida, and then into the Gulf of Mexico, but it had stalled out and now a stronger storm was taking its place, this one aiming straight for the Atlantic Seaboard.

Focusing on hurricane preparedness gave Jessi an excuse not to dwell on Allan. Which was difficult, because the last thing she wanted was for any of this to start to feel normal. But that was exactly what had happened. Worst of all, she couldn't wait to wake up each morning and have coffee with Allan while Fawkes did his crossword and baby Hannah drank her bottle.

He was quiet in the morning until he'd had his first

cup of coffee, which had surprised her because he was so chatty the rest of the time. And Fawkes had thawed toward her. If she had to pinpoint the moment when it had happened, she thought it was at the funeral, when she'd wrapped her arm around Allan's shoulders to keep him from breaking down. She didn't like to remember that moment when he'd seemed all too human and vulnerable.

But that time had passed and she was well aware that they were existing in a sort of vacuum as they waited for the custody of Hannah to be approved, and they wrapped up the rest of Patti and John's business matters. Fall seemed just around the corner. Jessi had even surprised herself by buying a tiny Halloween costume for Hannah to wear—an Elvis wig and leather jacket, which she thought would crack Allan up.

They had become that family unit she'd sort of been afraid of, and yet at the same time they hadn't. There was a tension between the two of them that couldn't be explained away. And no matter how nice it was to sit quietly in the kitchen in the morning, usually the rest of the day would reinforce in one way or another that they were still members of two different families embroiled in a feud.

It looked as if Jessi wouldn't be able to get back to L.A. for the meeting with Jack White, and Kell wasn't budging on his timeline. For an entire day she'd debated returning and giving up her rights to Hannah, but in the end she realized she'd only decided to try to keep her job at the merged company for Hannah's sake, so it made no sense to sacrifice her.

On Tuesday morning, Allan and Jessi were sitting at the kitchen table with Hannah and Fawkes, settling into their usual routine, when Allan asked, "Why are you staring at me?"

"I'm still marveling at the fact that you can be quiet for more than a second," Jessi said. "Every morning it's like discovering a new treasure."

He lowered his eyebrows, but didn't say anything, just took another sip of his coffee and went back to reading the *Wall Street Journal* on his iPad. Or at least that's what she thought he was reading, until Hannah slammed down her bottle and formula splattered across the table and onto the tablet. Jessi grabbed a towel and leaned over to wipe it off, noticing in the process that he was reading a book.

"You rat," she said.

"What?"

"*Baby 411!* That's what you've been reading every morning? No wonder you're so much better with Hannah than I am."

"I'll take Miss Hannah into the other room," Fawkes said as he got her out of her baby seat.

"Why?" Allan asked.

"She shouldn't hear you two fighting," he said as he walked away.

"Are we going to be fighting?" Allan asked when they were alone.

"I don't want to, but honestly, why would you go behind my back like that?" Jessi said. "I wondered why you knew what to do, but I figured you were going on gut instinct like me. Is being able to best me so important to you?"

"I don't like to lose," he said with a shrug, putting the cover over his iPad before standing up and taking his mug over to the Keurig machine. He made himself another cup of coffee as she watched him.

"I thought things were changing between us, but you're still the same," she said as he leaned back against the kitchen counter.

He stared down into his cup before putting it down. "I'm not the same. I downloaded the book because I knew nothing and was totally afraid I'd do something wrong. I can't be in a situation without knowing as much as I can about it."

"Why not just say that? Or suggest I read up on baby care? Clearly, I'm not a natural mother," Jessi said.

"Jess, you are wonderful with Hannah. Even when you screw up, you course correct and make it into something that is okay."

"Still, I wish you'd said something."

"If I had suggested you read a book on baby care you would have exploded and told me not to boss you around," he said.

"True. But I thought you were just supersmart when it came to kids," she said. "I'm kind of glad you're not. I was beginning to think you really were the superman you believe yourself to be."

"Ah, now you see the chinks in my armor? I suspect you knew they were there from the first moment we met," he said.

She thought back to that day. She'd never in her life been so scared. Her best friend had found her soul mate, and Jessi had known that she and Patti would never be as close again. And then there was sexy Allan acting all chummy with Patti and John. Jessi had heard of him before because of their family history, but hadn't expected him to be this obnoxious. She'd felt isolated... left out again, and it hurt.

"Only once you started talking," she said.

He threw his head back and laughed. "You're a pain in the ass. You know that, right?"

"I try. So what's that book say about when she can have real food?" Jessi asked, because she'd rather talk about the baby than about him and her. It had been so hard to keep her distance for the past week, but she'd done it because she already liked Allan too much, and allowing the physical bond between them to get any stronger would only lead her down the path to love.

And that frightened her more than anything else she'd experienced in her entire life. She just didn't think she was ready to give over her heart and her happiness to a man who kept so much of himself hidden.

"Let me look," he said.

She watched him for a minute and then realized what she was doing. "I'll go get Fawkes and Hannah."

She left the room without looking back.

Allan didn't dwell on feelings; he'd never been that comfortable with emotion. And nothing that he'd experienced since he'd arrived on Hatteras had changed his mind. Emotions were uncomfortable and created a lot of stress. The more he cared for Hannah and Jessi, the more he worried about them. Over the past few days he'd tried a couple times to lure Jessi back to bed, but she'd resisted, and frankly, he thought that was for the best.

What he needed was to get back to L.A. so he could have a little distance from Jessi. In terms of finalizing custody of Hannah, he was rattling cages, but he had no connections in North Carolina, and the local judge wasn't going to be rushed. Even though Patti and John had asked in their will that Jessi and he become guardians, the state wouldn't simply give the baby over to them without paperwork and visits. They'd had two in-home visits, and Reggie was doing all he could to speed the process along, but Allan was ready to get back to California.

He wanted life to return to normal. He'd never admit it aloud, but he was starting to like the routine of living with Jessi. Hannah was the sweetest thing, too, and he felt safe admitting that he loved that little baby as if she was his own daughter. But there was something almost surreal about sharing that bond with Jessi.

She'd changed since they'd been here. Her rocker chick clothes had given way to a wardrobe of casual jeans and blousy shirts. He realized she'd brought them with her, so she must have just been wearing her badass clothes to rile him.

Which she had. And that was part of the problem between the two of them. She was fire where he was concerned, and though he knew he'd get burned, he kept moving closer to her. In fact, he didn't mind being singed by her heat.

"Allan, you better come in here," Jessi called from the living room.

He went into the other room and saw that she was sitting on the floor playing with Hannah, while Fawkes sat in one of the armchairs. But they were both watching the television.

"What's up?"

"Hurricane warning. One of the tracking models has it heading straight for us."

"Great. I'm going to call Reggie and see if this will finally convince the judge to move on the custody ruling," Allan said.

"Let's switch over to the Weather Channel and see what it means for us. I think that the models are often unpredictable," Jessi said.

"Even if the Weather Channel has a different prediction, we don't want to take any chances," Allan said. "We both want to get back home, right, Jessi?"

She nodded, but there was something in her expression that made him wonder for a moment if she might not be in that big a hurry. But he doubted it. She had her own life, and the other night she herself had said that it would be easier with Hannah once they got back into their own routines.

He left her with Fawkes and walked back to his room to make the call. Allan sat on the edge of his bed and pondered whether he should try to convince Jessi to sell the bed-and-breakfast. He didn't think they were going to be able to manage it from across the country.

"Reggie Blythe." The attorney answered his phone on the second ring.

"Reggie, this is Allan McKinney. We just saw the weather bulletin about the possible hurricane. Any chance this will help the judge hurry his decision?"

"I was thinking along the same lines and already sent my secretary over to see if we can get on the docket for today or tomorrow. You and Jessi will need to leave the island if there is an evacuation."

"Really?"

"Yes, it's illegal for a nonresident to stay on Hatteras if that happens," Reggie said. "I think maybe the weather is going to work in your favor."

"I hope so. We want the right decision for Hannah, but we're also ready to get back home. Hannah needs to start adjusting to her new environment."

"I agree. I'll let you know as soon as we hear something more," Reggie said.

"One more thing," Allan said. "What does John and Patti's will say about the bed-and-breakfast? Does it have to be held for Hannah until she comes of age? Can Jessi and I sell it and put the money aside for her?"

"I'll look into it, but I do know that John hoped you'd keep the place open," Reggie said.

"That's all well and good, but neither Jessi nor I know a thing about running a hotel. I'm just trying to figure out what makes sense," Allan said. "I want to honor John's wishes...."

"I'll see what I can come up with. I might be able to find a caretaker for the property who can be paid out of the profits until Hannah is of age," Reggie suggested.

"That might work. Let me know if I can help in any way."

"I will."

He ended the call and then dialed Kell's number.

"What's up, Allan?"

"It looks like the hurricane in the Atlantic is headed straight for us," he said.

His cousin gave a mirthless laugh. "Seems like Jessi is never going to get back to L.A."

"It actually might speed up our leaving the island. We are using it as a reason to force the judge to make a decision. I just wanted to keep you posted."

"Thanks," Kell said.

"Kell?"

"Yeah?"

"Why do you hate Jessi so much?" Allan asked. It was one thing to have been upset about what happened with the past generation, and he knew that Jessi could be irritating, but he had no idea why his cousin didn't like her.

"Because she's a Chandler. I don't know her personally," Kell said.

"She's a great woman, Kell. Talented and dedicated to the company—"

"Don't tell me you've fallen for her. You hate her. You said she's a pain in the ass," Kell said.

"I did, didn't I." But he finally realized that "hating" Jessi had been a self-defense maneuver to protect himself, because she was too easy to respect and like and fall for.

"Yes. So don't desert me," his cousin declared. "I have to listen to Dec telling me how great all the Chandlers are every time we get together."

"I won't. I'm still staunchly a Montrose heir."

"Good to hear it," Kell said and ended the call.

Fawkes went out for supplies, and Jessi called a local handyman to see if he could come and make the bed-and-breakfast hurricane-ready. He was listed in the notebook where Patti had kept all the local services she used, including housekeeping and lawn maintenance.

"I'll be there as soon as we know it's headed this way," James the handyman said. "I know that property well, since it was in my family before the McCoys purchased it."

"Have you considered acting as a caretaker here?" Jessi asked, remembering that Allan had floated that as a possibility.

"Perhaps. I have my own business now and I'd have to ask the wife," he said. "She gets mighty pissed if I don't run things past her first."

Jessi smiled to herself. "How long have you been married?"

"Twenty years. Still feels like we just got back from our honeymoon," he said.

She smiled to herself. Happy couples made her feel better about the possibilities. And then she realized that for the first time she wasn't thinking of love and togetherness in vague terms, but specifically in terms of herself and Hannah and Allan.

His faults still loomed in the back of her mind, and she knew he hadn't said a word about them dating when they returned to California, but a part of her knew things had changed between them.

She thought back to this morning in the kitchen, when he'd admitted, well, that he was human. That he had flaws and that he didn't want her to see them. It was enough to fan the flames of the secret desire in her heart. She wasn't entirely sure when something as ill-advised as falling for Allan had started to be...well, something she wanted.

She liked that her heart raced every time he entered a room or that she got a little thrill from flirting with him and teasing him. True, she'd been cautious and tried to keep him at arm's length, but a part of her was very sure that Allan and she were...what?

Even to herself she couldn't admit it. Even in her own head she was afraid to let it be true.

She was falling in love with Allan.

Hannah made her little gurgling noises, and Jessi smiled over at the tiny baby. She scooped her up and held her in her arms, leaning close to take a deep breath of the fresh clean baby smell.

"You did good, Patti," she said out loud. She hadn't let herself hold Hannah or even talk to Patti about the baby much when her friend had been alive. Jessi had always thought she'd lived her life on her terms—no fears, no regrets—but now she realized how paralyzing that lie and the fear underlying it had been. It had been strong enough to make her miss out on sharing this joy with Patti because she'd been terrified of even holding the newborn.

Her entire self-view shifted in that instant, and Jessi understood that she'd been cowardly her entire life. Being here with Hannah was making it crystal clear how much she'd missed by keeping everyone at bay. Instead of facing the things that scared her, she'd fought with them, told herself she didn't need them and walked away.

She'd done it this morning in the kitchen. When her gut had told her to move toward Allan she'd backed away.

Hannah was starting to get sleepy, her little eyes drifting closed, and for a moment Jessi debated sitting on the porch and just holding the little girl. But then she decided she wanted to get some work done.

She took Hannah upstairs, stopping under the picture of Patti and John that Allan had hung above the crib. It had just appeared there two days ago. And when she'd asked him about it, he said that he didn't want her to forget their faces.

It had been a sweet sentiment, but then he'd spoiled the moment by making a pass at her. Now that she thought back on it, Jessi realized that Allan ran from emotion the same way she did.

Maybe that meant that he was starting to care for her. She put Hannah in her crib and sat down in the rocking chair to think. Was she going to keep running away from life or was she going to be the woman she'd always believed herself to be and face the thing that scared her the most?

Ironically, it was Allan. She'd fought with him and dared him and taunted him since the moment they'd met, and it was only now that she could recognize she'd done all of those things to keep herself from falling for him. And they hadn't exactly been successful. There had always been a part of her that had wanted to see him again.

She pushed herself up from the chair, resolute in her conviction that she wasn't going to run anymore.

Walking down the hallway to his bedroom, she paused on the threshold as she realized he was on the phone. She didn't want to eavesdrop, but heard him say that he was still a true Montrose heir.

Jessi knew better than to listen at doors, but she couldn't deny what she'd overheard. It was a fierce reminder of something that she already knew. No matter how he acted when he was here, he was still her… frenemy.

Eleven

She started for the stairs, but then remembered her new promise to herself. No more running away.

Resolutely, she strode back to Allan's room and found him still sitting on the edge of the bed, looking contemplative.

"So you're a staunch Montrose heir?" she asked.

"That's not exactly news," he said, tossing his phone on the bed and standing up. "Why were you eavesdropping?"

"Sorry. I didn't mean to. I kind of thought we'd changed in our attitudes toward each other...well, at least I know that I have. I no longer view you as one of those nasty Montroses."

She put her hands on her hips and looked at him, daring him to lie to her.

"You're right. We have changed toward each other. But at the end of the day we're still business rivals— no, that's the wrong word. But things aren't going to magically fix themselves. I know you're working hard to change Kell's image of you, but it's still down to financial gain as far as he's concerned," Allan said.

What exactly was he saying? "You're not being very clear. Even if I get Jack White to agree to a deal, the money won't come in this quarter or probably even the next. Is all that work for nothing? Because I'm fine with not keeping that meeting and letting you guys go hang," she said.

"That's not what I was saying. Potential profit will satisfy the terms of your probation," Allan said. "Why are you being so argumentative?"

"You shook me. I've just been thinking about my life and myself, and I made some discoveries I didn't necessarily find comfortable. But I was thinking you and me—we'd both... Never mind. I just sound like some sappy schoolgirl."

"You are the furthest thing from sappy I've ever met. Finish your thought," he said, closing the gap between them and touching her chin. "I like you when you are at your most honest."

"I like that quality in you as well, but I don't get to see that guy as often as I'd like."

He dropped his hand and thrust it through his thick hair. "What do you want me to say? I learned early on that when you care for someone they have power over you."

"Do I have power over you?" She felt a shot of pure adrenaline as she asked the question that had been burning in the back of her mind since that kiss they'd shared on his plane. Living so openly and so honestly gave her a rush of excitement, but she also saw the potential for a lot of pain.

"You know you do," he said. "All week I've been trying to get you back into my bed, but you keep pushing me away. Why is that? Do I have some sort of power over *you?*"

He wanted to keep things even and she couldn't blame him, but with her new knowledge she realized that if she was truly living bold and large she couldn't hedge her bets or hesitate. She had to go all-in.

"Yes, you do," she said quietly. "And it's not just about sex, but influences every corner of my life. I really hope that I'm not just making you into the man I want you to be, because you are becoming very important to me."

Allan looked at her in shock. She saw the fear in his eyes—or at least that's what she hoped it was, because otherwise it might be pity.

Oh, please don't let it be pity.

He stepped back from her, turned away and walked over to the window that overlooked the garden in the backyard.

"I don't know what to say to that," he said after a few minutes had passed.

"It's not that hard," she said softly. "If you're honest with yourself you know exactly what to say, and if you're brave enough you'll be able to say it."

She heard the dare in her words and decided she was okay with that. She couldn't completely change her attitude in one day. And if he was man enough to be with her, man enough to actually be there for her as she really hoped he would, then he'd have to be as honest with her as she'd been with him.

"I… You want something from me that I've given no one else, not even my parents or my best friend," Allan said, still not facing her.

She saw the proud set of his shoulders and thought

that he'd never be able to say the words she desperately wanted to hear. She hesitated and wondered if him saying them made a difference to what she was already feeling, and knew that it didn't.

Her heart sped up as she walked over and put her arms around him, linking them together over his chest as she rested her head between his shoulder blades. He was tense for a few seconds, but then brought his hand up to cover hers. He didn't say another word, and neither did she.

For this moment it was enough. She didn't need to hear the words from him, but the small knot in the pit of her stomach warned that she would need to sooner or later, and she only hoped that he'd be able to give them to her when it was time.

He turned in her embrace and stepped away from her, and that tiny knot grew as she realized that her gamble hadn't paid off. Allan wasn't the man she thought he was. She'd taken a chance on love and in the end it would have been better if she'd simply kept running from the emotion, because it seemed it wasn't for her.

"We've got a lot to do," he said at last.

"Of course," she replied, swallowing hard. "I've called a handyman to come and make the house hurricane-ready. He's waiting until the final warnings are issued. Also, he might be interested in applying to be the caretaker here."

Allan nodded.

Jessi turned and walked out the door, hoping he'd call her back and pretending she wasn't disappointed when he didn't.

Allan almost wished he was a different type of man. The kind of guy who'd run after Jessi and bring her back. But he wasn't. And he knew he couldn't be. He'd seen his father devote himself solely to one person's happiness, and in the end that devotion had killed him. His dad hadn't been able to live without his mom.

He knew that women often thought that was romantic or sweet, but he'd seen the other side of it. How his father wouldn't leave the house for days while his mom was on business trips. His dad had a career of his own, but had been crippled by loneliness when his mother had traveled out of town. And then there was the almost manic way he'd act when she was back. He'd never let her leave his sight. That kind of dependence on someone was something Allan vowed to never experience.

He had promised himself a long time ago that he'd never let any woman have that control over him. And if he was being completely honest with himself he'd have to admit that Jessi was already starting to make him feel a little like that. He refused to let it go further.

If he hurt her feelings now, he was sorry, but he knew that in the end no woman could live with that kind of obsessive love. He wasn't guessing or speculating; his mother had told him that when she'd left their family home to go back to her own father. It was just an odd twist of fate that she'd died in a car crash on her way there.

Allan rubbed the back of his neck. Damn, he never thought about those two—his parents, who had been so doomed in love. He had plenty of other things to occupy his mind. The hurricane brewing out in the Atlantic. Finding a caretaker for this place. Raising baby Hannah. And what to do about Jessi.

There was no way that he could force her from his thoughts. And part of him feared that he might be just like his dad, because the past few days had proved how much he really enjoyed being in her company. Every morning he got out of bed a little more easily than he ever had before, and actually looked forward to sitting in the quiet kitchen with her across the table from him.

There was something about her that called to him, and no matter what he said or how he acted toward her, he couldn't change that. So that made priority number one getting off Hatteras Island and keeping Jessi from satisfying the objectives in her probation. He wanted her to fail—needed her to.

Somehow the thought of seeing her every day at work and in his personal life was too...tempting. And he didn't like it. He'd always known that he wasn't good at personal relationships but he hadn't understood until this moment the real reason.

He didn't like the vulnerability that came with letting someone past his guard. Not just anyone—Jessi. She made him feel weak and unsure because he needed her and that wasn't acceptable.

But he knew he wouldn't be able to force her hand or to *make* her fail. He just had to hope that she ran out of time. It seemed unlikely, given the type of woman she was.

And that made him realize that he also had to decide if he was going to keep his guardianship of Hannah. Maybe he should let that go, as well...though John wouldn't have liked that.

In fact, if his friend were here right now he'd probably punch Allan in the shoulder and tell him to stop acting like an ass.

He paused in front of the mirror and stared at himself. He looked nothing like his father, but that didn't stop him from following in his footsteps where obsession was concerned. His grandfather, too, had been obsessed—with business. Allan didn't want to be like either of the main male influences in his life.

Was it impossible for him not to be like them? It seemed that obsessive personality trait ran deep. He knew from his own rigid attempts at control that he had somehow mastered it after all these years, until Jessi.

She threatened him. Threatened his sanity and his control and his core belief in himself. And now she wanted him to… What exactly did she want? He both admired and envied that she was able to be transparent and come to him and ask how he felt.

He knew that took more courage than he had. Because even though she'd sort of said what she was feeling toward him, he still couldn't bring himself to let her know what she meant to him.

He didn't care if that made him a coward—sure, he'd have kicked anyone's ass who said he was one, but he couldn't deny it to himself. It didn't change anything. He wouldn't let it.

But the words felt hollow and empty as he went downstairs and saw Jessi in the backyard, talking to the handyman and then working beside him to gather up loose articles in the yard.

She wore a pair of ridiculously high heels, skintight jeans and a white tank top paired with a black leather vest. She was back to her rocker chick clothing. He took a deep breath, acknowledging to himself that he was glad.

This was the Jessi he knew how to handle. He could challenge her and bet with her and probably even take her to his bed. She was the woman who gave as good as she got, and never let him forget it.

But another part of him was sad. He realized he'd missed a chance with Jessi. A chance to really know her and maybe find some sort of happiness.

Who was he kidding? He'd never really be happy. Not with Jessi Chandler. Not just because of the Chandler connection, but also because she did challenge him and dare him, and she'd never have settled for only half of what he was. She'd never have accepted the small bit of himself he'd have felt comfortable giving her, and a part of him was glad.

Because the way he felt about her, he wanted her to have it all. All the happiness and love that she deserved. And he knew he wasn't the man to give it to her.

With the hurricane warning slowly turning into a real threat, James had suggested they go ahead and do a few preventive things, such as get anything loose in the yard stored. And since it was either work with her hands or choke Allan, Jessi decided to dig in and help. She had the baby monitor speaker attached to her hip as she worked, putting away hoses and chairs and piling up loose tree limbs.

She could see as she puttered about the yard why her friend had enjoyed this pace after years of working eighteen-hour days and striving so hard to make her business a success. Jessi was glad that Patti had decided to sell her interior design company and come down here to the Outer Banks. The past two years were probably some of the happiest of her friend's life.

"Want some help?" Allan asked, coming up behind her.
"No."

"Jessi—"

"I'm mad at you. I'm not going to pretend we're okay or anything like that. You might want to go and talk to James and see if he needs your help," she said. There was one thing about being so honest, and that was that she felt freer than she had in a long time. She sort of liked it.

"No."

"What do you mean, no?"

"Just what I said. You changed the rules on me in one second and expected me to keep up with whatever was going on inside of you. That's not fair. Just this morning in the kitchen you walked away instead of staying," he reminded her. "I'm trying to catch up, Jessi. But I'm a guy. And these are emotions, and I'm not even going to pretend that I will ever be comfortable with them. Yes, I have them. No, I never want to talk about them."

She stopped what she was doing and looked up at him. He had his sunglasses on so it was hard to tell if he was sincere. But his words made a lot of sense to her. She had made a radical change of heart and she'd wanted him to immediately catch up to her. In fact, she wondered if she'd been a little bit cowardly by trying to force him to. His reaction had given her the freedom to feel superior and also the safety to back away again.

"I just have no idea what to do with you."

"Me, either," he admitted. "I guess for once we're both in the same place."

"We're always in the same place when we are warring, and I liked that for a long time," she admitted. "But now I want something else. And it scares me because you're still you."

"Yes, I am. But I'll let you in on a little secret.… You

scare me, too. I have no idea how I came to be in this position," Allan said. "I don't like it. I'm going to do everything I can to figure out how to get us back to where I feel comfortable. And it's not because I don't care."

She took his hand and led him from the yard up to the back porch, where they were hidden from the view of the handyman. "I want to know two things…first, where do you feel most comfortable with me, and second, how much do you care?"

"Right here," he said, pulling her into his arms and bringing his mouth down on hers.

It had been too long since they'd kissed and since she'd really held him in her arms. That one-sided hug upstairs hadn't done anything for her. But in his embrace she thought she heard all the things that he couldn't or wouldn't say out loud to her. And it was enough.

She saw this as a first step to something new and exciting. Something worth the scary knot that she felt in her stomach when she looked into the future and thought she saw Allan by her side. It wasn't anything concrete, but she felt as if it was the start of something.

"Uh…excuse me," James said in a gruff voice. "I don't mean to interrupt."

Allan slowly let his arms fall from her, and turned to face the other man. He was about six feet tall, and weathered from a life spent outdoors. His face had sun and laugh lines on it and he wore his faded jeans and work shirt well, as if he was very comfortable with the man he was.

"Yes?" Allan asked.

"There's been a weather update and the storm is confirmed to be heading straight for us. Landfall is in less than four hours. I'm going to go and get the storm shutters to cover the windows. You two should make plans to head off island."

"I'm not sure we can," Allan said. "Until we hear from our attorney."

"I'll get Hannah ready," Jessi said. "And then call Reggie. I also read some stuff on hurricane preparedness, and I've bought water and some nonperishables at the grocery store. Is there anything else I should do, James?"

"Fill the bathtubs with water in case something happens to contaminate the local supply. Also gather a radio, flashlights, candles and that sort of stuff all in one room. I'd pick one without windows."

"Okay," Allan said. "Do you need my help?"

"Yes," James said. "We have to secure everything in the yard and get the windows covered."

Allan squeezed Jessi's hand before he walked away, and she watched him go with a smile in her heart. It didn't matter that a big hurricane—Hurricane Pandora, it was now officially called—was heading straight toward them. Sure, she was scared, but having Allan there to help her reassured her a little because he wasn't the type of person to just sit passively by. She knew there was still so much that had to be settled and figured out between them. But for the first time in her life she had someone by her side.

A man she could count on. It was something that she'd never guessed she'd find. That the man was Allan McKinney was even more surprising, but there it was.

She gathered all the supplies that James had listed, as well as enough diapers for a week, and put them in the small study at the back of the house. The room had bookcases on all the walls and no windows.

She piled up pillows and blankets and a spare bassinet she'd found in Patti's closet for Hannah to sleep in. Then she called the attorney.

"Reggie Blythe's office, this is Reggie," he said.

"It's Jessi Chandler. I was hoping to find out if you'd had an update from the judge," she replied. "We've been told we're going to have to leave the island."

"As I mentioned to Allan, you can't leave with Hannah. It's not allowed until we get the paperwork. The farthest you could go would be to a hotel farther inland—is that what you both want? You can leave her with her foster family, or if you want, stay with her, I'll bring over the notice from the judge so that the police don't try to clear you off. I'm afraid all the judicial offices are sort of shut down while everyone prepares for this storm."

"Should we be scared? Should we go inland?" Jessi asked. "I don't know what to expect."

"I'd stay here. That bed-and-breakfast has weathered many late-season hurricanes. You'll be fine as long as you follow instructions and do what you're told. Do you have enough water and food for a few days?"

"I think so." She thought of the stocked cupboard and cases of water and soda she'd purchased. How much food would they need?

"I'll stop by to check on you," Reggie said.

"That would be nice, but only if you have time. We sort of have a handyman helping us out."

"Very well. I'll call as soon as I hear something from the judge."

Jessi busied herself getting ready for the hurricane

and tried to ignore the storm inside her as she adjusted to everything that was happening. Not the least of which were her feelings for Allan, and that they were all each other had in the coming storm.

She was scared by that, because if she took this gamble with her heart and it didn't pay off, she had the feeling she'd never again take a chance on loving a man.

Twelve

Allan sent Fawkes off island as Hurricane Pandora came toward them. The bed-and-breakfast was secured and they'd done everything possible to get prepared. Now all they could do was wait.

Reggie had finally gotten the judge to sign the papers that gave guardianship to both Jessi and Allan, but it had been too late to leave Hatteras when that happened. The rains had already started falling heavily and the road leading off the island was washed out.

Now they were sitting tensely in the study with a transistor radio on, because the electricity had gone out. They had flashlights and water. For a long time Allan pretended to be reading on his iPad, but the sound of the wind whipping through the yard and the harrowing noise of tree branches scraping against the house distracted him.

Jessi sat on the floor next to a sleeping Hannah.

"I don't like this," she said at last. "It sounds creepy outside and it's so dark and gloomy in here. Distract me, Allan."

"How am I supposed to do that?"

"I don't know. Tell me something about you that no one else knows."

"Okay, and then you'll tell me something?" he asked.

"Sure. Anything is better than listening to the storm," she said.

He got off the couch and came and sat on the floor next to her. "What do you want to know?"

"Tell me about your first kiss," she said. "Ballsy guy like you, it was probably remarkable."

He shook his head. "It was awkward. One of those moments in middle school when I thought I knew everything. It was at Amy Collins's thirteenth birthday party. It was a boy-girl party—a big deal. Her parents were trying to be cool, so they left us all alone in the converted third-floor game room. Jose kept watch at the door while we played spin the bottle, and I got to kiss the birthday girl.

"We went behind a bookcase that held DVDs and stared at each other. Finally, I leaned in and kissed her. Sort of missed her mouth and ended up kissing her cheek and then her mouth. It was over really quickly and both of us looked at each other, wondering if that was it."

Jessi smiled. "My first kiss was sort of like that, too. At a birthday party. Tons of other kids around. Patti liked this boy in our class, but he wasn't about to make a move, so I organized a game of truth or dare, intending to help Patti get her kiss. But instead I got dared to kiss Bobby and I did it. It wasn't bad. A bit like yours, where we sort of smashed mouths and then backed away. Isn't it funny, that age? I felt so ready to be a grown-up, but after that kiss I knew I'd end up waiting before I tried it again. It was scary, letting a boy that close to me."

"I bet. Boys have cooties at that age," Allan said. He had felt energized by the closeness with Amy that day and had become determined to get another kiss, which he had. But as he looked over at Jessi and the sleeping Hannah, he felt differently. "I definitely am not going to be the 'cool' dad where Hannah is concerned. I know how boys are and will keep my eye on anyone that gets too close to her."

Jessi laughed. "Good. You protect her and I'll teach her how to protect herself, in case one slips by us."

"Deal," Allan said.

"Did we just agree on something?" she asked with a smirk.

"No, you're mistaken.... I was about to ask about your tattoo. When did you get it and why?" He liked the intimacy created by the storm raging outside and the quiet ambient light inside. For this moment they were the only two people in the world, and that suited him.

"I got it when I turned eighteen. My parents wouldn't allow me to have one, but on my second day at the University of Texas in Austin I went and had it done anyway. I wanted something to commemorate the fact that I was on my own, free and flying toward the future."

"Why did you get it here?" he asked, touching her collarbone. He liked touching her and used the tattoo as an excuse to do it now.

"I wanted to see it every time I looked in the mirror so I'd remember the promises I made to myself."

"What promises?" he asked.

"That's another question," she said. "And it's my turn to ask."

"I'll tell you whatever you want to know," he said. "Just tell me what promise you made to yourself."

She stared at him for long moments and then shifted up on her knees and leaned forward so that barely an inch separated them. "I promised myself I'd never again let someone make me be something I'm not."

"You certainly have lived up to that," he said.

"It hasn't always been easy. You make it hard for me," she said quietly.

"Good, because you're always keeping me off my guard," he said. "Every time I think I've figured out how to deal with you something changes."

"Ha."

"Ha?"

"That's just a nice way of saying you can't manipulate me," she said.

"Perhaps. But I've discovered I'm not a big fan of manipulating you," he said. It hadn't taken him long to figure out that he wanted the real responses from Jessi instead of the bad-girl attitude she gave everyone else. "What's your question for me?"

She glanced over at Hannah and then moved a little bit closer to him. "Will you answer me truthfully?"

"Yes," he said.

"Then my question is this, Allan McKinney. How long are you going to keep pretending that everything in your world hasn't been changed by the past two weeks?" she asked.

It was a gutsy question and left no doubt as to what she really needed from him. He put his hands on her hips and drew her closer.

But she stopped him with a hand on his chest. "No funny business. I want your answer."

But funny business was the only answer he had. He wasn't going to confess his feelings, which he'd thought he'd made plain to her earlier in the day. Instead, he tangled his fingers in the back of her hair and drew her forward, kissing her with all the emotion that was pent up inside of him.

He cared for this complicated woman who had the ability to make him feel things—things he didn't want to feel. And he wasn't about to let her have the upper hand now.

Something hit the side of the house hard and they pulled back from each other, startled by the sound.

"What was that?" she asked, moving to pick up Hannah.

"I'll go and check," he said. It was impossible to really see through the windows, which had been boarded up, but he knew there was a tiny window near the front door that they had only taped. The handyman had told him the tape would keep the window in one piece, preventing it from shattering if it blew out of the frame.

When Allan got to the front hallway and looked through the window, he saw that a large tree limb had fallen on the front porch. He took a step back as the wind continued whipping branches and other debris down the street

"Are we going to be okay?" Jessi asked from down the hallway, where she held Hannah in her arms.

"Yes," he said. Suddenly, his determination not to show how much she meant to him seemed stupid. Their best friends' death had proved how short life could be, and the storm raging outside seemed a reminder to him to grab on to what was important to him while he still could.

He walked to her and wrapped an arm around her shoulders, leading her into the living room, where he pushed a love seat into the corner, away from the windows, and then gestured for Jessi to sit down. She did, and he settled next to her, wrapping his arm around her and pulling her and Hannah back against his chest.

"I'm not going to let anything hurt you or the baby. I'm going to protect you both," he said. And he repeated that vow inside himself, knowing it was one he'd never break.

"I'm scared," Jessi said. "This storm isn't something I know how to deal with. Plus it lasts so long, not like earthquakes."

"Spoken like a true Californian," he said. "I feel the same way. Give me an earthquake over this any day."

The storm seemed to be getting more intense, and he held her closer, wrapping his arms around both her and Hannah, until he heard Jessi mumbling something under her breath.

"What's that you said?" he asked.

"I'm praying," she said, tipping her head back to make eye contact. "Usually I'm not spiritual at all, but if anything makes me believe in a higher power it's this kind of storm."

"It makes me reprioritize my life, too. Family hasn't really mattered—"

"Yeah, right. You do everything with your cousins," she said.

"That's true, but our bond feels more like one brothers have. We've always been united with a common goal, and no matter what you think, our 'family' has had some problems over the years," Allan said. He'd never wanted to be tied to his cousins other than through the business. But they were friends and they'd shared the bitterness of their grandfather's goals for so long they couldn't be anything else. "What I was trying to say is that I always liked my money and my expensive adult toys, but being here with you and Hannah has made me realize that I can enjoy the quiet things, as well."

"Facing death makes you more accepting of certain things," Jessi murmured.

"Indeed," Allan said.

Jessi went back to her quiet prayers, and he held her and Hannah in his arms, watching over these two females who'd become so important to him in such a short time. He didn't know if these feelings would last beyond the storm or even beyond the time here in North Carolina. But he did know that they were very real and he liked them. He didn't have to talk about it to anyone, and as the storm raged outside, his feelings finally settled down inside.

He didn't need to know anything else at this moment.

"You're quiet," Jessi said.

"Just thinking," he said.

"About?"

"Stuff," he said.

"Stuff…what's that mean? Something weighty or something naughty? I can tell it's a subject you don't want to talk about," she said.

"Then why are you asking me about it?"

"Because I'm nosy and I like needling you."

"You certainly do a very good job of it," he said.

"Thanks."

He squeezed her and dropped a quick kiss on her neck, biting the spot just next to her tattoo. "Keep it up and I might have to give you what you're asking for."

"And that would be?" she asked in that cheeky tone of hers.

"Something naughty," he said.

"I like you when you're naughty," she responded.

"I like you that way, too," he said.

He leaned in close and whispered exactly what it was he would do to her, in detail. He could tell she was interested by the way she settled back against him. He kept talking, seducing her with his words.

He felt a little sad as he realized he'd never met another woman who suited his many sides and his many moods. Jessi's sexual drive was as fierce as his. Her loyalty to her sisters and her company was as laudable as his was. Her closely guarded emotions were hard to ascertain and made her as vulnerable as his did. And he didn't mind right now. At the moment that seemed exactly as it should be.

The worst of the winds seemed to pass a little after midnight, and they decided to sleep in the study with Hannah. The radio was still on and every once in a while they heard something else fly around in the yard. Jessi was feeling so much at this moment that she feared she was going to implode. She was worried and scared, and it seemed her awakening a day ago was timely, because this storm just reinforced that she wanted to live her life and stop being scared of things.

She needed to be more honest with the people who mattered to her, and she vowed once the storm was over she would do just that.

Allan made a quick trip through the house to check on the storm as she got Hannah into bed.

"Jess, come here," he called to her.

She walked down the hall to where he stood at the entrance, where that small window gave them a glimpse of the street and the world in the eye of the storm. He wrapped his arm around her and pointed outside.

"This reminds me that no matter how much research I do there are always going to be situations where I'm not in control," he said.

"It makes me feel small," she said. "And as you saw earlier, makes me believe in God."

"Did you make a bargain with Him?" Allan asked.

She turned in his arms. The faded scent of his aftershave, a fragrance she associated only with him, assailed her senses. "I did."

"I did, too," he said, surprising her.

"What'd you ask for?"

"I told God that if he got us through this then I'd stop…running from life, and give happiness a real shot."

Jessi narrowed her eyes as she watched him. "I don't believe that. Sounds a little too pat."

"Now you're judging what I asked for?" he demanded.

"It's like saying you wanted money when you already have enough," she said. "You haven't run from anything in your life. You stay in place and manipulate everything around you."

He tipped his head to the side and studied her. "You're right, but inside I run away and lock myself in a place where I don't have to engage. You said pretty much that very thing to me earlier."

"Fair enough. I shouldn't have judged. You just always seem so strong and so brave it's hard to think of you as someone who would run from trouble," she said.

"You seem to be the exact same way," he commented.

"You couldn't be further from the truth," she said. "And I promised God that if he kept us all safe I'd be better."

"Better?"

"Yes," she said, "Nicer to my sisters and to you and your cousins. I'd stop being afraid for Hannah and embrace loving her, even though I know that I can't always keep her safe."

Allan didn't say anything, just pulled her close and hugged her so tightly she couldn't breathe. She hugged him back with the same strength. Then she tipped her head up so she could see his face, and the expression on it made her breath catch in her throat.

He'd said earlier that he couldn't express his emotions, but right now there was something stark and raw in his eyes that she couldn't describe as anything other than love. And it awakened that same well of feeling inside her.

"Allan—"

He kissed her, his mouth moving over hers with purpose and she knew that he couldn't talk about whatever was in his heart. But for her it was enough that she'd seen in his eyes the emotions she'd been afraid to admit she wanted from him.

His hands moved over her body, not in a calculated seduction, but in a frenzied burst of passion, and it awakened the exact same frenetic desire in her. She quickly freed his sex from his pants, and he fumbled with her zipper. For the first time since they'd become intimate partners he wasn't smoothly seductive, and that rawness turned her on like nothing else could.

He lifted her and her pants fell to the floor and she shimmied out of her panties before he lifted her again. "Wrap your legs around me."

She did as he asked and felt the world spin as he turned them so her back was against the wall. His mouth captured hers, his tongue plunging deep as he thrust heavily into her. She clenched down hard on him, holding tight to his shoulders with her arms, and his waist with her legs.

He pulled his mouth from hers and kissed his way down the column of her neck, stopping at her tattoo—a spot that she was slowly coming to understand he loved. He laved it with his tongue and then leaned down to kiss and suck there.

Thought left her and instinct took over. With each thrust of his body he drove her closer to her orgasm and made his way deeper into her soul.

There was nothing of the Allan she'd come to expect in this fast coupling. When he lifted his head from her neck, she stared into his silver eyes and watched his pupils dilate as the first wave of her own climax washed over her.

Her orgasm seemed to trigger his and he started thrusting even harder, driving them both to the brink and then over it again as he spilled his seed inside her. It was warm and filled her with his essence.

She didn't even mind that they'd forgotten to use protection. It would have been an intrusion in this moment when their souls had united and their hearts had taken small steps toward each other.

It was not a moment she could regret, because for the first time in her life she felt as if she'd found a man she could depend on. And she was so glad it was Allan McKinney.

Thirteen

The next afternoon, once the winds had subsided, Jessi was glad to get out of the house and away from Allan for a few moments. Neither of them had spoken about what had happened in the hallway or afterward, when he'd carried her back into the living room and they'd fallen asleep in each other's arms, watching over Hannah.

Now that the storm had passed, she knew that everything was going to change. They were cleared to leave Hatteras, and Fawkes was on his way back to the island to help them make arrangements to return to L.A.

She stared outside at the sand that had been pushed up onto the street and into the front yard and the water that hadn't subsided with the tide. It was hard to imagine this place ever getting back to normal.

Downed branches and debris were strewn everywhere she looked. She remembered that howling wind and driving rain and wanted to keep Hannah as far away from this area as she could.

The hurricane had been big and scary. The only thing that had made it tolerable had been Allan, and Jessi was afraid that she was really relying too much on him. He was the man who didn't believe in love. He was the son of her family's sworn rivals. And he was truly the only one that she wanted.

Jessi was surprised when her phone started ringing. The cell towers must already be working again.

"Jess—thank God. Are you okay?" Cari asked when Jessi answered the call. "I've been dialing your number every half hour trying to get you."

She could imagine her younger sister carefully watching the clock and making sure she didn't miss a chance to call. "I'm okay. Allan is assessing the damage, but I think we made it through without too much."

"What was it like?" Cari asked.

"Intense. Loud and scary," Jessi said. "I wouldn't want to go through one again. We can't even drive on the main road. We have to walk everywhere."

"You won't have to once you come home. You're staying here, right?" her sister asked.

"Of course. Why wouldn't I?"

"I didn't know if you'd decided you'd had enough with the gaming world and wanted a change."

"No. My life is there. And I am working toward my objectives to satisfy my probation. I'm pretty sure I'll be joining you on the safe list soon," Jessi said. There was no way that securing a big money deal with a Hollywood producer wouldn't save her, and she had managed to reschedule the meeting with Jack White before the full force of the hurricane hit.

"Emma said you're on the cut list. Something about missing a deadline yesterday," Cari told her.

"What are you talking about? There was a hurricane and all the communications were down on the island. Hell, the entire southern Atlantic Seaboard was cut off," Jessi said.

"I know. Believe me, I think it's ridiculous and I've already raised my objection. If Kell doesn't back down I'm going to take it to the board."

"Fat lot of good that will do you," Jessi said. "I'm sure…I'll figure it out. Rest assured, I'm going to be back home to stay."

"Good. I miss you. And I really want to get to know little Hannah. She is so cute," Cari said. "Are you adjusting to being a mommy?"

"No," Jessi said bluntly. "I love her and I am doing stuff for her like I should, but it doesn't feel natural to me. I still hesitate before I do everything. I'm afraid I'll screw up."

"That's just part of being a parent," Cari said. "We all get overwhelmed sometimes.

"Emma doesn't feel like that," Jessi said.

"Emma's not human. She's a perfect oldest child who exists solely to make us feel inadequate," Cari said with a laugh.

"It seems that way sometimes," Jessi agreed, glancing at herself in the mirror. She had on a pair of artfully faded designer jeans with rips in the knees, and a silk blouse that she'd tied at her left hip. She'd put the combat boots on because walking in debris was going to be tricky.

As she glanced at her own reflection she admitted to herself she hardly looked like a mom. But inside she felt fiercely protective of Hannah, and she knew that moms came in all kinds of packages.

"Thanks for calling, Cari," she said.

"I love you, Jessi. I miss you and I was very worried about you."

"We were safe from the hurricane. I think this house has been standing for a long time, and John made sure to keep it up-to-date regarding hurricane codes."

"That's not why I was worried. You haven't been yourself lately. You've been a lot…harder than normal."

Harder. She knew what her sister meant and it just reinforced what she'd discovered recently: that no matter how well she thought she was doing at making the world think she was doing okay, she wasn't fooling anyone. "Life's been tough lately."

"Yes, it has," Cari agreed. "Doesn't seem fair that Grandfather sowed all this bad karma and we're the ones who are reaping it."

"No, it doesn't," Jessi said. "But no one ever said life was fair."

"It should be," Cari insisted. "We will do our best to make sure it is. I'm going to camp out in Kell's office until he agrees to take your name off the cut list."

"Thanks, little sis, but that's not for you to do. I already have a meeting scheduled that will change his mind. It's funny to me that a big-shot Hollywood producer understood that I had to reschedule due to Mother Nature, but the CEO of a gaming company couldn't," Jessi said.

"Kell hates us more than a normal person should," Cari said. "He's not all bad, though. He is nice to D.J."

"He's probably secretly brainwashing him to hate us," Jessi said.

"Jess—that's not true. I've got to go. I have a meeting in a few minutes. Love you."

"Love you, too," Jessi said, disconnecting the call.

She couldn't believe that Kell was being so stubborn about that timeline he'd developed. Did he really hate her so much? She'd hardly met the man. Was he that bitter just because of her last name?

She wasn't too worried, though. She'd win Jack White over, and surely after all they'd been through together Allan would be on her side. He had some sway over his cousin. She knew that and expected him to use it to help her.

And the two of them had a new bond. One that was stronger than ever. She felt confident that the man she'd spent the past tense night with was on her side. She knew she'd seen love in his eyes, and there was no way that someone who was in love would let his partner be hurt.

Partner… That almost sounded scarier than being in love. Was Allan her partner now? Did they have a true bond that would make them both stronger? Or was she kidding herself again? All her doubts made her feel small and insecure, and she wasn't going to give in to them. She couldn't.

She had to believe in Allan and in herself.

Allan had never seen this many downed limbs or this much standing water. It was the first time he'd seen damage like this. He'd grown up with mudslides and fires, but this was different. And the storm last night had been so loud…so intense. They were lucky the bed-and-breakfast was still standing.

He continued walking around the yard and searching for damage. He felt glad that now that the storm was over, he could get out of North Carolina. Frankly, he was ready to get away from Jessi.

Last night had been intense. He'd never been more alive, never felt every sense come awake like that. But this morning, with the sun shining down from the clear blue sky, he felt too exposed. Too vulnerable to the one person in the world he needed to be the strongest around.

He looked down at Hannah as she kicked her arms and legs in the carrier he was using to keep her with him as he surveyed the land. She seemed in good spirits this morning, and he had to admit the baby was a joy.

But at the same time he was always a little scared to let himself care for her. If things got sour between Jessi and him, one of them was going to have to give up their rights to the baby. Him, he thought. It was the perfect out. An easy way to hide from the emotions he felt toward both of them. He wasn't sure he could handle being that vulnerable. Both of them made him weak.

And though the judge had granted guardianship to both of them, in the back of his mind Allan was braced for the moment when he might lose Hannah. Lose them both.

If his life had followed one pattern, it was that no one he cared about stayed around forever. His mom had left; his dad had followed by taking his own life. His grandfather had been distant; Allan had never been close to the bitter old man. He was close to his cousins, but they all lived their own lives and went their own way.

Better that he make the break now before he let them both any deeper into his life and his heart.

And then there was John. John was probably the final blow, in that he was the one person who'd known Allan best. The one person he'd trusted to have his back. And now he was gone.

Why then would this little girl be any different? Or for that matter, Jessi? They'd both tried to make the situation between them into one that they could live with, but they both knew they were too different.

Last night, with a storm raging outside and that feeling that the world was just the three of them, it had made sense to let his guard down and make love to Jessi. Really make love. They'd had sex prior to that, but last night he'd felt as if he could almost let the full force of his emotions free. And now today...that seemed stupid.

It seemed like the move of a man who didn't know how to control himself or his own future. And that was a mistake. He just wished he had a solid plan for fixing the situation.

He was going to have to handle things carefully or he'd leave himself open to a lot of hurt and pain from Jessi. And a part of him almost believed he might deserve that. A part of him last night had been swept away by things...dreams that he knew he'd never really attain. They weren't things he really wanted, no matter how much he thought he might have in that moment.

"Looks like the bed-and-breakfast weathered the storm pretty well," James said, coming up to him. The handyman had called earlier to say he'd come by and help take down the storm shutters.

"It did. This building is certainly sturdy," Allan said.

"Yes, it is. John did a lot of work on it before Patti came down here. That man just wanted to keep her safe," James said.

"There are no guarantees in life," Allan stated.

"That's true enough. I've been meaning to talk to you about something that Jessi mentioned," James said.

"Yes?"

"You still looking for a caretaker to keep the inn open?"

"Yes, we are. I've asked Reggie Blythe, the McCoys' attorney, to help in the search," Allan said.

"Well, I talked to the wife and we'd like a chance at the job," James said.

Allan liked the idea of James and his wife taking over the inn until Hannah was old enough to decide what she wanted to do with it. "I'll tell Reggie, and then we can get him to draw up a contract and all that."

"Sounds good," the handyman said.

"Allan?" Jessi called from the front porch. She sounded troubled. "Can I talk to you?"

"Go on then," James told him. "I can get the storm shutters down by myself and store them."

"Thanks," Allan said.

"No problem," he replied.

Allan walked toward the house and noticed that Hannah waved her arms as they got closer. He wondered if she recognized Jessi. The book had said that she should start doing so at this age.

"What's up?"

"Um…your cousin still has me on the cut list, supposedly because I missed a deadline yesterday."

"I haven't had a chance to talk to him," Allan said. "The lines have been down all morning. Do you have a signal on your cell?"

"Yes. Cari called me," Jessi said. "So you don't know anything about this?"

"No, I don't," Allan said. He was angry on her behalf, until he realized that if he played this on Kell's side Jessi would back away from him. He'd be left alone, but it might be better given the fact that he couldn't see a way for them to really move forward from this, except as coguardians of the child and nothing more.

He wasn't prepared to let Jessi be his heart and soul every day for the rest of his life. He wasn't sure he could exist, feeling that insecure and vulnerable. As James had just said, no matter how much a man tried to protect the ones he loved, somehow when fate wanted them, they'd always be taken.

"Let's go inside and discuss this," Allan said. He walked past her, taking Hannah from the carrier he wore and transferring her to his arms. For a moment Jessi just watched him and tried to keep herself from feeling so in love with him. He was all the things she'd hoped to find in a man, but had never wanted to admit she'd been searching for.

He handed Hannah to her while he took off the carrier, and then went into the kitchen to wash his hands and pour himself some sweet tea.

She followed him and watched, waiting for him to call Kell. But it soon became apparent he wasn't going to.

"Aren't you going to call your cousin and chew his ass out for not taking me off the cut list?" Jessi said when he went to pour himself a second glass of sweet tea.

"No. Listen, Jessi, I understand your point, but Kell has one, as well. In business there are deadlines and they have to be met. That's how successful companies stay successful."

"I'm not saying I shouldn't have to meet the objectives laid out for me, but when there's a hurricane I think even Kell Montrose will have to admit it's impossible to do business."

"Yeah, but Kell won't."

"What about you, Allan? Will you?"

"Will I what?"

"Back me up. Support me. That's what I really need from you in this," Jessi said. She went to the fridge as Hannah started to get a little fussy and took out a bottle she'd prepared earlier. After heating it up, she gave it to the baby and stared at Allan, waiting to hear what he had to say.

But Allan was simply standing there, watching her.

"You're a good mother," he said.

"Thank you, Allan. I really did need to hear that," she said. "I'm learning, but I'm nowhere near where I need to be, and I don't want to talk about mothering right now. I'm still trying to figure out if you're in my corner or not. I thought we had each other's backs last night in the storm…."

Allan scrubbed his hand over his face and turned his back to her, putting his palms on the countertop in front of him and lowering his head. She wasn't asking much from him, so couldn't really understand his reaction.

"I just want to know you're on my side," she said again, and then realized that his continued silence was his answer. "You're not, are you?"

"I am just saying that, legally, Kell's not in the wrong here."

"We're not talking about Kell. We're talking about you and me. And if you feel what I do, then the answer is simple. You should want what's best for me. Even though you are being a complete ass right now I still care for you, Allan. I'd still defend you."

"That's good to know. I've never had you in my corner," he said.

She literally started shaking as his words sank in. Anger swept over her and she was livid. "I can't believe you're going to be flip about this. The last few weeks have been intense. They've changed my life and made me see things in a completely new way.

"I thought last night when we talked we shared something deep and meaningful, and yet right now you're acting like nothing has changed at all between us," she said.

She had to put Hannah in her baby chair with her bottle, because she didn't feel steady as her emotions got the better of her.

He turned back around to face her, but quickly averted his eyes. "Calm down," he said.

"Don't say that to me," she retorted. "I am calm. I just need answers from you."

"Well, I don't know what to say. Our time together has been intense, but it's not real. We both know that our lives are in California, and no matter what I might say to the contrary we are too different from each other to have a relationship. These days have been great and I'll treasure them always, but this has no meaning in our real lives. No matter how much I want to pretend otherwise."

"Pretend?" she repeated. She let his words sink in for a moment and then shook her head. "Last night I thought I saw the real man. The man behind the big gestures and the witty banter. Last night I had a glimpse of a man who was strong not by waving around his money or whisking people to places they've never visited, but with the quiet strength to know that all he needed was the right people by his side."

"There is an element of truth to that," he admitted. "I do lo—care for you. It's just that we've been living under a very intense set of circumstances. This isn't real. I can't pretend it is and neither can you."

"We weren't pretending last night. Or at least I wasn't," she said.

"Last night we thought we'd die in the house. Today…"

"Today you are showing yourself to be the man I guess you are, Allan. You're a coward. I never thought you'd be so shady. No matter how much we butted heads I always had a sort of grudging respect for you. The way you cared about John and your cousins, I thought you were a man with a heart. A man who would be worthy of not only my admiration, but also my love. Yet I see now that you're nothing but a hollow shell of a man."

"Is that all?" he asked, crossing his arms over his chest.

"Yes, it is," she said. "I'm taking Hannah back home as soon as I can get off the island. We'll work out a visitation schedule through our lawyers."

Still she hesitated, waiting to see if he'd stop her from leaving, and maybe ask her to stay. But he didn't. Instead, he just nodded at her.

"That makes sense. I'm going to stay here and settle things with the insurance company. Luckily, there wasn't as much storm damage as there could have been. I'll contact you when I'm back in California. Unless you have any objections, I've decided to hire James as the caretaker for the bed-and-breakfast."

She shook her head. "You really are all about yourself, aren't you? I thought I got a glimpse of a man who wasn't so shallow, but it seems I was wrong."

Picking up Hannah, she left the kitchen and her broken heart behind. She'd known from the moment they'd met that he wasn't all he pretended to be. But a part of her had hoped she was wrong, and she was really upset at herself for believing in the illusion of Allan McKinney.

Fourteen

Jessi didn't have any time to sleep after she got back to California. Her sisters met her at LAX and they went straight to her house. As they sat on the patio catching up, Jessi started to have a new vision of herself rising out of the ashes of her humiliating confession to Allan.

"Can one of you watch Hannah for me this afternoon?" she asked.

"Of course," Cari said. "Why?"

"I've got that meeting with Jack White, and even though the Montrose cousins are busy acting like I've shirked my responsibilities, I'm going to go through with it and deliver what I said I would."

"I'll go with you," Emma said.

"Why?"

"Because you'll need someone to make sure the financials make sense. Kell will crucify you if they aren't solid. It's your deal. I'll just be there to verify things," her big sister said.

"Thanks," Jessi replied, going back to staring out at the Pacific. It was a beautifully sunny day here, and on the outside, it seemed as if nothing had changed. But inside she was aching. Aching for Allan, which made her angrier than she'd expected. She had to admit that it was anger and hurt that were really driving her right now. She wanted to do what she could to prove to herself to the Montrose heirs, but most especially to Allan, who'd been too much of a coward—

Stop it, she reminded herself. She wasn't going to let herself go down that path again.

"Tell us more about what happened in North Carolina," Cari said.

"There's not much more to say," Jessi answered. "It was tough dealing with Patti's funeral and checking in on her mom. And then that hurricane...I don't think I ever want to experience anything like that again."

"What about Allan? Did something happen between the two of you?"

"No," she said.

"Liar," Emma declared. "You look like Cari did when she was pretending that Dec was nothing to her or D.J. You can't fool us. What really happened with Allan?"

Jessi looked over at her big sister and suddenly felt as if she were eight again. Back then, she might have been the one to defend Cari, but Emma had always been the one who defended Jessi. "I fell for him, but he didn't feel the same. I screwed up and now I'm just trying to survive."

"Oh, sweetie," Cari said.

Emma got up, came around to where Jessi sat and wrapped her arms around her.

"Love sucks." Jessi sighed.

"Yes, it does," she agreed.

Emma's husband had been killed in a car crash. He'd

been a Formula One driver and had been ripped from Emma's life while she'd been pregnant with their son.

"It's worse for you," Jessi said. "I'm just being a baby."

"It's not worse for either of us. When you fall in love with someone and they aren't in your life anymore, whether they are deceased or not it hurts. And you just have to learn to move on from it," Emma said.

"How, Emmy? How am I supposed to do that? I've never let myself care about a man like this. I've always kept it light."

"It's different for each of us," she murmured. "I kept Helio's obituary on my nightstand and reread it any time I thought I'd just imagined that he was gone."

Jessi hugged her sister back. Emma always seemed so strong that it was shocking to hear how vulnerable she had been.

"What changed for you?" Cari asked. "Why did you let Allan in?"

"I didn't mean to. I guess I could blame it on Hannah, but the truth is, I've been restless for a while. The Playtone takeover made me realize how life was changing and so were my priorities. But honestly, I didn't mean to fall for Allan. He's good-looking and all that, but he can be an ass."

"You would know better than either of us," Cari said. "He's always been pretty nice to me."

Emma glared at Cari.

"I still hate him for what he did to you, Jess."

Jessi had to smile at her sisters rallying around her. And it drove home something that she'd been completely unaware of her entire life. She'd thought she was the rebel and the loner, but she'd overlooked the fact that her sisters always had her back. It didn't matter if they held a differing opinion on things or if they were fighting about something else—when the chips were down they were always by her side.

"Thanks, girls," she said, smiling at both of them. In the corner on a blanket she heard Sam talking quietly to his little cousins. She reflected on how two years ago there had been only the three Chandler sisters, but now there was a future generation. Jessi needed no further proof that life just kept moving on no matter how much you felt like checking out from it.

"You're welcome. But what did we do?" Cari asked with a smile. Her youngest sister had such a good, open heart that Jessi had thought she was weak at times. But the past few weeks had changed that, and now Jessi understood the true strength that came from loving someone. Hannah had shown her that, and even though she hated to admit it, so had Allan.

"You just reminded me that I'm not alone. And that no matter how many times I might have thought I was, you were both always here for me." Jessi stopped herself before she turned truly sappy and way too emotional. But after all those years of thinking she wasn't a good Chandler girl like Emma and Cari, she finally accepted that that was exactly who she was.

"Of course we were," Emma said. "We're sisters and blood is thicker than water."

"And more trustworthy than men," Jessi said.

She saw the doubt in Cari's eyes, but her youngest sister was in the first throes of a new love.

"You're the exception that proves the rule," Emma said to Cari.

"I don't want to be. I want you each to find a man

who loves you as much as Dec loves me, a man who makes you happy."

Jessi wished she could believe there was a man like that out there waiting for her, but she knew there wasn't. She was fickle in her emotions, and as Emma had said, getting over loving someone was hard. Jessi had the feeling she might never truly stop loving Allan, or being mad at him for not loving her back.

Allan looked around the boardroom at his cousins, but didn't join them in their small talk about the NBA scores. He had never felt emptier than he had since Jessi walked out of his life. And it was his own fault. He'd let her go. Hell, he had encouraged her to leave, thinking that if it was a clean break it would be easier. But he'd been wrong.

He'd never in all his days felt such pain as he did when he woke up every morning alone. He'd been avoiding her ever since he got back to L.A. because a few days earlier he needed to find out if he'd been successful in cleansing her from his soul.

God, he was starting to sound pathetic even to himself. He just knew that he missed her. He didn't want to, but there it was. And the fact that he was going to be able to see her today was the only thing that had made him come into the office. He'd been working from home, getting scruffier by the day and turning into a miserable hermit.

Next week he'd have Hannah with him for the first time since his return, and even that hadn't been enough to stir him from his malaise.

"Allan?"

"Hmm?"

"Snap out of it," Kell said. "I don't know what happened to you in North Carolina, but you've been acting strange since you got back, and I need you sharp and on the ball. I think Jessi is up to something. She was vague when she asked for this meeting, but determined that we all be here."

"She was pissed off the last time I saw her. I'm not sure why she wanted us all here," Allan said, and then thought about it long and hard. So much had changed since the hurricane almost a month ago. It felt as if a lifetime had passed them both by, and now he was faced with a new life. One in which Jessi wasn't his enemy, but was his—what? The answer eluded him and he knew today he had to figure it out. "I bet she's done something to prove us wrong, Kell. She's a fighter and we both backed her into a corner. She's coming out swinging."

"You think so?" Dec asked. The other cousin stood by the window looking out at the sunny October day.

"I know so," Allan said. For the first time since she'd walked out of his life he realized he felt a charge of energy coming back through him. He'd missed her more than he wanted to admit, but he also missed sparring with her. There was so much to Jessi that he had needed, and he'd let her go. "I was a fool."

"Probably," Dec said. "Your name is mud at my house."

"Cari hates me?" Allan asked. She was the sweetest of the three sisters, and he hadn't thought she was capable of disliking anyone.

"I don't think she has it in her to hate. But she's very mad at you and said she pities you."

Nice. Jessi's sisters probably knew all about him.

Knew that he'd been afraid to take a chance on loving her.

"What the hell happened down there?" Kell asked.

"We got close," Allan said.

"Close? Did you fall for her?"

"Obviously," Allan said. "But you don't have to worry about that. I backed you and stayed true to my roots as a Montrose heir."

At what cost? he asked himself. He'd known all along that he was just using Kell and the family feud as an excuse to keep her at arm's length, and now he knew he'd acted like a fool. He had wanted Jessi from the first moment they'd met. It was ridiculous to pretend now that he hadn't.

"Thanks for your loyalty," Kell said. "I know I've made things difficult for both of you."

"You have, but we started this journey together," Allan said. "I'm not cut out to share my life with someone. Not even a woman like Jessi."

"I don't know about that. Our fathers weren't exactly solid examples of how to love a woman and be happy," Dec said.

There was a knock at the door. "Can we continue this conversation later?" Kell asked irritably.

"Come in," Allan called out.

The door opened, and Jessi walked in, but Allan hardly recognized her. Her normally spikey hair was tamed into a sedate style and she wore a suit. A gray-and-cream-checked business suit that made it seem to him as if all the light had gone out of his Jessi. She wore proper makeup, too—no outrageous cat eyes or bright purple lipstick. She was subdued.

He'd done this to her, he thought. He'd killed that rebellious light inside of her with his words on Hatteras. By saying that what they'd experienced together was fueled by circumstance instead of real emotion.

Suddenly, all his fears disappeared, as he acknowledged to himself that she was *his* Jessi. And he wasn't a coward as she'd said. He didn't run away from something he wanted; he claimed it, and he intended to claim her. He tried to catch her eye, but she refused to look his way.

But as the meeting went on and she made her presentation about the deal she'd hammered out with Jack White over the past few weeks to make games out of his latest movie trilogy, Allan knew he'd lost her. She was cold and icy in the meeting room. When any of them asked a question she answered it in a calm, quiet voice and ignored him.

Allan was afraid he'd realized his mistake too late. That he'd never be able to win her back. But when she'd concluded her presentation she gave a quick peek over at him. If he'd blinked he'd have missed it, but it was enough to convince him she was still in love with him. She had to be. Jessi wasn't fickle and wouldn't be able to love lightly.

"We'll have to review this, but we'll get back to you shortly," Kell said.

"Of course," Jessi said, standing up and leaving the room without another word.

Allan reached for the folder in front of Kell, started skimming the numbers and saw that it was a solid business case. Jessi had done more than he'd dreamed she would, and he was impressed anew at her talents. She was strong and smart and sexy and a million other things that he couldn't name just then because he felt such a strong outpouring of love for her. All he could say was, "This is beyond what we asked of her."

"I know. I think we're going to have to offer her a role in the newly merged company," Kell said.

"Um…would you mind doing me a favor?" Allan asked. "I think it could take me months to win her back without a little help from you guys."

"Just tell us what you need," Dec said.

"Am I going to have any cousins-in-law that aren't Chandlers?" Kell asked, but there was a faint grin around his mouth.

"No," Allan said impatiently. "Will you just tell her that you'll have the decision for her tonight, and ask her to return at seven?"

"Okay," Dec said, going out to talk to Jessi.

Allan was energized with a plan and knew exactly what he had to do to win back the only woman he wanted by his side for the rest of his life.

Jessi wasn't sure what the big deal was on the decision, or why she had to come back to the Playtone offices at seven that night, but since the Montrose heirs held all the cards, she did as they asked.

She felt battered from seeing Allan today. She'd thought she'd had control over her emotions. That she'd finally gotten him out of her heart, but she knew now that would never happen.

The love she'd hoped was temporary was starting to feel like the real thing. And keeping a job where she was going to be forced to see him, well, it was tempting. She hated that inside she was so weak where he was concerned, but that was the truth of it. She liked

Allan McKinney and she wanted to see him every day even if it was just at work.

Cari was babysitting Hannah for her tonight, and when Jessi parked her BMW convertible in the parking lot she admitted to herself how hard it had been to be in the same room with Allan and not look at him this afternoon. But she was glad she'd resisted all but that one little glance, which had made her breath catch and her heart beat faster.

She wasn't any closer to falling out of love with him than she'd been on the first day she arrived back in California. In fact, if her racing heart had indicated anything this afternoon, she might be even more in love with him.

She was still mad at him, and realistic enough to know that he was never going to return her feelings, but that hadn't changed anything inside her. She had no idea how she was going to handle things next week, when she had to meet up with him to give him Hannah. Maybe she'd just send Emma with the baby instead of going herself.

Her sister would do it for her. Emma had been in full-on big-sister mode since Jessi had returned from North Carolina, and right now Jessi was wallowing in it. But that had to stop. She was hiding and letting her emotions get the better of her.

Whatever they told her tonight about her job, she was going to have to figure out how to get Allan out of her mind and out of her heart so she didn't raise Hannah to be just as pitiful when it came to love.

Jessi got out of the car and walked into the office building, expecting to find a security guard waiting for her. But instead there stood Allan.

His hair was still as thick as ever and brushed the

back of his collar now. He wore a stylishly slim-cut black suit with a narrow gray tie. But he looked tired, and for the first time since she'd known him he watched her carefully before talking.

"I guess you guys decided to fire me if you're here," she commented when he didn't say anything.

"Don't jump to conclusions," he said.

"Oh, believe me, I don't do that anymore," she stated.

He cursed under his breath.

"Do you trust me?" he asked her.

She could only stare at him, but then took a deep breath. "You want the truth?"

"Always," he said.

She nodded. "I trust you. I trust you to break my heart and to let me down."

"God, Jessi. That's not true. I never wanted to break your heart. How could I?"

She didn't answer that.

"I'm sorry," he said. "I should never have let you leave North Carolina under those circumstances, but I was afraid. You were right when you said that we'd changed in those weeks we were out there together. And the truth was I wasn't ready for us to be different. I was still dealing with the loss of my best friend and finding out that the one woman I'd always thought I hated was actually the woman I loved."

She listened to his words, hoping he was sincere, but then she remembered that Allan was always honest when he spoke. She felt a spark of hope when he closed the gap between them and went down on one knee in front of her.

"I'm begging you, Jess, please forgive me and give me another chance."

She stared down at him as a million thoughts ran through her mind, images of the two of them from the moment they'd met. There had been something between them from the very beginning, and it had taken their friends' deaths to force them both to look at each other in a different way.

"I've missed you, too. I think I got too used to our morning routines and just talking to you during the day."

"I'm sorry I didn't say something to you before. But I didn't want to admit I'd been wrong about so much."

"But you hurt me, Allan. And I'm not the kind of person who likes that emotional pain."

"I won't do it again," he vowed. "I love you, Jess. I thought if I didn't say the words then I couldn't be vulnerable to you, but that wasn't true."

She felt silly standing while he was kneeling at her feet, so she got down on her knees in front of him and wrapped her arms around his big shoulders and kissed him. "I'll give you a second chance, but if you screw up again..."

"I won't," he said, kissing her and running his hands through her hair. "Will you promise me something?"

"Maybe. Depends on what you want."

"I want you to be you. No more suits like this, okay?"

She laughed. "Okay."

They got to their feet. "I have something else to show you."

He led the way to the elevator and took her up to the boardroom where his cousins and her sisters waited. There was a banner with her name on it that said Congratulations.

"Welcome to Playtone-Infinity Games," Kell said. "You hit one out of the park for us."

"Thanks. You didn't make it easy."

"Nothing worth having ever is," Kell said.

Everyone took turns congratulating her, and Jessi felt as if she finally had something she'd always been searching for when she watched Allan take Hannah from Cari. He held the baby in one arm and her with the other. She had a man she could count on, sisters she loved and a family of her own making.

"Just one more thing," Allan said.

"What now?" Jessi asked.

He took a box from his pocket and handed it to her. "Will you marry me?"

She stared at him. Dammit, he'd surprised her and gotten the upper hand, and the grin on his face said he knew it.

"Yes, I'll marry you," she said.

* * * * *

MILLS & BOON®
By Request

RELIVE THE ROMANCE WITH THE BEST OF THE BEST

1017/05

MILLS & BOON®

Why shop at millsandboon.co.uk?

Each year, thousands of romance readers find their perfect read at millsandboon.co.uk. That's because we're passionate about bringing you the very best romantic fiction. Here are some of the advantages of shopping at www.millsandboon.co.uk:

* **Get new books first**—you'll be able to buy your favourite books one month before they hit the shops

* **Get exclusive discounts**—you'll also be able to buy our specially created monthly collections, with up to 50% off the RRP

* **Find your favourite authors**—latest news, interviews and new releases for all your favourite authors and series on our website, plus ideas for what to try next

* **Join in**—once you've bought your favourite books, don't forget to register with us to rate, review and join in the discussions

Visit **www.millsandboon.co.uk**
for all this and more today!

THE GRUNTS
in Trouble

Praise for *The Grunts in Trouble*

"Fans of Andy Stanton's *Mr Gum* and Roald Dahl's *The Twits* will delight in this disgusting but amiable family." *The Guardian*

"... as always with Ardagh, there is the clever word-play, irony and plain silliness that make his books such fun ... To add to the enjoyment [it's] full of wonderfully incisive and daft illustrations by Axel Scheffler ... LOL." *The Telegraph*

"Axel Scheffler's illustrations impart a quirky comic charm to Ardagh's daft and comic story about the Grunts." *The Sunday Times*

Look out for:

THE GRUNTS ALL AT SEA

THE GRUNTS IN A JAM

THE GRUNTS ON THE RUN

Philip Ardagh
THE GRUNTS
in Trouble

Illustrated by
Axel Scheffler

nosy
crow

For FCRC,
with thanks for his permission
to use the name "Ginger Biscuit"

First published in the UK in 2012 by Nosy Crow Ltd
The Crow's Nest, 10a Lant Street
London, SE1 1QR, UK

This edition published in the UK in 2013 by Nosy Crow Ltd

Nosy Crow and associated logos are trademarks and/or registered
trademarks of Nosy Crow Ltd

Text © Philip Ardagh, 2012
Cover and inside illustrations © Axel Scheffler, 2012

The right of Philip Ardagh and Axel Scheffler to be identified as the author
and illustrator respectively of this work has been asserted by them in accordance
with the Copyright, Designs and Patents Act, 1988

Printed and bound in the UK by Clays Ltd, St Ives Plc

Papers used by Nosy Crow are made from wood grown in sustainable forests.

ISBN: 978 0 85763 272 2

Check out the buzz at
www.meetthegrunts.com

CONTENTS

1. Meet the Grunts   1

2. Throwing Things   21

3. Bigg Manor   42

4. Bees a-Buzzin'   60

5. Attack!   75

6. The Fall   98

7. Blunderbuss!   117

8. On the Trail!   142

9. One Rung at a Time   161

10. Round, Round, Get Around!   181

11. Fingers   195

12. Boom! Boom!   212

13. Law in Action   233

14. All Change   253

Chapter One
Meet the Grunts

Mr Grunt woke up with his head down by the footboard and his feet up by the headboard. He didn't realise that he'd got into bed the wrong way round the night before, so he thought someone had turned the room round in the night. And who did he blame? His wife, Mrs Grunt, of course.

Mr Grunt was FUMING. He reached over the side of the bed and, feeling something fluffy and stiff, curled his hairy fat fingers around it. It was Ginger Biscuit's tail. Ginger

Biscuit wasn't a biscuit and, although he was great-big-ginger-cat-shaped, he wasn't a great big ginger cat either. Ginger Biscuit was a doorstop: a doorstop stuffed with sawdust and *very heavy* (as doorstops should be). Mrs Grunt loved that old cloth moggy so much that she made Mr Grunt stuff him with fresh sawdust every time he sprung a serious leak. (Whenever Mr Grunt refused, she hid his favourite hat in the back of the fridge until he did.)

Mr Grunt struggled out of bed and stomped over to the window, accidentally brushing Ginger Biscuit's tail against Mrs Grunt's nose. She was snoring like an old boiler about to break down any minute, and had her mouth half open showing a jumble of yellow and green teeth. "Wh— What?" she spluttered, sitting up with a jolt. "What are you playing at, mister?"

"Teaching you a lesson, wife!" grunted Mr Grunt, opening the window and throwing the stuffed cat straight out of it.

Mrs Grunt watched it go with a mixture of puzzlement and anger. "Lesson? What lesson?" she demanded. (She had hated lessons at school, except for science when she could make explosions – she *loved* a good explosion – and certainly didn't want Mr Grunt teaching her a lesson first thing in the morning.) She swung her legs over the side of the bed and rammed her feet into a moth-eaten pair of old bunny slippers.

"I can't remember what lesson!" said Mr Grunt, which was true. He couldn't. "I want my breakfast."

(I don't usually eat breakfast myself, but there are those people who say that it's the most important meal of the day. One thing you can be sure of, though, is that people who say that about breakfast have *never* eaten one of the Grunts' breakfasts.)

Mrs Grunt snorted. "Then MAKE some breakfast," she said.

"But it's your turn!" Mr Grunt insisted. "I made us that lovely badger porridge yesterday morning." (The Grunts usually made meals from things they found squashed in the road. Squashed squirrels were a favourite, but even old car tyres didn't taste too bad to them, if they added enough salt and pepper.)

"It was badger STEW, not porridge," grunted

5

Mrs Grunt, "and you made it for *lunch* not breakfast, so it's YOUR TURN."

"Huh!" grunted Mr Grunt grudgingly. Mrs Grunt was right. He could now remember the bird-seed-and-sawdust cereal she'd served up the previous morning. Not bad. Not bad at all. He watched her stomping off in those tatty old bunny slippers of hers. She looked beautiful. Well, she looked beautiful to *him*. "Where are you going?" he demanded.

"I've got a cat to collect," said Mrs Grunt. She stepped out of the bedroom, tripped over something on the landing and promptly fell down the stairs.

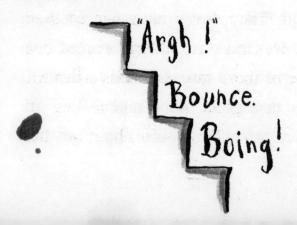

"Argh!"

Bounce.

Boing!

THUD!

(Another)

"Argh!"

Roll.

(An even bigger)

"Argh!"

The something she'd tripped over was
Sunny. Sunny wasn't the Grunts' flesh-and-
blood child. They didn't have one of their
own, but Mrs Grunt had always wanted one
and on one of those rare occasions when Mr
Grunt was in a good mood and feeling all
lovey-dovey towards his wife, he'd got her

7

one. Well, *stolen* one. (Not that he'd planned it, you understand. Oh no, it wasn't planned. It kind of just *happened*.)

Mr Grunt had been out pounding the pavement in search of something else – I've no idea what – when he'd glanced over a garden wall (or maybe a fence, he could never remember which) and caught sight of a washing line. On that washing line had been an assortment of things hanging up to dry, one of which he was pretty sure was a spotted sock and another of which had been a child. The child was held in position by large, old-fashioned clothes pegs clipped to each ear. And before you could say, "Put that child back, it's not yours . . . and, anyway, it's not dry yet!" Mr Grunt had leaned over the wall (or fence) and whipped that child off the line.

Mrs Grunt had been very pleased. Sunny

was the best present Mr Grunt had ever given her (with the possible exception of a pair of very expensive gold-coloured sandals and some old taped-together barbecue tongs, which she used to pull out her nose hairs). Mrs Grunt didn't know much about children but she could tell this one was a boy.

Mrs Grunt knew that boys should always be dressed in blue so she took a bottle of blue ink out of Mr Grunt's desk and tipped the contents into a great big saucepan full of boiling water. Next, she found some of her old dresses back from when she was a little girl and added them to the mix. She'd kept the dresses to use as cleaning rags, but now they were dyed they didn't look bad. Then, because she didn't like to waste things, she went on to serve up the boiling blue water to Mr Grunt, who'd liked it so much he had seconds. But he wasn't so happy when he had a blue tongue and blue lips for eight weeks.

Sunny was already an odd-looking boy, what with his left ear being higher than his right ear and that kind of sticky-up hair which NEVER goes flat, even if you pour glue into it and then try taping it into position with rolls of sticky tape, but in a badly made, badly dyed blue dress he looked really, REALLY odd.

Here, let me spell that for you:

O-D-D.

(Perhaps you could jot it down on a piece of paper and keep it under your beard until I ask you for it later. If you don't have a beard

then perhaps you could ask for one for your birthday.)

Sunny had been very young when Mr Grunt had snatched him from that washing line, so he didn't remember much about his real parents. He couldn't remember his father at all (though he did have a memory of a pair of amazingly shiny polished black shoes). As for his mother, what he seemed to remember most about her was a nice warm snuggly feeling and the smell of talcum powder. Once in a while, snatches of a song would drift into his mind on little wisps of memory. The song was something to do with fluffy little lambs shaking their lovely little lambs' tails, and — in his mind — it was his mother singing it. She had the voice of an angel who'd had singing lessons from a really good teacher.

The Grunts were very fond of Sunny in their

own way, but their own way was a *strange* way. Let me give you some examples (and if you don't like my examples you can always give them back).

For example: Mr and Mrs Grunt knew that boys don't like washing, so they never made Sunny wash. They knew that boys don't like tidying their bedrooms, so they didn't give him a bedroom. They made him sleep on the landing outside *their* room.

The truth be told, there wasn't room for a second bedroom in the Grunts' house because they didn't live in an ordinary house. They lived in a caravan.

Not a lovely, pretty, brightly painted wooden caravan.

No, not one of those. Put such thoughts out of your mind.

Nor a sleek, modern, metal caravan.

No, not one of those either.

They lived in a caravan Mr Grunt and his dad (Old Mr Grunt) had built together out of *stuff*. Stuff that included an old garden shed, the sidecar of a motorbike-and-sidecar, the less interesting half of an ice-cream van and some bobs (from a collection of bits and bobs) including an old dog kennel, some wooden planks and a frothy-coffee-making machine. The end result usually made most sensible people run away if they saw it being towed round the corner by the Grunts' two donkeys, Clip and Clop.

Ah, Clip and Clop. I was wondering when I'd get a chance to tell you about them, and now here we are.

Clip and Clop were sister and brother and/or brother and sister. They both had ridiculously long, lovable ears and big, lovable noses.

For a long time the Grunts thought that there was only one of them – that they were one and the same donkey – and they called "it" Clip-Clop. It was only when Sunny pointed out they could see them both at once, next to each other, that they realised that there must be TWO donkeys.

(This may not make much sense to you or me, but it's the Grunts we're talking about here, remember. They're not like the rest of us. Well, certainly not like ME. I can't be sure about you, come to think of it. I've no idea how ODD you may be. Which reminds me. I hope you've still got that piece of paper tucked safe and sound under your beard.)

The easiest way to tell Clip from Clop at a glance was to imagine that their ears were the hands of a clock. Clip's ears appeared to be saying eleven o'clock and Clop's said one o'clock. If you've no idea what I mean – and, amazingly, this does happen sometimes – here's a picture to explain it.

See? Good.

It was one of Sunny's many jobs to unhitch Clip and Clop from the caravan every evening so if the donkeys decided to go for a little wander in the night, the Grunts' house stayed put.

Back in the days before Mr Grunt took Sunny from the washing line and gave him to Mrs Grunt, it was up to them to unhitch the pair. And as you've probably realised by now, Mr and Mrs Grunt aren't the two most reliable people in the world.

More often than not, Mr Grunt would think that Mrs Grunt had unhitched the donkeys and Mrs Grunt would think that Mr Grunt had done it, so the job wouldn't get done and they'd wake up MILES from where they thought they'd parked their house the night before.

On one memorable occasion they woke up

on a golf course to find Clip sticking her nose down one of the holes, Clop thoughtfully chewing the little flagpole next to it, and a VERY angry, VERY red-faced man running towards them with a double-barrelled shotgun.

Mr Grunt knew that it was a double-barrelled shotgun because the man was firing at them WITH BOTH BARRELS! It took Mrs Grunt a week to dig the buckshot – the little round pellets inside the shotgun cartridges – out of Mr Grunt's bottom with a pair of rusty eyebrow tweezers. (And please don't ask me how you get rusty eyebrows because that'll make me almost as angry as

the golf-club groundsman had been with them
and the donkeys.) Mrs Grunt had a big grin on
her face every time Mr Grunt went "Ouch!" as
she dug out another tiny pellet, but that's not
to say she didn't secretly love him as much
as he secretly loved her. (Shocking, I know,
but true.) How much Mr and Mrs Grunt loved
Clip and Clop was unclear. Lately, Sunny had
heard Mr Grunt grumbling about the pair "not
being as hard-working as they used to be"
and muttering, "What good are donkeys that
won't do the donkey work?"

Now, where were we?

Oh, yes.

When Mrs Grunt tripped over Sunny outside
the bedroom door and went tumbling down
the stairs, she ended up tumbling out of the
doors of the caravan and on to the ground.
She narrowly avoided a patch of extremely

stingy stinging nettles but did land head-first in a mole hill.

"If you're going to fall downstairs, then do it *quietly*, wife!" Mr Grunt shouted from the bed. "Some of us have more sleeping to do." He pulled the duvet over his head, rolled over and fell on to the floor.

He landed on Sharpie, Mrs Grunt's stuffed hedgehog. A real one.

"OUCH!" yelled Mr Grunt.

His cry of pain could be heard as far away as Bigg Manor (if you were an exotic bird with very good hearing). That's BIGG MANOR, with two Gs. But more about *that* later.

Lots more.

20

Chapter Two
Throwing Things

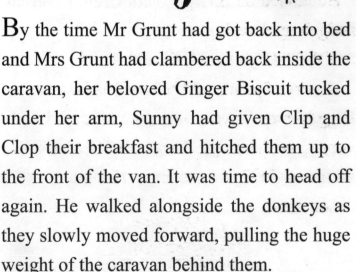

By the time Mr Grunt had got back into bed and Mrs Grunt had clambered back inside the caravan, her beloved Ginger Biscuit tucked under her arm, Sunny had given Clip and Clop their breakfast and hitched them up to the front of the van. It was time to head off again. He walked alongside the donkeys as they slowly moved forward, pulling the huge weight of the caravan behind them.

The sun was shining and birds sang in the trees. Well, *some* birds, at least. Others were

busy trying to pull reluctant juicy breakfast worms out of the ground, and yet more of them were flying away in horror at the sight of the Grunts' home-made caravan trundling along the asphalt road. Their little beaks were all a-quiver.

Mr and Mrs Grunt never really seemed to care much where they went, as long as they were going *somewhere*, though sometimes Mr Grunt would leave them for a few days – often on a rusty old bike made up from the parts of three separate rusty old bikes – then miraculously find them, wherever they'd ended up.

The Grunts didn't like staying in one spot for too long because whenever they did, they usually ended up getting into trouble. They didn't MEAN to, but they didn't go out of their way to avoid it either – like the time they

23

walked through the middle of a re-enactment of a famous battle involving three thousand people dressed as soldiers, and there was something about the way they joined in that seemed to upset people.

And not just people.

Sometimes animals too.

Once Mr Grunt upset a glow worm so much that it deliberately kept him awake all night by hovering above his bed, flashing on and off, on and off, on and off, on and off, on and off, on and off, on and off, on and off, on and off, on and off, on and off, on and off, on and off, on and off, on and off, on and off, on and off, on and off, on and off, on and off.

(And I suspect you're beginning to get an idea of *just* how irritating that can be. I went to make myself a cup of coffee part way through.)

Soon the Grunt residence was trundling up a hill, which was quite hard work for Clip and Clop but they didn't seem too bothered. Sunny had made sure that they'd had a good feed before they went to sleep and a good feed when they woke up – and the sleep in between had been peaceful – so they were in a good mood. Sunny was wandering along beside them, but before starting the uphill climb had double-checked that the bottom part of the stable-like door to the caravan (at the back) was bolted shut.

Why?

I'll tell you why. (That's what I'm here for, as well as to add a bit of bearded glamour.) He checked that it was bolted because if it hadn't been, once the caravan started going uphill the door might have swung open and lots of stuff would have rolled out of the doorway and into the road . . . which is what used to happen a lot before Sunny became part of the family.

Unfortunately, Mr Grunt had decided to have a bath. He was sitting in the tin tub just before the whole caravan had tilted backwards and begun the climb. The tub was fixed to the floor, so there was no problem with it sliding about, and it had a detachable lid with a hole for his head to stick out of so the water didn't slop everywhere, but he had left a big cake of soap resting on the floor.

Now the soap slid across the floor and right into the path of Mrs Grunt. Mrs Grunt wasn't one for looking where she was going even at the best of times. At that particular moment, however, she was carrying some rolls of turf she'd borrowed from a village green – which was now more of a village *brown*, because without its lovely layer of grass it looked plain muddy – so she couldn't have been watching her step even if she'd wanted to. She stood on the cake of soap, which skidded away in front of her, taking one foot forward and leaving the rest of her behind, like an ice-skater doing the splits.

She landed on top of the lid of the tin bath with a resounding CLANK (or THUNG!). The noise was like the sound you might get from a very fat knight in a roomy suit of armour being hit on the breastplate with a big, spiky truncheon-like thingy.

Next, the rolls of turf that had been in her arms went flying up in the air and came flopping down on her and on Mr Grunt and the surrounding area.

"Idiot woman!" said Mr Grunt.

"Rude man!" said Mrs Grunt. She had just spied the cake of soap on the floor and realised what must have happened. "This is your fault."

"Yours."

"Yours!"

"Yours!"

"Yours!" Mrs Grunt repeated, just as Sunny appeared through the doorway. He had heard the terrible CLANG (or THUNG!), stopped Clip and Clop as soon as he reached a not-quite-so-steep part on their uphill journey, and had come to investigate.

"Your father tried to trip me up," she protested.

"But he's in the bath," Sunny pointed out, "so how could he?"

"Through trickery!" cried Mrs Grunt. "That's what it was! Trickery!"

Sunny looked from the roll of turf on top of Mrs Grunt's head to the roll of turf on top of Mr Grunt's head and then back again. "Why are you both wearing grass wigs?" he asked. Mr Grunt gave out a big grunt and flung his piece of turf across the room. It landed on the doorstop cat, knocking him sideways.

"Ginger Biscuit!" cried Mrs Grunt, struggling off the bath lid and hurrying over to her beloved sawdust-filled moggy.

Sunny sighed and, safe in the knowledge that everything was pretty much normal (as far as the Grunt family was concerned, that is), went back outside – carefully bolting the bottom half of the stable-style door behind him – and returned to Clip and Clop.

Ten minutes or so later, Sunny found himself

leading the donkeys down the country road that led past the entrance to Bigg Manor. (Remember the name?

B-I-G-G ? Yes, that one.)

Up ahead a tallish, thinnish man was standing in the middle of the road with a neat pyramid-shaped pile of rocks. His name was Larry Smalls and he was wearing a badly crumpled, coal-black top hat on his head (of all places) and an old white T-shirt. On the T-shirt were the words:

"BIGG AIN'T BEST"

in faded red letters.

"Hello, kid," said Larry Smalls as the

caravan approached. (The truth be told, he couldn't tell whether the child with the wonky face, sticking-up hair and blue dress was a girl or a boy.) "Want to throw a rock?"

"Where?" asked Sunny.

"Here," said Larry Smalls, pointing to the pile. "One of these."

"I meant where should I throw it?" asked Sunny.

Larry Smalls sighed. "At the gates to the Bigg house, of course," he said, looking as sad as a box of ignored kittens.

Sunny looked over at the impressive entrance to the long and winding driveway leading up to the manor house: two big brown stone pillars either side, topped with white stone lions, and two gates of black metal railings with impressive gold-coloured spikes on top.

He looked back at Larry Smalls in his BIGG AIN'T BEST T-shirt. "Excuse me," he said a little hesitantly, "but WHY, exactly?"

"Why?" said Larry Smalls with a gasp. He was wondering a "Why?" of his own. He was wondering why this odd boy – he'd worked out Sunny was a boy – was wearing a strange blue dress. (Or *any* kind of dress, come to that.)

"Why would anyone want to throw rocks at the gates?" asked Sunny.

If you must know, Sunny was very tempted to throw a rock or two. He knew that throwing rocks at things was usually wrong, but there wasn't any rock-throwing in his life, and the neat pyramid-shaped pile of them did look very *throwable*.

Each rock was roughly the size and shape of a tennis ball; just the sort of size you'd want a chuckable rock to be. (Not that I EVER throw rocks, even when one seems to be saying, *"Throw me! Throw me!"* in a tiny voice inside my head which only I can hear.)

"Why should you throw them at the gates?" said Larry Smalls. "You ask me WHY?" He looked a mixture of puzzled and outraged and a bit like one of those birds that stands on one leg just because it can. "Because that is the gateway to the home of the Bigg family. *That's* why."

"Which big family?" asked Sunny, which was yet another perfectly reasonable question.

"Not *a* big family," said Larry Smalls, who had picked the topmost rock off his pyramid-shaped pile of rocks with his long, thin fingers and was now tossing it from one hand to the other. "THE Bigg family. The family called Bigg."

"Oh," said Sunny, though his "oh" made it obvious that he wasn't any clearer as to why this meant that he should throw rocks.

Except, perhaps, for the fun of it.

Looking at the man's expression, though, Sunny didn't think that FUN had anything to do with it. He eyed Larry Smalls' T-shirt. "So the 'BIGG' on your T-shirt means the Bigg family then?" He'd assumed it had just been a case of bad spelling.

"Humph," said Larry Smalls. The smell of his breath somehow reminded Sunny of the smell of a *circus*, which was rather strange. "Don't you know your history, boy?" he asked.

Not having been to school, Sunny didn't know much about anything except what Mr

34

Grunt, Mrs Grunt and Mr Grunt's dad (Old Mr Grunt) had told him, along with the things he'd learned for himself over the years, of course.

And one of the most important things that he'd learned for himself was to believe *half* of what Mr Grunt, Mrs Grunt and Mr Grunt's dad (Old Mr Grunt) told him.

Sunny was just about to get an answer as to why it might be a good idea to throw rocks at the gates to Bigg Manor, when Mrs Grunt went and spoiled it all.

She appeared in the doorway of the caravan. For some strange reason – if there *was* a reason – she had a mouldy old carrot stuck in her unkempt hair. "You're blocking the road, big nose!" she shouted.

Larry Smalls – whose nose was no bigger than Mrs Grunt's – looked rather startled. He was about to protest when Mr Grunt stuck his head out of a window in the roof. "Why have we stopped, wife?" he shouted. "What have you done NOW?"

"I haven't done nothing but *breathe*," said Mrs Grunt, "and everyone has to breathe."

"Except for dead people," snapped Mr Grunt, leaning dangerously far out of the window.

"Except for dead people," his wife agreed.

"*And* except for rocks and fridges and stuff," Mr Grunt added. Because he doesn't know much about anything, this felt like a very clever conversation he was suddenly having with Mrs Grunt. Quite *intellectual*, in fact.

Clip and Clop brought him back to earth with a bump.

Quite a big bump.

They had decided that it was high time to

36

walk forward a few donkey paces, causing Mr Grunt to lose his balance, fall out of the window and bounce off the caravan roof on to the road.

He stood up, adjusted his belt (which his father had made for him out of two smaller belts sewn together) and stood next to his wife.

"WHAT ARE YOU DOING BLOCKING OUR WAY?" Mr Grunt shouted at Larry Smalls.

Before Larry Smalls had a chance to say anything about Bigg not being best, Mr Grunt marched over to him in six purposeful strides and tripped over the pyramid of rocks almost as though he'd done it on purpose.

Mr Grunt hit the ground like a sack of mummified cats, with a terrific THUD! and an accompanying GRUNT! The rocks went everywhere: some flying through the air, some rolling across the ground and just about ALL of them heading for Larry Smalls.

Yelping like a cartoon dog who's had his tail nipped by a crab, Smalls ran for safety. He took a giant leap and scrabbled to the top of his intended target: one of the gates to Bigg Manor.

"Lunatics!" he shouted, shaking one fist as he held on to a gold-painted spike at the top of the gate with the other. "You're all lunatics!"

Somehow the wiry man's belt had got tangled up in the spikes, looping around one of them. He was stuck, and in trying to wriggle free, lost his grip and found himself hanging from the top of the gates like a dog's chew toy on a display hook in a pet shop. The "BIGG AIN'T BEST" on his T-shirt was now facing downwards.

Mrs Grunt twisted her head round to try to read the letters the wrong way up. "Bigg ain't best at *what*?" she demanded. She didn't like it when other people knew something she didn't, which was most of the time.

"Bigg ain't best because I is!" shouted Mr Grunt, and laughed as though he'd just said the funniest thing in the world.

Mrs Grunt certainly found it funny and laughed so much that her yellow teeth – and even some of her green ones – rattled inside her head.

Now Larry Smalls' already crumpled top hat fell from his upturned head to the ground, revealing a bald patch. It landed upright. Moments later, Mr Grunt was wildly throwing Smalls' carefully selected rocks at it.

"You shouldn't throw rocks!" said Mrs Grunt scornfully. "That's dangerous." She grabbed the one from Mr Grunt's hand and threw it as hard as she could at the hat, snatching another off the ground. Fortunately for Larry Smalls, despite the Grunts being such terrible shots, none of the rocks accidentally hit him.

In fact, the only person to get hit by one of the rocks was Sack, Lord Bigg's gardener. He had got up early in the morning to hide behind a really big patch of leaves and one of the rocks had gone sailing over the wall and landed on his head. He thought Lord Bigg must have thrown it, so he reluctantly headed off to find his wheelbarrow.

How Sack *hated* gardening.

Chapter Three

Bigg Manor

Bigg Manor was very big and, as you know by now, named after the Bigg family, who had lived in the manor for hundreds and hundreds of years. (Not all at the same time, of course. For one thing, it would have got ridiculously crowded. No, as the old Biggs died, younger ones took their place and then when *they* grew old and died, the next lot took over, and so on.) Now the only Bigg left in Bigg Manor was Lord Bigg. His wife, Lady Bigg (who referred to herself as "La-La"), had got fed up with him a long time ago and had moved out to live in the pigsty in the garden.

Poppet the pig already lived there, but she didn't seem to mind sharing (though she did think Lady Bigg's table manners were pretty appalling).

Don't get the wrong idea. The pigsty at Bigg Manor wasn't your average pigsty. It wasn't a small shack with a corrugated iron roof. It was a very fine pigsty built by a very famous English architect called Albert Docks, who designed the giant rabbits that were originally going to go at the bottom of Nelson's Column in Trafalgar Square in London, until it was decided to have lions instead. But it was still a pigsty.

Lord Bigg didn't miss Lady Bigg much any more, and Lady Bigg found Poppet the pig charming company compared to her husband, so all in all everyone in Bigg Manor (and the gardens) was pretty happy.

Except for the servants.

So, if you think about it, that meant that only two people (and one pig) were happy, and the rest of them were pretty miserable. And, oh yes, there were the birds in Lord Bigg's bird collection. *They* seemed happy enough but, then again, His Lordship did treat them much, much better than he did the servants.

Back in the old days, when men wore top hats – not short, crumpled ones like Smalls' – and had big beards, and the women wore layers and layers of frilly things, there were over one hundred servants working at the manor.

Now there were just five. Count them.

There was:

Peach, the red-headed butler (1)

Agnes, the cook and maid (Two jobs, one person) (2)
Jack, the handyman (also known as Handyman Jack), who used to be the boot boy (3)
Sack, the gardener (4) and
Mimi, the (newish) boot boy. Mimi was in fact a girl but there's no such title as a "boot girl", so a boot boy she was (5).

And that certainly adds up to five (unless you count at least one of them more than once, or leave one or more out.)

The Bigg family used to be very rich. They made their money from metal railings. You have to sell a lot of metal railings to make a lot of money, and that's exactly what they did.

The government had put the very first Lord Bigg in charge of coming up with a way of stopping people falling off cliffs, and he had a brainwave.

The first thing he did was get the law-makers to pass a law saying that all cliffs had to have safety railings built along the top of them.

Then he begged, stole and borrowed money to set up a factory making safety railings.

Next, he awarded this factory – *his* factory – the job of making ALL the railings to run along the tops of all the cliffs in the country.

But the first Lord Bigg's brainwave didn't end there. The final part of his brainwave was almost genius: Lord Bigg made sure that Bigg Railings were good, but not *that* good. For the first ten years after they'd been put up, they were just the sort of railings you'd want to use to stop people falling off cliffs: big and strong and railing-like. After ten years *and one week*, though, they'd go all floppy, like the stems of wilting flowers, and then droop to the ground, completely useless. This meant that every ten years the railings had to be replaced with a lot of *new* Bigg Railings! See what I mean? Clever or what?

Because different stretches of cliff top were fenced at different times – they couldn't all be done at once – there was *never* a time when the government wasn't paying Lord Bigg's safety-railings factory for more Bigg

Railings!

And so it went on for years and years and years. All the next Lord Bigg had to do – and the one after that, and the one after that, and so on – was to make sure that someone was running his factory and making railings so that the money kept on rolling in. All *he* and the Bigg family had to do was to spend, spend, spend, which was the fun part.

One day, however, the government decided to stop wasting money on fencing off cliff tops. They decided to spend the money on guns and cannons and smart new uniforms for their soldiers instead . . . and the Bigg Railings factory was left full of railings (which went floppy just over ten years after they were made) with no one to buy them.

Because the Bigg family had no idea HOW to work, having never had to give it a go,

they decided the best way to make money was by selling off some of the stuff they already had.

The latest Lord Bigg's grandfather sold off the family tropical island, the fifty-bedroom town house and a fleet of vintage motor cars. Next, Bigg's father sold off all his wife's jewellery, his silver foil collection and some of the grounds. (He'd tried to sell his wife only to find that she'd been trying to sell him at exactly the same time. And no one had wanted to buy either of them.) This left next to nothing for the current Lord Bigg to sell, except the railings factory itself and the occasional painting or piece of furniture.

Because he paid for the servants' food and drink and let them live in Bigg Manor with him, Lord Bigg really didn't like having to pay them wages as well. He thought that they should be paying *him*. But Peach, Agnes, Jack, Sack and Mimi didn't see it that way. They said they would leave if they didn't get wages, so Lord Bigg paid them *just enough* to make them stay. He also made them each sign a very complicated, official-looking contract – with plenty of rubber stamps, and a big red seal at the bottom – which stated that if they thought of leaving without permission, *they'd* owe *him* far too much money to dare try.

So they added the contract to their usual list of grumblings, stayed at Bigg Manor, and felt even more cross and miserable.

Peach the butler was usually moaning about his corns and bunions (which were lumpy things on his feet).

Agnes the cook and maid was always going on about her different allergies, which made her eyes and nose run and brought her out in all kinds of interesting spots and exciting blotches in the shapes of different counties.

Jack was forever breaking different parts of himself – arms, legs and, once, an ear – while climbing ladders when trying to mend everything from holes in the roof to a dripping tap. (This didn't put him in the best of moods.)

Sack the gardener hated plants and flowers. Actually, he hated most things. This was because he was a really good inventor. His inventions included the hat and the motor car. The only trouble was, someone had already invented hats and cars before him, and when he found this out he got terribly upset and blamed everyone and everything around him (including the daisies, marrows, peas and carrots).

And Mimi, the boot boy, found polishing everyone else's boots VERY BORING INDEED. She was also fed up with everyone calling her a *boy*, which is why she wore an ENORMOUS pink bow in her hair and pink-framed glasses with tinted pink lenses. She had also got Sack the gardener to give her all the old rose petals, which she boiled up in a big saucepan to create her very own home-made girly-smelling perfume. It smelled so sickly sweet that a quick dab behind each ear was enough to attract all the hummingbirds in the district. (All two of them. They were called Frizzle and Twist and they were part of His Lordship's bird collection.)

On top of all these gripes and groans, the servants at Bigg Manor lived in the part of the house that didn't have any glass in the windows and had very few planks on the floor. (Lord Bigg used the planks from that part of the house for firewood. I've no idea what happened to the glass.) They also had very little furniture. With the exception of the furniture in his own rooms, Lord Bigg had sold off all the valuable stuff and burned a lot of the cheaper stuff for fuel too (when he ran out of planks).

The servants' beds were made of old sacks stuffed with straw and old beard hairs.

His Lordship's rooms were nice enough, though, and he did have a best friend in Monty the parrot.

Monty the parrot was actually as grumpy as the servants but Lord Bigg didn't seem to notice. Monty bit him hard and often and it didn't seem to bother His Lordship in the slightest. He simply stuck another sticking plaster on the cut (which was why Lord Bigg

was usually covered in the things). If a servant had bitten him so much as ONCE, he'd have exploded in a terrible rage.

That day, Lord Bigg was woken up by

a squawk from Monty, who had in turn been disturbed by the distant, but still loud, "OUCH!". You know the one: it was the "OUCH!" from Mr Grunt when he'd rolled out of bed and landed on Sharpie the stuffed hedgehog. The house was at the end of  a long driveway, some distance from the road, but as well as having beady, birdie eyes Monty had *excellent* birdie hearing.

Lord Bigg slept in a huge bed that looked more like a giant wooden sledge. He sat up, let out a great big yawn, leaned against his pile of plump pillows, and yanked a bell-rope.

Down in the dark, dank kitchens, a little bell tinkled. It was the signal for Agnes to cook and take up his breakfast. She was asleep at the kitchen table (an old packing crate), her head slumped over a copy of *Dull* magazine. *Dull* magazine was a weekly magazine full of such boring articles that it was supposed to make you feel better about your own life. Agnes had been reading a piece about a woman who spent thirty-five years inside a hollow tree counting ants. Suddenly, working for the horrible Lord Bigg inside nasty Bigg Manor hadn't seemed quite so bad.

The annoying tinkling of the bell woke her up. She had been having a lovely dream about having a pet frog that burped up gold coins. When she realised that it had been just that – a lovely dream – she felt very upset, and came out in a whole new set of blotches. She dragged herself out of her chair and banged a frying pan down on to the top of the great big iron range stove to cook His Lordship his morning eggies.

Lord Bigg had finished his eggies and was sharing a piece of toast with Monty the parrot when there was yet *more* noise. This time it was the distant sound of the "thunk-phwut-thwacks" made by the Grunts' rock-throwing, and it got the parrot into another flap. He squawked and ruffled his feathers, then flew over to the window, where he tapped the glass with his beak.

"What is it, Monty?" asked Lord Bigg. He lifted the tray off his lap, threw back his bedclothes and stepped out on to a threadbare rug. "What's all the fuss about?" He slipped a blue silk dressing gown over his red-and-white striped pyjamas, and strode across to the window. Monty flapped up on to his shoulder.

With money in such short supply, Lord Bigg had bought the dressing gown second-hand from an Internet auction site. (A rather dodgy Internet site, where not everything on it was being sold by people who actually had the right to sell them, if you see what I mean. As in: they probably-weren't-theirs-to-sell.) What *hadn't* been stated in the ad was that the dressing gown must have been worn by a boxer into the boxing ring. So when it arrived and Lord Biggs unwrapped it, he was surprised to find that it had writing on the back. The big black letters said:

Barney
"The Bruiser"
Brown

No wonder the photo on the website had only shown the dressing gown from the *front*.

At first, Lord Bigg had been very angry. Then he decided that, because he only ever saw himself from the *front*, it didn't really matter. What's more, Barney "The Bruiser" Brown had been quite a GOOD boxer in his day, before he had retired and got himself a new job with a smart blue uniform.

Standing at the window, Lord Bigg pulled a small pair of mother-of-pearl-coated binoculars from a dressing-gown pocket and held them up to his eyes. He surveyed the scene. Through the trees he could just make out the entrance to the grounds. What he spied was the Grunts and Larry Smalls. What he thought was: *trouble*.

Chapter Four

Bees a-Buzzin'

By the time Lord Bigg had tramped all the way out of the house and down the drive to the entrance gates, Mr and Mrs Grunt, Sunny and the donkeys were long gone.

All His Lordship found was Larry Smalls hanging from the top of one of the gates, and tennis ball-sized rocks dotted all over the ground.

"What in blazes are you doing up there, man?" demanded Lord Bigg.

"Squawk!" added Monty the parrot for good

measure.

"Bigg ain't best!" shouted Larry Smalls, who was very proud of his slogan and couldn't think what else to say anyway.

"Oh, it's *you*, is it?" said Lord Bigg with a sigh.

"Of course I'm me," said Larry Smalls.

"You're the man who threw the cauliflowers at me at the village fête, aren't you?" said Lord Bigg.

Larry Smalls nodded proudly. "And who tried to drown you at the swimming gala!" he added.

"And posted me that very realistic rubber tarantula!" spluttered Lord Bigg.

"And smeared full-fat yoghurt on the saddle of your bike!" said Larry Smalls.

"And tried to push me into that vat of marmalade on the factory outing!" said His

Lordship.

"And forced your motor car into a ditch that wet Wednesday!" Smalls nodded with glee.

"And locked me in that cupboard at the art gallery that dry Thursday!" fumed Lord Bigg.

"And—" began Larry Smalls, only to be interrupted this time.

"And I think I'll go and call the police," said Lord Bigg. He looked down at his feet. There on the ground in front of him was a coal-black, short, crumpled top hat. "Yours, I take it?" he said, looking up at Smalls.

"Mine!" agreed Smalls.

Lord Bigg picked the hat up, crumpled it some more, and somehow managed to squodge it into a large outside pocket of his dressing gown.

"You can't do that!" Larry Smalls protested.

Lord Bigg chose to ignore him.

Monty the parrot, on the other hand, took immediate action. Up until now he'd been perching on Lord Bigg's left shoulder. He flapped up into the air and sank his beak into Larry Smalls' nose.

"ARGGGGGHHHHHHH!"

screeched Mr Smalls, then added a few very rude words, which I'm FAR too polite to repeat here and now. (Maybe later, when no one else is around, if you ask me nicely.)

"I want you off my land – I mean, off my *gate* – within the hour," said Lord Bigg, "or I really will call the police. One hour."

"But I'm stuck!" protested Larry Smalls. He clutched his bleeding, swollen nose in both hands.

"That's not my problem," said His Lordship. He turned and walked away. Monty the parrot swooped low and landed back on his shoulder. From the top of the gate, his belt looped over a railing spike, Mr Smalls read the back of Lord Bigg's dressing gown with a puzzled frown.

Barney "The Bruiser" Brown?

Lord Bigg was Barney "The Bruiser" Brown?

Blimey.

Smalls hadn't even known that Lord Bigg was a boxer, let alone a fairly well-known one, recently retired from the ring. That would help explain why Bigg was covered in little crosses of sticky plasters. Boxing injuries!

Larry Smalls would never admit it, but he was impressed that Lord Bigg was Barney "The Bruiser" Brown. Only a *tiny* bit impressed, but impressed none the less.

A mile or so away, meanwhile, Mr Grunt was climbing up on to the roof of the moving caravan for a better view of the road ahead. He often sat up there and often fell off, which was usually Mrs Grunt's fault, Sunny's fault or Clip and Clop's fault, but never HIS fault. (According to Mr Grunt, that is. Funny that.)

Today was no exception; as the caravan went over a small bump, Mr Grunt found himself sliding off the roof with a "Wooooooaaaaah!", which was swiftly followed by an "Ahhh! Ahh! Argh! Ouch!" as he landed in a roadside gorse bush.

A gorse bush is a very prickly bush. It has a few pretty yellow flowers, but apart from that it's just about all thorns. If he'd been a sack full of jelly, Mr Grunt would have sprung some serious leaks.

Sunny sighed and told Clip and Clop to stop. They were happy to, which surprised Sunny a little until he saw what they'd seen: an especially fine patch of roadside thistles. So while he did his best to help free Mr Grunt without getting too prickled himself, the two donkeys enjoyed a mid-morning snack.

Once freed, Mr Grunt felt a need to kick something solid. Sunny remembered the time Mr Grunt had kicked a statue in the middle of a town square. It wasn't in the middle of a town square any more. It was now in pieces in the town's rubbish dump. Not that Mr Grunt's foot hadn't suffered too. For the following three days, Mrs Grunt'd had to give him a piggyback up and down stairs, and the rest of the time he'd shuffled around on his bottom like a toddler who couldn't quite toddle (so wasn't *really* a toddler yet, I suppose).

Today, however, Mr Grunt decided to kick an electricity pylon because, apart from a couple of spindly-looking trees, it was the nearest solid thing. Electricity pylons – metal towers supporting electric cables high above ground – can be dangerous things, as Mr Grunt was about to find out. He gave the pylon a mighty kick, and guess what happened . . .

Oh, go on. Guess.

Just for me.

Mr Grunt gave the pylon such a big kick that it vibrated, making the ground vibrate, causing a swarm of bees to leave their hive in a nearby tree to find out what was going on.

Did you guess right? Of course you didn't. (And if you *did* think "bees" you're either one of those people who can see into the future, or you've read this before. And that's not proper guessing, so it doesn't count.)

So the bees swarmed out of their hive to find out what was going on and, because Mr Grunt was what was going on, they decided to take a closer look. They landed on his face, creating what looked like A GIANT BEARD OF LIVING BEES.

What Mr Grunt wanted to do was to SCREAM, but even Mr Grunt wasn't stupid enough to do that because screaming would have meant having to open his mouth. And one of the last things he wanted was a mouthful of stingy bees. It was annoying enough that a few of the bees were thinking

about exploring his nostrils. So he *imagined* himself screaming and simply went beetroot red instead.

In fact, his face went *so* red that it was enough to make Clip and Clop stop chewing their thistles and stare at him with a gleam of casual interest in their donkey eyes. Or perhaps it was the enormous buzzy beard he'd suddenly grown that attracted their attention.

Mrs Grunt, meanwhile, burst out laughing. You may have heard the phrase "to laugh like a

drain", which has always confused me because drains don't laugh. I can't really describe *what* Mrs Grunt's laugh sounded like but I can say that with her mouth that wide open it *smelled* like a drain.

"Shave that thing off, mister!" she said between the guffaws. "It makes you look stupid!"

Saying that Mr Grunt looked stupid is like saying that France is "a bit French". For Mrs Grunt to have said that Mr Grunt looked stupid, then, must have meant that he looked really, *REALLY* stupid.

Sunny, meanwhile, was taking matters more seriously. He imagined that if a lot of the bees decided to sting Mr Grunt, this would be very bad – as well as very painful – for him. So how could he help?

Sunny ran back inside the caravan and

grabbed a big jar of honey off the breakfast table. The Grunts had discovered long ago that a smear of honey could make even the toughest squashed magpie even tastier, so they'd bought the biggest jar they could find. And bees like honey, don't they? (Or is that bears?)

"Here, bee, bee, *bees*!" said Sunny, waving the open honey pot in front of Mr Grunt's buzzing face, trying to attract the stripy insects' attention. "Here, bees! Lovely honey, honey, *honey*!"

And this was the scene that met a certain young lady as she rounded the bend in the road: the strangest, most worrying-looking caravan she'd ever clapped eyes on; a cackling yellow-and-green-toothed woman; a bright-red man with an enormous beard of BUZZING BEES; and an extraordinary-looking boy, wearing an extraordinary blue dress, leaping about with a big pot of honey.

In the girl's hair was the biggest pink bow Sunny had ever seen.

Yes, you guessed it: she was Lord Bigg's boot boy, Mimi. She was skipping down the lane with two tiny hummingbirds buzzing around her head like the excited bees. On seeing this most amazing sight, she stopped in her tracks and her eyes widened behind the pink-tinted lenses of her pink-framed glasses.

Waves of her cloying home-made rose-petal perfume wafted through the air. Mrs Grunt *hated* the smell. Mr Grunt couldn't smell anything except BEE. And Sunny thought it was rather nice.

But the bees?

The bees?

They LOVED IT!

Before anyone quite knew what was happening, they'd wiped themselves off Mr Grunt's face – as if he'd had an instant, magical shave – and were heading for Mimi faster than Sunny could shout, "Run for your life!"

Chapter Five
Attack!

Sack the gardener was hiding in the potting shed and he didn't want to come out. After being hit by a tennis ball-sized rock that some IDIOT had thrown over the wall, he'd gone to the shed to get ready for work, but ended up trying to get back to sleep. Lying among the terracotta pots, staring up at the cobwebby roof, he found himself inventing stuff. He just couldn't stop it.

In the space of half an hour, he'd invented the collapsible ironing board, toast, fingerless gloves and lightbulbs. Eventually, he decided that he'd better do some gardening. Unfortunately for Sack, although he really hated it, he was very good at gardening. If he threw away an apple core it would eventually grow into a tree. If he spat out a grape pip, in next to no time a vine would start curling out of the ground where it landed. He had what his gran called "green fingers".

Sack's gran (Granny Sack) was not very good at telling greens from browns, or recognising people's faces unless they were pushed up very close to her own, but she was right about the green fingers part. It's a phrase that describes someone who seems to have a natural ability to get plants to grow beautifully, without necessarily even trying that hard. (I meant the green-fingered folk don't have to try hard. The plants have to, of course. They always do. All that turning-sunlight-into-food and stuff.)

So when Sack had to garden – when there was no way out of it – he did it very well. He had just picked up his least favourite garden tools and put them in his least favourite wheelbarrow and was wheeling it across the loathsome front lawn to one of his least favourite flowerbeds when he heard Mimi.

She was sprinting down the road the other side of the wall, wailing as she went. Or was it a word? What was she saying? Was it "*Beeeeeeeeeeeeeeeeeeeeesss!*"?

The walls around the Bigg Manor estate were high: brick-built with no obvious footholds or hand-holds. Those gates with their fancy gold-topped spikes were there for a reason and not just for show. When they were closed, entrance was pretty much by invitation – or by ladder – only.

Or would have been, if there hadn't been a hole in the wall, hidden on both sides by evergreen bushes. The hole was so well hidden that Lord Bigg himself didn't know about it. But the servants, Peach, Agnes, Handyman Jack, Sack and Mimi, knew about it. And it was through this hole in the wall that Mimi suddenly appeared – well, *charged* – still crying, "*Beeeeeeeeeeeeeeeeeeeeesss!*"

Sack watched in amazement as the bright-pink, rose-petal-smelling, big-bowed Mimi was pursued across the lawn by a swarm of eager bees. Hummingbirds Frizzle and Twist hovered around her ears, snapping at the buzzing insects with their tiny beaks. Moments later, a boy in a blue dress appeared through the hole, clutching the biggest jar of honey Sack had ever seen, and waving a spoon in the air.

Sunny had a dozen or so bees buzzing around him, but they obviously found Mimi *far* more interesting. Then he spotted the fish pond. There was a big lake in the grounds of Bigg Manor, but that was round the back of the house. Here at the front there was a large, formal, circular stone fish pond. It had a fountain shaped like a dolphin in the middle, which had long since stopped squirting water.

"The pond!" Sunny shouted.

"Jump into the pond!"

He wasn't sure whether Mimi had heard him. She certainly didn't veer off in that direction. So he shouted it a few more times: "Jump into the pond! Jump into the pond!"

Finally, Mimi seemed to get the message. Flapping her arms as she ran, she zigzagged across the grass, then with one last cry of "*Beeeeeeeeeeeeeeeeeeeesss!*" she threw herself into the water with an almighty SPLASH! A startled goldfish or two found themselves momentarily in mid-air, and some lily pads flew around like plates in a Greek restaurant, then all was still.

At first, Mimi kept her head above water, but the bees still swarmed around her. It was only when she ducked it below the surface that the bees lost interest and looked around for somewhere else to go. It was then that Sunny lobbed the huge jar of honey high in the air in a graceful arc. It landed on the gravel drive a fair distance away, breaking the glass and revealing a wonderful, golden, gloopy mass of honey. *Now* he had the bees' attention. They forgot all about Mimi and buzzed over to the honey.

Sunny and Sack reached the pond at about the same time. Frizzle and Twist hovered above the water where Mimi's head had disappeared moments before, their wings flapping at such a speed they seemed a blur.

As Sunny and Lord Bigg's gardener leaned over the stone surround, Mimi broke through

82

the surface of the water, gasping for air. Sack took one hand and Sunny the other and together they heaved her out on to the grass. She couldn't have looked more soaked. Her clothes clung to her like a flabby second skin, her hair dripped straight and long, and her once-proud bow looked more like a squashed, pink, soggy *something*. And gone was the smell of her rose-petal scent, to be replaced by the faintest whiff of pond water.

The first thing Mimi did was look around nervously for the bees through the pink-tinted lenses of her pink-framed spectacles.

"Don't worry about them," said Sunny, pointing towards the broken honey jar on the driveway. "That should keep them busy for a while."

Mimi's whole body suddenly seemed to sag and she lowered herself on to the stone rim of

the pond, sitting down with a bump.

"Thanks," she said, looking up at Sunny, who was panting from the chase. "Thanks for rescuing me."

"Rescuing?"

"For suggesting I jump in the pond. I would never have thought of it," said Mimi. She seemed to be taking in the boy's appearance for the first time: the sticky-up hair, the sticky-out ears and the blue dress. "I'm Mimi."

"I'm Sunny," said Sunny. "Pleased to meet you."

"And I'm Sack," said the gardener. "We'd better get away from here before His Lordship starts wondering what's going on.'

Sack headed off in the direction of his potting shed, with Sunny and Mimi following close behind. Every step she made was accompanied by a squelch from the water in her shoes.

"Do you know the man with the beard?" Mimi asked Sunny.

"What man?" asked Sunny.

"The man with the beard of bees that decided to chase me?"

"Oh," said Sunny, looking a little crestfallen. "He's my dad. He doesn't usually go around with a beard of bees. I'm pretty sure this was his first time. He kicked an electricity pylon that annoyed them, and they took a liking to his face—"

"Until I came along," said Mimi as she squelched.

"Well, you do have a much nicer face," said Sunny, then turned an interesting shade of pink when he realised what he'd just said.

"You think so?" she asked.

"Yes." He blushed some more. "And

obviously the bees thought so too. And you smell – well, you smell*ed* – fantastic."

"You liked that? It's my very own home-made rose-petal scent."

"It smelled delicious," said Sunny.

"You're not supposed to drink it!" Mimi laughed.

"You know what I mean," said Sunny.

"Yes." Mimi nodded. "I know what you mean."

"Do you work here?" Sunny asked.

"She's the boot boy," said Sack, who'd come to a halt and was fumbling for a key in his pocket.

"But she's a girl!" said Sunny.

Mimi beamed. "My point exactly!" she said, and proceeded to give Sunny a big hug, the end result being that the front half of his dress looked a far darker

87

blue than the back half because of the wetness (and now he too had the slightest whiff of pond water about him).

Sack and Sunny waited outside the potting shed, while Mimi slipped inside, reappearing at the door a few minutes later dressed in one of Sack's overalls. "I'll put the kettle on," she said.

Soon all three were sitting around a little camping stove, three chipped enamel mugs in front of them and the kettle well on its way to boiling.

"So you live with your family in that – er – that—"

"Caravan?" said Sunny. "Yes. Dad built it himself, with a little help from *his* dad, Old Mr Grunt."

"It's unlike any caravan I've ever seen," said Mimi, which was no word of a lie.

Sunny didn't really get much of an opportunity to talk to other people so, despite the unusual circumstances, he really enjoyed his time with Mimi and Sack that afternoon. He enjoyed the tea too, when it had brewed. The so-called tea they drank back in the caravan was usually made of any old leaves Mr or Mrs Grunt decided to pick, dry and put

in the tea caddy, and Mrs Grunt sometimes simply held a corner of her dress over a cup, and poured hot water through it to give the water a bit of colour and taste. The tea he drank in the potting shed that day was real tea made from real tea leaves. It was delicious.

Sack's conversation was less enjoyable. He spent most of the time moaning about how mean Lord Bigg was, which was fair enough, I suppose, because Lord Bigg WAS very mean. He told Sunny about the servants' terrible living conditions and bad pay. And what a big old empty shell the manor really was.

"It looks so impressive from the outside," said Sunny.

"It must have been an amazing house once," Mimi agreed. "But almost everything's been sold and most of what's left has been chopped up or ripped to pieces."

"Peach and Agnes say that Lord Bigg's bedroom and sitting room are still beautiful," said Sack, "but I've never been allowed in either, what with being the gardener. My place is out here."

"And my place is down with the boots and the polish," said Mimi. Her hair was already drying out and getting some of its bounce back.

"Why don't you both leave?" said Sunny, taking his last sip of tea. "Resign? Give up your jobs?"

"We have contracts," said Sack.

"Signed documents that could land us in a load of trouble if we quit without His Lordship's permission," Mimi explained.

"You could always run away," said Sunny.

"But what would I do?" asked Sack.

"Well, you wouldn't have to garden, that's

for sure," said Sunny (who'd had an earful of just how much Sack hated, hated, *hated* gardening).

"But that's all I'm good at." Sack sighed. "If I mow a lawn I can't help doing it perfectly, even if I don't try!"

"But what would you *like* to do?" asked Sunny.

"Wait here," said Sack. He got up from the large upturned flowerpot he was using as a seat, and disappeared behind some wooden shelving, reappearing with a black plastic seed tray piled high with papers. Sitting down again, Sack grabbed a bunch of papers from the top of the pile and handed them to Sunny. "Take a look at these."

Sunny studied the beautifully drawn diagrams. There was one of a screwdriver and screw; one of a light switch; and one of a folding umbrella. All of them had their working parts carefully labelled, with lots of arrows and written explanations. "These are really well done, Sack," he said when he'd finished. "So you want to be an artist?"

"An inventor!" said Sack. "I want to invent things!"

Sunny frowned. "You – er – invented all these yourself?"

"Yes," said Sack, suddenly looking glum. "And don't tell me that someone already invented them before me, because I know that *now*. That's the trouble with all of my inventions so far!"

"But just because someone beat you to it,

doesn't mean that you're not a genius for coming up with the ideas all on your own," said Mimi.

Sack smiled again. "Mimi always says encouraging stuff like that," he said.

"She has a point," said Sunny. "What about you, Mimi?" He placed his empty mug between his feet on the potting-shed floor and twisted to face her more directly.

"What about me?" she asked.

"I mean, what would you like to do if you left Bigg Manor?"

Mimi thought for a moment, taking off her pink-framed glasses and giving the lenses a good wipe with a cloth she'd pulled from a big front pocket of her borrowed overalls. "Well," she said at last. "I love animals and I'd like to see the world, so something involving animals and travel, I suppose."

"Ah, I was meaning to ask you about those," said Sunny, pointing up at Frizzle and Twist. Now that Mimi had washed off her rose-petal perfume in the fish pond, the two hummingbirds had stopped flying around her head, but they still liked to stay close to her. They were currently hovering high above the three of them, in the pitch of the roof.

"Lord Bigg has an aviary – a bird collection," said Sack.

At that precise moment, the door to the shed was thrown open from the outside. Framed in the doorway, in brilliant sunlight, was the silhouette of a man with bushy side-whiskers.

95

Before Sunny knew what was happening, something flapped right up to his face and pressed its big beak against his nose. It was Monty the parrot.

Sunny's eyes had quickly become accustomed to the sunlight, and he could see that the face of the man in the doorway was covered with tiny little crosses of sticking plaster.

"Who the blazes are you?" demanded Lord Bigg. He sounded far from friendly.

Chapter Six

The Fall

Lord Bigg wasn't a big fan of children. He and Lady "La-La" Bigg had once had a boy, but they'd mislaid him, which had rather pleased His Lordship and rather upset Her Ladyship. (It was one of the reasons why they were both happy with the arrangement of his living in the house and her living in the pigsty.)

There were many reasons why Lord Bigg didn't particularly like children. Firstly, they cost money. You had to feed and clothe and maybe even educate them. Then there was the fact that they didn't behave like adults. They charged round pretending to be kings or queens or aeroplanes, and had imaginary friends. They asked stupid questions, such as, "How many beans make five?" or difficult questions, such as, "Why's the sky blue?" Or stupid, difficult questions, such as, "Why aren't carrots called oranges when they're as orange as oranges are, and got here first?"

At meal times, they spent as much time *under* the table as at it, or they curled up in a ball and squirmed on their chair. More food ended up on the table, the floor and themselves

than in their mouths.

They somehow managed to get their clothes dirty within thirty seconds of putting them on. They collected bugs and mud and little scraps of paper with "important" squiggles on them.

They talked when you wanted them to be quiet and were quiet when you wanted them to say something. They gave off strange smells and said embarrassing things, such as "Why isn't Mr Morris dead yet?" when Mr Morris was standing right next to them; or "How come you have big sweat patches under your arms, Mrs Sawyer?"; or "Are you really as dumb as my daddy says you are?". And that was just for starters . . .

So no, Lord Bigg wasn't one of those lordships who wanted a son and heir who would one day take over Bigg Manor from him and keep the family name alive.

It wasn't as if he had a fortune to pass on, like in the old days when the Bigg family was still making railings. If Lord and Lady Bigg hadn't mislaid their son somewhere – and neither of them could remember which one of them had been supposed to have been looking after him when they did – he'd have inherited an empty house, some beautifully gardened gardens, a handful of servants and, probably by then, some serious debts. So it had all worked out rather well really.

Lord Bigg eyed the strange child sitting before him now. "I said, who the blazes are you?"

Sack and Mimi had jumped to their feet, and Sunny now did the same. "My name is Sunny," he said.

"And what are you doing on my land?" demanded His Lordship.

"I – er—"

"You're not with Smalls, are you?" Monty had landed on Bigg's shoulder and they both leaned forward as one, their two pairs of beady eyes boring into Sunny's. "You do look somehow familiar."

"S-S-S-malls, sir?" asked Sunny.

"An odious little man with a BIGG IS BAD T-shirt," said Bigg.

"AIN'T BEST," Sunny corrected him. "BIGG AIN'T BEST."

Lord Bigg's eyes widened and flickered with rage. "So you *are* part of his little circus."

"No!" said Sunny. "I've read the T-shirt, that's all."

Bigg looked far from convinced, and Monty was itching to bite the boy's nose. "Then who are you?"

"He saved me from the bees, Your Lordship,"

said Mimi.

"It's true, Your Lordship," said Sack. "Young Sunny here was only trying to help your boot boy, at great personal risk to himself."

"Personal risk?" Lord Bigg snorted. "I was stung by a wasp once and didn't even cry."

"But there was a whole swarm of them," Mimi protested.

"A whole hive's worth," the gardener added.

"There *were* a lot of bees, My Lord," said Sunny. He was feeling more confident now, and was distracted by all the little crosses of sticking plaster. He imagined joining them up with lines to make a picture on the man's skin, like in a dot-to-dot puzzle.

"What did you do?" said Lord Bigg. They'd caught his interest now. "Shoot them? Trap them?"

"At first I tried distracting them with honey,

but they found Mimi far more interesting," Sunny explained.

"Mimi?" asked Lord Bigg. "Who's Mimi?"

"I am, Your Lordship," said Mimi.

"Oh. And you're the boot boy, right?"

"Well, yes and no," said Mimi.

"You either are or you aren't!" said His Lordship.

"I mean I'm a boot *girl*."

Lord Bigg snorted like Poppet the pig (or Lady "La-La" Bigg). "No such thing," he said. "You're simply a boot boy who happens to be a girl."

Mimi looked sad. "Yes, Your Lordship.'

"So if the honey didn't work, what did you do?" Bigg asked Sunny.

"I made her jump in the pond. Cover herself totally with water. That did the trick."

"Clever." Lord Bigg nodded. "Where are

the bees now?"

Sunny thought of the broken jar of honey on the driveway. "We're not sure, My Lord," he said.

"They just flew off," said Sack hurriedly. "Could be anywhere."

"If I get stung, I shall hold you personally responsible," said Bigg. "Where do you live?"

"All over the place," said Sunny. "I mean, we're always on the move."

"Aha!" said Lord Bigg. "You're one of those No Fixed Abode chaps."

Of course, Sunny had NO idea what His Lordship was on about, because although he knew a "chap" was a male person, he wasn't sure what an "abode" was, fixed, broken or otherwise.

"Am I?" asked Sunny.

"You just said you were," said Bigg, nodding

his head. On his shoulder, Monty the parrot tried a little head-bobbing of his own.

"Then I must be, I suppose," said Sunny. ("No fixed abode" means "homeless", more or less.)

"So if I DO hold you personally responsible for my getting stung, and I do get stung, then it'd be a real bore having to track you down . . . so do you know what?"

Sunny didn't know what, so he shook his head. "No, My Lord," he said, "I most definitely don't know what."

"I don't think I'll hold you responsible after all. Now, please leave my property. Sack will show you out."

Sack visibly relaxed. He had been worrying that Lord Bigg might wonder how Sunny had got on to the estate in the first place, and that they might have to admit to the existence of

the hole in the wall. But it didn't seem to have occurred to him.

"Thank you," said Sunny.

Lord Bigg turned and walked away from the potting shed. Monty, however, twisted his birdie neck so that he could keep a beady eye on the newcomer as they made their exit. You could just tell he WANTED TO SINK HIS BEAK INTO THAT BOY'S NOSE.

"Well," said Sunny, once Bigg had gone a fair distance back towards the house, "I'd better be off then."

"Nice meeting you," said Sack, shaking the boy warmly by the hand. He sounded like he meant it.

"Goodbye," said Mimi. She flung her arms

round Sunny and gave him a nice dry hug this time. "It'd be very nice to see you again."

"It would," said Sunny, because it most certainly would.

Both Mimi and Sack walked with Sunny towards the main gates. They passed the broken honey jar on the driveway, but the honey appeared to have gone and there was no sign of the bees.

As they neared the gate, they could hear mutterings and the occasional yelp.

"That'll be Mr Smalls," said Sunny. "The man in the BIGG AIN'T BEST T-shirt. I'd no idea he'd still be up there."

"Should we help him get down, do you think?" asked Mimi, looking up at the man on the spikes.

"Good idea," Sunny agreed.

"Not sure how we could," said Sacks. "And anyway, if Lord Bigg wanted him down he'd have told us to do it."

"Best leave him then," said Mimi, but she didn't look sure.

Sack dug his hand in his pocket and pulled out the gate key. He turned it in the well-oiled lock and it opened with one satisfyingly smooth action, without so much as a "click". He then swung one of the gates inwards. The one with Larry Smalls on top.

"Hey! What? Who? Get me down!" Larry Smalls yelled, shaking a fist. He recognised Sunny at once (which isn't surprising with the blue dress and all). "Oh, it's YOU!"

"Ignore him," said Sack.

"IGNORE ME?" shouted Mr Smalls. "You can't ignore me!" and to make sure they didn't, he starting to sing a song about a sad clown who falls in love with a stilt-walker who's afraid of heights. Despite the fact that he was hanging from the top of a gate by his belt and that, in my opinion, the song itself was sentimental twaddle, he sounded rather good.

"Bye then!" said Sunny above the noise.

"Bye," said Mimi.

Sunny strode out on to the lane, and Sack swung the gate closed behind him (to cries of "Traitors!"). He locked the lock and slipped the key back into his pocket.

Sunny raised his arm in a final farewell, then headed off back in the direction where he'd last left Mr and Mrs Grunt.

"Don't leave me," pleaded Larry Smalls, his voice more of a whimper.

To tell the truth, Sunny felt sorry for Larry Smalls. It had been the Grunts' rock-throwing that got him stuck up there in the first place. He stopped and walked back over to the gate.

"How am I going to help you get down, Mr Smalls?" he asked. "I don't—"

"How do you know my name?" asked Larry Smalls.

"Lord Bigg called you that."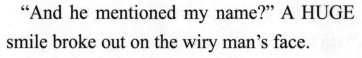

"Lord Bigg spoke to you?"

"Yes."

"And he mentioned my name?" A HUGE smile broke out on the wiry man's face.

"That's good?" asked Sunny.

"That's excellent," said Mr Smalls. "I've been bugging Bigg for years. Really trying to get under his skin. Hanging around like a

111

bad smell and he's never admitted to knowing who I am, until now . . ." He gave an even BIGGER grin.

"Er, about getting you down," Sunny reminded him. "How am I supposed to help you get down?"

"If only the Chinn Twins were here. They'd have me down in an instant. Them or Fingers."

"The Chinn Twins?"

"Oh, never mind. Those two grown-ups you were with," said Larry Smalls. "The frightening woman and the worrying man?"

"Mum and Dad, you mean?"

"They're your *parents*?" said Mr Smalls with obvious surprise.

"Near enough," said Sunny, not wanting to go into the whole taken-from-a-washing-line explanation right there and then.

"Them. Do you think you could persuade

them to come back and help me down? If they drove their – er – " He fumbled for the right word.

"Caravan?" said Sunny.

"Is that what it is?" said Larry Smalls. "If they could drive it right up against the gates, I could easily climb down from here."

Even from up there, Mr Smalls could see the doubt on Sunny's face. He thought back to Mrs Grunt's cries of "Big nose!" and their throwing rocks at his hat. "It's not going to happen, is it?" he said.

"I don't think I'd be able to persuade them, I'm afr—" Sunny began.

He was interrupted by a terrible tearing sound as Larry Smalls' belt – which had been supporting him all this time – finally gave up under the stress, and Larry Smalls came tumbling down.

In that split second, Sunny instinctively put out his arms to try to catch the man. And amazingly, Mr Smalls did land in Sunny's outstretched arms. Not surprisingly, both man and boy ended up on the ground with Sunny the worse off, because he was the one underneath. Larry Smalls rolled off him and jumped to his feet. "You caught me!" he said in amazement. "You caught me."

Sunny lay on the hard road surface gulping in new supplies of air (which was surprisingly painful).

"I can't believe you were willing to catch me!" said Mr Smalls. "Thank you. Thank you so much!"

When Sunny just carried on lying there, Larry Smalls' euphoria turned to concern. "Are you OK?" he asked.

"I'll . . . I'll . . . be . . . f-f-fine," Sunny managed.

Mr Smalls helped Sunny to his feet.

"Are you sure you're OK?"

"I'm good," said Sunny. And it was true. He felt really good. Not just good as in OK, but good as in he felt good about himself. He'd helped save Mimi from the bees and, even though it had been more of a reflex action followed by an accident, he'd helped Mr Smalls too.

Life – like honey – was sweet.

Buzz. Buzz.

Chapter Seven

Blunderbuss!

When Sunny finally caught up with Mr and Mrs Grunt they were outside the caravan about a mile and a half further down the road from where they'd been attacked by bees, having a tug-of-war with Ginger Biscuit. Clip and Clop were busy chewing some brightly coloured flowers in the flowerbed of a pretty cottage garden.

"Give it here, wife!" Mr Grunt was shouting, trying to pull the doorstop cat from Mrs Grunt's grasp.

"He's MINE," Mrs Grunt protested, "and he ain't an *it*, he's a *he*—"

"It's nothing but a moth-eaten sawdust-filled doorstop!" roared Mr Grunt (who was secretly quite fond of Ginger Biscuit too, but was never going to tell Mrs Grunt that).

"I'm back!" said Sunny.

Mr Grunt stopped tugging, causing Mrs Grunt to topple backwards on to the ground.

"HA!" laughed Mr Grunt. "Serves you right!"

"I meant to fall over," said Mrs Grunt, sitting up and dusting herself down. "I *loves* falling over . . . Where did you run off to?" she asked Sunny as she got to her feet, clutching Ginger Biscuit in one hand and rubbing her head with the other.

"I was trying to help Mimi – the girl being chased by the bees," said Sunny. Hadn't it

118

been obvious?

"You took our honey," grunted Mr Grunt.

"She needed help!" Sunny protested.

"Why?" asked Mrs Grunt. "What does she have to do with us?"

"It was Dad who kicked the pylon and that's what upset the bees," said Sunny. "We were responsible. And anyway, shouldn't we help people?"

Mr and Mrs Grunt looked at each other then burst out laughing. "Help people? You do get some funny ideas sometimes, Sunny!" said Mr Grunt. "Now, go and hitch up creaky old Clip and Clop, will you? We have an appointment to keep."

That was the first Sunny had heard about any appointment. "We do?" he asked.

"We do." Mr Grunt nodded.

Sunny was trying to get the two donkeys

out of the cottage garden when Elsie Spawn, the elderly owner of the cottage – a very angry-looking woman with very blue hair – threw open her bedroom window and started shouting.

"Vandals!" she shouted. "Turnip-heads! Vagabonds! Hoodlums! Looters! Pillagers!" She was getting more and more purple in the face.

What Mr and Mrs Grunt and Sunny didn't know was that Elsie Spawn had been doing a crossword when she'd spotted Clip and Clop eating her lovely flowers. And, along with a sharp pencil (with a rubber on the end) and a nice cup of tea, there were two things Elsie Spawn always kept close to hand when doing a crossword: a dictionary and a thesaurus.

She used the *dictionary* to check the spelling of words she was trying to fit into the little

white squares. She used the *thesaurus* to find words with similar meanings to other words in the clues, because that's what it's there for. She quickly looked down the page of the thesaurus for more insults: "Mischief-makers! Plunderers! THIEVES!"

Mr Grunt had been merrily ignoring the insults raining down on Sunny as he led the donkeys back to the caravan, but he couldn't let the word THIEVES pass without action.

He stomped off the asphalt into the garden, trampling flowers as he went. "No, lady," he bellowed. "THIS is what *thieves* do!' He wrapped his arms round a pretty flowering bush and with one swift tug pulled the whole thing out of the ground. And using his poshest voice – the one that he usually saved for talking to judges in court – said, "I'll thank you to remember the difference." He began lugging the bush back to the caravan, fuming indignantly.

Elsie Spawn was aghast. She was agape; agog; dumbstruck; dumbfounded. (You get the picture.)

As well as the day's crossword, a nice sharp pencil, a cup of tea, a dictionary and a thesaurus, there was something *else* Elsie Spawn had readily to hand.

Perhaps I should have mentioned it earlier, but I have a lot to think about, you know. My shiny shoes don't polish themselves.

She had a blunderbuss loaded with black peppercorns.

Before you could say, "Ready! Take aim! Fire!", she'd lifted the firearm to the open window and pulled the trigger. There was a bang loud enough to wake a sleeping chicken, and an almost blinding flash followed by a cloud of soot-like smoke.

When the smoke cleared, Elsie Spawn's hair no longer looked blue, and Mr Grunt had dropped the bush and was dancing around in circles clutching the seat of his trousers with both hands, howling like someone who'd just been shot in the bottom with a hail of black peppercorns. Clip and Clop had been frightened by the sudden flash-bang-wallop, so bared their teeth, started "Hee-haw"-ing, and kicked the nearest thing, which happened to be Mrs Grunt. She went flying through the air, past her dancing husband, and – much to her utter amazement – landed in a seated position on the top step of the caravan.

Back in her bedroom,

meanwhile, Elsie Spawn was looking around for something to reload the blunderbuss with. She spotted a jar full of hairpins on her dressing table and quickly tipped the contents into her arthritic fingers, stuffing them down the trumpet-like end of the blunderbuss.

Soon she was ready to fire a second time, and thrust the nose of her weapon through the open window once more. Her face dropped in disappointment when she saw that the boy in the blue dress had managed to hitch up the donkeys and the blaggards/brutes/rascals were getting away!

She fired the blunderbuss just for the fun of it anyway, the lethal hairpins glinting in the fading light, like a flash of silvery fish darting through clear waters. They landed harmlessly in the garden, embedded in the lawn, flowerbeds and the trunks of trees.

The flash and the bang were less
harmless though: they caused
Elsie Spawn's once-blue hair
to catch alight.

She snatched a bedside jug of water and tipped it over her head. There was a hiss like frying bacon.

Elsie Spawn looked down on her damaged garden in dismay and at the bush lying in the middle of the lane. She then caught a glimpse of her reflection in her dressing-table mirror. She looked as if she'd been rolling in the ashes of a camp fire.

The elderly lady sighed. She didn't know their names but she certainly wouldn't forget the Grunts in a hurry. Whoever they were, they were nothing but *trouble*.

The appointment Mr Grunt had talked about was round the back of a dingy old barn about two hours' ride away by caravan. If the barn was dingy, round the back of it was dingier still. Mrs Grunt gave Sunny a large nettle-and-goat's-cheese roll and a bottle of home-made conker fizz, and Mr Grunt told him to wait round the back for a Mr Lippy.

"Don't talk to anyone else," he said.

"How will I know he's Mr Lippy?" said Sunny.

"Ask him his name," said Mrs Grunt.

"But if he turns out *not* to be Mr Lippy then I'll have talked to someone who isn't him, and Dad said—"

Mrs Grunt frowned. "You think too much,

Sunny," she said. "Bad for your brain. If you want to grow up smart like your dad, don't think so much."

"You'll know Mr Lippy is Mr Lippy when you see him," Mr Grunt assured the boy. "Now leave us be."

Sunny left Mr and Mrs Grunt in the caravan, huddled in front of the television set. The television was one of those old box-shaped ones – not a flat screen – but the actual telly part had been taken out long ago and replaced with a fish tank that fitted inside it perfectly.

Beautifully lit, the Grunts loved watching the handful of colourful fish dart around inside it, between plastic weeds. Mrs Grunt was always sure to stick her beloved Ginger Biscuit on the sofa between her and Mr Grunt, his glass eyes facing the little fishes.

The barn and surrounding field were used for everything from dances to amateur plays, fêtes to pig races, and dog shows to prize-vegetable competitions. All over the outer walls there were torn remains of posters announcing these various events, which had been pasted up, then pasted over with new ones, over the years.

As the summer evening light began to fade, Sunny found himself finishing off his roll and trying to make sense of the snatches of words: *FOR ONE OR TWO NIGHTS ONLY . . . back by fairly popular demand . . . CHILDREN*

ALMOST FREE . . . You Won't Believe Your Half-Closed Eyes . . . PAY AT DOOR OR SNEAK IN LATE . . . in its 3rd quite good year . . . Singing! Dancing! Falling Over! . . . Nearly All You Can Eat! There were also the names of various actors, singers and performers dotted among the shreds of poster, but one name seemed to leap out at him: *THE REMARKABLE CHINN TWINS.*

Where had he heard them mentioned before?

"Boo!" said a voice.

Sunny gave a little jump and turned to find himself face-to-face with a man with unnaturally curly hair and an *enormous* pair of bright-red lips. In the failing light, Sunny could see that his skin was a pale, chalky white.

Sunny suddenly felt nervous. Mr Grunt had told him that he'd know Mr Lippy was Mr

Lippy when he saw him, and here was a man with enormous lips. This could, of course, mean that the man's real name wasn't Mr Lippy but that he *called* himself Mr Lippy on account of his lips . . .

. . . the only problem was that if the man with the humongous lips *wasn't* Mr Lippy and Sunny asked him if he *was* Mr Lippy, he might not take too kindly to someone asking such an apparently rude question. And he might punch Sunny on the nose.

"Are you looking for a Mr L?" asked the man.

"Y-yes," said Sunny. "A Mr Lippy."

"Then you found him! I'm Lippy by name, Lippy by nature!" said the man in a sing-song tone that somehow suggested to Sunny that he'd said it a thousand times before.

Mr Lippy looked at Sunny closely, taking

in the sticky-up hair, the wonky ears – the left much higher than the right – and, of course, the blue dress. "Have you got something for me?" he asked.

"Er, no," said Sunny. "Am I supposed to have?"

"Are you sure you haven't been given something to give to me?"

"All Dad gave me was a nettle-and-goat's-cheese roll and a bottle of home-made conker fizz," said Sunny.

"Is that it?" asked Mr Lippy, pointing at an old bottle filled with a rich, brown, gravy-thick liquid and stoppered with a small cork. It was propped up against the tree stump where Sunny had been sitting.

"Yup." Sunny nodded.

"Aren't you thirsty?" asked the big-lipped Mr Lippy.

"It's not because I'm not thirsty that I'm not drinking it," said Sunny, tying himself in "nots".

"Then why not?"

134

"Because it tastes disgusting," said Sunny.

"May I?" said Mr Lippy.

"Be my guest," said Sunny.

Mr Lippy bent down, put the neck of the bottle between his super-ginormous lips, pulled out the cork with them, spitting it into the grass, and then glugged down the conker fizz in one go. When he'd finished, he smacked his lips – and that was one BIG smack – then wiped them on his sleeve – with one BIG wipe.

"Ah!" said Mr Lippy. "You're absolutely right, son. That was truly horrible."

For a fleeting millisecond, Sunny wondered whether Mr Lippy had called him son because he was his real father, or because he was someone who called most boys son if he didn't know their names. As a reflex action, he found himself glancing down at the man's feet to see if he was wearing super-shiny black shoes (as he thought he remembered his father had worn). It turned out Mr Lippy was wearing shoes far bigger than any human being's feet could ever hope to be. And they were lime green.

Sunny suddenly had a thought. A good one. "Er – Mr Lippy?" he asked. "Are you by any chance a clown?"

"What on EARTH gave you that idea?" asked Mr Lippy, roaring with laughter. "My tight curly red hair? My lips painted bright red, my huge shoes, or my comedy squirty-flower?"

"What comedy squirty-flower?" asked Sunny.

Mr Lippy looked down at the lapel of his slightly threadbare mauve jacket. "Oh, botheration!" he snapped. "It must have dropped off on the way here."

"Aren't you off duty?" asked Sunny, more than a little intrigued.

"How do you mean?" asked Mr Lippy.

"I mean, you're here to meet me, but you're still in—"

"My clowning clobber? Not all of it. I'm not in my comedy trousers and funny stretch braces. It's difficult to ride my bike when I've got them on."

"Isn't it difficult to cycle wearing those?" asked Sunny, looking down at the huge pair of lime-green shoes.

"Oh, not if I splay out my feet and pedal with my heels," said Mr Lippy. "And, anyway, I couldn't find my proper shoes. I think Trunk might have hidden them for a joke."

"Is Trunk a circus elephant?"

Mr Lippy shook his head. "No, no. Not him.

Don't let Trunk hear you call him that! He's a circus strongman. No neck to speak of. His body sort of ends and his head sort of begins with nothing in between."

"Oh," said Sunny (because he thought he should say something).

"But as much as I'd love to stay and chat, you're supposed to have something for me."

"Maybe Dad forgot. Would you mind waiting here?"

"As long as you're quick," said Mr Lippy.

Sunny dashed round to the front of the barn and down a small track, veering off across the field to a clump of trees behind which the Grunts had parked the caravan out of sight.

"Did you get it, Sunny?" asked Mr Grunt, eagerly looking up from the sofa.

"He seems to think we've got something to give him, not the other way around," said

Sunny.

Mr Grunt smacked himself in the middle of his forehead with the heel of his palm. "The envelope!" he said. "I forgot to give you the envelope. It's in the top drawer of the kitchen dresser."

Sunny went over to the dresser and pulled open the top drawer. On top of the usual mess of bits of string, bottle tops, takeaway menus and a single clothes peg was a sealed envelope. He pulled it out. "This one, Dad?" he asked.

"That's the one, Sunny," said Mr Grunt. "You go and give him that. There's a good lad." He turned his attention back to the fish in the television.

It was suddenly getting really dark now as Sunny made his way around the back of the barn. He was half expecting the clown not to be there, but Mr Lippy was sitting on the tree stump. "Got it?" he asked, rising to his (big-shoed) feet.

"Got it," said Sunny, handing him the envelope. "Though why Dad couldn't just give it to you himself . . ."

"Better this way," said Mr Lippy. "This way, if anyone asks, we can honestly say that he and I have never met and certainly didn't meet this evening."

"And why should anyone ask?" asked Sunny.

Mr Lippy handed him a similar-sized envelope in return. "Elephants often lead to lots of questions," said Mr Lippy.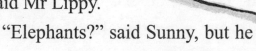

"Elephants?" said Sunny, but he

was talking to thin air. Mr Lippy was already climbing on to his bicycle. Moments later, the clown was pedalling off into the night.

Chapter Eight

On the Trail!

"It's a map," Mr Grunt explained, opening the envelope at the kitchen table, unfolding the piece of paper from inside it. Mrs Grunt and Sunny sat either side of him.

"Map?" asked Sunny excitedly.

"You heard your father," said Mrs Grunt. "M-O-P, map."

"That's a mop," snorted Mr Grunt.

"No it isn't," said Mrs Grunt. "I know a map when I see one. And anyhows, a mop wouldn't fit in an envelope that size!"

"M-O-P spells mop!" said Mr Grunt.

"Of course it does," said Mrs Grunt. "But that's got nothing to do with—"

Mr Grunt banged his fist on the table. "You just said 'M-O-P, map'," he said.

"Didn't," said Mrs Grunt (who secretly suspected she might have).

143

"Did," said Mr Grunt.

"Didn't!"

"Did!"

"Didn't!"

"Did!"

"Didn't!"

"Did!"

"Didn't!"

"Did! Did! Did!" said Mr Grunt.

While they were busy arguing, Sunny studied the hand-drawn map lying on the table. The most interesting part was where the big X was, next to what looked like a small wooden building. The other side of the X were two words: ELEPHANT HERE.

"Dad?" he asked.

"What?" asked Mr Grunt.

"Did we just buy an elephant?"

"No."

"No?"

"No, Sunny. *You* just bought an elephant," said Mr Grunt. "Nothing to do with me or your mother."

"If you say so," said Sunny.

"He did say so!" snorted Mrs Grunt. "I saw his lips move and everything."

"But it wasn't my money," said Sunny.

"Money?" said Mr Grunt (with a grunt). "Who said anything about money?"

"Sunny just did," said Mrs Grunt helpfully.

Mr Grunt glared at her.

"Well, if it wasn't money in the envelope, what was it then?" asked Sunny. "What else can you pay for a circus elephant with?"

"Ooooh," said Mrs Grunt. "So it's not just any old kind of elephant – it's a CIRCUS elephant. I had no idea."

"Of course you had no idea, wife," said Mr

145

Grunt. "Because this buying-of-an-elephant business was nothing to do with us, was it?"

"I thought you said—"

"WAS IT?" Mr Grunt glowered.

"Um . . . No. You're right, mister," said Mrs Grunt with genuine pride at her husband's scheming.

"I'm only guessing it's from a circus," said Sunny, "because you . . . we . . . I bought it off Mr Lippy, who is a *clown*."

"We have taught you well, Sunny!" said Mr Grunt.

"What was in the envelope, if it wasn't money, Dad?"

"Another map, drawn by *me* this time," said Mr Grunt triumphantly.

"A map leading to something Mr Lippy wants?" asked Sunny. "So it's a sort of swap?"

"S'what he just said!" said Mrs Grunt.

"Kind of," said Mr Grunt.

"Why only 'kind of', Dad?" asked Sunny. He had an uneasy feeling in the pit of his stomach.

"Because although my map is real, what it leads to isn't *exactly* what I'd promised it would be," said Mr Grunt.

Now Sunny was feeling really uneasy. "What did you promise to give him in exchange for the elephant?" he asked.

"It doesn't matter, because what he's actually getting is close enough. Just not *precisely* what we agreed!" Mr Grunt laughed.

"Exactly!" said Mrs Grunt, who spent much of the time not really knowing what was going on but doing her best to pretend she did.

"But that's cheating!" said Sunny. "That's wrong."

"I'll tell you what's wrong, Sunny," said Mr

Grunt. "Stealing an elephant from a circus is what's wrong. Do you really think the elephant was Mr Lippy's to swap in the first place?"

"Not necessarily—"

"So you could argue that we're –" Mr Grunt tried to think of the right words. "We're teaching him a lesson."

"A lesson that you should never trust people!" said Mrs Grunt proudly.

"Quiet, wife," said Mr Grunt. "You're making a fool of yourself."

"No more than you are!" Mrs Grunt retorted.

"Numbskull!" said Mr Grunt.

"Toolbag!" said Mrs Grunt.

"Armpit!" said Mr Grunt.

"Trench coat!" said Mrs Grunt.

"Don't you think Mr Lippy will come looking for us when he finds out he's been tricked?" Sunny interrupted.

"He may not even notice. And if he does, we'll be long gone from here by then," said Mr Grunt.

"But circuses travel around too, and surely we won't be that hard to find," said Sunny.

"Why not?" said Mr Grunt.

"Because we'll have a hulking great elephant with us," said Sunny.

Mr Grunt was about to say something, but stopped. He looked flummoxed. He didn't have an answer to that.

The following morning – after a night in which both Mr and Mrs Grunt slept beautifully in their bed, and Sunny lay awake for much of it outside their door with a mixture of worry and excitement – the Grunts actually set off for a particular destination for the second time in two days.

Sunny was used to hitching up Clip and Clop and simply going where the donkeys and the Grunts' moods might lead them. Today, however, they were following Mr Lippy's map to collect *an elephant*.

Mr Grunt had given Sunny the task of reading the map and making sure that they were going the right way. He didn't trust Mrs Grunt to be able to do it, and had "important things" to do himself, apparently.

Sunny certainly heard much hammering, crashing and bashing, along with the occasional cry of pain when Mr Grunt must

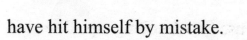

have hit himself by mistake.

The clown's map wasn't particularly detailed but what details he had drawn were very useful. He'd shown landmarks to look out for (linked together by dotted lines and arrows), with instructions for what to do – turn left, straight on, turn right, etc. – once they were reached. (So it wasn't really a *proper* map. It was not to scale, with places in the right place or anything.)

The starting point was the old barn and the next landmark Sunny had to look out for as he led Clip and Clop westward was a crossroads by a windmill, where they'd have to turn right. They stopped briefly at the mill to give Mr and Mrs Grunt time to laugh and point at the miller in his flour-covered smock, and for Mr Grunt to kick one of the sacks of grain stacked at the roadside. (Mrs Grunt

usually liked to save her kicking-of-things for
extra-special occasions.) They then hopped
back inside the caravan, ready for Sunny to
negotiate the bend.

It was quite a tight turn for the Grunts'
extraordinarily higgledy-piggledy house on
wheels. The roads were narrow, and the one
he was supposed to be taking them down
had high hedges on both sides. Sunny had
to manoeuvre the caravan backwards and
forwards quite a few times (which wasn't the

easiest thing in the world when working with donkeys, especially ones that weren't quite as young as they used to be). Sunny talked to Clip and Clop, gently coaxing and praising them, and promising them juicy carrots in the not too distant future. He also gave them hearty pats on the haunches, stroked their muzzles and, when he *really* needed the pair to go beyond the call of donkey duty, scratched them between the ears. The Grunts' home was a big haul for Clip and Clop, even though there were actually two of them.

After the windmill crossroads, Sunny had to look out for a left-hand turn just after crossing a three-arched bridge, and a right-hand fork in the road next to a waterfall. He found these, along with the entrance to a shortcut by a fallen tree and a turning by a statue of a white stag – a deer with antlers – into a forest. The statue had recently been given a fresh coat of white gloss paint, so looked very shiny and unrealistic.

Sunny enjoyed following the map instructions: seeing places first as black-and-white drawings on paper, and later as the real thing. He liked being on the move with a purpose – and such an exciting purpose . . .

He found himself thinking of Mimi, imagining her not as he'd last seen her (in Sack the gardener's borrowed overalls) but as he'd first caught sight of her before the bee attack, at her very pinkest, when she was still smelling of roses, with the pink ribbon proudly tied in her hair. She'd said that she liked animals and she'd like to travel. And what was he doing right there and then? Travelling with two donkeys on his way to collect an elephant! It would have been great if she could have come too.

Thinking about Mimi made him think of Bigg Manor and of Larry Smalls hanging from the gate. And then – *bam!* – he remembered where he'd heard mention of the Chinn Twins before he'd read their name on the remains of a poster on the barn wall. Larry Smalls had said that if only *the Chinn Twins* had been there, they'd have been able to get him down from the gate easily (or something like that).

Maybe they were acrobats? On the poster they'd been referred to as being "remarkable". Sunny imagined one identical twin leaping up on to the back of the other and unhooking Larry Smalls from the top of the gates to Bigg Manor in one swift, graceful movement. What a sight that would have been!

After ten minutes or so of clip-clopping down the forest track, Clip and Clop decided that it was lunchtime, and they stopped. Sunny knew that there'd be no point in trying to make them go any further until they'd rested and eaten. And anyway, he was hungry too.

Mrs Grunt threw open an upstairs window. "Why have we stopped?" she demanded.

"Lunchtime," said Sunny.

Now *Mr* Grunt threw open a downstairs window. "Why have we stopped?" he demanded.

"Lunchtime," said Mrs Grunt.

"Good!" said Mr Grunt. "Make me an omelette, wife!" He pulled in his head and slammed the window shut.

"Make it yourself, mister!" shouted Mrs Grunt, slamming her window too.

In the end, Mr Grunt gathered some old fir cones from the forest floor while Sunny fed Clip and Clop. Mr Grunt then tossed the cones into a blender, ready to make some woody soup or other. Unfortunately, he forgot to put the lid on, and bits of fir cone shot around the kitchen like pieces of shrapnel. Mrs Grunt screamed and dived under the kitchen table, letting out an even BIGGER scream when she landed on Sharpie, the stuffed hedgehog.

"What's Sharpie doing under here?!" she yelped the moment Mr Grunt had fumbled with the off switch of the blender, and all was quiet.

"Not a lot, I expect," said Mr Grunt. "He's dead."

"I mean, who put him here?" said Mrs Grunt, rubbing her arm where the spines had gone in.

"Then say what you mean, wife!" Mr Grunt grunted.

"I just did," said Mrs Grunt.

"Oh, well done!" said Mr Grunt. "Do you want a medal?"

"Yes."

"Well, I can't make you one because I'm too busy *making lunch because my wife is too lazy to do it*," said Mr Grunt with enough menace in his voice to frighten the weevils in the cheese. (To be fair, though, cheese weevils are easily frightened, or so I've heard.)

"Too busy shooting chunks of fir cone about the place, more like!" said Mrs Grunt. "And I still want to know why you put Sharpie under the table."

"What makes you think it was me, wife?"

"Well, I didn't do it, and Sharpie's dead, so he can't have walked there by himself . . . so that leaves you, mister!" said Mrs Grunt.

"What about Sunny?"

Mrs Grunt gave a puzzled frown. "He's not dead," she snapped.

"I mean, who's to say that *Sunny* didn't move him?" said Mr Grunt.

"Because Sunny isn't an idiot," said Mrs Grunt.

Mr Grunt slammed the lid on the top of the blender, trapping what remained of the fir cones. "Are you saying that I am?" he demanded.

"That you are what?"

"An idiot!"

"Are you call me an idiot?" Mrs Grunt bristled.

"I was calling *me* an idiot!" said Mr Grunt. "No, I mean, I was asking to know whether *you* were calling me an idiot."

"Work it out for yourself," said Mrs Grunt, adding the words "you idiot" under her breath. They were drowned out by the noise of the blender when Mr Grunt hit the on switch again.

Chapter Nine

 # One Rung at a Time

It was with only a slight tummy ache that Sunny set Clip and Clop off again along the track after lunch. It was late afternoon when they left the forest, the trees as close together at the fringes as in its very heart.

Because of the nature of the map – it only showing landmarks to guide them by, leaving out everything else in between – it was impossible to gauge time and distances. On the map, for example, the distance between a blue house they'd had to turn right at and a tunnel they'd had to pass through was the same (on paper) as the distance between the windmill and the three-arched bridge. But on the ground, it took hours longer to get from house to tunnel.

Once out of the forest and following the road to the right (which was east), Sunny was on the lookout for what looked on the map like a large column with a statue on top. That should be easy enough to spot, he thought. And easy enough as it was – for reasons that will soon become clear – it looked rather different from the picture. There was something like a lay-by – a parking place and resting spot – at the side of the road, where the side of the hill behind had been carved out into a semicircle, with a low stone wall running along the base. In the middle of this area was the impressive column, which was about twenty metres tall.

Sunny led the donkeys into the lay-by, and stood and looked up at the statue on top of the column. It was of a man with side-whiskers and a big top hat. He appeared to be holding a giant bunch of wilted flowers in his right hand. Unlike the column, statue and surrounding wall – which were all obviously made of stone – the wilting flower-like-thingummies were made of some kind of metal. Only they weren't supposed to be flowers, of course. This was a statue of one of the early Lord Biggs, proudly clutching a handful of his railings, and they had wilted ten years and a week after they'd been made.

Sunny wasn't familiar with how the Bigg family had made their fortune, so might not have known this was a statue of one of the Biggs if it weren't for three things.

Firstly, the statue of this particular Lord

Bigg looked extraordinarily like the Lord Bigg he'd come face-to-face with in Sack's potting shed back at Bigg Manor (though it didn't have little stone sticking-plaster crosses all over its stone face).

Secondly, there was a big plaque screwed into the base of the column, which read: "LORD BIGG: He Made Our Cliff Tops Safe". (Well, what it actually said was: "LORD BIGG: He Mad Our li   ps Safe", because some of the letters had worn away.)

And thirdly, dotted all around the semicircle of the lay-by were handwritten placards that read: "BIGG AIN'T BEST". One placard was even tied round the statue's neck with old blue nylon rope. The statue's stone hat was also partially covered by an orange-and-white traffic cone, which had been plonked on top of it at a jaunty angle.

"Mr Smalls," said Sunny to himself, a slight smile appearing on his lips. He couldn't help having a sneaking admiration for the man (in much the same way that Larry Smalls had had a sneaking admiration for Lord Bigg when he mistakenly thought that he was the ex-boxer Barney "The Bruiser" Brown).

"What?" said Mr Grunt, tumbling out of the caravan. When he picked himself up, he found himself looking up at the statue with the traffic cone headgear. "Who's the wizard?" he asked.

"Lord Bigg," said Sunny. "Not the latest Lord Bigg. Not the one I met, but another one."

Mr Grunt looked at him blankly. He had *no* idea what the boy was on about. "We'll stop here for the night," he announced. "Tomorrow we collect Fingers."

"Fingers?" asked Sunny.

"Fingers." Mr Grunt nodded.

"Fingers?" asked Sunny. Again.

"The elephant," said Mr Grunt.

"That's a funny name for an elephant," said Sunny.

"Know many elephants, do you?" asked Mr Grunt, pleased with himself for his quick thinking and clever comment.

"Aren't they usually called Jumbo, or, er . . .?" Sunny couldn't think of any elephant names other than Jumbo, so he stopped there.

Very little traffic passed that way that night, and even Sunny slept soundly until he was awoken by the pop-pop-pop of a passing motorcycle at around three o'clock in the morning. Luckily, he managed to get back to sleep.

First up, Sunny went outside to see what

Clip and Clop were up to (which turned out to be chewing things), only to come face-to-face with a middle-aged man with snow-white hair, a yellow checked waistcoat and an arm in plaster.

"Mornin'," said the man. "You've gotta be Sunny!"

"How do you mean?" asked Sunny.

"The way Mimi described your mobile home and your – er – blue dress an' that," said the man, finding it difficult to take his eyes off Sunny's head, with his sticky-up hair and wonky ears (which were probably something else Mimi had mentioned).

"You know Mimi?" asked Sunny. The world somehow felt that bit sunnier to Sunny, simply at the mention of her name.

"Know her?" said the man. "I taught her everything she needed to know to become an excellent boot boy." He put out a bandaged hand. (The one on the end of the arm that wasn't in a plaster cast.) "I'm Jack the handyman," he said, grasping Sunny's hand, "also known as Handyman Jack."

"You work at Bigg Manor?" Sunny asked.

"Yes. I used to be boot boy until Mimi took

169

over," he explained.

"So what brings you this far?" asked Sunny.

"Far?" said Jack, raising a snow-white eyebrow. "If you carry on down this road another half-mile and take a right, you'll find yourself on the edge of the Bigg estate."

"Oh," said Sunny. The map had given no suggestion of that. They must have been going around in circles.

"I've been instructed to clear up this mess," said Jack, looking around at the "BIGG AIN'T BEST"'s dotted all over the place.

"I see you brought a ladder," said Sunny, looking at Jack the handyman's vehicle. It was an adult-sized black-framed tricycle with a matching black metal trailer attached to the back, with a large number of ladders either side and a heap of tools in the middle.

"I certainly came prepared," said Jack.

"Would you like a hand?" asked Sunny, looking at the bandage and the plaster cast. "I don't think they'll be awake for a while." He jerked his head in the direction of the caravan.

Jack tilted his whole body back to look to the very top of the column. "I could do with someone holding the ladder when I go up there," he said.

"I'd be happy to," said Sunny.

Handyman Jack had to fit all the ladders together to make one long one to reach all the way up to the statue. He slipped them into position quickly and efficiently (despite the plastered arm and bandaged hand), but Sunny still felt a little doubtful.

"Will that be safe?" he asked.

"You sound like my wife," said the handyman, referring to Agnes, the cook and maid back at Bigg Manor. "It'll be a lot safer than if you weren't holding it for me, that's for sure!"

Sunny gripped the sides of the ladder and gave it a shake. The top, some thirty or so metres above them, wibbled and wobbled (though I'm not absolutely sure "wibbled" is a real word).

"Here I go!" said Jack. "That Larry Smalls has a lot to answer for! If I break my neck, there's only him to blame!" He sounded very cheerful about it. When Jack's feet were on the fifth or sixth rung – level with Sunny's eyes – the boy found himself staring at the shiniest pair of black lace-up shoes he'd ever seen.

Shiny black shoes.

He also noticed that Jack was wearing one spotted sock and one plain. He found his thoughts returning to his one memory of his father.

"Jack?" he called up, almost afraid of the answer before he'd even asked the question.

"Yes, Sunny?" Jack called back down.

"Do you have any children?"

"No," said Jack.

No? thought Sunny. *Oh*, thought Sunny. Then another thought occurred to him. "Did you ever lose any?" he asked.

"I'm sorry?"

"I mean, I know you just said you don't have any children but I was wondering if you meant that you don't have any children *now*. That you might have had one once and – er – lost it," said Sunny.

"Oh, like His Lordship, you mean?" asked

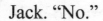

Jack. "No."

Like His Lordship?

"What's that about Lord Bigg?" asked Sunny, tightening his grip on the ladder, making his knuckles whiten.

Jack kept on climbing as he talked. "He and Lady Bigg had a son but they mislaid him years ago. They can't remember where they put him," said Jack.

"How old is he?" asked Sunny.

Jack stopped. He'd now reached the halfway point, about fifteen metres above the ground. "Er, I suppose he must be about your age," he said.

Sunny suddenly had a funny feeling in his tummy, and he was sure that it was nothing to do with the fir-cone soup this time. He simply stood there in silence, holding the ladder, while Jack reached the top and then

174

somehow managed to knock the orange-and-white traffic cone off the statue's stone hat – "Watch out below!" – and cut the blue nylon rope off the placard around the statue's neck. This done, he tossed the placard to the ground.

Caught in a tiny eddy of air, it spun over to the Grunts' caravan and landed on its roof, before skittering to the ground with a thwack. As Jack made his way back down the ladder, Sunny spoke again. "What's Lord Bigg's son's name?" he asked.

"Horace," said Jack.

"You remember him?"

"Course I do. My wife, Agnes, used to look after him sometimes. Wash him. Change him. Sing to him."

Just as Handyman Jack said the words "sing to him", his shiny shoes had reached Sunny's eye level again.

"Sing to him?"

"Oh yes, my Agnes has the voice of an angel. She could sing you the list of anti-allergy pills and medicines she has to take, and it would sound beautiful."

A man with shiny shoes.

A woman with the voice of an angel.

What if these memories weren't of his actual mother and father, but memories of SERVANTS of his mother and father's? What if he was the missing son of Lord and Lady Bigg!?!

Just behind Sunny came a belch loud enough to frighten the beetles in the undergrowth.

There was a familiar
smell of pickling
vinegar and open
drains.

"Pardon!" said
Mrs Grunt with such glee that it was obvious
she didn't mean it. "Where did you get that
ladder from, Sunny?" she asked. "It's the
longest I've ever seen." She peered at it more
closely. "Did you know that there's a funny
little white-haired man attached to it?"

"This is Handyman Jack from Bigg Manor,"
said Sunny. "Or Jack the handyman."

"Make your mind up!" snapped Mrs Grunt.

"He's both," Sunny explained. "It's his
ladder."

"Pity," said Mrs Grunt. "You can never go
wrong with a good ladder."

Jack took the final few rungs to the ground.

"Pleased to meet you, ma'am," he said.

"Pleased to meet her?" bellowed Mr Grunt, emerging from the caravan. "Then you obviously don't know her!" He snorted with delight at his witty repartee. "The woman is nothing but walking trouble."

Mrs Grunt went off foraging for food for breakfast (returning later with a basketful of what she called "mushrooms" but which Mr

Grunt informed her were "highly poisonous toadstools". She went on to insist that they were perfectly fine to eat and that her cousin

Lil had regularly eaten mushrooms *just like them*. When Mr Grunt asked which one of her many cousins Cousin Lil was, Mrs Grunt replied, "The one who died from poisoning.").

Sunny, meanwhile, took the opportunity to ask Handyman Jack more about Horace.

"What did he look like?" he asked.

"Why the interest?" said Jack, who was busy gathering up the remaining BIGG AIN'T BEST placards.

"Oh, I just wondered," said Sunny unconvincingly.

"He was little more than a baby," said Jack. "And between you and me –" He lowered his voice and leaned in close – "all babies look pretty much alike to me."

"Oh," said Sunny. "No birthmark or anything?"

"Distinguishing features?" said Handyman

Jack, rubbing his chin. "No, not really. Apart from his ears."

HIS EARS?!?

"His ears?" asked Sunny.

"Yup." Jack nodded. "He had three of them."

Sunny's jaw dropped.

"Only jokin'!" said Jack with a loud guffaw. "He only had two of 'em and they were perfectly normal."

Sunny's heart sank. "Unlike mine," he said, barely above a whisper.

"There's nothing wrong with your ears, Sunny!" said the handyman cheerily.

Sunny rather suspected he was just saying that to be nice.

Chapter Ten
Round, Round, Get Around!

Soon the column and Handyman Jack were far behind Sunny, Mr and Mrs Grunt, and Clip and Clop as their journey in search of Fingers the elephant entered its final phase.

One of the pictures on Mr Lippy the clown's map-that-wasn't-quite-a-map was what appeared to be a giant tomato at the side of the road. Ever since Sunny had first seen it, he'd been looking forward to finding out what it was for real and now here it was . . .

. . . and it appeared to be just that: a giant

tomato. Not big as in "Cor! That's a big 'un! How did you grow that?" but big as in BIG ENOUGH TO LIVE IN.

Sunny stopped the caravan and walked over to it. Even close up it looked incredibly lifelike. He gave it a tap; it sounded hollow.

"Fibreglass," said Mr Grunt, leaning out of an upstairs window. "I'll bet it's fibreglass."

"What do you reckon it's *for*, Dad?" asked Sunny.

"Dunno," said Mr Grunt with a grunt. He came out of the caravan and gave the giant pretend fruit – tomatoes aren't vegetables, you know – a good kick. (Or, I should say, a *bad* kick, because one shouldn't go kicking things, apart from footballs and the like, and even then only when you're supposed to.)

The kick had an immediate effect. A very small man appeared from the other side of the

tomato and without so much as a word kicked
Mr Grunt very hard in the shins.

This was so unexpected, and so painful, that
Mr Grunt not only fell to the ground like a ton
of turnips but he also burst into tears. This was
enough to bring Mrs Grunt on to the scene to
find out what all the fuss was about.

"What's this fuss all about?" she demanded.

"He kicked me!" Mr Grunt managed to say between sobs and gulps of air.

"He kicked my tomato first!" said the small man.

"That's true," said Sunny, who was helping Mr Grunt to his feet.

"Which is true?" asked Mrs Grunt.

"They're both telling the truth," said Sunny.

Mrs Grunt glared at her husband. "You can't go kicking other people's tomatoes and expect to get away with it," she said, swinging back her leg and giving the giant fibreglass tomato an almighty kick. (See? I said she saved her kicks for special occasions, and what occasion could be more special than one where she could kick the tomato of someone who'd just kicked her lovely husband?)

"Stop it!" cried the man. "Please stop it! You'll break it!"

"Oh, boo-hoo!" said Mrs Grunt. "You shouldn't go kicking my husband then, should you?"

"Why doesn't everyone stop kicking everyone and everything else?" said Sunny. "Just a suggestion."

"And a good one," said Mr Grunt, who'd stopped blubbing now. "And I wasn't crying, by the way. I had something in my eye."

"Yeah," said Mrs Grunt. "Tears from crying."

"Didn't you just hear what I said, wife? I said—"

"I'm Sunny," said Sunny, putting his hand out for the little man to shake. The man shook it.

"I'm Jeremy," he said.

"What's this tomato doing here?" asked Sunny, who was dying to know. It was so big.

And so shiny and red, glinting in the afternoon sunshine. It appeared to have been lovingly polished.

"It was used in a TV advertisement for a tomato sauce a few years back," said Jeremy, "and when they didn't need it any more I offered to buy it from them."

"Wow," said Sunny.

"And in the end they actually gave it to me for nothing as long as I arranged to have it taken away," said Jeremy.

"What do you use it for?" asked Sunny.

"Use it for?" asked Jeremy.

"I mean, it looks great, but I wonder if you got it for a particular purpose?" said Sunny.

"I got it for a *very* particular purpose," said Jeremy. "I live in it."

"Oh," said Sunny. He hadn't been expecting that.

"It's boiling hot in the summer and freezing cold in the winter," said Jeremy.

"Is that a good thing?"

"No. That's a terrible thing. And stuffy. Look." Jeremy led Sunny round to the other side of the tomato, where there was a proper door. "I had this door put in, but decided that adding windows would stop it looking like a tomato, so I didn't."

"Didn't?"

"Add any."

"Oh," said Sunny. "Why do you live in a tomato?" he asked, trying to sound as polite as possible.

Jeremy looked over to the Grunts' caravan. "Is that your home?" he asked.

"Yes." Sunny nodded.

The little man shrugged. "Well, we've all gotta live somewhere," he said. He caught sight of Mr Lippy's map in Sunny's hand. "What's that?" he asked.

Mr Grunt, who'd obviously overheard the question, appeared at his side. "That," he said, snatching the map from Sunny's grasp, "is none of your business. That's what that is. Put it away, Sunny," he said, handing it back to the boy. "Keep it away from prying eyes." He glared at Jeremy.

Sunny folded the map and stuffed it in the pocket in his blue dress.

"It looked like Mr Lippy's writing, that's all," said Jeremy.

"You know Mr Lippy?" asked Sunny.

"We, on the other hand, have never heard of him," said Mr Grunt. He gave Sunny a stare. "Who is he?"

"Just some clown," said Jeremy, "with handwriting just like that." He pointed at the top of the map sticking out from Sunny's pocket.

"Well," said Mr Grunt. "We must be going." He appeared to be walking away, then suddenly turned and ran towards Jeremy to give him a get-his-own-back kick . . .

. . . but Jeremy was too fast and neatly stepped to one side at the very last moment, like a matador teasing a bull.

When Mr Grunt's foot failed to come into contact with a person as planned, it kept on moving, causing him to fall to the ground a second time – not that anyone was counting – with an "UMPFF!".

Mrs Grunt simply stepped over him. "Stop lying around, mister," she said. "We've an elephant to find."

"Keep your voice down, idiot wife!" he hissed through gritted teeth.

But if Jeremy had heard her mention an elephant, he didn't let it show. He slammed the front door – the *only* door – of the tomato behind him as he went inside.

"Charming!" said Mr Grunt, now upright. He turned to Mrs Grunt. "Wife, no more blabbering about a certain E-L-I-F-A-N-T." Next, he turned to Sunny. "And you keep your lips closed about knowing Mr Lippy," he reminded him.

"Sorry, Dad," said Sunny.

Mr Grunt gave him a slap on the back. "No harm done," he said.

The rest of the trek to reach Fingers was uneventful. Sunny led them to the right when he reached the crooked house; took the twisty, almost-back-on-yourself left at the rock shaped like a toad; and finally led them down the path to the barn.

Not *a* barn. *The* barn. The barn where they'd started out from. Of course, this barn was drawn in a completely different place on the map because – remember – it wasn't really a proper map with everything in its place relative to everything else. It was more an illustrated list of instructions, showing landmarks and where to turn. So on the piece of paper there were TWO barns. The one showing where to start from – where Mr Lippy and Sunny had met – and this barn, which was shown as being NOWHERE NEAR that one . . . Only, in real life, it was one and the same.

Sunny had a sinking feeling as they approached.

"Dad!" he called out. "Good news and bad news."

Mr Grunt opened the top of the stable-like door. "What is it?" he asked.

"We're nearly there."

"That's the good news?"

"Yes, Dad."

"What's the bad news?" Mrs Grunt demanded, pushing Mr Grunt aside, and sitting her sawdust-filled doorstop, Ginger Biscuit, on the top of the bottom half of the door, for a better view.

"We're back at the barn we started from."

"That doesn't matter so long as there's an elephant inside," said Mrs Grunt.

"It might be bad news, if Mr Lippy brought along the elephant," said Sunny.

"Why's that, Sunny?" asked Mr Grunt, elbowing his wife out of the way. Ginger Biscuit nearly toppled off, but Mrs Grunt managed to catch him by the tail.

"Because you gave him a map that led him to something which – according to you – isn't quite what you promised it would be."

"Oh, that," said Mr Grunt. "Yes, that *is* bad news." He didn't sound too bothered.

"So what do you want me to do?" asked Sunny.

"Do? Keep going till we reach the barn," said Mr Grunt.

"Yes," said Mrs Grunt. "Get on with it!" Now both of them were crammed in the doorway.

"You never know," said Mr Grunt. "We may have luck on our side!"

Since when had the Grunts EVER had luck

on their side, Sunny wondered, but he didn't say anything.

In next to no time he'd pulled up near the barn with a mixture of excitement and dread.

Chapter Eleven

Fingers

It probably comes as no great surprise for you to learn that Mr and Mrs Grunt decided Sunny should be the one to go into the barn. There was no sign of life outside so, if there was going to be any elephant action, or funny business – there was potential clown involvement here, remember – it was likely to occur behind those two mighty closed doors.

Mr Grunt insisted that they hide the caravan behind the trees as before, though it being broad daylight and their having had to cross an open field, it was unlikely that anyone on the lookout would have failed to spot them.

"Good luck, Sunny," said Mr Grunt.

"Be brave," said Mrs Grunt, "and leave your shoes behind, will you? It'd be a shame to waste them."

"Waste them?"

"Your mother means in case you don't come back," Mr Grunt explained.

Sunny didn't bother arguing. He kicked off his non-matching shoes – one slip-on and one blue-laced lace-up – and felt the grass between his toes. "What is it exactly that you want me to do?" he asked.

"Be friendly. If it's Mr Lippy, smile as

though you haven't a care in the world. If it's someone else, simply say that you're here for the – er – elephant."

"And if whoever-it-may-be asks about the stuff you gave him not being the stuff you promised?"

"Protest your innocence!" said Mr Grunt, using the very piece of advice his lawyer had given him the time he was arrested for stealing a statue carved from Cheddar cheese. (Fortunately for him, some hungry mice ate the evidence before there could be a trial. Mrs Grunt had bribed the mice to do it. She'd promised them as much cheese as they could eat.)

"Stand firm!" said Mrs Grunt.

"And if things turn nasty?" asked Sunny.

"Then run like Billy-o!" said Mrs Grunt.

"Billy-o?" asked Sunny.

Mrs Grunt shrugged. "I think Billy-o must have been a really fast runner," she said. ("Running like Billy-o" was simply a phrase her own mother had used and – like you and Sunny – she had no idea what it really meant.)

"Did he run in bare feet?" asked Sunny.

Neither Mr nor Mrs Grunt said anything. Mrs Grunt had spotted a dead crow and her thoughts were turning to an early supper.

Sunny had a quiet word with Clip and Clop, patting their muzzles and scratching them between the ears, then headed off to the barn.

Though huge, the right-hand door to the barn was unlocked, and swung open surprisingly easily. Sunny stepped nervously inside. Sunlight poured through some of the gaps between the planks in the walls, or the holes where there had once been knots in the wood, but much of the inside of the barn was in shadow.

Fingers, however, was easy enough to spot.

It's hard to hide an elephant, even in a big barn.

"You!" said a surprised voice.

It was a familiar voice too. But it didn't belong to Mr Lippy. It was a voice that Sunny was more used to hearing say, "BIGG AIN'T BEST."

"Mr Smalls!" he said. "What are you doing here?"

"Sitting on an elephant," said Larry Smalls.

Now that Sunny had become more accustomed to the light, he could indeed see Mr Smalls astride the elephant. And what a lovely-looking elephant he was too. All friendly.

"What about you?"

"What about me, Mr Smalls?"

"What are YOU doing here?"

"I've come to collect the elephant," said Sunny.

Larry Smalls smiled. He actually smiled. This was probably the first time Sunny had seen Larry Smalls smile and the transformation was amazing. He looked like a different man. He didn't look like a man with a grudge who spent his time writing placards and throwing rocks and being all bitter about Lord Bigg. He looked *happy*.

"You? You're the mystery buyer?"

"Kind of," said Sunny.

"It makes perfect sense, I suppose," said Larry Smalls, sliding off the side of Fingers on to one of a number of bales of hay that had been lined up in rows to form seats (for an upcoming play).

"It does?" said Sunny, surprised.

"Of course!" said Mr Smalls. "I was wondering who'd want to buy an elephant, apart from a circus or zoo or wildlife park, I mean. Having seen the size of your – er – caravan, though, it makes perfect sense!"

"You think Dad's bought him to take over from Clip and Clop?"

"The two donkeys?" asked Larry Smalls.

Sunny nodded.

"An elephant would find the job a whole lot easier!" said Smalls.

Sunny smiled. He could just imagine Fingers pulling along their home as easy as pie. Then his face fell. What would happen to Clip and Clop? Would the Grunts simply abandon them now that they didn't need them? Hadn't he heard Mr Grunt grumbling about them getting old and not wanting to do the donkey work any more? A little knot of worry formed in the pit of his stomach. Sunny suddenly realised just how much he loved the big-eared pair.

"Won't Fingers mind lugging a great big house around?" he asked.

"Mind? He'll love it," said Larry Smalls rummaging in his pocket and pulling out a fist full of peanuts (still in their shells). Fingers' trunk swung into action, snuffling them up surprisingly elegantly and putting them in his mouth, all the while watching them with his highly intelligent eyes. "I rescued Fingers from a rich animal collector when he was a baby," Mr Smalls explained. "You see, I never took animals from the wild. That would be wrong. He was chained up in a tiny cage, but with me he's had a life on the open road!

He'd pull the circus trucks. Help erect the tent poles for the big top."

"You used to work in a circus?"

"I used to *own* a circus," said Larry Smalls. "Smalls' Big Top. All our animals had been rescued in some way or other."

"But isn't it cruel to make them do tricks?"

"Not the way I did it," said Smalls. "We let the animals find their own talents. Why make a sea lion balance a ball on his nose if he prefers doing card tricks? Why make a lion jump through a hoop when he might prefer to hold a brush in his mouth and do a little painting?"

Fingers wasn't waiting for Larry Smalls to give him more peanuts. He put his trunk directly into the man's other pocket and pulled out some for himself.

"So what happened?" asked Sunny.

"What do you mean?" asked Larry Smalls.

"What happened to Smalls' Big Top?"

Larry Smalls' face passed into the shadows. "Lord Bigg is what happened," he said. "Him and his railings."

At the mention of Bigg's name, Fingers stopped chewing.

"I don't understand," said Sunny.

"Then let me explain," said Larry Smalls. "Sit."

Sunny made himself as comfortable as he could on a nearby bale of straw.

"People often think that fences around enclosures and bars on cages are there to protect people from animals and, of course, that's partly true," said Larry Smalls. "But they're also there to protect the animals from the people. You see, stupid people do stupid things. They try to feed animals the wrong

kinds of food. They prod them when they're sleeping. They flash cameras in their faces. The tease them. Upset them." Smalls himself looked upset at the thought of this, and paused for a moment. "So bars work both ways. And the metal bars – the metal railings – we used for our cages when the animals were on the move, and for the enclosures when we were camped, were made by the Bigg Railing Company."

"Lord Bigg makes railings?" asked Sunny.

"Used to," said Smalls, and he told Sunny *all* about it, pretty much as I told you many, many chapters ago (though probably not quite so well as I did, what with my being such a brilliant author).

"So did the railings on your cages go floppy after ten years and a week?" Sunny gasped.

"Yes," said Larry Smalls. "We had no idea

that was going to happen, of course. One night we went to bed with all the animals safe and sound. The next morning, disaster! In the night the bars had gone floppy, the animals wandered out and . . . and . . ."

"And?" Sunny leaned forward on his straw bale.

"We'd pitched the circus in a field as part of a steam tractor festival. There were huge-great steam-powered machines everywhere . . . including steam*rollers* . . ."

"You mean, the animals . . .?"

Larry Smalls nodded. "Many of them were as flat as pancakes."

Sunny imagined a squashed lion in the middle of the road. How terrible! Then he couldn't help himself. He imagined Mr and Mrs Grunt shovelling it up between them and making a casserole. He could picture the tail sticking out of the cooking pot.

"No wonder you hate Lord Bigg!" said Sunny. "I'm so sorry, Mr Smalls."

"Thank you, Sunny," said Larry Smalls. "I knew you were a good kid from the moment you – er – kind of caught me."

Sunny felt like a fraudster and a cheat, remembering that the "payment" for Fingers wasn't what Larry Smalls would be expecting. He tried not to think about it. "So what happened to the rest of the circus?" he asked.

"Mr Lippy, who you met, does children's parties, and he runs the odd errand for me. The Chinn Twins – my acrobats – trim treetops and repair telephone lines. Sammy the sea lion works in a call centre—"

"A call centre?"

"Yes, when people complain to one of the telephone operators and demand to speak to their supervisor, he barks down the phone at them. Most effective, apparently."

Mr Smalls then went on to list some of the others in their new roles, including Trunk the strongman, who had opened a specialist shirt shop for men with no neck to speak of, and Jeremy the juggler, who now lived in a large fibreglass fruit.

"So Fingers is the only animal you have left?" said Sunny.

"Yes," said Smalls. He probably wasn't even aware of it, but he was gently stroking the elephant's trunk as he spoke. Even in this dim light, Sunny could see the glint of tears in the man's eyes.

"So why are you selling him?" Sunny wanted to know. "Why don't you keep him?"

"Because I want him settled in a new life before I go to prison."

"Prison?" Sunny gasped. "Why are you going to prison?"

"For blowing up Bigg Manor," said Larry Smalls.

"You've blown up Bigg Manor!?!" said

Sunny. He was stunned.

"Not yet, I haven't," said Larry Smalls, his voice barely above a whisper. "But I'm about to."

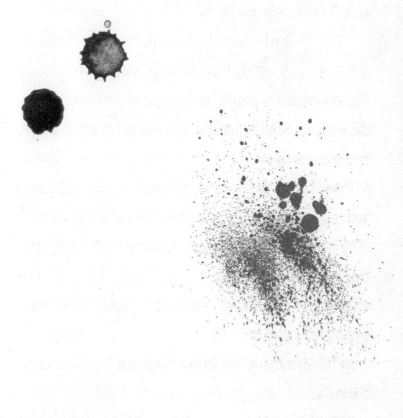

Chapter Twelve

Boom!
Boom!

Sunny found himself with more worries than he knew what to do with: Larry Smalls was planning to blow up Bigg Manor; he, Sunny, was about to take delivery of an elephant that they hadn't actually paid for; Larry Smalls was planning to blow up Bigg Manor; he might never see Mimi again; Larry Smalls was planning to blow up Bigg Manor; he didn't know what would become of Clip and Clop; and Larry Smalls was planning to blow up Bigg Manor.

Sunny's priorities were clear. He imagined sweet-smelling, bright-pink Mimi under a smouldering pile of bricks. "You can't go around blowing up houses, Mr Smalls!" he protested.

"Oh, but I can," said Larry Smalls. "The dynamite is in position and everything." His voice had gone back to sounding like the Larry Smalls Sunny had first met, preparing to throw those rocks at the gate of Bigg Manor.

"But Mimi . . . Mimi and the others!"

"I'm not planning on hurting anyone," said Larry Smalls. "I simply plan to reduce the house to rubble!"

"But what's the point?" protested Sunny.

"It's just an empty shell. Lord Bigg won't care and you'll go to prison for nothing."

"An empty shell?"

"Yes. Sack – he's the gardener – and Mimi – she's the boot boy – were telling me there's nothing in it. So all you'd be doing is destroying a useless building."

"It'll still be a Bold Statement though," said the ex-circus man. "It'll still Get People's Attention. Then I can tell the world what a crook Lord Bigg is!"

"But you can't blame today's Lord Bigg," said Sunny, trying to reason with him. "You said yourself that it was his *family* who started the business, hundreds of years ago, and, from what you say about his father and his father's father having to sell off stuff, they must have stopped making those useless railings long before he was b—"

A thought suddenly struck Sunny like a Scotch egg hits a frying pan (if you're playing tennis with them).

"What?" asked Larry Smalls. "What is it, Sunny?"

"The railings last ten years and a week before they go all floppy, right?"

"Right." Mr Smalls nodded. "Ten years and a week."

"But the last of the Bigg Railings must have been made long, long, ago. So surely the railings you used for your cage bars would have gone floppy and become useless long *before* you ever bought them! In fact, you wouldn't have bought them in the first place!"

"Which is EXACTLY why I hate this Lord Bigg so much," said Larry Smalls. "A while back, he actually managed to sell the factory but, before he did, he made *one last batch of railings* with the leftover metal lying around. And, even though he knew we were going to use them for cage bars, he sold them to the circus."

"But that's—"

"Criminal?"

"That's—"

"Outrageous?"

"That's WRONG!"

"Yes, Sunny. That's wrong," said Larry Smalls grimly. "He sold us railings for cage bars that he knew were unsafe, and animals – my animals – died because of it."

"But blowing up a building is wrong too," said Sunny.

"One thing at a time," said Smalls. "First, let's talk elephant." He pushed the barn door wide open and sunlight flooded the place, causing all three – two humans, one elephant

– to blink. He walked outside and Fingers followed, with Sunny close behind.

'But, Mr Smalls—"

"Elephant," he repeated.

Sunny gave a very sad sigh. "Mr Smalls, the truth is, I don't think my parents—"

"Those people really are your parents?" Larry Smalls interrupted.

"Sort of," said Sunny. "I don't know who my birth parents are."

"Aha." Smalls nodded.

"Anyway, I don't think they'd necessarily be the best people to look after Fingers. They're too . . ."

"Weird?" said Larry Smalls.

"Set in their ways," said Sunny. "They do everything *their* way."

"Then I want you to promise me something, Sunny."

"What?"

"Whether or not I blow up Bigg Manor – whether or not I go to prison – I want YOU to look after Fingers. He's yours now. So if you ever decide to part company with – with . . ."

Sunny supplied their names. "Mr and Mrs Grunt," he said.

"If ever you and the Grunts decide to go your separate ways, you must take Fingers with you. He's your responsibility. Is that a deal?"

Sunny was bubbling with excitement. His very own elephant! "But what if Dad has other ideas?"

"Don't worry about that," said Larry Smalls. He took Fingers' trunk in one hand and Sunny's hand in the other. Then he put them both together, Sunny curling his fingers round the end of the elephant's trunk. It was a bit like they were now holding hands, except that one of the hands was actually a trunk. "You two are together now, and Fingers knows it, don't you, boy?"

Fingers pulled the tip of his trunk from Sunny's grasp and put it round the boy's shoulders, giving him a kind of elephant hug. He knew it, all right.

"And even that Mr Grunt of yours isn't going to argue with an elephant, is he?"

Sunny supposed not. And now was the time to mention that the same Mr Grunt hadn't kept his part of the bargain.

"Mr Smalls—"

"No time," said Larry Smalls. "I've talked long enough and there's somewhere I have to be." The truth be told, he also hated long goodbyes. Now Fingers was safely in the care of the funny kid with the wonky ears and

blue dress, and the funny kid with the wonky ears and blue dress was safely in the care of Fingers, it was time for Larry Smalls to move on.

Of course, if Larry Smalls hadn't liked the look of whoever it was who was buying the elephant – he'd left those arrangements to Mr Lippy the clown – he would have kept Fingers, and simply wouldn't have kept *his* side of the bargain. This probably would have been a comfort to Sunny had he known it.

"But—"

"No, really, Sunny. This is goodbye." He jogged over to a pop-pop-pop motorcycle, over by a wire-mesh litter bin, and climbed on to the seat. "You'll find some bags of feed and caring instructions over there." He pointed. "Bye, Fingers!"

The elephant, standing by Sunny as if they

were old friends, his front leg pressed up against the boy's body, raised his trunk and waved.

"Come on, Fingers," said Sunny. "It's time to meet the Grunts."

Mr and Mrs Grunt couldn't have been more delighted when Sunny reappeared with the elephant. In fact, the boy couldn't remember a time when he'd seen them happier (and that included the day they managed to sink each and every remote-controlled boat at the annual Huntsworth Mayday Picnic).

"You've got him!" said Mr Grunt with such a smile.

"Hello, Fingers," said Mrs Grunt. She reached out and gave the elephant a hearty pat on the nearest part of him – a knee – which would have been enough to flatten an Irish wolfhound.

Fingers returned the compliment by feeling her hair with the tip of his trunk.

"That tickles!" said a delighted Mrs Grunt.

"Your head could do with a good hoovering!" said Mr Grunt. "Hope you don't give him fleas."

Sunny was forgotten in all the excitement so he slipped inside the caravan to look for his shoes. He found them in a box on the kitchen table labelled "JUNK", and put them back on his grass-stained feet.

When he went outside again, he found Mr Grunt leaning against Fingers as though he were a wall, chatting to the elephant. All the while, Fingers looked at him with his intelligent eyes.

"So no trouble with Mr Lippy then?" asked Mr Grunt when he saw the boy.

"No, Dad," said Sunny. "It was Mr Smalls who gave me Fingers, and I think everything's sort of OK, except for the fact that he plans to blow—"

"Who's Mr Smalls when he's at home?" demanded Mrs Grunt. "And what does he plan to blow? A raspberry? A kiss?"

"He's the man whose hat we threw rocks at," Sunny said. "The one who ended up hanging from the gates of Bigg Manor, and he's planning to blow—"

"Oh, him," said Mr Grunt with a raised eyebrow. "Small world."

"Small*s* world, more like," Mrs Grunt cackled. "I should be a comedian!"

"You're certainly a joke," said Mr Grunt.

"Dishcloth!" shouted Mrs Grunt.

"Earwax!" shouted Mr Grunt.

"Knuckle-head!" shouted Mrs Grunt.

"Herring!" shouted Mr Grunt.

That surprised Mrs Grunt. "You've never called me a herring before," she said quietly.

"I meant spongebag, you old spongebag!" said Mr Grunt.

Mrs Grunt seemed satisfied with that, and they carried on name-calling.

Sunny sighed and took Fingers over to a thistle patch to meet Clip and Clop. He knew he wouldn't get a word in edgeways when the Grunts were behaving like that, however urgent it was. The donkeys didn't seem at all bothered by a giant animal with a stretchy nose, and Fingers seem pleased to meet them. He sniffed their faces with his finger-like trunk. So, all in all, Sunny was happy with how that went.

It was then that he noticed a new trailer hitched to the back of the caravan. Not new as in shiny new, but new as in recently made, and new to Sunny. He'd never laid eyes on it before. It was very much in keeping with the caravan itself. It was made in the same style (or lack of style), as in loads-of-old-stuff-badly-put-together.

This must have been what all the hammering and bashing that was going on inside the caravan had been about. But what had Mr

Grunt built the trailer for? Storing elephant feed? Sunny seriously doubted that Mr Grunt would be that well organised.

"I see you're admiring my craftsmanship," said Mr Grunt, appearing at his side. He was wiping what appeared to be mud off one side of his face.

"Very nice," said Sunny. "What's it for?"

"What's it for? What's it *for*? Isn't it obvious what it's for?" asked Mr Grunt. He was trying to rub off the mud with an oily rag now.

"Not really, Dad," said Sunny, "which is why I asked."

"It's more of a *who* than a what," said Mrs Grunt. She had a mouthful of currant bun, having discovered the sack of them Larry Smalls had left for Sunny to feed Fingers.

"Who?" asked Sunny, wondering whether the "who" in question might actually be him, and that the trailer might be his very first bedroom. Sure, it was small and outdoors, but—

"It's for Clip and Clop, of course!" said Mrs Grunt. "Now that Fingers is going to pull our home, they can have a well-earned rest." She stared at Mr Grunt. "What's that all over your face, mister?"

"The remains of that mud you threw at me, wife!"

Mrs Grunt gave a triumphant leer, showing off her teeth – the yellow *and* the green ones – to great effect. "I had no idea I was such a good shot."

"Don't leer with your mouth full," grunted Mr Grunt, who'd seen more than enough half-chewed currant bun in hers.

Sunny, meanwhile, was feeling a flood of relief. So the two donkeys would still be part

228

of the family. . .

Family.

Now, there was a word. Because, in their own strange way, of course, that's exactly what that odd collection of people and animals was: a family.

"A trailer for Clip and Clop! That's a great idea," said Sunny. Then he paused and took a deep breath. It was time to try again. "I know you're not big fans of helping people, but I really, really think we need to get to Bigg Manor as soon as possible—"

"Why on earth should we do that?" Mrs Grunt interrupted.

"The boy was about to tell us when you interrupted him," said Mr Grunt.

"Then shut up and let him speak," said Mrs Grunt.

"That's exactly what I was telling YOU to

do, wife!" fumed Mr Grunt.

"We need to warn them that someone is planning to blow up the house!" said Sunny.

"Blow it up?" said Mrs Grunt.

"YES!" said Sunny.

"Then of course we must go there," said Mrs Grunt.

"Definitely," said Mr Grunt. "I wouldn't want us to miss a good explosion. I love a good explosion!"

"Me too!" said Mrs Grunt, thinking back to her science lessons at school. "Come on!"

Now, Sunny could have wasted time arguing that the whole purpose of his getting to Bigg Manor as soon as possible was to try to STOP there being a big explosion, but a waste of time was all it would have been. With Mr and Mrs Grunt excited at the prospect of witnessing a big bang, Mrs Grunt was quick to get Clip and

Clop aboard their new custom-built trailer at the back, while Mr Grunt and Sunny hitched Fingers up to the newly adapted harness at the front of the caravan.

"A perfect fit!" said Mr Grunt. "Let's get going!"

So off they headed, a slightly puzzled Clip and Clop enjoying the view and feeling the wind whizzing between their ears, and an excited elephant pulling them at impressive speed, eager for adventure.

Chapter Thirteen
Law in Action

When they arrived at Bigg Manor, Sunny felt that they were as late as one could be without actually being too late. Sticking out of every window of the house was . . . was . . .

"Dynamite!" Sunny gasped.

Up above the rooftop, brilliantly coloured birds circled and swooped, and squawked in dismay. Sunny could clearly make out Monty, the parrot that had been eyeing his nose in the potting shed, his beautiful plumage catching the fading rays of the sun.

There was no difficulty in Fingers pulling the Grunts' caravan, trailer and all, up the drive because the gates – those hated gates – hung crooked, broken and wide open where something had rammed them apart. One of the lion-topped pillars was badly scraped, the fresh scars showing white against the weathered stone, where something had hit it hard. And that something was stationed on the lawn before them now, right by the pond where Mimi had hidden from the bees.

It was a giant of a mechanical digger with a huge yellow scoop on the front with jagged teeth of metal. And it was in that scoop – now raised in its highest position – that Larry Smalls stood. Yes, he was wearing his BIGG AIN'T BEST T-shirt but (quite apart from the crazy glint in his eyes) there was something very different about him: it was the bow and

arrow he was brandishing. Instead of being pointy, the tip of the arrow was wrapped in cloth. And, from the way that the cloth was burning, it had obviously been dipped in something . . . something like *petrol*.

Sunny could see the servants crowding round the base of the digger. There was Sack the gardener, Jack the handyman (also known as Handyman Jack) and a woman he took to be Jack's wife, Agnes the cook and maid, and someone else – a spiky red-haired man – who must be Peach the butler.

There was no sign of Mimi. Sunny gulped. Was she still inside the building?

He had already jumped down from the caravan and was rushing towards the digger. The servants were being prevented from reaching Larry Smalls by a small but dedicated group of ex-circus performers.

Jeremy the juggler was running up and down, juggling flaming clubs and nasty-looking knives. There was also a very large man who had no neck to speak of – his head just seemed to join his body – who was wearing

a beautifully tailored pink-striped shirt, and a frightening expression on his face. He was bending enormous metal bars as if they were as floppy as Lord Bigg's ten-year-and-one-week-old railings. And there was Mr Lippy, in full clown clobber – including a squirty plastic rose on his lapel – cycling around the digger on a tiny bicycle, firing green gunk from a super-soaker at anyone foolish enough to try to get too near.

Hitched to the front of the Grunts' caravan, Fingers caught sight of his old friend Mr Smalls, raised his trunk and let out a mournful trumpet.

Larry Smalls turned and saw Sunny and the others. "Oh, you came!" he shouted. "And you're just in time!"

"Wait!" shouted Sunny. "Where are Mimi and Lord Bigg? How can you be sure the

238

house is empty?! WAIT!"

"Fire the arrow! Fire the arrow!" shouted Mr and Mrs Grunt in an unusual example of unity. "Do it now! Do it now! Do it now!" they chanted.

There was sudden movement at the right-hand side of the house, and Sunny could make out two figures climbing from a window on the middle floor and shimmying down a drainpipe with the speed and agility of acrobats.

The Chinn Twins! thought Sunny. *It must be the Chinn Twins!*

And how right he was. Having reached the lawn, the Chinns were now cartwheeling and somersaulting to a safe distance.

"Ready?" shouted Larry Smalls from on high.

"Ready!" replied the far-off voices of the twins.

"This is for the animals of Smalls' Big Top!" cried Larry Smalls. But Sunny hadn't been idle all this time. As far as he knew, water put out flames, and what was that fish pond over there filled with? Plenty of the wet stuff. He knew from an article (in a newspaper that Mr Grunt had used to wrap up a dead badger before cooking) that elephants were good at sucking up water in their trunks and spraying it everywhere. So all he needed to do was to combine the two: to get Fingers to suck up the water from the fish pond and to squirt out Mr Smalls' blazing arrow . . .

. . . but Sunny wasn't altogether sure where Fingers' loyalty lay. Certainly, he and Fingers were together now, but the elephant had years of history with Larry Smalls and, even if Fingers *was* now loyal to him rather than Larry, he didn't feel too comfortable about making him act against his old friend Larry's wishes.

What decided it for Sunny was Mimi. Or the absence of Mimi. For all Sunny knew, she was inside the manor stuffed to the gills with dynamite, about to be blown to smithereens.

So Sunny hurried Fingers to the fish pond and the elephant sucked up water at incredible speed. Sunny turned Fingers to face Larry Smalls . . . but it was too late.

As the jet of water squirted from the perfectly aimed elephant trunk towards the flaming arrow tip, Larry Smalls let loose the arrow and it arched through the air landing gracefully

in the wide-open front doorway, where it spluttered and sparked, before erupting into the first of a sequence of stupendous explosions.

"NO!" screamed Sunny.

"Nice one!" screamed Mrs Grunt.

"Yay!" shouted Mr Grunt.

Handyman Jack, Peaches, Agnes and Sack stopped trying to reach Larry Smalls now – there was little point; the damage was done – and they turned to watch the spectacle. Mr Lippy stopped pedalling the tiny bicycle, Jeremy stopped his dangerous juggling, and Trunk ceased the bar-bending and grimacing (though he continued to wear his very nice pink-striped shirt). All eyes were on the big event.

As they watched open-mouthed, Lord Bigg

suddenly appeared at a window and – without so much as a second glance down – jumped. If Lady "La-La" Bigg hadn't at that self-same moment appeared round the side of the manor – presumably from the pigsty – with Poppet the pig in hot pursuit, he may well have done himself a serious injury. As it was, he landed directly on top of the pig, who seemed more disgruntled – and grunty – than damaged by the whole experience.

But there was something odd about these explosions. All but one of the onlookers were expecting crumbling masonry and thick black smoke as Bigg Manor collapsed in an inferno. But instead, as each stick of so-called dynamite ignited, it shot in the air – or wherever it could – with a trailing of glittering sparks, like a firework . . . which was hardly surprising because that's exactly what they were: fireworks.

As everyone suddenly realised that they were watching a fabulous firework display, the mood of the onlookers changed. The servants, Jeremy and Mr Lippy started "Oooo"-ing and "Ahhhh"-ing. Trunk looked absolutely delighted, and a childish grin spread across his face. Sunny let out a sigh of relief, and even Mr and Mrs Grunt settled down on the grass to watch. But Larry Smalls was incandescent with rage. If you didn't know what "incandescent" meant, you do now, because that was just how blood-vessel-burstingly, humongously ANGRY Larry Smalls was.

Standing in the scoop of the metal-toothed digger, he grabbed fistfuls of his BIGG AIN'T BEST T-shirt and began tearing it apart with his bare hands. Soon it was little more than tattered shreds, revealing his string vest beneath. He howled. He ranted. He screamed. He yelled. Then he sat down with a thud and started to sob. It was at this point that three police cars arrived, sirens blaring and lights

flashing (which is exactly what you want from a police car, really). Sitting in the front passenger seat of the first car was none other than Mimi, with Frizzle and Twist humming round her head as usual.

Sunny dashed forward as she clambered out of her seat. "You're all right!" he yelped. Although he'd been worried about everyone at the manor, he'd been worried about the sweet-smelling, extraordinarily pink Mimi most of all.

"All right? Yes, I'm all right," she said distractedly, looking up at the whiz-bangs in the sky. "Fireworks!" She gawped. "They're nothing but fireworks! I told the police it was dynamite!" For it was Mimi who had grabbed Handyman Jack's tricycle and pedalled as fast as she could to the local police station. While the others had been running round in a what-shall-we-do kind of way, she'd taken pink, sweet-smelling action.

And a tricycle.

"We *all* thought it was dynamite!" said Sunny and before she knew what was happening, he gave her a big hug. Before he knew what was happening, she gave him one right back. The hummingbirds hovered above them both.

The police, meanwhile, had poured out of all three cars and were charging about trying to look busy and important, and enjoying the free show.

"Who's in charge here?" shouted a policeman, a bent-nosed, cauliflower-eared man by the name of Brown.

"I am!" boomed Lord Bigg, wearing his dressing gown, which had a perfect impression of a pig – legs splayed out sideways – on the front, in mud. "I demand that you make arrests immediately!" His sticking-plastered face looked even stranger in the blue glow of the police cars' flashing lights.

"This is your property, sir?" said Inspector Brown, eyes narrowing. He was staring at the dressing gown with great interest.

"Yes, yes. I am Lord Bigg. This is Bigg Manor."

"And do you have a licence for this firework display, sir?"

"I am not a 'sir', I am a 'lord'! And no, of course I don't have a licence for this . . . this . . . *display*, you nincompoop!" Lord Bigg spluttered.

It's never a good idea to call a policeman a nincompoop. "Turn round, please, Your

Lordship," said Inspector Brown, scratching his bent nose.

"WHAT?" demanded Lord Bigg.

"You heard me, Your Lordship. Turn round, please," said the policeman.

"I will not!" said Lord Bigg.

"That wasn't a request," said Inspector Brown. "I am instructing you to turn round in the name of the law!"

"This is preposterous," said Lord Bigg, but something in the policeman's voice suggested that he might punch Bigg on the nose if he didn't do as he was told. So he turned round.

When the policeman saw the words BARNEY "THE BRUISER" BROWN

written in nice big letters on the back of Lord Bigg's dressing gown, he nodded in an I-thought-so kind of way . . . because he thought he'd recognised that dressing gown the minute he clapped eyes on it, Poppet-the-pig-shaped mud stain or no Poppet-the-pig-shaped mud stain.

"Lord Bigg, I am arresting you for holding an illegal firework display and on suspicion of theft or of receiving stolen goods—" began Brown.

"STOLEN GOODS?" Lord Bigg bellowed. "What stolen goods?"

"Is your name by any chance Barney 'The Bruiser' Brown, My Lord?"

"Of course it isn't, you . . . you buffoon!"

"I thought not, Lord Bigg. Because *I* am Barney 'The Bruiser' Brown and that's MY dressing gown you're wearing."

"Oh," said Lord Bigg, his mouth itself forming the shape of a little "o". There wasn't much he could say to that.

"And not only am I the rightful owner of that dressing gown," Inspector Brown added, "I am also arresting you." He sounded rather happy about it.

Moments later, Lord Bigg found himself being led away in handcuffs.

Larry Smalls witnessed the whole thing from his excellent vantage point up in the digger scoop, his eyes filling with tears of joy. Soon he was whooping with delight, which led to Jeremy the juggler, Trunk the strongman, Mr

Lippy the clown, and the Remarkable Chinn Twins to whoop too, and before they could stop themselves the Bigg Manor servants – including Mimi – found themselves whooping, which started Sunny off, which finally made Fingers start trumpeting, and everyone burst into song.

"Do you have a licence to hold an outdoor concert on your premises?" Inspector Brown asked Lord Bigg in the back of the police car.

"Of course I don't have a— Er, no, officer," said Lord Bigg, ending more meekly than he'd begun.

"Then I'm afraid I'm going to have to add it to my list of charges," said Inspector Brown, looking very pleased indeed.

Chapter Fourteen

All Change

Once the police cars had gone, Sunny turned to Mr Grunt. "Dad?" he said. "You know that stuff you gave to Larry Smalls in return for Fingers, which wasn't quite what you'd promised it would be?"

"Yes," said Mr Grunt with a grunt.

"You didn't promise him dynamite and give him fireworks instead, by any chance, did you?"

"Might have," said Mr Grunt. And he might even have smiled. Larry Smalls had climbed down from the digger, and now strode across to them both. He'd removed the remains of his BIGG AIN'T BEST T-shirt and was now wearing a colourful one emblazoned with the words "SMALLS' BIG TOP" across the front. He gripped Mr Grunt's hand and shook it.

"I couldn't be happier with today's outcome," he said. "I couldn't be happier!"

Mr Grunt put his free hand on Larry Smalls' arm. "I'm pleased for you," he said. "Does that mean you don't want the elephant back?"

"He's Sunny's now," said Mr Smalls.

"Sunny's?" said Mr Grunt.

Larry Smalls nodded. "And Bigg is in trouble! Bigg is in *BIG* trouble! I couldn't be happier . . ." The delighted ex-circus owner turned and strode off, humming a victory march.

Just then, a large woman with a large,

wide-brimmed, flowery-crowned hat came bounding over, closely followed by an even fatter (and extremely muddy) pig. They both stared up at Fingers with interest.

"Hello!" she snorted. "So they carted off the old man, did they?"

"If you mean Lord Bigg," then yes," said Sunny.

"Excellent! Excellent!" she snorted. "Glad to see the back of the pompous old plaster-face. All he cared about were his silly old birds."

Sunny didn't know what to say, so said nothing.

"I'm Lady Bigg," said the woman, "but you can call me La-La! This little poppet is Poppet." She pointed down at the far-from-little pig, who was still looking up at Fingers in amazement. She'd never *seen* such a big pig (or what she *thought* was a pig).

"Oink," said Poppet.

"Trumpet," said Fingers.

"Oink," said Poppet. She was in love.

La-La Lady Bigg looked around. "Peach!"

she called. "PEACH!"

The red-haired butler appeared out of the chaos. "You yelled, m'lady?" he said.

"You're fired," she said.

Sunny was SHOCKED. She'd seemed such a nice lady and now she was kicking the butler out of his job.

"You, Agnes, Handyman Jack, Sack and Mimi. The lot of you. You can leave any time you wish," she went on.

"We can?" said Peach, raising a bushy red eyebrow in surprise.

"If you like. You're welcome to stay if you *want* to, any of you, but otherwise you can just go!"

Sunny smiled. Now she was making sense.

"But our contracts, m'lady," said Peach. "His Lordship made it absolutely clear that if we left we'd be in breach of contract, and that he could sue us for every penny—"

At that moment, the flames must have found a new batch of fireworks. There was a series of bang-bang-bangs and the skies filled with a whole new shower of multicoloured sparks.

"Sue you for every penny you *don't have* in the first place?" asked La-La.

Peach smiled. "You have a point there, m'lady."

"And do you know where the contracts are, Peach?"

The butler nodded.

"Then tear 'em up, Peach! I'm moving out of the pigsty and back into the manor! With the boring old plaster-face out of the way, things are going to change around here." Lady Bigg turned back to Sunny. "And who are you?" she asked. "You do look rather familiar . . . and I like your elephant."

"Thank you," said Sunny. "And I like your pig."

"You're not my son, are you? Only I lost him a long time back and he must be your age by now."

"No," said Mrs Grunt, barging between them. "This is my boy, Sunny."

"Yes," said Mr Grunt. "This is Sunny, our son."

"Just wondered," said Lady Bigg with a shrug. "It's nothing to get het up about, is it, Poppet?" She patted her beloved pig.

Sunny was about to protest – what if he *was* Horace? – when La-La went on: "Whoever you are, you and your elephant and family and friends are all welcome to stay at Bigg Manor as long as you like. You all are."

There were claps and cheers and more whoops of delight, some from the servants, who Peach had just told about the tearing up of the contracts.

Mimi turned to Sunny. "You know," she said. "I might like it here if I don't have to be the boot boy. I think I might stay."

And stay they all did, even the Grunts. But matters didn't end there. Of course they didn't. Lord Bigg wasn't under lock and key for ever, though he did end up in jail for a long time. Then there was the fact that wherever the Grunts went, trouble was never far behind and when they *didn't* go anywhere, trouble soon found them anyway.

Like the first time they ran out of elephant-feed and decided to take the caravan to Hunnybun's Bun Factory to stock up on – you guessed it – some currant buns (stale ones if they were cheaper). It took them past a very pretty thatched cottage with a messed-up front garden. Although Mr Grunt wasn't sure he recognised it, he found his bottom tingling at the memory of being peppered with peppercorns . . .

. . . and before he could say, "Silly old bat!",

Elsie Spawn had her blunderbuss pointing out of the window, ready to fire.

What she hadn't bargained for was a smart elephant, such as Fingers. Before she'd even had the satisfaction of pulling the trigger, a large trunk had wrapped itself around the weapon's trumpet-like muzzle and had pulled it from her grasp.

"Monster!" she bellowed, peering over the windowsill. "Brute! Ogre!" Because, in all the good ways, Sunny was nothing like Mr and Mrs Grunt, he made sure that Fingers returned the weapon to the elderly lady – once he'd tipped out the gunpowder and drawing pins – but, the truth be told, it never worked again. Fingers' elephantine grip had left the muzzle all crudnuckled (which isn't a real word, but one that best describes the state it was in).

The delay meant that they didn't reach the

Hunnybun's factory until after closing time.

"It's all your fault!" Mrs Grunt shouted from the bedroom window.

"Yours!" Mr Grunt shouted back from the factory's sloping forecourt. He wanted to kick something, and chose a piece of wood. It was a large cheese-shaped wedge under the back wheel of a delivery van. He kicked it clear. The van began rolling slowly backwards towards him.

"Look out, mister!" Mrs Grunt shouted from the caravan, before she could stop herself.

"What?" shouted Mr Grunt. "How do you expect me to hear you when you MUMBLE, wife?"

"Nothing!" Mrs Grunt replied, with a flash of green and yellow teeth.

Mr Grunt grunted, and only jumped clear thanks to Sunny's last-minute warning cry of,

"Dad!"

The van rumbled past him and hit a bollard, causing its back doors to burst open. Sunny read the words on the nearest one: SUPPLIERS OF FRESH HONEY TO HUNNYBUN'S.

What Mr Grunt said next was drowned out by a sudden loud buzzing noise, but Sunny could guess what it was. It was a single word, shouted loud and long. It was: "*Beeeeeeeeee eeeeeeeeeeeeeeeeeeeeeeeeees!*"